HER MEMORY OF

HER MEMORY OF

KATHERINE SCOTT JONES

Published by Redemption Press, PO Box 427, Enumclaw, WA 98022

Toll Free (844) 2REDEEM (273-3336)

Redemption Press is honored to present this title in partnership with the author. The views expressed or implied in this work are those of the author. Redemption Press provides our imprint seal representing design excellence, creative content, and high quality production.

ISBN: 978-1-68314-164-8
978-1-68314-165-5 ePub
978-1-68314-166-2 Mobi

Library of Congress Catalog Card Number: 2017933730

For women everywhere
who cannot speak for themselves.
You are seen.
You are known.
You are not alone.

The Lord will fight for you; you need only to be still.
—Exodus 14:14

CHAPTER 1

Langley-by-the-Sea, Washington, 2010

The jangling of the distant bell beckoned as it always did, only today the sound carried a note of urgency. Ally let the screen door slap behind her, an exclamation point to mark the end of her shift, and hastened down the bistro's rough steps. An autumn wind whisking up from Saratoga Passage cooled her face. After six hours of hustling in and out of the steamy kitchen filling orders, she'd have enjoyed a few minutes to savor the breeze, but the bell's lingering echo told her she couldn't afford even a moment's respite.

She hurried on foot across the parking lot. *Shoot, shoot, shoot.* She'd been doing so well too, keeping a close eye on the clock, closing her stations well before quitting time. But her last customer sabotaged her efforts. She might have stood a chance had it been anyone but Margit Olsson. Margit loved to chat, and now Ally was late.

Her tote thumped against her hip as she broke into a jog. She turned off Front Street away from the bay, where sailboats were scattered like dice across the water. A few blocks later, she stepped aside to let two bicyclists pass through the narrow schoolyard gate before taking her turn. Once inside, boisterous kids surged past her like a river around a rock. Ally followed the gravel pathway around the brick building to the kindergarten classroom, passing the blue-and-yellow Big Toy, where two girls swung from the monkey bars.

Ally felt a lift of relief when she saw a woman in pink sweats and a baseball cap hurrying from the opposite direction toward the kindergarten wing. At least she wasn't the only mom running late. But a qualm tightened her stomach as she rounded the corner. Even from here, Ally could see that Jack was crying while his teacher, Mrs. Nichols, held his hand. Another little boy wearing a Seahawks windbreaker waited with them, but as soon as he caught sight of his mom in the pink sweats, he grinned and ran to join her.

As Ally drew near, Jack wiped his eyes with the back of a grimy hand. "Sorry I'm late, Bubba." She dropped to her knees and folded him in her arms, a throb in her chest feeling as if someone had bumped a bruise. "Were you worried?"

When he didn't respond, Mrs. Nichols touched his shoulder. "Know what, Jack? I never got around to erasing the whiteboard this afternoon. Would you do that for me?" Mrs. Nichols gave Ally a look over Jack's head.

Jack turned his face up to Ally, questioning with his eyes.

"I'll be right here," she promised. He headed back into the classroom, shoulders slumped beneath the straps of his

Spiderman backpack. Ally turned to Mrs. Nichols. "I'm so sorry, I got held up at work."

The teacher offered a thin smile. "Jack had a rough day today."

Ally frowned. "In what way?"

"He took a swipe at another little boy on the playground during afternoon recess."

"He—he hit someone?" The news caused an uneasy jump somewhere between Ally's heart and her stomach.

"Well, he tried to, and that's not like him. Forgive me for asking, but is everything all right at home? No significant changes?"

"I—no, none." What exactly was she suggesting? "Other than starting kindergarten, of course."

"No new boyfriend, or a grandparent dying…?"

"Nothing like that." Ally crossed her arms, ignoring the apprehension that tightened her insides. "Would you mind telling me exactly what happened? Did someone provoke him?"

"A first grader was teasing Jack at recess, but instead of telling a teacher, Jack tried to hit him. When the other boy swung back, a teacher stepped in."

So, he *was* provoked. "Why wasn't I called?"

"Since it was a first offense, we thought we could wait to tell you. We've spoken to both boys and trust the issue's resolved."

"What was the boy teasing Jack about?"

"Neither of them would say."

Jack emerged from the classroom. "All done, Mrs. Nichols."

"Good boy." Mrs. Nichols' smile etched grooves around her pale blue eyes. Then she crouched so she was eye-to-eye with Jack. "What happened today on the playground isn't going to happen again, is it, Jack?"

He shook his head. Ally ached to pull her small son close, to press her lips into the soft, sweaty skin of his neck.

"Didn't think so." Mrs. Nichols straightened with a smile. "We'll see you tomorrow for a better day, all right?"

Ally thanked the teacher and reached for Jack's hand then led him from the school. Not until they'd turned onto Front Street, far away from Mrs. Nichols' keen eye, did she allow her pent-up anxiety to tumble free. Her son picking fights in kindergarten? Even if he had been provoked, how could this be? Part of her wanted to disbelieve Mrs. Nichols. But Jack's teacher, with her long cotton skirts and sensible clogs, struck Ally as eminently trustworthy. If she said it was true, it must be.

Ally glanced down at Jack, who kept his gaze fixed on his Spiderman sneakers. "Mrs. Nichols said you got into trouble today on the playground. Want to tell me about it?"

He shook his head.

"She said another boy was teasing you. Is that true?"

"I guess."

"What did he say?"

No answer.

"Jack, you know I won't tolerate fighting. I can't help you if you won't tell me what's going on. Can you at least tell me why you were crying when I got there?"

He shrugged and shook his head.

It wasn't like him not to talk to her. She watched him, searching for a clue to unlock the riddle. Even provoked, what would make him try to hit another little boy? She'd taught him better than that. Was it pure instinct that made him lash out, the fault of the blood that ran through his veins?

Stop it. Just because he tussled with another boy doesn't mean he'll turn out like—

No. She couldn't go there. She wouldn't.

At the corner post office, as they waited for a stream of cars to pass before they could cross the street, Ally wished for the umpteenth time they'd lower the speed limit along this stretch of road. Once they reached the other side, she put herself between Jack and the curb.

"So, Bubba." Ally spoke in a new tone, determined to put this day's troubles behind them. "I was thinking about what to fix for dinner. I've pretty much settled on asparagus sandwiches. What do you think?"

"Asparagus?" He squinted up at her.

"No? Not even if I told you I had artichoke ice cream for dessert?

"Eww."

"Well, then, liver soup? I know liver soup is one of your favorites."

A shudder coursed through his slight frame. "*Gross*, Mom."

"I'm stumped then, because the only other thing I can think of is mac-n-cheese with hotdogs. But I thought for sure you'd prefer asparagus ice cream."

"You said asparagus sandwiches, Mom." Jack rolled his eyes. "Not ice cream. But I'll take mac-n-cheese and hot dogs."

Ally touched his soft, blond hair, so different from her own. "Good choice, little man."

Seashells crunched beneath their feet as they turned onto their lane, passing the stand of alder trees that shielded Penny

Watrous's property from the road. They walked by their landlady's clapboard house and empty carport on the left. A short path branching from the drive led to their cottage, a cedar-shingled converted boathouse nestled at the base of the sloping yard. Below the cottage, a rocky beach met the blue-gray waters of Saratoga Passage, which stretched to the snow-capped Cascades.

As Ally followed Jack, she eyed the half-acre of lawn, which seemed to have sprouted four inches in the last week, a final hurrah before the first frost. Ally sighed, adding "mow the lawn" to her list. If she didn't get it done this weekend, Penny would certainly have something to say about it.

She dug into her handbag for her keys, finding them buried beneath her soiled work apron. On the front porch, they dropped their sneakers into the shoe basket. Then Ally turned the key in the lock, and the door swung wide.

Salty air breezed across her face, a draft coming from inside the house. *From inside the house?*

"Jack, wait!" She grabbed his arm as he started over the threshold.

"Mom! Ow!"

She kept her grip as her eyes swept their small domain and settled on the space where their television used to be. The truth hit her like a punch to the gut. *We've been robbed.*

Her heart catapulted into her throat. Was the intruder still in the house? She waited, listening, but she heard only the rhythmic slosh of waves on the shore below and the rush of blood behind her ears. The living room windows were shut tight, but the draft told her another somewhere in the back was open.

Jack seemed rooted to the porch. "Don't move," she ordered.

Ally crept inside, her socked feet soundless on the hardwood floor. Careful to keep Jack in sight, she made a wide circle around the living room until she could peer around the divider into the kitchen. There she saw the source of the breeze. The glass in their back door had been smashed. Shards lay scattered across the yellow linoleum.

She raised a trembling hand, reminding Jack to stay put as she moved into the short hallway. In her bedroom, the only evidence of the intruder was a ring of dust made noticeable by her missing jewelry box. A glance into Jack's room and the bath told her no one lurked there.

Breathing easier, she returned to the living room and scanned the area again for anything else out of place. As her gaze passed over the built-in bookcases, something flitted across her brain. She looked again, but the thought skittered from her grasp.

In the kitchen, she skirted the table with Jack's box of peanut-butter crunch cereal still at his place and stepped closer to their shattered door. *Penny's going to freak.*

"Mom?"

She jumped. "Ow!" White-hot pain ripped through her foot and raced to her spine. "Jack! I told you to stay put."

"But I wanted to see—" His gaze traveled to her foot. "Mom, you're bleeding."

A crimson splotch spread across her white sock. As she yanked out a chair and sat down, a new, sickening thought occurred to her. *My viola.*

"Jack, quick, go make sure Lola's still here."

He didn't move, his alarmed gaze fastened on her foot.

"Jack!"

He scampered off. As soon as he was out of sight, Ally bent over the wound. The glass remained embedded in the ball of her foot. Blood dripped from the edge of her sock to the floor. She fought back a wave of nausea. What if she'd severed a tendon or something?

Then Jack was back, a dust bunny clinging to his hair, a black hourglass case clasped to his chest. "She was there," he panted. "Under the bed."

"Put her on the table. Watch out for the glass. Now Bubs, I need you to bring me my bag from the porch."

When he returned, he thrust it at her. She rooted through it for her cell phone, even emptied the contents onto the table. No phone. Where was it? Then it hit her. Brittany. She'd loaned it to her at work today and forgot to get it back.

"Jack, listen carefully." She tried to keep her voice steady as the puddle of blood spread. "I don't have my phone, so you're going to have to run to Miss Penny's. Go straight there, then back. Understand?"

"But Mom—"

"Now, Jack." Pain swelled, and her vision went gray around the edges. "Run!"

CHAPTER 2

The cramping began as Darcie drove east on Saratoga Road, toward home. It started subtly, more of an ache than a pinch, so that at first she didn't recognize the feeling. But by the time she pulled off of Saratoga onto their gravel driveway, the pain had morphed into a tight fist clenched low in her belly.

She eased beneath the carport, angling her Camry beside Paul's green Dodge pickup before stilling the engine and resting her forehead on the steering wheel. *Please, Lord, let it be something else—the shrimp I ate for lunch, a kink in my system, anything. Anything but this.*

But who was she kidding? She was a nurse, trained to interpret the body's signals. And she knew these cramps for what they were.

The beginning of her period.

Her limbs felt weighted as she got out of the car. This past week, she'd actually allowed herself to believe this month was the one. At four days late—two days later than she had ever been—she'd even dared to calculate a due date. May 15. A spring baby. God choosing to smile on them at last.

Letting herself in by the front door, she headed straight to the master bedroom with its adjoining bathroom. *Please, please, God, no,* she begged as she shut the bathroom door. *Not this time. Not again.* Her hands shook.

But on her panties: blood.

Searing disappointment clawed her, as if a beast had reached its talons inside her body and ripped a section of her gut right through her skin, leaving a jagged, seeping wound. It always surprised her, the strength of the pain. She'd thought that over time, it would get easier. That she'd improve with practice. But it didn't work that way.

How can I miss someone I've never met? Each month, Darcie asked herself the same question, feeling as though someone vital to her existence was being withheld from her, leaving her alone to find a way, somehow, to carry on.

Part of Darcie embraced that God had designed women this way, each round of grief intended to create a sense of urgency to propel her forward into the next month, to try again. But another part wished the grief would just go away. Wished she could forget this dream and move on to a more fruitful one.

Darcie reached beneath the sink for a sanitary pad, then into a drawer for clean panties, using the rote activity as a dam against the surging tide of disappointment. After she finished, she lingered in the stillness of the bathroom, hoping to hear a word of comfort from the Spirit to loosen the choking cords of desolation. *I'm not getting any younger, Lord. Neither is my husband. Make us wait much longer and Paul will be doddering around with a cane at our child's graduation. Is that Your best for us? Remember, a hope deferred makes the heart sick, but a longing fulfilled is a tree of life.*

Life was what she longed for. New life, in its most literal sense.

She sighed and looked once more at the evidence of this month's failure before flushing it down the toilet.

She swallowed two Advil with a swig of water and briefly considered changing out of her scrubs, but then decided she didn't have the energy. Taking a deep breath, she stuffed the unwieldy bulk of her disappointment back into the dark hole where it lived and emerged from the bedroom.

Moving down the shadowy hall, she paused at Rees's door, listening for signs of her brother's presence. Perhaps she heard a rustle and a sigh, or maybe it was just the heat kicking on. Either way, she knew better than to knock. Rees had made it clear he valued his privacy. When his door was shut, it signaled do-not-disturb.

In the kitchen, smells of cinnamon and vanilla lingered as reminders of breakfast. On the counter, two jumbo-sized muffins hugged in plastic wrap squatted on a china plate. Paul had made the pastries from scratch, using blueberries picked early last summer from the untended fields above their property. With a pang, Darcie recalled eating one of those muffins, imagining if she *was* pregnant that the product of their land was nourishing the product of their union. The thought, both earthy and primeval, had pleased her.

She reached now for another muffin, peeling the wrap away as she moved toward the sink. Outside the window, she caught a flash of white, causing her heart to sink low in her chest. Paul, wearing his favorite bucket hat, moved with a pair of clippers among his rhododendrons. Moses and Aaron, their black Labs, nosed around the beauty bark. Not until that moment did Darcie realize she'd been so focused on her own worries she'd failed to register that the dogs hadn't been at the door to greet her. Or that Paul's truck had been in the carport before hers.

How long had he been home? This made the third time in a week he'd returned early from the shop. Glancing around the kitchen for clues, she saw a pound of ground hamburger thawing in an inch of water in the sink. On the counter, Paul's favorite cookbook was open to a baked enchilada recipe. She poked a finger into the mound of meat, leaving an indentation. The hamburger was completely thawed, which meant her husband had been home for some time. An hour, at least, and it was now just past four o'clock.

As resentment brought a rush of bitterness to her mouth, she set her half-finished muffin on the counter. She thought about yet another month's hopes dashed. She thought about her brother holed up in his room and her husband snipping at rhodies without a care in the world. Since Paul *was* home early, couldn't he at least have Rees out there with him? Hadn't they agreed allowing Rees too much time alone was doing more harm than good?

The doorbell startled Darcie from her dark thoughts. When it rang again, twice more in quick succession, she hastened to the foyer. Through the stained-glass window, she recognized their little neighbor boy.

What on earth? Fumbling with the lock, she tried to summon his name. Jake? No, Jack. He and his mother moved into Penny Watrous's mother-in-law cottage when the boy was just a baby, but despite the fact they were neighbors, Darcie hardly knew them. About the only thing she did know was that Ally—the name popped into her head—worked at the Front Street Bistro.

The chain lock tumbled free and Darcie opened the door. "Jack? What—"

"Miss Penny's not home!" he gasped, his face bleached with fear.

"Miss Penny?"

"And there's glass!"

"Glass? Where?"

"My mom's hurt."

Darcie bent to his level, placed her hands on his trembling shoulders. "Your mom sent you to get me?"

"To get Miss Penny, but she's not home. Mom needs help." He blinked wide brown eyes to keep tears from falling, and Darcie's heart flared.

"All right." She straightened, welcoming the clinical calm that descended like a curtain, temporarily separating her from her own reality. "Tell me what happened."

"A piece of glass. Mom stepped on it, and it's stuck in her foot."

"Is she bleeding?"

"There was a lot of blood on her sock."

How deeply had the glass penetrated? Had Ally severed a tendon? The possibilities spooled through Darcie's mind even as she asked the next question. "Is she conscious?" She doubted there had been any serious loss of blood, though the sight of it sometimes made people faint. When Jack only stared, she realized he didn't know what she meant. "Is she awake?"

"Yes."

"All right, good. Thank you. Now Jack, look at me." She waited for his gaze to meet hers. Even in this moment, she was struck by his uncommonly thick, dark lashes. What a beautiful child. Again, her heart squeezed. "Everything's going to be okay." His shoulders felt so narrow between her hands, his face so pale beneath the freckles. "My medical kit's in the car. I'll grab it while you run back and tell your mom I'm on my way."

He ran.

"Be careful crossing the street!"

He never looked back.

CHAPTER 3

Ally bit her lip as blood soaked though yet another wad of paper towels. After Jack had disappeared, she'd managed to hop to the counter, pull down the roll of paper towels, and use them to stanch the bleeding. It seemed to have slowed some, but with the shard still in her foot, she was afraid to apply much pressure.

What if she'd cut something important? Or needed surgery? Without health insurance, even a relatively minor procedure would drain her savings account. Not to mention that her feet were her livelihood. What would she do if she couldn't work for the next month or more? Penny was flexible regarding the rent, provided Ally made up for it by doing additional work on the property. But if Ally was unable to walk, even that option would be out of the question. As the grim possibilities flooded in, a band of anxiety tightened around her chest.

With both back and front doors thrown open, the narrow kitchen served as a wind tunnel. The briny air brought goose bumps to her flesh. Why hadn't she thought to ask Jack to bring her a sweatshirt?

And then a new worry struck. Ten minutes had passed since Jack ran out the door. Where was he? He should have returned by now.

All at once, she visualized Penny's empty carport. And she remembered: It was Tuesday, Penny's day to work the cashier counter at the Good Cheer thrift shop in town.

Finding Penny's house empty, Jack must have gone to find help elsewhere. But where? Their nearest neighbors had already headed mainland for the winter, which left only…

Their neighbors across the street.

With a sick lurch, Ally remembered the busy road above their lane, with its speeding cars and blind curve, that Jack was forbidden to cross alone. In his determination to find help, would he have tried anyway?

Oh, God.

Jack burst through the door. "Mom!"

"Right here, Bubs." Her eyes closed in relief. "Is someone coming?"

"The lady across the street!" His face was pink with exertion. He must have run all the way.

She heard the front door latch and the wind tunnel abated. Then the woman Ally knew as their neighbor appeared in the kitchen doorway. Her honey blond hair escaped in wisps from a ponytail, her ample chest heaved with each deep breath. She wore a white cardigan sweater over teal scrubs and carried a canvas medical kit. "You're a doctor?" Ally asked.

"Nurse," she corrected. "I'm Darcie." She skirted the smeared blood on the linoleum to reach Ally, propped against a cupboard door. "You look chilled. Here, take this." She removed her sweater and draped it, still warm, across Ally's shoulders. "Now, let's see what we've got here." Gingerly, she lifted the wad of paper towels from Ally's foot and removed the bloody sock. "A nasty gash." Reaching behind her, she opened her bag, withdrew a pair of latex gloves and slipped them on. "Wiggle your toes for me. Yes, that's good." She pinched Ally's big toe. "Capillary refill, also good. What about tingling or numbness?" Ally shook her head. "All right, doesn't look like you've sliced through anything important. First thing is to get that glass out. Let's get you up off the floor. I'll take you to urgent care for stitches."

"Wait. If we just get the glass out, won't it heal up on its own?"

"Eventually, but it'll take much longer without stitches. Plus, the tissue won't close together correctly, leaving a pretty big scar. You don't want that."

"You're sure we can't just leave it?"

"I'm sure. You'll probably need a tetanus shot, too."

Ally looked down at her bare hands. "I don't have health insurance."

"Oh." A pause lengthened. Then, "I'm sure they can work something out. You really should be seen."

What Darcie really meant was the clinic would work out a payment schedule for the cost of their services, which would surely run into the hundreds. Even if they gave her a year, it was an expense she couldn't afford.

A new thought struck her. "Could you—would you do it?" She glanced at Darcie's medical kit. "Stitch me up, I mean?"

"Me?"

Ally felt Darcie's regard, sensed her putting the puzzle pieces together. And her ears pricked with embarrassment as she imagined the picture emerging: single mom, part-time waitress, no insurance, irresponsible. "Sorry, I shouldn't have asked. You're probably worried I'll sue you or something—"

"No. No, I'm not worried about that. Here, I need you to keep applying pressure." Darcie guided Ally's hands to the gauze pad she'd been holding over the wound and got to her feet before pulling a cell phone from the deep pocket of her scrubs. She smiled at Ally, her blue eyes clear and kind, though faint lines radiating from the corners hinted at something deeper. She had the sort of round face that looked young from a distance but closer examination proved older. "I don't blame you for asking. It's just I don't carry that sort of thing with me. But I do have suture material and lidocaine back at the house. I'll just call up there and have someone bring it down." She moved away as she punched a number into the phone. "Hey, it's me. I need you to do something..." Her voice faded as she walked into the living room.

Jack appeared in the doorway, clutching his stuffed beagle, Fluff. His pose, reminding her of the way he'd held Lola, caused Ally's glance to flicker to the hard-shelled case on the table. "Jack, would you mind putting Lola back in my room? Watch the glass."

Darcie returned in time to hear this last part. "I'll get that mess cleaned up for you." She opened the pantry door to scan its contents. "Where's your broom?"

"Oh." Ally kept her eye on Jack, making sure he skirted the shattered glass. "In the hall closet."

"Thanks." Darcie's gaze followed Jack as he slid the case from the table. "You play violin?"

"Viola, actually."

Darcie fetched the broom and dustpan. "You any good?"

"Used to be." Ally's voice faltered, unnerved not only by the unrelenting pain but by the abrupt shift in conversation. "In another life."

"I have a friend who plays with a group. They do gigs around here, weddings and stuff. One of their players moved back to Seattle last summer. I can ask my friend if he wants to audition you."

"Oh, no. Thank you, but no."

"Why not?"

"Well—" Ally drew back, feeling cornered by Darcie's persistence. "It's been years since I've played for an audience. I just play for myself now, and Jack. Anyway, it'd be too hard for me to find someone to watch Jack while I rehearsed."

Darcie frowned and seemed about to argue, but a scuffle of boots on the back porch deflected her attention. A *thunk* sounded as something heavy landed against the side of the house. Ally startled.

"Don't worry," Darcie said quickly, reading her apprehension. "It's just my brother." In the doorway stood a man wearing jeans and a green North Face windbreaker over a white t-shirt. Nice-looking guy, broad-shouldered and fit, with blue eyes like his sister's and light brown hair spiked over his forehead. From one hand dangled a large tool box, from the other a plastic bag, which he handed to Darcie.

"That was quick." Darcie's tone had an edge Ally didn't understand. If he got here so fast, shouldn't she be pleased? "Ally, this is my brother, Rees Davies. Rees, Ally."

"And this is my son, Jack." She pulled him to her side as he returned from her bedroom. "Sorry to put you to this trouble."

"No trouble," Rees said, a little shortly.

"While I work on your foot," Darcie went on, "Rees is going to fix your back door."

"Oh, please don't do that." Already unsettled by the tension she sensed between brother and sister, she squirmed at the idea of putting them to further trouble. "I can do it myself as soon as … as soon as I'm back on my feet again."

Darcie flicked her a glance. "You don't think we're going to leave your door like this overnight, do you? You're in no shape to fix it yourself, and I'd wager Penny Watrous isn't the one to do it either. Rees will rig up something so you'll be safe tonight. Then he and my husband will be back in the morning to fix it properly."

Ally looked at Rees to see what he thought of this plan, but his tanned face remained unreadable as he peeled off his windbreaker. As he tossed it onto a chair, Ally saw what she hadn't at first: a discolored line of flesh. A scar stretching upwards from his neck to his right cheek. "I don't know how I'll repay you."

"No need for that." Darcie unwrapped a vial from the small parcel Rees had given her. "This is what neighbors do." She glanced at the label on the vial and nodded, satisfied. "Rees, will you please help me carry Ally into the next room?"

"Oh, no." Ally hoisted herself up before Rees had a chance to move. "I can do it." Using the table to support herself, she hopped toward the living room, ignoring the pain that shot clear to her knee. "Jack, come with me, please."

In the living room, she lowered herself onto the sofa. "This okay?" she asked as Darcie came behind her, carrying all the medical supplies. Hammer blows sounded from the kitchen.

"Fine." Darcie pulled on fresh gloves before laying out a small towel, suture twine and tweezers on a sterile cloth. "Okay, turn onto your stomach. We'll prop your foot here." She pushed a throw pillow beneath Ally's foot and laid the towel across it before turning on a lamp, flooding the room with burnished light. Ally felt Darcie's firm hand grasp her foot, a moment of pressure followed by a stab of pain. Ally gasped, and Darcie gave her ankle a squeeze. "Good girl, glass is out. Step one done." Darcie kept firm pressure over the wound for a minute before checking the area again, dousing it with something cool and wet.

Jack sidled up beside Ally, eyeing Darcie's movements with an expression Ally couldn't decipher but which made her realize her son didn't need to be watching this. "Hey, Bubba, why don't you put on *Finding Nemo* while Miss Darcie's helping me."

He stared at her. "But I can't."

"Why not?"

"They took our TV, 'member?"

Darcie's ministrations stilled. Though she couldn't see her, Ally sensed her neighbor's sharp interest. Ally hurried on. "Well, then, how about listening to a VeggieTales CD in your room?"

"Can I watch the man fix the door?"

"I don't think that's such a good idea—"

"Please?"

"Rees won't mind," Darcie interjected, patting Ally's leg. "Okay, you can sit up now. We'll give the lidocaine a few minutes to take effect before stitching you up."

Ally readjusted herself on the couch, aware of her son watching her hopefully. "Okay," she conceded, "you can go into the kitchen. But please stay out of Mr. Rees's way."

He skipped into the kitchen, Darcie waiting only until his back was turned before lasering Ally with a glare. "*That's* how this happened? Your house was broken into?"

Taken aback by her intensity, Ally stammered, "Y-yes."

"Why didn't you say so? I thought it was an accident, a baseball going through the door or something. I assume you've called the police."

"I—I left my phone at work. That's why I sent Jack for help."

"Well, here, use mine." She pulled hers from her pocket and thrust it at Ally. Ally took it but made no move to dial. "You're not dialing."

"The only things missing are the television, my jewelry box, and some costume jewelry." But even as she said it, her stomach bottomed out as she remembered her grandmother's wedding rings. Normally, she wore them at work as an easy way to keep unwanted interest at bay, but this morning she was rushed and had forgotten. Though not worth a lot of money, they were precious to her.

Ally swallowed. "It's not worth getting the police involved."

"Don't you want to at least try getting your things back?"

"I told you, it's not worth the trouble. Besides, all they'll do is file a report. I know, I used to know someone in law enforcement."

Darcie shrugged. "Have it your way." She took back her phone, dropped it in her pocket, then held aloft a needle, threaded with suture. "Ready? Let's get you back on your stomach."

As Ally reflexively turned from the sight of the needle, her glance snagged on the bookcase, where once more her brain registered something amiss. More than just the television gone, something was out of place. But what? She couldn't think of anything valuable that might have been stolen. In fact, on the top shelf stood her Chihuly glass sculpture that Sam had given each of his employees last Christmas. That was probably the most valuable knick-knack she owned, and yet the thief had passed it by.

She gave up on retrieving the memory and settled onto her stomach. "You do know how to do this, right?" For the first time, it occurred to her to ask.

"Sure. In theory."

"In theory?" She sucked in a breath as Darcie picked up her foot. "What—exactly what kind of nurse are you, anyway?"

"Hospice."

Chapter 4

Scents of cumin and chili powder embraced Darcie as she walked into her own kitchen an hour later.

"Just getting ready to call out the cavalry." Paul lifted a heavy Corningware dish from the oven before turning down the jazz on the radio. "Rees told me what happened."

Saliva flooded Darcie's mouth as she looked at the line-up inside the pan, the beef enchiladas baked golden brown, smothered in cheese and simmering in sauce. She sighed, calculating calories. Another woman might be grateful for a husband who loved to cook, one who, quite honestly, preferred his own cooking to hers. Problem was, Paul—drat his skinny hide—possessed the metabolism of a nuclear reactor and could enjoy the fruits of his labor with impunity. She, on the other hand, metabolized like a hibernating bear and had gained seven pounds last year. At this rate, she'd weigh as much as a Seahawks lineman by the time she turned forty.

Darcie dropped her medical kit on the counter as Moses and Aaron rose from their blue, donut-shaped cushions. Nails clicking on the hardwood floor, they lumbered over. "Sorry to be so late." She rubbed each dog hard on his ebony haunches. "The Brennans needed something for dinner, so I made sandwiches."

"She going to be okay?"

"Oh, yes. Only a minor cut that bled a lot. Looked a lot worse than it was, but she'll be pretty sore for the next week or so." She gave each dog a final pat. As they flopped back onto their donuts, her eye fell on her half-eaten blueberry muffin, which Paul had neatly re-wrapped and returned to a china plate on top of the microwave. It reminded her that they had been denied parenthood once again. With a sick feeling, she wondered when she should tell Paul. But as she also remembered him puttering happily among his rhodies, she felt a flare of pique at his cluelessness. Why should she have to tell him? Eventually the truth would become self-evident. Even to Paul.

She crossed to the dinette table, where Paul had set a pitcher of iced tea beside two tumblers. She'd avoided caffeine for the last three weeks, just in case, but there was no good reason to deny herself anymore. Ice clinked against the glass as she poured a full glass. "Noticed you were home early this afternoon." Sipping her tea, she eyed her husband over the rim of her tumbler. He set a green salad on the table. "Any particular reason?"

"Business was slow so I asked Diego to close up." He shrugged, turning away.

The gesture struck her as evasive. "How slow?"

"I was going to mention it." A beat. "Richard stopped by today."

Darcie set down her tumbler. "He did?" Their accountant rarely made a personal appearance unless he had something unpleasant to say.

"Last week I asked him to run some numbers for me." He went to the sink, turned on the tap. "They're not great."

"*How* not great?"

Another beat, this one longer. "If business doesn't pick up by year's end, the shop's going to be in trouble." He glanced at her, a weak smile touching his hazel eyes. "Forestalling a miracle, that is."

She ignored this last comment. Miracles were slow to come their way lately. "But business *won't* pick up." Darcie crossed her arms. "Not this time of year." Paul's boat shop did most of its business during the summer months, when tourists rented kayaks and canoes. With winter on its way, he would supplement the shop's income with detailing and repair services for the locals who moored their vessels at the Langley small boat marina. But that was peanuts compared to what they needed if they didn't have a good cushion to begin with.

"If worse comes to worst," Paul pointed out, "we can always get a loan from my brothers."

"No, we can*not.*"

Her vehemence brought two faint furrows to his brow, same as always when she caught him off guard. "Hon, we've been through this before. You know we'll pull through one way or another."

Sure, by the skin of our teeth. From the start, Paul's business had struggled, but because he'd not said anything in months, she'd assumed it was doing better. That was her first mistake. "We will not be asking your brothers for help."

"Not that I'd want to—"

"You won't." She looked him full in the eye. "We'll go belly-up before we go that route. It was hard enough for you to break from them in the first place. We won't become indebted to them now." Or listen to them crow. Paul's brothers meant well, but they never hesitated to show anyone the error of his ways. Especially when that someone was their youngest brother. "Do I need to take on more clients? I could ask Carla to give me more hours." Currently assigned only three clients, Darcie worked twenty-five hours a week. She could easily take on one more client, maybe two.

Paul frowned. "What about your other commitments?"

When they'd moved from Seattle to Whidbey Island six years ago, they agreed Darcie would limit her work hours to part-time in order to have more time for community involvement. She now co-chaired the South Island Harvest Festival every fall, in addition to serving on several committees at their church. "The festival's done next month. I can cut back on some of the other stuff at church, at least until we get over this hump." Part-time employment was a luxury she enjoyed, but only if they could afford it. "Seems a logical solution to me."

Paul turned back to the sink, adding soap to the water. "I'd rather we held off doing anything drastic quite yet."

She stared at his back, the way his shoulders flexed with every motion of his hands. She used to love watching him work, admiring the way he maintained his youthful physique long past the age when most men grew a pot belly. "I'm going to go change." She pivoted on her heel, only then noticing the table held only two place settings. "Rees isn't joining us?"

"Not tonight."

"Why not?"

"Says he's not hungry."

"That boy." She allowed aggravation to spill into her tone. "He's turning into a recluse."

"He's hardly a boy."

"Why does he keep shutting himself away?" She raised her voice, uncaring whether Rees could hear her words. Maybe if he understood how much it bothered her, he'd open up to her the way he used to.

"Not everyone's the extrovert you are, hon."

"He needs to talk about it." That much had become clear to her over the last three weeks. Though the red gash on Rees's face was healing quickly, his silence about how he'd gotten it made her believe whatever had happened in Mumbai had wounded more than just his skin. "Surely even you can see that."

"What I see," Paul said evenly, "is that he needs time. He'll talk when he's ready."

"I'd like to believe that, but I'm afraid this is going to destroy him."

A brief silence settled between them. "Because of Julie?" Paul asked quietly.

"Yes." Of course because of Julie.

"It won't."

"How do you know? Has he talked to you?" The thought that he may have talked to Paul before he talked to her sent a jealous dart through her heart.

"I know because he's stronger than that." Paul took his place at the table.

"I just can't stand to see him go through the fire again." If only she had some idea what was bothering him. Why did he persist in keeping it from her? It was so unlike him, her little brother, who from the time they were small came to her to solve all his problems, from a skinned knee to a broken heart. She pulled out her chair and joined Paul at the table.

"He's fortunate to have a sister who cares so much." Paul paused. She bowed her head, waiting for him to say grace. When the pause lengthened, she looked up and found him staring pointedly at her midsection. "Aren't you going to change first?"

She glanced down and saw what he saw: Ally's blood smeared across her scrubs. With a sigh, she laid her napkin beside her plate and rose to change into something clean.

CHAPTER 5

Jack's face, small and white, nestled on his *Cars* pillow as his eyelids drooped at half-mast. Ally replaced the Magic Tree House book she'd been reading aloud on his nightstand. "Sleep tight, no bedbugs." She kissed his nose. "Been a long day." She felt the truth of it in every molecule of her body, the afternoon's trauma and her injury making her want to crawl beneath her own duvet as soon as possible.

But Jack's dark lashes swept up again and worried eyes peered at her. "Mom?"

"Yes, Bubba?" She brushed the blond hair off his forehead, marveling, as always, at the smooth perfection of his skin.

"What if that man comes back?"

Her hand stilled. *That man*. The same question kept rippling through her own mind. The rational side of her knew the odds of the burglar returning were practically nil. He'd gotten what he'd come for. But the protective-mom side of her, the side that considered it not only her prerogative but her duty to worry, had gained the upper hand.

Hoping to distract him, she deliberately misunderstood his question. "Well, Miss Darcie said Mr. Rees would be back tomorrow to fix our door for good. We won't see him, though, because you'll be at school and I'll be at work."

But Jack would not be distracted. "Not Mr. Rees." His head moved impatiently against the pillow. "The man who took our stuff. Do you think he was in my room?"

"I don't know, Bubs. But whether he was or not, he's not now, so there's nothing to be afraid of."

"I'm not afraid, I just want to be ready. What happens if he comes back when we're sleeping?"

"He won't. People who take from other people are cowards. He won't come back while we're here." She prayed it was true, even as she marveled at her son's courage, greater than her own. "Besides, whoever broke into our house wanted to steal, not hurt us. And you saw how Mr. Rees nailed that plywood over our door. No one's getting in that way again."

Jack looked to the ceiling, where his lamp cast a circle of yellow light. "Do you think he took our TV because he didn't have one of his own?"

"Probably." No point explaining the thief had not wanted their TV and jewelry for himself but for the quick cash they would provide. No doubt both were already sitting in a pawn shop somewhere in downtown Seattle. She didn't care about the television, but she did regret the loss of her grandmother's rings, one of the few links to her past. They were surely worth much more to her than to the thief. "The main thing is he wasn't after us. He just wanted our stuff, and who cares about stuff, right? We're storing up our treasures in heaven."

Jack tucked Fluff more firmly beneath his chin as he thought about this. "What kind of treasures?"

"Oh, relationships. And character qualities, like being loving and patient and forgiving. Jesus says these things will last forever, which means they're the only things that really count."

All at once, the full weight of her burden settled around her shoulders like a lead cape. Times like these, it became easy to second-guess her decision to raise her son all by herself. Not that she questioned her decision to single parent. In that, she'd had no choice. But had she done the right thing in coming to Langley, so far away from family and friends and everything familiar? Had she done the right thing in keeping them isolated and alone? This afternoon, when Darcie had started asking questions, Ally worried she'd probe too far.

If Ally had chosen differently, would moments like this be any easier? It was hard, doing it all by herself. Raising this child. Teaching him the values and truths she'd come to embrace.

Still, looking down at his sweet, sleepy face, she knew Jack was worth it. Worth the doubts. Worth even the heartache. Ally shook off the moment of melancholy and smoothed the blanket over him and Fluff. "Think you can sleep now?"

"Maybe. If you played Lola…?"

She smiled at his wheedling. "Only for a few minutes." Bone-tired as she was, she knew Lola was what he needed. *And what I need, too.* She rose gingerly, touching her thickly swathed foot to the floor. Darcie had told her to stay off her feet, but clearly Darcie was not a mom. Stay off her feet while she had a young child to care for? Impossible.

Ally hobbled into her bedroom and pulled Lola from beneath the bed, holding her case briefly to her heart. Thank God the thief didn't find her. If he had...

She didn't like to think what she'd do without her instrument. Might as well try to sing without a voice.

A knock sounded at the front door. Her heart leapt into her throat as she imagined for a split second that the intruder had returned. Then she chided herself for being ridiculous. As if he would knock.

"Mom?" Jack called from his room, worry lacing his voice. "Someone's at the door."

Through the thin veil of curtain, Ally saw the lumpy contours of Penny Watrous. "It's just Miss Penny." She pinched back a sigh. Would the demands of this day never cease? "I'll see what she wants, then be right with you."

Ally set Lola on an end table and opened the door. "Hi, Penny."

"Darcie Nielsen called and said something about a burglary?" In one hand, her landlady clutched a wrinkled, plastic grocery bag, while her sharp brown gaze darted around the room, landing finally on Ally's foot. "What happened to you?"

"I stepped on broken glass." She wished Darcie hadn't called her landlady. "Everything's okay."

"Okay? Your stuff was stolen, the back door busted in, you're injured. What's okay about that?" She pushed past Ally into the kitchen. By the time Ally caught up with her, she was at the back door, inspecting Rees's repair job.

"That's only temporary. Darcie's brother will be back tomorrow to fix it properly. Don't worry," she added, anticipating Penny's next question. "I'll pay for it."

Penny's thin lips set in a small, tight hyphen. "Well, I guess that's all right then. I don't got insurance for this kind of thing, you know. What'd you tell the police?"

"I didn't tell them anything. We'll never get the stuff back, so it seemed like too much trouble to call."

"Well, fine. Just see that the door is fixed tomorrow." Penny paused before adding gruffly, "Glad you and Jack are okay. Here." She thrust the plastic bag at Ally. "This is for Jack."

Ally peeled back the bag to reveal a neatly folded sweater. "You made this?" She held it up, a crazy-quilt cacophony of primary colors with a yellow dump truck appliquéd on the front. Unspeakably gaudy, but the wool felt soft as fleece against her hands.

"Thought he could use it, with the cold weather coming on. Should keep him nice and snug."

"I'm sure it will." Despite the garment's questionable aesthetics, she felt warmed by the gesture. Penny's random acts of kindness tended to be—well, random. "Thank you, Penny."

She nodded. "You're welcome. My grandson didn't want it, said it didn't suit his *style*."

"I can't imagine why," she murmured, then pinched her lips tight.

Penny eyed her suspiciously. "If your boy doesn't want it, just say so."

"Oh, no. Thank you. Jack will appreciate this." She held it against her cheek. "He loves soft things."

"Should be soft, what I paid for that yarn. Hate to see it go to waste." Penny paused with her hand on the knob, looking down at Ally's bandaged foot. "Don't suppose you'll be up to mowing the lawn this weekend."

Ally widened her eyes, hoping she looked regretful enough to please Penny. "Probably not." She felt proud of her control. Given the pain radiating from her sole, she wondered how she'd get through her shift tomorrow, let alone mow a half-acre of grass. "I'll get to it as soon as I'm able, I promise."

After shutting the door behind Penny, Ally picked up Lola and headed for her son's bedroom. In the doorway, she stopped. Jack was sound asleep, lashes fanned across his cheek. She folded Penny's sweater on the bureau for him to discover as a surprise in the morning. Then she pressed her lips to his satin-soft cheek, turned out the lamp, and quietly shut the door.

CHAPTER 6

Paul had filled both their plates with steaming enchiladas by the time Darcie returned to the table in fresh jeans and a pink, scoop-necked sweater. She waited for her husband to say grace before picking up her fork. "Did Rees mention they were robbed?"

Paul's own fork stopped halfway to his mouth. "Who was?"

"The Brennans. A smash and grab. The thieves took what they could and got out."

"Couple of kids, you think?"

"Probably." This downturn in the economy brought out the worst in some people.

"What about Penny?" Paul took a bite. "Is she okay?"

"She wasn't home when I left Ally's, but everything there looked fine. Left her a message, told her what happened." A new thought occurred to her. "What time did you get home this afternoon?"

"Around three?"

"Did you see or hear anything?"

"No. But I was out back most of the time, wouldn't have seen anything from there."

"Ally's back door will have to be replaced. I told her that you and Rees would be by in the morning to take care of it."

"Sure, fine." Her husband forked another bite of enchilada into his mouth. "Any idea what their story is? Neighbors for five years and we barely know their names."

"Ally didn't volunteer much by way of information. Quite the opposite, in fact." As a hospice nurse, she found most people eager to talk about themselves and their loved ones. Understanding it to be part of the mourning process, she always welcomed their stories. But Ally had steered the conversation away from anything personal. And the few photos scattered around the house were of Jack, none whatsoever of grandparents or aunts and uncles and cousins. "Bit of a mystery, that one. I think she prefers it that way."

"Her son sure didn't get his looks from her, did he? Must take after his dad. I take it he's not in the picture."

"Not so far as I could tell." Darcie stood and carried her plate to the sink, which she filled with soapy water. Outside, darkness obscured Paul's rhodies and raindrops freckled the windowpane.

Her husband finished clearing the table and put leftovers in Tupperware containers. "Did you like the enchiladas? I added bell pepper and minced garlic to the sauce. I think it gave it an extra kick, don't you?"

"Everything was delicious."

Suddenly, he turned and wrapped his arms around her waist, pressing his cheek against her hair. "Please don't worry about the shop."

She sucked in a breath. "Who says I'm worrying?"

"I do."

His hands moved to her shoulders, kneading them. "Everything's going to be okay. Trust me?"

"Of course." She knew it was what he wanted to hear. She leaned into his touch, willing herself to believe him. Maybe he was right. Maybe she was reading too much into this slump. Every business went through its ups and downs, didn't it? And this recession had hit everyone particularly hard. Yet every day the papers reported businesses like Paul's rebounding, the strength of the economy reasserting itself. Her hormones, coupled with today's disappointment, could be shading the picture darker than it was.

He kissed her neck. "You're the best."

"You're second best." She managed a smile as she called on their familiar old joke.

"We got *Grey's Anatomy* on Netflix." He picked up a dishcloth from the dish drain. "Wanna watch with me?"

"Sure." He knew she enjoyed pointing out all the medical inaccuracies of the show—his way of smoothing over the tension about the shop. But this triggered another thought. "Hey, did we ever get rid of our old TV?" When Rees had come to stay with them, they removed the old set from the guest room and replaced it with a combination TV-DVD-player.

"Not yet. Keep meaning to drop it off at the Good Cheer but haven't found the chance."

"Let's give it to Ally. You don't mind, do you?"

"'Course not. I'll take it over tomorrow, if you like."

"No." Darcie handed him the serving platter to dry. "I'll ask Rees to take it over tonight."

Paul dried in silence for several seconds. She glanced at him and found a smile dancing over his lips. "What?" she asked.

"You're plotting something."

"I'm not."

"You sure? Attractive, young, *single* neighbor. Attractive little brother, also single. You're trying to get them together."

Despite her worries, Darcie laughed. "Um, *no*." Rees liked brainy, leggy blondes, sophisticated women who enjoyed travel and the arts, who loved Jesus and wanted to make a difference in the world. Women like Julie. Ally Brennan, sweet and pretty as she was, wasn't her brother's type at all. "It's just that I told Ally to stay off her feet for the next couple of nights and thought she might miss her TV."

Paul's smirk said he didn't believe her. His smugness irritated her, but a retort died on her tongue as her cell phone trilled from the depths of her handbag.

"Want me to get that?" Paul asked.

"No thanks." She clipped her words as she peeled off her dish gloves. "Probably work." Either that or Lauren, her co-chair for the Harvest Festival, calling to update her on bake sale volunteers.

Her first guess was right. "I've got a new-patient assessment for you tomorrow," said Carla, her scheduling supervisor with Island Hospice and HomeCare.

"Hold on, let me grab a pen." She reached for the white binder by the phone and opened it to a new page.

"Seventy-two-year-old female, type two diabetic, end-stage renal failure. Hospital sent her home, her daughter's staying with her for the duration." Carla gave her the address.

"Got it." She shifted to the sink as Paul called to Aaron and Moses before grabbing his hat from its peg. He flipped on the porch light, ushered the dogs outside. Through the window, she watched her husband wait, hands in his pockets while the dogs sniffed around to find the perfect spot to do their business. Despite the rain that pattered down, speckling his hat and shoulders, Paul would stand there all night if he had to. From the day she'd met him, Darcie had known patience was one of her husband's virtues. Lately, it took effort to feel grateful for it.

"Carla? There was something else I wanted to tell you, since I've got you on the line." Darcie moved to the study, where she shut the door to speak with privacy. "Starting as soon as possible, you can send me more clients."

CHAPTER 7

When she knew Jack was sleeping soundly, Ally finally allowed herself to admit the fear she'd tasted, cold and metallic at the back of her throat, when she'd opened the front door that afternoon and realized something was wrong. She'd held it together for Jack's sake, had shoved fear into the tight, dark cave she'd walked away from twice before, with the promise never again to revisit. But this, this invasion of their home, had brought her closer to that cave than she'd been ever since. Her words to Jack about treasures in heaven had masked a visceral sense of violation.

A stranger had been inside her house. Inside her very bedroom, his hands on her things, touching, feeling, taking what wasn't his. She knew what it meant to feel that terrible slap of outrage to the gut, had vowed never to be so vulnerable again. It was why she'd chosen Langley-by-the-Sea. Quiet, remote, lazy Langley, where such personal violations weren't supposed to happen.

Leaning her head against the wall outside Jack's bedroom, she stayed motionless, willing the dread and doubt to recede. When she felt she'd regained some measure of control, she limped into the living room and laid the viola's hard-shelled case on the coffee table. As she lifted Lola from her red velvet bed, she experienced the usual throb of wonder that such an instrument belonged to her and felt slightly reassured by the familiar feeling. The gentle patina of the viola gleamed like warm satin. Even the mended crack along its back, which few people ever saw but which spoke of its history, did nothing to mar Lola's beauty.

Ally tightened first one peg and then another before drawing her bow across all four strings until they sang in harmony. And then she played, the mellow strains emerging from Lola's throat like a prayer. Before this moment, she'd been unable to pray, too mindful of her clenched emotions to be able to bring her concerns to God. But now, closing her eyes, Ally envisioned Him as she loved Him best, seated on His throne, His train filling the court of His temple. Music settled over her like a sweet memory. The notes she played lifted…lifted…until they touched the very hem of His robe.

It had always been like this. Well, not always, but ever since the day God had returned His gift to her, the gift of music. Her music. She'd tried to give it up out of misplaced grief and guilt. But He'd insisted she take it back. And no wonder. It was music, after all, that taught her so much about how to worship Him.

Music danced through her, imprinting God's messages on her heart so she'd remember them when she needed them most. Like a satisfying meal, a good song stayed with her long after it was done, nourishing her soul the way food nourished her body.

Ally started by playing a few random lines, scrap melodies of whatever came to mind, but these soon blossomed into something altogether different. As so often happened, Lola guided her toward music instead of the other way around. She rode the tide of melody, allowing the music to be her voice.

Alone in his room with the door closed, Rees stared at the words on his laptop screen, black-on-white blurring into gray. This was where he'd been when Darcie's phone call had interrupted him three hours ago—legs stretched before him on the full-sized bed, back propped on two pillows against the carved oak headboard.

Despite her good reason for needing his help, he'd been irked at having to drop everything when she called. He'd let it show, though he knew it unfair. How could Darcie have known he'd just received news from a Sanctuary colleague that hit him like a sucker punch to the gut?

Only vaguely aware of the savory aromas drifting beneath his door, he shifted his laptop, feeling its warmth through the denim of his jeans. He reread Sheela's email, finding her words no more palatable now than he had the first three times.

The fact that he'd received an email from Sheela Gupta in the first place had surprised him. Sheela had little reason to copy him on a routine report to her staff about the rescued women under her care. Normally her job as aftercare supervisor and his as legal investigator intersected only the day of a rescue. On those days, Sheela and her team were on hand at the brothel site to receive, literally into open arms, the victims Rees and his team freed during their raid. But Sheela, a friend as well as a colleague, had perceived the circumstances relating to Jayashri were anything but normal, and she rightly guessed Rees would want to know.

Rees closed his eyes as Sheela's words caught and tangled in his mind. *Jayashri remains resistant…very little progress…totally overwhelmed…won't speak of her mother's death…self-cutting…*

Jayashri was cutting. Or, to be more clinical, she was engaging in self-mortification. *Self-mortification.* That word seemed to him to carry religious overtones. He pictured medieval monks, haircloth, flagellation. But as Sheela had been careful to explain, ancient monks used self-mortification as a means, however perverse, to draw nearer to God. For emotionally traumatized women like Jayashri, it was a means to drive Him away. By slicing into her own skin, Jayashri, consciously or unconsciously, was wounding her *imago dei*, her being-made-in-the-image-of-God. In this sense, she was cutting God Himself.

"When a person is denied justice the way these women are denied justice," Sheela had told him, "she feels as if God—or gods, whomever she believes in—has abandoned her. So, she hates God. And what better way to express her hatred than to make Him bleed?"

Rees touched the line of puckered skin that ran across his cheek, a permanent reminder of the night Jayashri's mother died. Though still tender, his own physical discomfort would end soon enough, leaving only a faint scar.

If only Jayashri's spirit would heal as easily.

In his years as a legal investigator, he'd never questioned his role, never doubted that despite the setbacks and the risks to his personal safety, he was doing good. He felt confident—proud, even—of his part in the fight against injustice. Until now.

How much of Jayashri's pain could be traced back to his snap decision on that fateful night? A decision that now struck him as reckless, maybe even wrong. Though Sheela had never hinted she blamed him for what had happened, he couldn't help but wonder. To his shame, he lacked the courage to ask.

God, what have I done?

Opening his eyes, his gaze fell on the framed oil painting at the foot of his bed, a piece of work he had bought from an artist on the boardwalk of Mumbai's Chowpatty Beach. With deft, spare strokes, the artist had captured the view from Chowpatty, the fishermen at noonday, drifting in their boats offshore. Rees had purchased it specifically with Darcie and Paul in mind, giving it to them as a host-and-hostess gift on his last visit home.

Sometime in the two years since, Darcie had redecorated this room, making his gift its centerpiece. The blue-green comforter, the bamboo mats, the rust-colored walls—each highlighted the hues in the painting. All of which should have made him feel welcome and at home. That's how Darcie wanted him to feel. Instead, it only added to his restlessness.

A tap on his door halted the downward spiral of his thoughts. With a sigh, he closed his laptop. "Come in."

Darcie poked her head in. She'd changed from her scrubs and re-combed her ponytail. She started to say something, but reading his face, detoured into a quick, "What's wrong?"

"Nothing." To tell her anything else would invite her to try to fix things that couldn't be fixed. Darcie was a fixer, always had been, especially when it came to her baby brother. But she couldn't fix what troubled him this time. "Just thinking, that's all."

"About what?"

He hesitated. "Work."

"Work?" She moved farther into the room, leaving the door open. "You're supposed to be on vacation."

"Was there something you wanted?" He wasn't in the mood for this conversation tonight.

"Oh. Yes, I just wanted to thank you for coming when I called."

"You're welcome."

Her gaze swept the room, taking in the open suitcase in the corner, still not completely unpacked, and the rumpled bed. He tried not to feel the intrusion.

"Sure you're not hungry? Leftovers are in the fridge. Enchiladas. Paul's own special recipe."

In the flippant, sing-songy way she trotted out this last part, he heard a note of sarcasm directed, for some unknown reason, at Paul. Well, Rees refused to rise to the bait. He liked Paul even more than he liked his cooking, which was saying something. "I'll eat after my run."

"It's dark out. And raining."

"I'll wear a jacket."

To his relief, she didn't argue. Instead she said, "Since you're already going out, could I ask a favor?"

Five minutes later, dressed for his run, Rees found the TV in the carport beneath a blue tarp as Darcie had said. Keeping the tarp snug around its bulk to protect it from the drizzle, he set out for Ally's house, welcoming the lactic acid burn of his physical labor.

A single streetlight provided the only illumination, prompting him to pick his way carefully across the street until he reached the crushed seashells of Ally's lane. As he passed the stand of trees at the top of the road, he caught full-on the sharp wind blowing up from the water, causing the edge of his collar to scrape against the still-sore scar on his neck.

From fifty yards away, the lights of the cottage appeared like yellow pats of melting butter, blurred by the rain. He mounted Ally's front porch, his sneakers silent on the steps. Balancing the television against his knee, he lifted his hand to knock, but before his knuckles brushed the door, he heard strains of music. Beautiful music, made by a single, stringed instrument—a violin, maybe, or a cello. The sound held him in its grip, the gentle sloshing of the water on the shore providing a steady beat as the wandering melody transitioned into a new tune, sad and slow. Only then did he realize it wasn't a recording but someone playing. He felt a pulse of surprise. Ally?

He'd pegged Ally Brennan as an ordinary single mom focused on earning a living and raising her child, with little left over for anything like making music. Shame sliced through him. He of all people knew better than to judge by what could be seen.

He placed the television silently against the wall beside the door, well out of the way of the rain. He would let Darcie explain the television when Ally discovered it there in the morning. Rees couldn't—wouldn't—do anything to stop the music. There was something powerful in the way she played, something that conveyed not just desire but a soul-deep need for this melody.

He jogged lightly down the steps and into the darkness, carrying with him the haunting melody of Ally Brennan's music.

Chapter 8

Ally played on and on, until finally the last note shimmered and faded on the strings. She held her pose, letting those last strains work their magic on her soul. Opening her eyes, she found herself looking at the bookshelves on the far side of the room. And it clicked. The missing item she'd been unable to identify before. A photograph of her and Jack on the beach below their cottage, held in a cheap wooden frame she'd bought at a garage sale. The item had no extrinsic value. Why would anyone steal it?

She lowered the viola and bow, puzzling it over. Could Jack have taken it? He had a habit of rearranging things when she wasn't looking. Maybe he'd put it in his room.

She followed the impulse to check. From the doorway of his room, she surveyed his shelves by the light in the hallway, even moved inside to peek at his nightstand drawer. But she found only a blue LEGO brick and a stash of sand-dusted shells.

When a burst of wind tossed a spatter of rain against the window, she saw she'd forgotten to shut Jack's blinds. She crossed to the window and lifted her eyes to the trees, illuminated by the porch light, scanning for signs this might be anything more than a passing shower, waiting for the familiar prickling on her skin, the raising of hairs along her arms she recalled from the thunderstorms of her childhood. The warning that came as electricity filled the air, alerting her to a storm long before it arrived.

But the maple leaves only twitched in rhythm to the falling rain. No rustle of air pushing through the leaves, no gymnastic swaying of long-limbed branches. That would come when the winds arrived, as they always did in the fall. But not tonight.

A flash of light and movement at the corner of the house made her stiffen, and then relax. The porch light revealed Rees Davies in the North Face jacket he'd worn earlier, cutting across the property on his way to the beach. Despite the rain, he was dressed in shorts, which clung to his muscled form. Though he had only a flashlight to light his way, he didn't slow his stride across the rocky shore, and she envied his confidence.

CHAPTER 9

The next morning, despite two extra-strength Advil, a thick bandage, and her roomiest sneakers, Ally felt as if a dozen tacks pressed into her foot. As a concession to the pain, she drove her Saturn to the bistro instead of walking, wondering how she would make it through an entire day on her feet.

Faded smells of curry and onion met Ally as she hobbled through the back door. "Morning, Sam." She greeted her boss as she hung her tote on a peg by the door.

Sam paused in his rhythmic chopping of vegetables for the daily soup—crab bisque, judging from the mound of shelled crabmeat resting beside the stove. His white chef's cap tipped over his broad forehead, gray-streaked brown hair tucked behind both ears. His keen blue gaze immediately took in her limp. "What's wrong with you?"

Ally tied her apron over her low-waisted black pants before answering. "Stepped on some broken glass yesterday."

Sam grunted, the angles of his fleshy face pulling long in sympathy. "Looks pretty bad."

"It's not." She brushed off his concern, afraid if she admitted how much it hurt, he'd send her home. She couldn't afford that.

"You gonna be okay today?"

"Of course." She offered him a bright smile.

He frowned at her through narrowed eyes. "Go ask Brit if she can stay a few extra hours today to give you a hand."

She shrugged to disguise her relief. "Thanks, Sam."

He waved off her thanks with a work-reddened hand and went back to chopping his vegetables.

Sam bought the Doghouse Diner in 1985 and transformed it from a dive to the Front Street Bistro. Every weekday plus Saturday, Brittany Williams served espresso concoctions and pastries in the alcove, starting at six. The restaurant opened at eight, doing crossover business with the espresso counter until Brittany closed after the lunch rush. Ally worked her shift in the restaurant from nine-thirty until three-thirty to accommodate Jack's school schedule.

This morning, only a family of four was eating breakfast in the restaurant. Susan, the morning waitress, had them covered, so Ally moved to the espresso stand to give Brittany a hand. The alcove was unusually crowded for a Wednesday, customers at every table. The line for coffee stood five people deep. Ally moved from table to table, clearing used cups and wiping down tabletops as customers finished and left. As the last customer in line took his beverage and claimed a just-vacated table, Ally joined Brittany behind the counter to help with tidying up after the rush.

Brittany, her blond hair caught up in a clip, gave her a frown similar to Sam's. "Why are you limping?"

"Cut my foot on some glass last night. Sam asked if you'd be willing to stay on a few extra hours to give me a hand."

"Sure. I could use the extra tips. Oh, and before I forget—" She pulled Ally's cell phone from her apron pocket. "Found it in my purse this morning. Sorry."

"Thanks." Ally slipped it into her own voluminous pocket as the bell over the door signaled another customer. They both looked over as a tall sheriff's deputy entered, doffing his wide-brimmed beige hat to reveal Marine-short, sandy hair.

"Hi, Ally. Brittany." His gaze skimmed over Ally to land on Brittany, where it lingered, taking in her artfully-messy up-do, the figure-skimming lilac tee, the jean-clad hips. Ally smothered a smile as she moved past him to bus the table by the window. Men. Did they have to be so obvious?

"Morning, Denny." Brittany smiled as she gave the steamer's spout a swipe with her damp cloth. "The usual?"

"Am I that predictable?"

"As Seattle rain," she said cheerfully. "That's okay, you make my job easy. One hazelnut mocha comin' up." She measured out the dark grounds, set the milk to steam.

Denny leaned an elbow on the counter, his Adam's apple bobbing as he cleared his throat. "Say, Brit."

"Yeah, Denny?" She pumped four squirts of flavoring into the bottom of his paper cup.

"So, a bunch of us are getting together tonight at Melrose's." His ruddy cheeks deepened to crimson. "Want to come?"

"Oh, I don't think so." She didn't look up. "But thanks for asking."

"Oh." He looked down at the hat in his hands. "Okay. Maybe next time, then."

Ally's heart squeezed as she watched Denny's expression fall. She quickly placed the dirty mugs in the black bin against the wall before moving behind the cash register. "That'll be three-fifty, Denny."

The deputy gave her a strained smile and a five-dollar bill. "Keep the change." Then, as she dropped the bill and coins into the tip jar, Denny included her in his invitation. "How about you, Ally? Want to come?"

"Me? Oh, no. Thanks, but I'd have no one to watch Jack."

"Oh, sure. Right."

"Here you go, one hazelnut mocha." Brittany slipped the cup into a cardboard sleeve before handing it to Denny.

"Thanks, Brit."

"Welcome, Den."

He left. Ally watched him get into his blue and white patrol car. "He likes you, Brit."

"Ya think?" Brittany removed the used grounds from the machine and thwacked them out against the side of the plastic garbage can.

"So why do you keep turning him down? He's a sweet guy." Not bad-looking, either. Broad shoulders. White smile.

"Not my type." Brittany reached behind her head to refasten the clip holding her hair. "Besides, I'm seeing someone."

"Since when?"

"Last week."

"How come you didn't say anything?" Brittany wasn't one to keep secrets.

Brittany's mouth flattened. "After Rand, I wanted to see if this one would stick." She'd dated Rand McPherson for four months—until his wife showed up at Billy's Bar-n-Grill, looking for her husband who hadn't come home for dinner. Brittany dumped him faster than he could say, "Let me explain"—but not before keying a ring around his new Mazda Miata. "I'm a nice girl," Brittany had told Ally, "just don't make me mad."

"And this one's going to stick?" Ally asked.

Brittany's pink-glossed lips twitched. "I kind of think so."

"Details, please."

"Blond hair, gorgeous eyes, tight build. In all the right places, if you know what I mean."

"Where'd you meet him?"

"Friday a bunch of us went out and ended up at the Melrose. He was sitting at the bar. Came here from the Midwest looking for work."

"For work? Not likely to find much here, is he?"

"Said he likes island living."

Don't we all? So long as we can afford it. "What line of work is he in?"

A frown traced grooves in Brittany's smooth forehead. "That part's a little sketchy, but he said he'd take any kind of work, so long as it paid decent. So, if you hear of something, be sure to let me know." Brittany slid Ally a glance. "Maybe I'll see if he's got a friend so we can double-date."

"No thanks."

Brittany opened her mouth to say something, but another customer walked in. She moved away to clear tables while Ally served the woman her Americano with cream. The woman left, and Brittany returned to the counter. "You could at least pretend to think about it, you know."

Ally shrugged. "Men aren't worth the trouble."

Brittany planted her hands on her hips, shaking her head. "This isn't about trouble, Ally. It's about trust."

"You're saying I don't trust you to set me up with a nice guy?"

Brittany picked up Ally's left hand, her eyebrows lifting. "Where are your rings?"

Ally pulled her hand back. "Forgot them at home," she fibbed, not wanting to admit they were stolen. No point opening that can of worms.

"Makes two days in a row you've 'forgotten.'" Brittany tossed her head. "Maybe there's hope for you yet."

"Your point?"

"You hide behind those rings because you're afraid to trust a man. Afraid to take a chance that someone might actually make you happy."

"I am happy."

"Oh, sure. On your feet all day waiting tables, then home to a landlady who makes you do all her yard work so you can afford her rent. A five-year-old boy, who I'll grant you is adorable, but adorable gets you only so far. No dates. No men. When was the last time you went out, just for fun?"

Never. But she couldn't admit that to Brittany or she'd never hear the end of it. Ally ran her damp cloth over the far end of the counter. "I have more than just my own happiness to think about, you know."

"Exactly."

She straightened to meet Brittany's light blue eyes. "What are you saying?" Allowing sarcasm to edge her tone. "Jack needs a daddy?"

Brittany raised both hands, palms up. "Why are you so afraid to take a chance? You never do, afraid you'll get hurt. Or Jack will. How is he ever going to learn to be a man if he sees you avoiding risk at all cost?"

Ally opened her mouth as the bell over the door announced another customer, sparing Ally's answer. As if she'd had one.

CHAPTER 10

Brittany not only agreed to work the extra morning hours but also offered to handle the lunch crowd while Ally tended the espresso stand, which required less walking. Ally was grateful. Her foot throbbed. She couldn't wait to get off it for good.

At eleven o'clock, Margit Olsson, wearing a straw hat and an ankle-length sundress over a yellow blouse, came in for her daily mocha. "You're early today." Ally pumped three squirts of chocolate syrup into a paper cup.

"Catching the noon ferry." Margit handed her a bill. "Keep the change."

Ally looked down. "From a twenty?"

Margit waved her hand. "My way of saying thanks for serving the best coffee in town for the last twenty-five years." At Ally's puzzled look, she added, "I'm leaving."

"Margit, no. Serious?"

"Have to. My shop's been struggling for a year now. I was hoping things might pull around over the summer, but—" She shrugged. "Lease was up. Thought I'd better get out while I'm still ahead."

Regret washed over Ally as she recalled with a tinge of guilt her impatience at Margit's chattiness yesterday. "What'll happen to your shop?"

The plump shoulders lifted. "Spent all night packing, but I'm all cleared out. Up to the landlord now."

"I'm so sad." Ally always loved stopping in at Books & Such with its smells of mellowing pages and candle wax, the yellow lights and overstuffed chairs inviting customers to come in and stay a while. Not to mention Margit herself, her kind brown eyes, ubiquitous hats and voluminous dresses. She never failed to give a lollipop to Jack and a list of recommended books to Ally. "Where will you go?"

"My sister runs a tea shop in Seattle. She's letting me put in a book nook, so I'll still have my books. Just not so many of them."

"I can hardly stand the thought of Books & Such not being here anymore. You're a Langley institution." The little shop on the corner of Second and Front Street had been there long before she and Jack arrived. She'd assumed it would always remain.

Margit shrugged again. "It's just a change, that's all."

Ally frowned. "I don't like change." At twenty-four, she'd lived through enough change to last until she was eighty.

"Don't you?" As Margit pushed back her hat, a wisp of brown hair fell over her forehead. "I suppose we all gravitate to the familiar. Maybe that's why I always order a grande double shot skinny mocha." She picked up her drink from the counter and poked a straw through the lid. "Maybe when I get to Seattle, I'll try something new. Caramel macchiato, how's that sound? Maybe really go out on a limb and make it decaf."

Margit's eyes traveled the room. Ally knew she was seeing the string of twinkly lights framing the long front windows, the menu of daily specials on the easel by the door. The walls painted in colors of shrimp and sage, the framed posters of contemporary French and Italian art. The metal chairs with vinyl seats clustered around the plain tables, which gave the impression that the decorator had started with a vision of European chic but ran out of money and filled in the gaps with American diner. And yet somehow it worked.

"I remember when this place was the Doghouse," Margit went on. "A dive, nothing but greasy burgers and fish 'n' chips, but I loved it. Then Sam bought it and turned it into a family establishment, adding the espresso stand, which back then was some newfangled idea from Seattle. Never thought it'd work, not in little ol' Langley. Took years before I sipped my first latte; thought I preferred my coffee the old-fashioned way, brewed straight up, thank you very much. But gotta hand it to Sam, he had vision, understood the tides of change. And now look. Espresso's here to stay, and I was one of your best customers."

Was. "I'll miss you, Margit."

"Miss you too, sweetie. Stop in and see me next time you're on the mainland."

After the lunch rush, Sam kept an eye on the tables so Ally could take her break. She found Brittany on the back stoop, smoking.

"Those things'll kill you, you know." Ally plopped down beside her, taking a long draw from her blue Nalgene water bottle.

Brittany blew a stream of smoke, never taking her eyes from the water view. Yesterday's glowering clouds had dissipated, though the sound's color, more gray than blue, hinted that stormier weather would soon return. "Make you a deal. I'll give up cigarettes when you go out with Jamie and me on a double date."

"Guess you're headed for an early grave." Despite her razzing, Ally didn't really mind Brittany's smoking. The smell reminded her of her father. Of home. "By the way, thanks for staying today, giving me an extra hand."

"No problem. How's the foot?"

"Hurts." She fished two Advil from her pocket and downed them with a swallow of water. "Did you know Margit's left?"

Brittany's blond eyebrows winged up. "Left Langley, you mean? For good?"

Ally nodded. "I loved her bookstore."

"It's happening everywhere."

True. For Lease signs occupied every street in town. "If I'd known she was struggling, I'd have made it a point to visit her store more often." Not that she could ever afford more than a used book or two. Ally took another swig of water and scanned the tangle of wild blackberry bushes that formed a hedge between the bistro's parking lot and the cliff's edge. "Any sign of Stormy?"

"Haven't seen her."

"Wonder if something's happened."

"Hope not." But she didn't sound all that hopeful. Ally knew she was thinking of the coyotes that roamed the nearby Saratoga Woods, not to mention the speeding cars that posed a constant threat to all of Langley's four-legged inhabitants. Most likely Stormy the stray cat was gone for good.

Another change, Ally thought sadly. She'd first seen the cat at the start of the summer, a creature so scrawny Ally had taken pity on her, feeding her scrap morsels as she left work each day. After a month, the cat had fleshed out, and had in fact become so plump that in recent weeks, Ally wondered if she needed to cut back. She'd named her Stormy because her coat so closely resembled the clouds that sometimes piled up over Saratoga Passage, exactly like the ones mounded now across the distant Cascades.

It'd been a week since Ally had last seen the gray cat, though the food she set out always disappeared by morning. But that could mean anything. A dog might be getting it, or a raccoon.

Brittany finished her cigarette and went back inside. A shaft of wind drifted from the water. Ally inhaled the fragrance, salt and sweet combined. The sweet came from the blackberry patch: though past its peak, it still retained the last berries of the season. Maybe this weekend she'd bring Jack here to pick them. Whatever they didn't eat she could freeze for pies and muffins this winter.

She stood, gingerly tapping her injured foot on the ground, relieved to find the pain bearable. Good enough for her last two hours of work. She started back inside. But then, more to satisfy herself that it was a lost cause than because she had any real hope, she called out, "Stormy! Dinnertime, Stormy!"

Nothing but Sam's off-key whistling from inside the kitchen. Ally opened the door, her heart bumping with regret over the little cat's disappearance. Then, a sound. Just the wind? But no, it came again, a rustling in the brambles as a sleek gray cat emerged from the tangle of vines.

"Stormy!" Ally exclaimed, but softly, not wanting to spook the animal. "Look how skinny you are! What's happened to you? Where've you been?" As the cat angled toward her, Ally suddenly understood. Stormy's teats dangled beneath her, elongated and limp. Kittens. "But where are your babies?" she murmured. "For you to leave them, you must be starving." Ignoring the stab of pain, she turned and hurried into the kitchen. "Sam! Where are those scraps I set out?"

He pointed to the plastic tub of chicken parts. She grabbed it, hoping Stormy hadn't disappeared in the time it took her to return. But the cat waited at the bottom step, tail switching in anticipation. As soon as Ally set the container down, Stormy wolfed the whole lot.

"So that's where you've been, taking care of your babies. If I'd known, I wouldn't have worried so much." As the cat licked the last bit of gravy from the bowl, Ally stroked the soft fur. Stormy's muted purr vibrated beneath her palm. "I know," she crooned. "Motherhood changes everything, doesn't it? You'll do anything for your little ones."

"Been looking for you." The male voice, too loud and too sudden in the stillness, caused Ally to jump and the cat to skitter into the bushes. Rees Davies stood at the edge of the parking lot, hands shoved into the pockets of his denim shorts.

"I'm sorry?" Straightening from her crouched position, she caught her weight on her injured foot and hitched a breath.

"Been looking for you," he repeated. Today he wore a light, zippered sweatshirt with its collar turned up so his scar was all but invisible. "Brittany said I would find you here."

"Why were you looking?"

"To give you these." He held out a pair of keys. "You'll need them to get into your house today."

"My house…?"

"We changed both locks, front and back."

She fingered the keys hooked onto a ring with a plastic tag in the shape of a sailboat bearing the inscription, Paul's Boats & Moor, hoping he didn't see how it unsettled her to accept this favor from strangers. "You could have just left them under the mat." That at least would have saved him the trouble of tracking her down.

"Considering what happened yesterday, I didn't want to risk someone getting into your house."

She looked away, feeling foolish. Of course he was right. She dug in her apron pocket for tip money. "How much do I owe you?"

He took a step back. "Nothing."

"Not even for materials?"

"Paul had a refinished door in one of his sheds. We used that."

"Paul?" She caught a whiff of aftershave, clean and cedar-scented. The man did not smell like someone who'd spent the day on a handyman project. She, on the other hand, reeked of coffee and grease from the grill. And though she hadn't looked in a mirror since leaving the house this morning, she knew her dark hair swirled in untidy tendrils around her face, and her swipe of lip gloss had long-since vanished.

"Darcie's husband. We had to shave a couple of inches off the top but we made it fit. And Penny rounded up an extra set of deadbolts. Said she'd been intending to replace the old ones, actually."

"Oh. Well, thank you."

"Glad to help. By the way—" His gaze traveled to her sneakered feet. "Does Darcie know you're working today?"

"I didn't tell her I was or wasn't."

An eyebrow lifted. "She'd worry if she knew."

Ally lifted an eyebrow back. "I don't have much choice. There's no such thing as short-term disability in my line of work. Unless *you'd* like to pay me a day's wages for sitting on my duff." She gave him a half-smile.

"Wish I could." His mouth tipped sidewise in a way that made her realize that even with the scar tracing down his cheek, Darcie's brother was a very attractive man.

"Well, so do I." She gave a good-natured shrug. "But wishing won't pay the bills." She scooped up the empty take-out container from the bottom step and moved up the stairs, favoring her good foot but trying not to show it. "All the same—" She paused on the top step to look down at Rees. Her chest tightened when she found him looking back at her. "No need to mention you saw me here today, is there?"

He smiled, and then pulled an innocent face while making the sign of a zipper across his lips. "None at all."

CHAPTER 11

Rees leaned back on the wooden bench overlooking Langley's boat marina, stretching his khaki-clad legs. One hundred yards below, the crescent-shaped marina formed a protective cove around sailboats moored for the winter, their masts spiking like toothpicks into the overcast sky. The waterfront wasn't busy this time of year; most of the hobby boatmen were done for the season. Only diehards and professional fishermen ventured out on the water on cloudy days like this.

He'd walked from Paul's boat shop, where he'd been lending a hand since Paul's part-time employee, Diego, had gone home sick at lunchtime. After Rees helped winterize six of the kayak rentals, Paul told him to go on home. But somehow, Rees wasn't ready for that. So he'd come here, to watch the fishermen at work. With Puget Sound's mainland stretched along the horizon, separated from him by the great, gray expanse of water, this place imparted a feeling of peace.

And it beat staying holed up in his room, trying to stay out of his sister's way.

Darcie didn't know he came here. Didn't know a lot of things, in fact. Not about his being in touch with his Sanctuary colleagues back in Mumbai. Nor about last night's Skype with Sheela, in which he'd asked to return to India a month ahead of schedule.

"I understood you to be on holiday, Rees," Sheela had greeted him in her lilting English, her round, earnest face filling his computer screen. Behind her he saw the familiar trappings of the Sanctuary conference room—the map of Kamathipura, Mumbai's red-light district, with thumbtacks identifying the locations of planned brothel raids, the whiteboard filled with scrawled notes in red and blue ink. "Don't you have better things to do than to spend your time talking to me?"

Rees ignored her gentle teasing. "I wanted to let you know I appreciate you copying me on the report about Jayashri."

"You're welcome, but you could have put that in an email." Dark eyebrows lifted elegantly above the gold rims of her glasses. "I expect the reason you requested this Skype was to inquire as to how she's doing now."

"Yes," he admitted, grateful she cut straight to the point.

Sheela's sigh carried to him from twelve time zones away. "About the same, I'm afraid. That is to say, she's enormously ticked off. I saw her again last night. She called me every name in the book. My ears are still burning."

Rees closed his eyes. Memory formed a picture of Jayashri the last time he'd seen her. The budding breasts, the straight black hair, the startling golden eyes, liquid with fear. That fear fueled the anger. "Is she still cutting?"

"No, but only because we put her under twenty-four-hour surveillance. Otherwise, I'm sure she'd still be carving away."

Rees shook away the image of the blade drawn across smooth, cappuccino-colored skin, the crimson rivulets offering a pain-filled high, a temporary escape from a never-ending nightmare. "Where'd she get the knife?"

"It wasn't a knife. It was a shard of broken pottery. Her roommate was learning how to throw pottery. She brought a finished vase back to their room." After a brothel raid, the rescued victims were taken to Sanctuary, a safe house tucked within a wooded compound away from the swarming city streets. Each woman was paired with a roommate, her care monitored around the clock by counselors and social workers. There she received care not only for her physical needs, but her emotional and spiritual ones as well. Each woman was also trained in a skilled labor—jewelry- or pottery-making, accounting, cooking—so she could support herself once she moved on from Sanctuary's care. "While the roommate was in her group therapy meeting, Jayashri broke the vase and used it for her own purpose. Obviously, we've tightened our vigilance. We're doing all we can. As you know, reaching these girls takes time, especially the ones who don't embrace their new freedom."

Rees had a hard time accepting this part of his work. After all the risks he and his colleagues took to free these women from their lives of bondage, some were so entrenched, so brainwashed, their spirits so crushed by their oppressors that they resisted the new life freedom offered. Women like Jayashri were taught from the time they could speak they had no worth in the world except to feed a man's sexual pleasure. When that purpose ended, they felt worthless. Worse than worthless. Without hope.

Confronted with such psychological obstacles, Sanctuary had to be careful in its approach. While Rees wanted to believe Christ's love in action was enough to turn anyone around, it didn't always work that way. Often, it initially made these women angrier. Most of them had been so abused that they'd added layer after layer of hardened armor to protect their souls. To touch them again, the layers had to be peeled back, one by one.

"I want to come back," Rees said.

"What, you mean now?" Once more, Sheela's eyebrows rose. "Cut short your holiday?"

"Why not? I've no specific plans. No reason to stay here."

"Rees." Sheela gentled her voice. "I know you're troubled about Jayashri, and I understand why. But what could you do for her that's not already being done?"

She was right. Nigel Helmsley had assembled an international team of top-notch lawyers, investigators, therapists and case-workers. *Just because we're a non-profit organization*, Nigel would say, *doesn't mean we settle for second-rate employees.* Each person who worked for Sanctuary loved Jesus and was passionate about his work. Each willing to sacrifice a great deal to free helpless souls from unspeakable bondage. What pearls of wisdom could Rees possibly offer Jayashri that his clever, compassionate colleagues had not?

Even so, Rees felt he had to try. "Is Nigel in his office?" Once a high-powered, London corporate attorney, Nigel had given up his high-on-the-hog lifestyle when he met Jesus fifteen years before. But though almost everything else in his life had changed, Nigel remained a notorious workaholic. Even at this early hour, not even eight a.m. Mumbai-time, he'd probably been at his desk an hour already. "See if he'll talk to me."

"I will be happy to let you talk to Nigel. But I say honestly that I will advise him against allowing you to return. Let me tell you something, Rees, and this is me speaking as a therapist now, not merely as your friend." She leaned toward the video-cam, so close he could make out the clean, straight part of her hair. "I know you feel responsible for this girl, but you're taking on too much. You've not taken off two days together in the last two years. While all of us appreciate your dedication, you need this holiday. Call it a mental-health break if it makes you feel any better. We want you to come back refreshed and ready to fight the good fight once more."

Rees pushed both hands through his hair. "If it's my mental health you're concerned about, then you need to know that living with my sister isn't helping."

With anyone else, the comment would have elicited a knowing smile, a commiserating shrug. He should have known Sheela would read it differently. She frowned. "Is it not good being with your family again?"

Rees dropped his gaze from hers. "Not as good as it should be."

"Why not?"

"I don't know."

"Don't you?" In her tone, a challenge. *Come, my friend, you can do better than that.*

He tried. "Things are—different. Not what I expected." His gaze found hers again. "She's different. I'm different."

"Is that so surprising? How long has it been since you last saw your sister?"

"Two years."

"Enough time for you to change, and she as well. We are all altered by our circumstances. If you find your sister different, I would ask, why? Have her circumstances changed since you last were together? Is she happy in her marriage? With her children? Her job? How is her walk with Jesus? These are the questions you should be asking. They will tell you much about your sister's happiness."

Rees opened his mouth to reply then snapped it shut so quickly his teeth clicked together. To be honest, he hadn't the faintest idea how to answer any of her questions. He'd assumed Darcie was fine because she always had been fine. Had that changed? If so, when? And why? And what did it say about him that he hadn't taken the trouble to find out?

When his silence elongated, Sheela continued gently. "And as for you—" She lowered her chin, peering at him over the tops of her gold-rimmed spectacles. "You have not faced, I think, that what happened to Jayashri's mother has had a deep and lasting impact on you. Have you told your sister about it? About what happened that night?"

And this, Rees thought, was what made Sheela so good at what she did. She had an uncanny, almost supernatural way of putting her finger on the pulse of the problem. Sometimes it seemed as if God Himself whispered in her ear. "I haven't told her."

"Why not?"

Why not? At first, it was because the accident was a wound too fresh to probe. Then when he did feel ready, Darcie's interest had morphed into something less appealing. An eagerness…no, an insistence he tell her, as if it were her right to know. Quite frankly, it had turned him off.

When again Rees offered no answer, Sheela said, "You have told me of your close relationship with your sister in the past. If that has been true, she must feel very hurt by your silence. And she must wonder, naturally, what is behind it."

Rees couldn't argue with her. She knew about his unorthodox childhood, his mom dying of cancer when he was young, Darcie's taking on the mantle of raising him. Though only two years older than he, she'd been a little mother to him, a role she seemed uniquely suited for. "I do feel bad for not telling her."

"Then tell her, my friend. Otherwise, what you hold inside will fester like an unclean lesion. Worse, it will tear apart your relationship. There." She nodded. "That is my advice. I give it to you for free."

In all this conversation, it hadn't escaped his notice that Sheela had never said what she thought of his role in the events that led to the death of Jayashri's mother. "Do you think I was wrong to do what I did that night?" He felt his breath catch and expand inside his chest as he waited for her answer.

It came quickly, so quickly he wondered if she had prepared for such a moment. "It is not my place to decide whether what you did was wrong or right."

He released his pent-up breath. "That doesn't answer my question, you know."

She nodded. "I believe you did what you thought was right in that moment, that situation. What more can anyone do? Hindsight always provides perfect vision."

Rees couldn't help but feel disappointed. He'd hoped for more from her, one way or the other.

In the end, Rees had not bothered to speak to Nigel about returning early, knowing if Sheela advised against it, Nigel would not be persuaded. So, he'd stay in Langley—for another month, anyway. That would make Darcie happy, at least. Although given the way they'd been bickering, maybe even she would prefer he leave.

This thought scuttled through Rees's mind as he pulled aviator shades from his pocket, donning them against the overcast glare. Behind him came a child's piping voice. When he turned to look, he saw Ally Brennan and her son in a Spiderman backpack passing by on the sidewalk fifty yards below. She limped slightly. If she looked up, she'd see Rees, but the boy had her full attention. She lifted a hand, as graceful as a bird, and rested it briefly on Jack's golden head before letting it drop to her side again.

As the pair moved out of sight, down the slope that led to their home, Rees recalled the melody he'd heard coming from Ally's cottage a few nights ago. When he'd seen her yesterday to give her the new keys, he'd not said anything about it, though he'd wanted to. Her ability to draw music from horsehair and wood seemed miraculous. Since that night, the memory of that melancholy refrain had come to him at odd moments. He was no musician, but he knew enough to recognize virtuosity. No, it was more than skill. Her music had power. Which begged the question: Why was a woman with talent like Ally's hiding in tucked-away little Langley-by-the-Sea?

The steady chugging of an outboard motor alerted him to the approach of a crabbing boat. From a distance, the white boat with green trim looked like a plastic bathtub toy, but as it neared the marina, Rees saw the crab pots on deck weighted with harvest. He'd watched this boat often over the last few weeks. Normally, two men worked together—brothers, he surmised from their banter and similar thick-waisted builds. Today, however, only one manned the helm.

Rees left his bench and sauntered down toward the marina as the crabber cut the motor and coasted to the dock. After tethering his boat in place, the crabber hopped ashore, strode to the adjacent parking lot, and backed a battered half-bed pickup truck to the dock. When he began unloading the crab pots from his boat to the truck, Rees spoke up. "Need a hand?"

The crabber turned his head, pushed back his cap. "Could use some help, sure." He wore a wool sweater, the color of oatmeal, and rubber boots. A toothpick protruded from wind-chapped lips and stubble covered his cheeks, but the graying hair beneath the denim cap was neatly trimmed. "Brother's laid up today with the flu. Thought I could handle the job on my own, but it's been pretty slow going."

Rees stepped aboard. With the vessel swaying under his weight, he handed the next pot up to the crabber.

"Name's Rusty, by the way."

"I'm Rees."

"Appreciate your help, Rees. You look like you know what you're doing."

"My dad used to own a boat. We'd go crabbing together sometimes, when the weather was right."

They worked for several minutes in silence. Rees realized how good it felt to be moving his muscles again. Since returning to Langley, he made it a point to get out every night for a run, but he missed this kind of physical exercise, the taut swing and pull of his muscles beneath his skin. He thought again of Sheela, who knew of his passion for jogging and liked to tease him about it. *Why are you so concerned with this idea of fitness? Your body won't last forever, you know, no matter how many miles you run.*

When Rusty had emptied the last crab into the large container on his truck, he surveyed the pink light just starting to paint the horizon. "Looks like I have time for one more run. Want to come?"

Rees did.

Rusty motored about fifteen minutes from the harbor before dropping the first pot into the water. "You don't strike me as from around here," Rusty observed.

"I'm not." Rees zipped his jacket up to his chin. Out here in the Saratoga Passage, there was nothing to break the power of the wind. The thin layer of overcast had thickened in the last hour, shrouding the land and water in gray flannel.

"So, where're you from?"

"Originally, Mercer Island." The affluent community nestled between Seattle and Lake Washington's east side. "But more recently, Mumbai."

"Mumbai, eh?" The man squinted. "What'dya do in Mumbai?"

"I'm a legal investigator."

"Huh." Rusty shifted his toothpick to the other side of his mouth. "Not one of them fellows doing something about the sex trade over there, are ya? Human trafficking and all that."

Rees looked at him, surprised. "Yes, actually."

"Read about it in *Newsweek*." Another pot splashed into the water. "Bad business, that. Prostitutes no better than slaves. They say the slave trade now is worse than it was two hundred years ago. Can't say I've got much stomach for folks who use defenseless people like that for profit. Breaks my heart considering all those women and children who'll never know the touch of a man. The tender touch, I mean. All they know is the unholy hunger of a man out to get what he can get." Two more crab pots into the water. "Must seem pretty hopeless sometimes."

Hopeless? Of course it seemed hopeless, from a human perspective. The sheer numbers were enough to prevent most people from trying to change a thing. By some count, there were over 200,000 sexual slaves in Mumbai alone. But numbers didn't consider the entire toll on human souls—trafficked, trafficker, buyer and rescuer alike. The unstoppable lust and greed, the black despair that rendered life seemingly worthless. Was it any wonder so many rescued women attempted suicide? Some days the only thing keeping hope alive at Sanctuary was knowing that God Himself was on their side. The side of justice. His very words were inscribed on their walls, on the heart of every person on staff. *Is this not what I have chosen, to loose the chains of injustice, to set the oppressed free and break every yoke? The glory of the LORD will be your rear guard. You will cry for help, and He will say: Here am I.*

As Nigel liked to say, rescue was the easy part. Much more difficult was the process that followed: the restoring of wounded souls to wholeness. Which brought Rees back once more to Jayashri. He knew the pattern. If they couldn't get through to her within a matter of months, she'd return to her former life, the only one she'd ever known. Only this time, she'd be worse off than before because it would be a life she'd now chosen. Her soul would be that much more deeply shackled to darkness.

If only they could find a way to get past her defenses, to peel away those protective layers. He understood Sheela's point; they were doing all they could. He didn't mean to doubt her ability to succeed. But the therapy, the life-skills lessons—these approached the issues directly. What happened when a woman's defenses were so high they were impenetrable by frontal assault? Did that make her situation hopeless?

Rees refused to believe the answer was *yes*. What they needed was to find a way in through the backdoor.

"They say," Rusty went on, "that a lot of these girls are sold by their own father or brothers or uncles, people they trust, and usually for no more than a week's wage. How do you begin to get beyond that?"

"One rescue at a time."

"One at a time?" Rusty turned the boat toward open water. "That's a mighty slow process."

"It is." Rees held on as the vessel picked up speed. "Sometimes it's downright excruciating."

Chapter 12

With a plate of chocolate chip cookies balanced in one hand, Ally knocked on Darcie Nielsen's front door, setting off a din of barking inside. She shot a glance at Jack, who was using a twig to draw stick figures in the dirt around the Nielsens' azalea bushes. Hearing the dogs, Jack abandoned his artwork as a calm male voice commanded, "Moses! Aaron! Quiet." A short scuffle followed, and then the door opened to reveal a lanky man with steel-gray hair and wire-rimmed glasses. "Well, hello. Ally, isn't it? And Jack."

"And you're Paul." Two large, black dogs nosed their way forward. Jack surged to meet them as Ally pressed a hand to his chest, holding him back.

"Moses, Aaron, sit!" Paul commanded. "Stay. Good boys." Then, as if sensing Ally's nervousness about the dogs, he added,

"Don't worry, they won't bite. Unless, of course," he winked at Jack, "you bite them first."

Jack's eyes brightened as he ducked around Ally's protective gesture. "Wait, Jack," she admonished. "Let them smell your hand first. Be gentle."

After gaining the dogs' approval, Jack patted first one enormous black head and then the other.

"See? They like you. This one's Moses." Paul pointed to the larger of the two. "And that one's Aaron. Generally, Moses lets his brother do the talking, but get him riled and he speaks up quick enough."

Ally offered the cookies, still warm enough to give off a brown-sugar aroma. "We made these for you, as thanks for fixing our door yesterday."

"You didn't have to. But I'm kinda glad you did." He gave Jack another wink, and Ally decided she liked him.

"Is Darcie home? She wanted me to stop by so she could take a look at my foot."

"Oh, yes, she mentioned that. She's not back yet, but I expect her any minute. Please, come in." He ushered them inside. "How's your foot doing, anyway?"

"I'll be glad for Darcie to look at it." She was worried about a yellowish puffiness around the wound.

"Let me get you some coffee while you wait. Or would you prefer tea?"

"Coffee's wonderful."

Paul pulled out a chair for Ally at the oak table. She sat stiffly, somewhat uncomfortable with being waited upon. But as Paul started the coffeemaker, sending its enticing aroma into the room, she found herself relaxing and taking in her surroundings. The Nielsens' kitchen was large, with blue gingham curtains framing the window and walls painted a warm, golden yellow. In the adjoining family room, a russet sectional sofa, long enough to accommodate eight, was littered with a potpourri of burgundy and gold chenille throw pillows. A Turkish rug, rich in deep hues of blue and red, covered the hardwood floor, and floor-to-ceiling bookshelves dominated one entire wall. A friendly clutter of bric-a-brac and family photographs filled every other bit of real estate.

Jack followed the dogs to their blue donuts and settled himself cross-legged between them.

After a moment, Paul broke the silence. "So, you helped your mom make these cookies, Jack?"

Jack, intent on giving Moses a thorough belly rub, didn't answer.

"Sorry," Ally spoke up. "He's got a bit of a one-track mind when it comes to animals. Jack was in charge of the chocolate chips. A few might have actually made it into the batter."

"That's the way I cook, too," Paul confessed as his gaze settled on a white, loose-leaf binder lying open by the phone. Two vertical lines appeared briefly between his eyes as he closed it and slipped it into a drawer.

"Do your dogs know any tricks?" Jack asked.

"Tricks? Well, let's see. They shake hands. Want to try? First, you must get them to sit. Watch this. Moses, sit!" Paul lifted his hand from his knee to waist level as he issued the command, and the dog promptly hoisted himself into sitting position. "Good boy. Now—" He turned his hand, palm up, and lowered it to about a foot off the ground. "Shake!" Instantly,

Moses lifted a gigantic paw and placed it in Paul's palm. "Good boy!" He smiled at Jack's eager face. "Now your turn."

Jack scrambled to his feet and, following Paul's prompts, got Moses to repeat the trick. "Look, Mom! We're shaking hands."

"Good job, Bubba."

"Will Aaron do it, too?" Jack asked.

"Of course. Go ahead and try it out. And then maybe you'd like to take them into the backyard. They love to play Frisbee, and I haven't had time for a game today." Immediately, Jack moved to the door, calling the dogs as he went. "There's a Frisbee on the shelf right outside." Paul opened the door for them. In a wave of wagging tails, the dogs disappeared with Jack right behind them.

It happened so fast, Ally hadn't had a chance to question Jack's playing outside alone with two big dogs. But looking at Paul's easy demeanor, she decided it was okay. She'd seen enough to know Paul wouldn't have encouraged Jack if it weren't safe.

Quit worrying, she chided silently. She knew her over-protectiveness wasn't good for Jack, but some days she just couldn't help herself. Taking a breath, her attention was caught by a large, framed photograph to the left of the door. It depicted a sailboat on which stood a group of about a dozen grinning kids, ranging in age from six to twelve, each of them standing erect in sharp salute. In the center of them all, with a grin wider than any, stood a slim man in a white yachting hat. "Is that you?"

"That's me." Paul moved to the refrigerator and pulled a bag of broccoli heads from the veggie bin. "Long time ago. When I was younger and handsomer."

The caption beneath the photo read *Paul's Li'l Sailors*. "Who are they?"

"Before Darcie and I were married, my brothers and I owned a sailboat-making company in Seattle. Business was good and we wanted a way to give back to the community, so we started a summer program for underprivileged kids." Watching him chop the broccoli, she formed a picture of Paul Nielsen. He managed his own business, was fond of kids, and evidently knew how to cook. She started to feel Darcie was a fortunate woman.

"Sounds like fun."

"It was." Paul added water to the veggies in the pan, and then a dash of garlic salt before setting it on the stove. "We offered a week-long sailing camp on one of our boats, teaching the kids to sail. Even if they never set foot on a sailboat again, we figured it would teach them good things like teamwork and overcoming their fears." He paused. "One of the most rewarding things I've ever done."

She started to ask why he and Darcie didn't have kids, but when a car engine rumbled into the carport, she thought better of her question. After all, she never appreciated people's equally intrusive inquiries about Jack's absent father.

A moment later Darcie came inside, placing a pile of mail and a tinfoil-wrapped loaf beside the phone. "I see Jack's found the dogs. Hi, Ally. How's that foot?"

"So-so."

"Ally brought cookies," Paul interjected. Then, "How was your day?"

"Medium." She pulled a pitcher of water from the fridge.

"Certainly was a *long* one."

Darcie stopped, her hand on the refrigerator door. Until that moment, she'd worn an air of vague inattention, as if her mind were elsewhere, but now she glanced sharply at her husband. Ally wished she could fade from the room. The gaze between husband and wife caught and held, a tense silence pulsing between them. "Yes, well—"

The backdoor opened and Jack and the dogs rushed in, followed more sedately by Rees. At the sight of him, Ally's pulse gave an unexpected little hop.

"I brought dinner," Rees announced, setting a Styrofoam cooler beside the sink.

"What on earth?" Darcie's face lit up, the strange moment between her and Paul apparently forgotten as she opened the cooler's lid and peered inside. "Crab!" She looked at her brother, pleasure and surprise mingling on her round face. "Where'd you get these?"

"From Rusty, down at the dock." He bent to greet the dogs snuffling for his attention. At his sister's puzzled look, he added, "Long story, tell you later."

"Over dinner," Paul said. "We're going to feast tonight. Fresh crab and homemade cookies. Ally? You'll join us?"

Jack grabbed her hand. "Can we, Mom?"

No. The usual answer balanced on her tongue, a habit gained from years of keeping her distance. But Darcie still had to examine her foot, and looking into her son's shining face, she saw how much he wanted to stay. He didn't get many chances to eat with anything resembling a family. "Sure." She hoped she didn't sound as reluctant as she felt.

Jack cheered and Darcie suggested they move into the next room while the men got to work on the crab. "Let's take a look at that foot first." Darcie guided her to the couch and then knelt on the floor to remove the bandaging. "Hmm, not doing so good." She looked troubled. "Staying off it, aren't you?"

Ally shot a glance toward the kitchen, knowing that Rees knew the truth, but he had his back to her, apparently unaware of the conversation. "As best I can."

Darcie sat back on her heels. "Your best needs to do better, Ally."

"How?" From the stove, metal clanged as the crabs went into a pot. She glanced again at Rees and saw his shoulders had tightened. "I'm a waitress, plus I've got a little boy to chase." At least she'd driven to work these past two days. Normally she walked, rain or shine, to ease her gas budget.

Darcie frowned. "Your foot would be in much better shape if you'd stay off it like I told you."

"What do you expect me to do, quit my job?" Then, realizing she sounded defensive, not to mention ungrateful, she added, "Sorry. I know that would be ideal, but I just can't. I'll have to make the best of it, even if it means taking longer to heal."

"Can you at least stay off it at home? Instead of, oh, I don't know…baking cookies."

"I'll try." Ally smiled. "Though I'll hardly know what to do with myself."

"Try reading a novel." Darcie voice grew dry. "Or watching TV. Or—"

"Playing the violin," Rees said, coming suddenly into the room. Ally gave him a startled glance. So he *had* been listening. He'd removed his North Face jacket, revealing a thick blue turtleneck sweater that mirrored the color of his eyes. His hair looked windblown and his cheeks reddened, making the thin scar appear more white than pink against his skin.

"I think you mean viola." Darcie looked to her. "Doesn't he, Ally?"

"Yes." Ally's gaze locked with his. When he gave her the barest wink, she realized what he was up to: diverting Darcie's line of questioning. "How did you know I played?" The night of the break-in, she distinctly remembered Jack putting Lola away before Rees arrived to work on the door.

"When I left the television on your porch the other night, I heard you playing."

"Well—" Darcie applied antibiotic salve to Ally's wound. "Your secret's out now."

"It was never a secret," Ally insisted.

"You're very good," Rees said.

"Thank you."

Darcie applied a fresh bandage and handed Ally her sock. "If you're so good, why don't you play for real?"

"I do." Ally couldn't help a smile.

Darcie *tsk*ed impatiently. "I meant with a group. An ensemble or something."

"Well, I used to. Quite a few of them actually." Youth symphony, school orchestra, elite orchestra, string quintet. "Then I quit for a few years. When I started up again, I decided to play just for my own enjoyment. For now, it's enough."

"What made you quit?" Paul came in to place silverware and plates on the dinette table. "Motherhood?"

"Motherhood is actually what gave me back my music. I'd kind of lost my will to play when my mother died a few years earlier. But then Jack was born, and he was so colicky that one night I dug out my viola and started playing out of desperation. He calmed down, and I've played ever since."

"What a blessing you had Jack." Darcie stood abruptly, crumpling the bandage wrapper in her hand.

"Yes." She sensed an undercurrent to Darcie's words. Was this why she and Paul didn't have children? Not because they didn't want to, but because they couldn't? "I've come to believe having Jack was God's way of giving me back my gift. My voice, actually."

Darcie crossed the room to drop the wrapper in the trash can beside the chair where Rees sat. Ally saw something in his expression shift, grow more alert. He opened his mouth to speak, but then closed it again as Paul called from the kitchen. "Who's ready for crab? Come and get it, everyone."

"I wanted to apologize if I made you uncomfortable back there," Rees told Ally later that evening as he backed Paul's truck out of the carport. Rees had been surprised but pleased to find the boy playing with the dogs when he'd arrived home after his crabbing outing, correctly guessing that if Jack were there, his mother would be too. After gorging themselves on crab, Rees had volunteered to drive Ally and Jack home since

Darcie refused to let Ally walk even that short distance. They piled into the truck, Jack sitting on Ally's lap.

"Uncomfortable?" she echoed. "When?"

"When I brought up your playing the violin—viola, I mean. In front of Darcie." He'd done it half to stop Darcie from haranguing Ally for returning to work, half to bait his sister, a childish habit he really needed to get over. He was too old for such games. But when Darcie launched into bossy mode, she put blinders on and became oblivious to the effect she had on people. Anyone else would have seen Ally already felt guilty enough.

"I was glad for the diversion. Thank you." He felt her watching him in the dim light of the dash. "And I don't mind talking about my playing. I love music. I can't imagine life without it. It's just I don't usually talk about it with people who aren't musicians because I get frustrated when they don't 'get it' the way I do." A small pause in which he sensed her smile. "Pretty snooty, right?"

"Not really." He reached the busy street that separated the Nielsens' driveway from Ally's and paused to look both ways before crossing. "I feel the same way about my work. If someone doesn't share my vision or my passion, it's hard to feel like I'm relating at a meaningful level. And I'm not really interested in doing anything less, simply because it means that much to me."

"Exactly." The lift in her voice conveyed her surprise at his understanding. "Otherwise, it can be like trying to explain color to a blind person." Exchanging smiles with her over the top of Jack's head, he felt pleased they'd made this connection.

He pulled up to the cottage and parked. Jack, who'd been silent and sleepy, slid from his mother's lap to the ground. Ally was about to follow, but Rees touched her shoulder. "Do you have a minute? I know it's getting late, but I wanted to talk to you about something." Because Jayashri was never far from his thoughts, when Ally had spoken earlier about her return to the viola, it had sprung an idea. He wanted to explore it further. "It can wait until morning, if that's better."

"No, this is fine." When surprise again flickered across her face, he found himself thinking those big green eyes of hers didn't hide much. "Come on in."

Inside the house, she turned on a lamp and offered him a seat on the sofa. When he'd been here before, he'd been too preoccupied with repairing the door to notice anything about the house, but now he took the time to observe his surroundings. Framed prints, European landscapes, maybe, and earth tones on the walls. A worn, chocolate-brown sofa and a brick fireplace with ashes in the grate. Area rugs on the hardwood floors. A pile of LEGOs shoved into a corner.

From the hallway, Ally gave Jack his instructions. "Okay, Bubba, into your jammies and brush your teeth. I'll tuck you in as soon as I finish talking to Mr. Rees."

He waited for her to take a seat in the rocking chair opposite the coffee table. "What you said before, that you stopped playing when your mom died and then picked it up again. You said it was like music gave you back your voice. What did you mean by that?"

She pulled a gold throw pillow from behind her back and fiddled with a frayed seam. "Music speaks for me in ways I can't."

"How?"

"Well—" The dark wings of her eyebrows drew together. When she closed her eyes, he could almost see her swaying to music that filled the room, as if imagining the viola in her arms. Then she opened her eyes. "I'm able to tap into a part of me that hides away at other times. It's hard to put into words, but it's like music enables me to reach past my conscious emotions, drawing up feelings I can't reach any other way. After Jack was born, I went through a very difficult time. Not just a new baby, but, well, a lot of other stuff. Bad stuff. I was sad and angry and lonely, but at the same time filled with a new kind of hope and joy. All these emotions jumbled up inside me. Music allowed me to push them out so I could deal with it."

"Using music to tap into places in your psyche—you think that's something that can be taught, or is it something you're born with?"

Her head tilted. "I'm not sure. For me, it's natural, but we're all drawn to music to some degree, don't you think? That's one of the things that fascinates me about music, how people all over the world are drawn to it. It's universal." As she spoke, her hands moved as if shaping her words. She seemed completely unaware of it. "They've done studies, taking people from remote tribes in Africa who have had no exposure to Western music. They have them listen to music in a major key, which they say makes them feel happy. Then they listen to music in a minor key, and it makes them sad. How is that? It's not taught. It must be innate. So in answer to your question, I suppose I'd say that although some of us are more naturally gifted, music can be nurtured in anyone."

"Even someone who's been through a trauma of some kind?"

"Especially then."

From the bathroom came the splash of running water and the splat of Jack spitting toothpaste into the sink. Rees knew he was about to overstay his welcome, so he stood. "Thanks for talking to me. A non-musician, even."

She stood with him. "You kept up very well."

"Didn't frustrate you too much with my musical obtuseness?"

"No." Her pretty smile flashed. "Shocking, huh?"

Rees started for the door but then paused. "What was it I heard you playing the other night?"

She thought a moment and hummed a few bars. "Like that?"

That was the one all right. Hearing even that snippet of melody resurrected all his feelings at the time. His frustration with work, his irritation with Darcie, even the chill of rain on his skin as he stood in the dark, mesmerized by Ally's music. "I don't think I've heard it before."

"It's kind of an unusual piece, a modern Israeli composition."

"It sounded…sad."

"It's not a happy piece," she agreed. "I wasn't feeling very happy that night, so it matched. It's called *Neharot Neharot*. In Hebrew it means Rivers Rivers. It speaks of the rivers of tears shed by women mourning the fighting in Lebanon, which sounds so awful unless you follow the thread of the piece through to the end. The composer says that from rivers of tears flows hope. That by expressing our pain, we find healing. That message is buried, even in the music's title."

"Nehar—what?"

"Neharot. It comes from another Hebrew word, *nehara,* meaning ray of light. Loosely translated, it means, from weeping comes solace."

Rees stared at her, amazed she should relate so intimately with the music she played. He felt the questions lining up on his tongue. How did she know so much about this? Could she teach him? And with her level of talent, what was she doing in tiny Langley-by-the-Sea? But before any of these things could spill from his mouth, Jack padded into the room in spaceship-decorated, footed pajamas, carrying a ratty stuffed animal of indeterminate species. "Mom? I'm ready."

"Be right there." She offered Rees an apologetic smile. "Sorry. I probably gave you a lot more than you wanted, but see—you got me going."

"I'm glad you told me. It's helpful." He put his hand on the door.

"How is it helpful?" Ally took a quick step toward him. "I mean, if you don't mind telling me."

"I don't mind at all." Looking down into her eyes framed with long lashes, it struck Rees that Ally Brennan was a beautiful woman. The memory of her walking by the marina filled his mind, the way she tipped her head when listening to Jack as if his every word was important. It dawned on him that her habit of focused interest wasn't something she reserved only for her son. Her warm attention right now made him feel as if a bright light was falling on him. "I was thinking about a girl named Jayashri."

"Jayashri." The name rolled like music from her mouth. "What a pretty name. Why were you thinking about her?"

"Mo-om!" Jack's voice came from behind them. "I'm ready."

Ally looked at Rees with another apologetic grimace. "Another time? I really would like to hear about her."

"And I'd like to tell you."

CHAPTER 13

After Rees left to take the Brennans home, Paul disappeared into his home office while Darcie spent a few minutes putting the kitchen to rights, prepping the coffee maker, and letting the dogs out. Despite the lingering ache in her heart over this month's disappointment, she couldn't help but smile as she swept up the small mountain of cookie crumbs from beneath Jack's chair. Then she headed for bed.

To her surprise, she found Paul sitting on the edge of the king-sized bed, waiting. Her stomach tightened in a moment of misgiving. Whatever was on his mind, she didn't like the look on his face. "I thought you were in the study." She unfastened her watch as she moved to the dresser.

"I was waiting for you." He lowered his chin, regarding her sadly. "Do you have something to tell me?"

She felt a wash of relief as a lump of emotion, equal parts regret and gratitude, rose in her throat. *So you did notice.* She hadn't known until that moment how badly she wanted him to. "I figured you knew yesterday when I asked you to pick up another box of maxi-pads at the store."

"Box of..." Bewilderment rippled across Paul's face. "What are you talking about?"

Darcie turned from the dresser. "My period. It came the other day. I'm not pregnant." Now she was confused. What was *he* talking about?

The room went thickly quiet for a moment. Then—"Oh, hon." He held out a hand and pulled her close beside him on the blue floral duvet. "Why didn't you tell me?"

"I didn't want you to feel as miserable as I did." Though even as she said it, she knew Paul *didn't* actually feel as miserable as she did. How could he? He wasn't the one with the womb that remained empty month after month. He didn't feel the pain of that loss as a sharp knife twisted between the ribs.

"Honey." In his slow enunciation, she could almost see him tiptoeing through the volatile minefield of her emotions. "I'm on this journey with you, right? I appreciate you wanting to spare me pain, but I'd rather know these things when you do so I can help. I know how hard this is for you." He touched her cheek. "We'll keep trying, okay?"

She nodded, though the idea brought her no joy. *Even if you don't get pregnant, you'll sure have fun trying!* How many times had she heard *that* from well-meaning friends? The originator of the witticism had either been on Prozac or had never experienced the unique hell of infertility. If there was anything less fun than prescribed sex, she had yet to discover what it was.

"I'm sorry I didn't say anything." She offered her own apology to help bridge the divide. Then her eye fell on the white binder Paul had pushed behind him on the bed when he'd pulled her down beside him. The binder where she kept her client information. "Why is this in here?" Suddenly she recalled his hardened look of determination when she first walked into the bedroom. He'd been bracing for battle until she derailed him. "You know I asked for extra hours at work, don't you?"

He exhaled. Looked her in the eye. Nodded. "Why'd you do it when I specifically asked you not to?"

"Because we need the money." The hypocrisy of the situation struck her. "You just told me how important it is I communicate with you, but it works both ways, Paul. You need to talk to me, too. If the shop is struggling, I need to know so we can work as a team. If I'm willing to work more hours for the sake of our financial health, I think you should let me."

Paul thrust his fingers through his bristly hair, making it stand up on the sides. "I just hate the thought of you working so hard."

"You know I enjoy what I do." After nearly ten years in the hospice business, it still gave her immense satisfaction. If working more hours provided a way out of their financial bind, so be it. "Besides, we both know it won't be forever, right? One of these days, the shop will turn around. Then I'll go back to working part-time again."

Uncertainty registered in his clear hazel eyes. "Darce—" He broke off when they heard the truck pulling into the carport. A moment later, the backdoor opened and shut, and Rees's murmured greeting to the dogs floated back to them.

"Paul?" She put both palms to his cheeks, felt the emery-board grit of a day's beard, tried to draw him back to her. "What is it?"

But Paul shook his head. "Nothing." He rose from the bed, the moment lost. "Guess I better go let Moses and Aaron out." He left so fast she couldn't even tell him she'd already taken care of the dogs.

As the door clicked shut behind him, a new worry twisted beneath her skin. Something was wrong at the shop, something worse than simply not meeting their numbers for the year. Something Paul didn't want her to know. How long before he found the courage to tell her?

CHAPTER 14

Bundled in a green parka, Ally hunched over a picnic table at the South Whidbey Community Park. Several yards away, in the sprawling wooden complex of turrets and bridges known locally as The Castle, Jack and a handful of kids played a noisy, complicated version of tag. She'd been there fifteen minutes before she sensed a presence beside her and looked up into Denny Lewis's ruddy face. "Good book?" A smile touched the deputy's hazel eyes.

She glanced down at the medical thriller in her hands and closed it. "I wouldn't know." She'd been sitting with the novel open on her lap since they arrived and hadn't gotten past page one. "I just started."

He raised a paper coffee cup to his lips. She caught a whiff of hazelnut. "Don't imagine you get much time to read."

"Probably because I don't take better advantage of moments like these." Darcie had loaned her the book, promising a page-turner. It probably was, if Ally could just get her mind on it. Instead, her thoughts kept jumping to her son. Mrs. Nichols had stopped her after school again today to tell her about another incident with Jack on the playground. This time it was a hands-on wrestling match. The two boys were separated and lost their recess privileges for the rest of the week. Ally had been appalled, even more so when Jack still refused to tell her what made him do it. He wouldn't even tell her who started it.

After that, she knew she shouldn't reward her son with a trip to The Castle, but the truth was she needed this time for herself. To think. "What are you doing here?" she asked Denny. This part of the park was isolated, half a mile from the main road, with a baseball diamond and a stand of Douglas fir trees in between.

"Making the rounds." When other moms nearby glanced curiously at the uniformed deputy, he gave them a nod. "Been getting reports of car prowls; thought I'd take a pass through here. I'm due for a break, though. Mind if I sit down?"

"Please." Though she'd come here for mental solitude, she was glad for the interruption. She shifted her tote, and he straddled the bench.

"One of those yours?" Denny tipped his cup toward the kids.

"The one in the yellow jacket and jeans." With smeared mud on the knees, a ripped sleeve, and that stubborn lock of hair at his crown sticking straight up—every inch a boy. *Snips and snails and puppy dog tails…* the rhyme tripped through her mind. If Jack wasn't playing a rowdy game of tag, he was digging up clams from their beach or chasing garter snakes through Miss Penny's azalea bushes. And now, apparently, getting into fights.

Denny watched him a few minutes. "Cute kid."

Despite her troubled thoughts, she was able to smile. "God did a good job on him." Then, "You have kids, Denny?"

"Me?" He blew out a breath. "No. Someday, I hope."

She eyed Denny as he traced a groove in the pattern of the wood with a ragged thumbnail. She'd overheard him once tell Brittany he had two brothers. He might be able to answer some of the questions tumbling around inside her head. She drew a breath. "Denny, can I ask you something? Why do people do what they do?"

He raised his sandy eyebrows. "You're asking why I'm a cop?"

"No, I mean, why do some people do bad things? It seems like there are some people who are more predisposed to be troublemakers. Why is that?"

"Ah. The infamous nature versus nurture question."

"Yes, that's it. Do they teach you anything about that in cop school?"

"In cop school, no." Denny smiled a little as he lifted his coffee and took another sip. "But experience has given me theories on both sides. I tend to think it's a little of both. Why?"

She looked up at the sullen gray sky, unable to meet his direct gaze. "Jack's been getting into trouble on the playground, and it worries me."

"What kind of trouble?"

She told him.

"Sounds like pretty normal kid stuff to me."

"Really?"

He shrugged. "Sure. Unless you have some other reason to be concerned, I wouldn't worry about it."

Ah, but there's the rub. She had plenty of other reasons to be concerned. Namely, that Jack's very DNA could be making him behave this way. But she couldn't say so, not without inviting questions she didn't want to answer. "Sometimes I worry I'm not doing enough for my boy. He doesn't have a dad at home, and I didn't grow up with brothers, so…" She shrugged.

"I'm sure you're a great mom, Ally."

"Yeah? Even though on my best days I still feel completely inadequate?"

"I don't know much about parenting, but that sounds about right." Denny's eyes crinkled at the corners. "I can't offer advice, but I can tell you what my dad told me the day I graduated from the academy. 'Denny,' he said, 'whenever you're in doubt about something, go with your gut.' I think of that whenever I don't know what to do. So, go with your gut, Ally. Then you'll not go far wrong."

At that moment, Jack abandoned his game of tag to gallop over to them. "Mom, I'm thirsty!"

"Water fountain's right over there, Bubba." Then, "Jack, this is Deputy Lewis."

Denny held out fist. "Nice to meet you, Jack."

Jack pounded the rock and then sprinted off again, thirst forgotten. Ally smiled, knowing attention from the cop was what her son was really after. A moment later, he shouted to her from the top of The Castle. "Hey, Mom, watch this!" He waited until she was looking before leaping for the first rung of the monkey bars. Skipping every other bar, he swung himself across until he reached the other side. "Did you see me, Mom?"

She waved. To Denny, she said, "He's showing off for you."

But Denny didn't answer. Instead he stood quickly, his expression quickening. She craned her head to see what had caught his attention. "What's wrong?"

"Did you see that guy?" Denny kept his focus on the stand of trees to the south of the parking lot.

"What guy?"

"He's gone now. Ducked behind those trees."

"A man?" She glanced uneasily at the dark stand of fir behind them. "What did he look like?"

"Just caught a glimpse. Slight build, not real tall, maybe five-seven, five-eight. Baseball cap. Puffy red jacket. Jeans. Don't like it when I see strangers standing around watching kids."

She frowned. "Neither do I."

"Have you ever—" He broke off as his lapel radio beeped. A female voice sounded through the com. "Deputy Lewis, this is Dispatch. We've got a report of a 10-14 over on Ash. Repeat, 10-14 on Ash."

Denny touched a button near his collar to respond. "Dispatch, this is Lewis, on my way." He gave Ally an apologetic smile. "Gotta run."

"Duty calls."

"Just remember—" He tossed his empty cup into a nearby garbage can. "Go with your gut."

"My gut. Got it."

After he left, Ally kept her gaze on the stand of firs, wondering if the stranger would reappear. She hadn't liked the look of Denny's taut expression, but she saw no movement among the trees, only a sleek seagull dropping from the granite-gray sky to perch on one of The Castle's turrets. Several more minutes ticked by without any sign of a man in a red jacket, and then another seagull joined the first one. The gulls were moving inland. She knew what that meant. A storm was coming.

As the first splatter of rain fell, she rose from the table and called Jack to the car.

CHAPTER 15

"Mom? Mommy?" A small voice and soft hand roused Ally from sleep. Peeking from the covers, she peered at her son's anxious face, lit only by the nightlight in the hall between their bedrooms. "Can I sleep in your bed?"

The rain that had begun at the park had steadily increased to a driving downpour. By bedtime, the wind flung raindrops like pebbles against the cottage windows. Just a few yards from their backdoor, churning white waves crashed against the seawall. Altogether, it sounded like the roar of a Boeing 747 taking flight.

Without a word, she opened wide the covers and welcomed him inside. Then, tucking the soft curl of his small body into hers, she pulled him tight as he burrowed beneath the duvet.

For a while they lay silent, listening to the storm's fury, content to be safe and secure inside. Then Jack spoke drowsily. "Mommy?"

"Mmmm?"

"Was your mommy as nice as you?"

She smiled against his hair, which smelled of berry-scented shampoo. "Yes, Bubba." She felt again the familiar pang that her son would never know his grandparents.

"Was that how you got to be so nice?"

"Maybe. Or maybe it's because you make it easy."

He wriggled with contentment. "Does that mean you're not mad at me anymore for what happened on the playground?"

She went still, surprised he would bring it up. She'd banned him from TV for a week, yet even then he wouldn't tell her what it was all about. "I was never mad, Bubba." A lot of other things, but not mad.

"I thought you were."

"No. Though it concerns me that you won't tell me why you're fighting with other boys. That's not like you." At least it hadn't been. Until now.

A pause followed, so long she wondered if he'd drifted off. Then his voice came again, very small. "Do I have to?"

She pressed a kiss to the top of his head. "Don't you want to?"

His silky hair brushed her lips as he shook his head. No.

"Well. I hope someday you will."

The wind whistled without ceasing past their windows, and the cottage still smelled of wood smoke from the blaze she'd lit in the fireplace. She lay awake after Jack drifted off, listening to his even breathing, feeling him twitch in his sleep, thinking, *God, I don't know what to do.*

Go with your gut. As Denny's words came back to her, she mulled them over. Problem was, she didn't find that particularly helpful in this situation. Her gut told her to remove her child from the scene that was causing the trouble, but she couldn't do that. He needed to learn to resolve his differences in a productive way, not with aggression.

A tree branch scraped the side of the cottage. She found her thoughts turning to her mother. Funny that Jack had mentioned her. He rarely asked about her parents, probably because she mentioned them so seldom, letting him assume they were both dead. His questions would increase, she knew, as he grew older and became more interested in his roots.

Mom. She hardly ever allowed herself to go there, but when Ally closed her eyes, she could still see the movement of her mother's hands threading every expression, every story like melody lines, changing tempo and rhythm with the pathos of the tale. Memories like these helped to block the darker ones, such as the way her mom's mental health deteriorated after the stillborn death of Ally's baby brother when Ally was thirteen. How her mother slumped into a depression nothing and no one could pull her from. And then that terrible moment when Ally's father came to school to tell her that her mother was dead, drowned in her own bathtub. Accident or suicide? In the end, the coroner ruled it an accident, deciding she'd slipped and bumped her head, causing the loss of consciousness that led to her drowning.

Irrationally, this did nothing to dissuade Ally from her own suspicion that her mother had taken her own life, for which

Ally had blamed herself. Because on that fateful day, if she'd delayed going to school, if she'd lingered to keep her mother company as her mother begged her to, she might have been able to prevent her mother's demons from finally overwhelming her. Instead, Ally hurried to school so she wouldn't be late for Ms. Damiani's zero-period Advanced Symphony class. Ally had put her own interests ahead of her mother's. And her mother had died as the result.

Would she ever tell Jack about that? Or the years that followed, when she'd wished every day she could go back into that morning and do it over again? She doubted it. There were some things that were better for him not to know.

She must have drifted off again for a sound awakened her. The wind? No. Outside, she heard only the steady rush and pull of the waves on the beach, not the frenzied crashing of before. It was her phone, she realized as it rang again, that had penetrated her slumber. She stretched out a hand from beneath the covers. "Hello?" Her voice emerged raspy with sleep.

"Hey, it's Sam. Just heard from Brittany. She can't get to work this morning. Storm toppled a tree across her driveway."

Ally caught her breath. "Is she all right?"

"Yes, yes, fine, just can't get out and a flippin' mess to clean up. I'm not expecting a whole lot of business 'cause of the storm, but Susan's still sick, and I gotta have someone on the floor. Can you come?"

Ally rolled to look at the clock. Not even seven, and Jack still sleeping beside her, not stirring. "I'll be there as soon as I can, okay?"

Half an hour later, Ally wondered if she'd promised something she couldn't deliver. "Hurry, Jack, we're going to be late," she urged for the ninth time, but her son would not be rushed. He hadn't appreciated being roused so early, especially when she reminded him it was Saturday, which meant he'd be spending the day with Miss Penny. "Haven't you tied your shoes yet?"

"I ca-aan't." His whine made her molars ache.

She searched the ceiling for patience. "Why not?"

"My foot won't go in."

Pressing back an exasperated sigh, she dropped his red jacket to the floor and crouched to help. Almost immediately, she found the problem. "Are these shoes too small? Do your toes pinch?"

"A little."

Didn't she buy these shoes just last month, before school started? She'd spent more on them than on her own sneakers, and now he needed another pair. Great. "All right." She tied them as loosely as she could. "Come on, let's go."

But once she finally had him out the door, he moped ten feet behind her all the way to Penny's front porch. The lawn was littered with leaves and branches downed by last night's wind. At least the rain had stopped.

Ally mounted Penny's front steps, the wooden boards creaking beneath her weight. Her landlady opened the door to Ally's knock and grabbed a tabby cat as it tried to streak outside. Ally reached out a hand to encourage her son up the last two steps before bending to kiss him. "All right, Bubs, see you this afternoon. Maybe I'll stop by The Pizzeria on my way home, pick up dinner for tonight." Now that she was leaving him, she felt a pang of remorse for her earlier impatience. He couldn't help that he wasn't a morning person. "Would you like that?" Jack shook his head before burying his face in her abdomen. "Hey, what's wrong?" She threw a nervous look at Penny, whose crossed arms and stern mouth telegraphed her disapproval. "You need to tell me, Bubba. I can't help you if you don't."

"Can I whisper it in your ear?"

From the door, Penny said, "It's not polite to whisper in front of people, Jack."

Ignoring her, Ally gently guided Jack to the edge of the porch. "What's up?" She resisted the urge to look at her watch.

Jack put his mouth to her ear. His steamy breath tickled her neck as he whispered, "I don't want to stay at Miss Penny's."

Ally lowered her chin to look him in the eye. "Jack." Putting on her firmest mom voice. "There's no school today, and I've got to go to work. You've got to stay here."

His chin trembled. "But I don't want to."

"Come in, Jack. Now," Penny called from the doorway. "I'm letting all the heat out, and your mother's got to go."

Ally clamped her back teeth together, wishing Penny would let her handle this her own way. "I'll bet Miss Penny will give you a little snack if you ask her nicely." Penny clicked her tongue, but she didn't disagree. Jack, however, would not let go, clutching the ends of Ally's long green scarf between his hands. "Sweetie, I've really got to go. I'll see you this afternoo—"

His small face crumpled. "But I don't want to stay here!" he blurted, abandoning all attempt at secrecy.

Ally exchanged glances with Penny, whose mouth puckered as if tasting sour milk. "Jack, come on—"

As he revved up to a full-on wail, Ally felt heat creeping into her cheeks. "Jack, you're making Miss Penny feel bad." *And embarrassing me.*

"I don't care! I won't stay here." He ran down the porch steps. At the bottom, he glared up at her, his lower lip shoved out half an inch.

Ally stared back, completely at a loss, feeling the weight of her inadequacy as a parent. But what could she do? Short of bodily carrying him inside Penny's house, not much. Jack had had his share of childhood tantrums, but he'd never flat-out refused to go to Penny's, who had watched him every Saturday since his babyhood.

But Ally didn't have time to get to the bottom of this mystery now. "I'm so sorry, Penny. I guess we have a change in plans."

Penny tilted her chin and narrowed her eyes. "What exactly do you plan to do now, Ally?"

"Take him with me." What other choice did she have?

Chapter 16

As Darcie drove into Langley, far fewer leaves clung to branches after last night's crashing windstorm. Some trees were completely bare, making them look oddly vulnerable. Though the clouds had rolled back over the sound, the pavement remained dark with rain, and fallen branches littered lawns everywhere. As she searched for a parking space near the Front Street Bistro, she passed several shopkeepers with wide brooms, sweeping their sidewalks free of debris.

At breakfast that morning, Paul had suggested they meet for lunch in town, something he rarely did—not only because they could hardly afford it, but because he usually preferred his own cooking to anyone else's. So did she, to be honest, but sensing her husband's desire for her company, she'd agreed.

After parking, she walked the short distance to the bistro, where she paused to read the headlines on the newspapers in the row of sidewalk dispensers. *The Seattle Times'* lead story caught her attention.

Fall storm closes 2 passes in Cascades, kills Freeland woman

Frowning, Darcie fished three quarters from her purse and plugged them into the dispenser. Freeland was just down the road from Langley. She had clients there. After pulling a paper from the stack, she continued to read.

The storm that led to a freak accident in Freeland and flooding in the Hanst Valley also closed two passes in the Cascade Mountains on Friday.

Washington State Department of Transportation temporarily closed Stevens Pass early Saturday morning because of heavy snowfall and Snoqualmie Pass because of avalanche danger. Meanwhile, the National Weather Service says that while we'll get a break in the weather for now, more rain is on the way. Yesterday's windstorm arrived a month earlier than normal, bringing with it high winds, including gusts up to 50 mph.

One of those gusts caused the death of Eileen Wilkinson, 54, as she and her husband walked their dog in Freeland on Whidbey Island on Friday afternoon. Wilkinson was killed when a tree limb broke off and struck her.

Eileen Wilkinson? The name rang a bell. Then, as she mounted the bistro's front steps, she remembered why. Eileen had been the daughter of one of her patients.

She opened the restaurant door to the rich, burnt-brown aroma of coffee and the soft, buttery scent of things baking. Ally worked behind the barista counter, smudges of weariness beneath her eyes, but when she saw Darcie, she broke into a smile and came from behind the counter to greet her. "Just you for lunch?"

"Paul's joining me."

Ally grabbed two plastic-coated menus from the rack and led her to a table by the window. As Darcie slid into the booth, she caught sight of a tousled, blond head bent over a sketch pad in the far corner. "Is that Jack? What's he doing here?"

The tender wrinkles around Ally's eyes deepened. "My compliant child decided to grow an opinion this morning. Flat-out refused to go to Penny's. I had no choice but to bring him with me."

Darcie knew she shouldn't smile, but she couldn't help it.

Ally frowned. "It works for today, but I'm going to have to figure out another plan long-term."

"What are your options?"

"No clue." Ally blew out her breath, making the curls over her forehead dance. "Need to make some calls when I take my break to see about daycare options around here. But then I'll have to work more hours in order to pay for them. Bit of a conundrum, you see."

An idea bloomed in Darcie's mind. "It's only weekends you need someone to watch him? Whenever you're working and he's not in school?"

"Saturdays, mainly. Know of any place?"

"Yes." She nodded. "Mine."

But Ally was already shaking her head. "Thanks, Darcie, but no."

"Why not?"

"I couldn't inflict that on you. And anyway, don't you and Paul have to work?"

Why did parents always assume that their children were an affliction to others? Seemed like once people became parents, they forgot what a gift their child was. "Paul and I would like to do this for you and Jack." *For us, too*, she could have added, but didn't.

Ally lowered her chin. "Really?"

"Would he like that?"

"Oh, I'm sure he'd be thrilled. But what about when you have to work?"

"We'll figure something out." Isn't that what real parents did every day? "Besides, we've got Rees to help us out too, until he leaves."

At the mention of Rees, something flickered across Ally's face but was gone before Darcie could identify it. "I can pay you, at least a little."

"You will not." Darcie waved the words away.

Ally's face smoothed, her relief unmistakable. "You're a godsend." As she stooped to give an awkward hug, Darcie patted her back, touched and pleased. Then Ally straightened and took the order pad from her apron pocket. "What can I get you from the espresso bar? This one's on me." She took Darcie's order for an iced mocha then went to greet the couple who'd just come in.

While she waited for her drink, Darcie went over to Jack's table. "Whatcha working on?" She slid into the seat across from him.

"Drawing."

Darcie tipped her head to examine his work. He'd sketched a threesome of people—a curly-haired brunette, clearly Ally, a boy with yellow hair, Jack. And a man, as yet featureless. His father? "Good job making sure no underwear shows." His eyebrows quirked into a frown. "You haven't heard that? It means you color in all the right places, no white showing."

"No white…underwear!" He smiled, a brilliant moment. "I get it! Mom says I'm a good artist."

"Exceptional, I'd say."

He drew with confidence and whimsy, his hand flying over the page as he added bounce to Ally's curls with a few strokes of his brown crayon.

"Your mom told me you don't want to stay at Miss Penny's anymore."

"Her house smells funny." He eyed her narrowly, daring her to disagree.

Darcie smothered a snicker. *I'll bet it does. All those cats.* "So, your mom and I worked out something different. Would you like to spend Saturdays at our house?"

His brown eyes searched her face. "Serious?"

"Would I kid you about something like that?" *Egads, this child has eyelashes women would kill for.*

"Can I teach Moses and Aaron some new tricks?"

"They'd love it."

His forehead wrinkled doubtfully. "What if they're too old?"

"Oh, dogs are never too old to learn new tricks. People just say that because dogs are creatures of habit, so when they get older, it's harder to break them out of their old ways to teach them new ways. But it's never impossible."

"Cool." A small peace washed over his face as he chose a lime green crayon and colored in Ally's skirt.

"Cool," she agreed. She would have been content to linger, but Ally caught her eye and pointed to the iced drink she'd delivered to her table. Reluctantly, Darcie rose. "Guess I'll see you next weekend, okay?"

"'Kay." His gaze traveled over her shoulder. "Hey, there's that policeman again." Darcie looked. Denny Lewis was removing his hat as he stepped through the door. Ally approached him with a menu, but he waved it away and gestured toward the back. Frowning, Ally nodded and spoke briefly to Sam before disappearing through the swinging kitchen door. "He's talking to Mom again."

"He was talking to her before?"

"Uh-huh. Yesterday at the park."

Why would Langley's deputy sheriff want to speak to Ally? Had Ally decided to tell him about the break-in at her house after all? These questions flitted through her mind as she said goodbye to Jack and reclaimed her seat by the window. She took a sip of her mocha before unfolding the *Times* to read more about the storm that killed Eileen Wilkinson. She had finished that article and was almost done with the entire front page when Paul finally arrived, ten minutes late.

"Sorry to keep you waiting."

"Hey." Darcie pushed the *Times* across the table at him and pointed at the article. "Look at this."

Paul skimmed the first few paragraphs, looked up, raised his eyebrows.

"I knew her," she said.

"You knew…" he skimmed the article again to catch the name. "Eileen Wilkinson?"

"Her father was one of my first clients here on Whidbey. Over in Freeland. Nice lady." Eileen played the piano, she remembered suddenly. Her father had often asked for it, and Eileen would drop everything to play his requests.

"Feel for the husband." Paul shook his head. "Poor guy, he must have seen it happen. The storm struck pretty hard over there. It's actually the reason I'm late in getting here—"

He would have said more except that Ally arrived to take his beverage order. "Anything from the espresso bar?" she asked. "My treat."

"Well, that's mighty nice of you. I'll take a tall decaf latte."

"Would you like to order your lunch now, too?"

Neither of them had even opened their menus. "What would you recommend?" Paul asked.

"Chicken peanut stew's good," Ally said. "If you like curry and cilantro."

"Love curry and cilantro."

"Comes with cornbread or sourdough."

"Cornbread, please."

Ally looked at Darcie. "And you?"

"Same."

As Ally wrote down their orders, Paul noticed Jack for the first time. "What's your boy doing here?"

Ally tucked her pencil behind her ear. "Ask your wife." She smiled and left.

Paul looked at her inquiringly, and she filled him in. Halfway through, Paul began to smile in approval, as she'd known he would. "You don't mind, do you?"

"Not at all. In fact, it makes what I wanted to share with you easier to say." He reached across the table for Darcie's hand, surprising her. Her husband wasn't usually demonstrative in public. "Had an interesting discussion with Diego this morning."

"With Diego? On Saturday?" Normally his assistant worked weekdays only.

"I'll explain in a minute. First, I want to tell you what Diego and I talked about. We were discussing ways we might increase our business next year."

Darcie's heart lifted. So he *was* taking their financial concerns to heart. It gratified her to know he was trying to do something about it.

"As we were talking, I suddenly remembered the boating camps my brothers and I used to do back in Seattle. Ally was asking about them the other day."

She watched his face, trying to figure out where this was going. "You thinking of doing something similar here in Langley?" Hard to imagine how that might work. Langley wasn't Seattle, and besides Li'l Sailors was never a money-making venture. It was a gift back to the community.

"No, but it got me thinking. Those kids, a lot of them, were foster kids. You ever thought about us being foster parents?"

Of course she'd thought about it. Years before, when it became clear she wasn't going to get pregnant the easy way, she'd done some research into adopting. What she discovered was more discouraging than hopeful. For one thing, domestic adoption wouldn't be the simple solution for them that it was for many other couples. Paul's age, pushing fifty, would make many birth mothers skittish about choosing them as adoptive parents. Birth-moms worried about dad not being around long enough to provide a stable childhood.

International adoption wasn't much better. Because of increasing restrictions and red tape, the process could not only take years, but with travel and application expenses, it was just as pricey as domestic adoption. Or infertility treatments, for that matter. In any case, it was money they did not have. "Can't say it never crossed my mind," she said, answering his question.

Paul deflated a little. "You're not excited."

"It's just… fostering? We'd never know what we'd be getting. There are so many risks. Too many unknowns." It wasn't the unknown physical needs that scared her as much as the psychological ones. What if a child came to them who was addicted to his mother's drugs or abused beyond redemption?

"How is that any different than a child who came from us? No parent has control over the kind of kid they end up with." He stroked her hand with his thumb. "I know you want one of our own. Me too. But just because we say yes to a foster child doesn't mean it won't ever happen for us, right? And don't you think it might help to scratch that itch in the meantime?"

Scratch that itch? Is that what he thought it was? Frustration bubbled inside her chest as she leveled her gaze at her husband. "I just don't know if I could love a child who came to us with issues. Not love them the way a parent is supposed to." It sounded heartless, but there it was.

"Don't you think I have those same questions?"

"Not the same way I do, apparently."

A beat. "Don't you think we should at least think about it?"

She was spared having to answer as Ally appeared with their order. "Two chicken peanut stews, with cornbread." Ally set the dishes on the table. "Enjoy. I'll be back in a few minutes to check on you."

Darcie looked down at the chunks of chicken and carrots swimming in thick, peanuty broth. Fostering? That was his solution to their problem?

She waited for Paul's brief word of grace before reaching for her spoon. "You haven't told me why Diego was at the shop this morning."

"Oh, yes. Well." He was distracted now, bent over his stew, inhaling deeply. Finally, he looked up. "Turns out last night's storm did quite a bit of damage to the Freeland marina. Lot of boats got banged up. Jerry, the fellow with the repair shop over there, is swamped with work orders. He called me, asked if we could take some of their business. We worked out a deal. Looks like Diego and I are going to have our hands full for quite a while. Probably until the end of the year."

"Oh, Paul." She felt an unexpected lightness. "That's good, isn't it? Good for business, that is."

He smiled, but his eyebrows pulled together so the smile seemed worried. "Should be enough to get us over this hump." He picked up his corn muffin, eyed it from all angles and took a bite. He smiled again, a real one this time. "Holy cats. Have you tasted this?" He took a second bite, eyes closed. "Sorry, hon, but do you mind? I need to find out what Sam put into this. I'll only be a sec."

"Go ahead." She sighed and waved him away. This was the other reason they rarely ate out. Paul usually spent more time in the kitchen chatting with the chef than with her.

As he left, her gaze fell on the newspaper once more, prompting another memory about Eileen Wilkinson. During the last days of Eileen's father's life, when Darcie was tending him around the clock, Darcie had asked what she and Bill, her husband, would do when they no longer had to care for her ailing father. Eileen said they'd probably travel some around the U.S. But then she'd confided her greatest life's dream: to go to Europe to see the great cathedrals and castles she loved to read about.

"Then why don't you go to Europe?"

"It's Bill." Eileen pulled a face. "He's afraid to fly. He's perfectly willing to go anywhere I want, so long as we can drive. Since we can't exactly drive across the Atlantic, it's unlikely I'll ever go."

"You could go with a friend," Darcie suggested. "Or by yourself."

"Suppose I could," Eileen agreed. "But I won't."

"Why not?"

"It just wouldn't be the same."

And that, Darcie realized, was how she felt about foster parenting. Sure, it might get her to her intended destination: parenthood. But what if the experience disappointed her? What if she somehow disappointed the child? What if they failed to bond in a fundamental way? Ultimately, at the heart of it, it was as Eileen said.

Unless the child was her own, Darcie was afraid it just wouldn't be the same.

Chapter 17

What's happening to me? Ally wondered as she returned to the espresso bar after delivering Paul's latte. Had she really agreed to allow a couple she barely knew to take care of her son? She recalled her recent conversation with Brittany, who seemed to think she had trust issues. She wished Brittany were here now so she could show her otherwise. *See? I can trust people, when I have to. When they've done something to deserve it.*

Her musings were interrupted when Denny Lewis walked in, admitting a burst of cool air. "Hey, Denny." She came around the counter to pluck a menu from the stack. "You here for your usual or a late lunch?"

"Neither, actually. I'm here to talk to you." Only he didn't look too happy about it.

She felt a flutter of uneasiness. "Me?" She hoped he didn't want to talk about Brittany. She didn't want to be the one to tell him what her friend had confided yesterday, that she'd invited Jamie to move into her parents' house with her while her parents were on a two-month RV tour of New England. "Why?"

Denny's glance skimmed the alcove, where only one customer sat at a window table with an open laptop. "You due for a break anytime soon?"

"I could ask Sam to cover for me. We're not very busy today. Storm cleanup's keeping everyone home, I guess." All morning she'd caught sight of Langley's shop owners working to pick up downed branches from their property, while more than one utility crew had rumbled past in a white cherry-picker truck. "Everything all right?"

"Well, that's for you to tell me. Where would you like to talk?"

"I'll tell Sam I'm taking a break." At least this didn't seem to be about Brittany. "Meet me around back, okay?"

As soon as the screen door closed behind her, Denny got right to the point. "Don't know if you heard, but there's been a rash of break-ins around town."

"Break-ins?" Heat flooded her face. "You mean burglaries?"

"Smash-and-grabs. Guy seems to know what he's doing: strikes during the day when the homeowners are gone and takes only what he knows he can sell quickly for cash. Fact that he knows who's gone makes us think he's staking out the houses beforehand. Breaks a back window to gain access, grabs two or three big-ticket items within easy reach." One sandy eyebrow arched. "Sound familiar?"

She swallowed but said nothing.

"Thing is," Denny continued, "I was talking to one of the victims this morning. She has a little girl who claims someone at school was telling everyone at recess that his house had been broken into."

"Really?" It was cold, the wind whipping straight up off the water making her wish she'd thought to grab a jacket. She rubbed the goosebumps rising along her arms.

"What I found odd is that this girl said the boy claimed it happened several days ago. I know kids aren't good with telling time. Could have been a week ago or even the day before. But what troubled me was *I* had never heard about it. Thought it was worth following through on, so I asked her classmate's name. Jack Brennan, she said." He eyed her sternly. "Well? Is it true?"

Ally shrugged.

Denny cocked his head to one side. "Now why on earth wouldn't you tell me a thing like that?"

"I just didn't think it was important."

His voice notched up to incredulity. "Not even yesterday when I mentioned a car prowler?"

"I…didn't think there was a connection."

He sighed. "Listen. We're a community here. You know what that means? It means we look out for one another. We watch each other's backs. Rash of thefts like this, that's big news in these parts. Don't get much of this sort of thing, so when it happens, we *say* something. Not to be a newsmaker or grab the spotlight, but because we care and so it doesn't happen to somebody else. Understand?"

"Yes," she whispered. His words closely echoed Darcie's the night she stitched up Ally's foot. *This is what neighbors do. We watch each other's backs.* "I'm sorry."

He nodded, pulling a notepad from his front pocket. "Now that your cat's out of the bag, why don't you tell me about it. When exactly did this happen?"

"Tuesday. When Jack and I came home from school, we found the window in the back door had been smashed in." She held out her foot. "That's how this happened."

He frowned at her before jotting this down. "About what time?"

"Four, I think."

"When had you last been home before that?"

"At nine that morning, when we left for school and work."

"Did you lock up?"

"Of course." She always did. Even in Langley.

"So he got in by the back door. What did he take?"

"Our television. My jewelry box."

Denny jotted this as well. "Anything valuable in the jewelry box?"

"My grandmother's wedding rings. Not that valuable, really. Only to me."

"Describe them."

"Yellow gold, quarter-carat diamond. Wedding ring wraps around the engagement ring. Victorian-looking."

"File a report with your insurance company?"

"I don't have insurance." Her composure returning, she lifted her chin a notch. "That's why I didn't think it was worth reporting."

He merely gave her a raised eyebrow. "Anything else?"

She shook her head. "I'm going to have a talk with my son, though, about telling other people our private business." Did this have anything to do with his getting into arguments at recess? But no, that didn't make sense. Why would Jack's news of a break-in cause a fight?

"Don't be too hard on the kid. We all want to impress our friends sometimes." For the first time today, he smiled. Such a nice smile, too. Rows of white, even teeth. "Does anyone else know about this?" he added, pocketing his notepad. "Your neighbors, a friend?"

"My landlady, Penny Watrous. And the Nielsens. They live across the street and fixed my door."

"Good to know. I'll talk to them." Again, a stern look. "*If* that's all right with you."

She had the grace to blush.

CHAPTER 18

"Come with me." Darcie beckoned Ally to follow her to her bedroom. It was the following Saturday, the first Jack had spent with them while his mother worked. Ally had arrived to pick up Jack after her shift, but he and Paul weren't back yet from walking the dogs. "I've got something to show you."

"So it went okay today?" Ally trailed her down the hall. "Jack wasn't too much trouble?"

"We had a good time." She wished Ally would quit worrying about being a burden; she didn't know what it would take to convince her they were only doing what they wanted to do. Really, she found it the teeniest bit annoying. Darcie said only what she meant, so she expected people to take her at her word. "Jack helped Paul bake brownies, and then we read *Hank the Cowdog* and drew pictures on the whiteboard in the kitchen. Your son's quite the artist." Darcie pushed open her bedroom door and went to the carved wooden jewelry box on her mirrored dresser. She opened it and pulled out a small, black velvet box. From this, she withdrew a diamond wedding set. "Here, put this on." When Ally made no move to take the rings, she tried again. "Please. I'd like you to."

Ally's forehead furrowed, clearly puzzled by the request, but she took the rings and slid them on her finger. "Beautiful." She held them up for Darcie to admire. "See?"

"Looks good on you. They fit?"

"Yes."

She started taking them off, but Darcie stopped her. "They're yours."

"What?"

"I want you to have them."

"Don't be ridiculous." She slipped them from her finger.

Darcie pressed her hand over hers, stilling the action. "Please, I'd like to give them to you." She'd gotten the idea when Ally told her about the scolding Denny Lewis had given her, reminding her that Ally had lost her rings in the theft. "Though I know they won't mean the same to you as your grandmother's."

"I can't keep these."

"A loan, then, until your own rings are found. I'd like you to have them to wear."

"Why?"

"Because otherwise they sit here in my jewelry box doing no one any good."

"Why don't you wear them?"

Darcie tipped her head. "Um, because I don't think my husband would appreciate my wearing rings another man gave me?" As Ally's eyebrows winged upward, she nodded. "I was engaged to someone else when I met Paul. Even though I broke it off, the guy insisted I keep the rings. I've hung onto them all these years because I haven't known what to do with them. Didn't seem right to sell them. I certainly can't wear them." She smiled. "Paul's a pretty laid-back fellow but not *that* laid-back."

Ally frowned. "I feel guilty taking them from you."

"Well, you shouldn't."

Ally hesitated, and then finally nodded. "Well, thank you. What happened to the guy you jilted?"

"Joined the Peace Corps, married a dentist he met in Haiti." She so rarely thought about Doug anymore or the years they spent together in nursing school at the University of Washington.

Ally perched on the edge of the king-sized bed. "So what about Paul?" She picked up the ivory-framed wedding photo on Darcie's nightstand. "How'd you meet him?"

"I was his dad's hospice nurse." The bedsprings creaked as Darcie joined her on the bed. By the afternoon light slanting through the window over the bed, she examined her own face on her wedding day. It was a candid shot, taken by one of her new sisters-in-law, showing only Paul's profile as he looked at her with quiet pride. Darcie looked straight into the camera, her eyes alight with joy. "It sounds strange, maybe, if you're not in the hospice business, but when it's done right, death can be a beautiful thing. And making it beautiful mostly depends on the family. That's what Paul did for his dad."

She recalled those first months after meeting Paul. "The day of his dad's funeral, I knew I loved him. Paul, I mean." She remembered sitting through the long service, all the testimonies, the eulogy, thinking not about her patient who had just died but his son. About how, now that his father was dead, she had no reason to see him anymore. No reason to linger together in the warm kitchen after her official call was finished, no reason to call him on her days off, ostensibly to check on her patient's welfare, really just to hear Paul's voice. She'd known then if she didn't do something drastic, she'd spend the rest of her life wondering about this man who knew how to make death a lovely thing. If he could do that with death, what might he do with life?

Funny how often she forgot, in the ordinariness of the day-to-day, what had attracted her to Paul in the first place.

"That night, I broke up with my fiancé. The next morning, I called Paul to see if he wanted to meet me for lunch. He asked if he could cook dinner for me instead, and the rest…well, here we are." They'd waited only four months to get married, and after that, no time at all in trying to get pregnant. Both agreed they wanted a boatload of kids—four, maybe five. Though Darcie was only in her mid-twenties, Paul was already forty. They'd joked about how their kids would have an old man for a dad, which no longer seemed like much of a joke. "How 'bout you? Ever been married?"

"No."

"You must have been pretty young when you had Jack."

"Too young. It was never a relationship meant to last." She hesitated. "There was someone else, though. Once."

"What happened?"

"Oh…" She looked down at her fingers pleating the quilted bedspread. "Just didn't work out. He was meant for bigger things."

"Like what?"

"He was—is—a musician. A professional."

"What kind of musician?"

"Jazz."

"Really? Paul loves jazz. What's his name?"

Another hesitation, a longer one. As if Ally was weighing the wisdom of sharing so much about herself. "Josh Mitchell."

"The guitarist?"

Surprise rippled across Ally's face. "You've heard of him?"

Darcie laughed. "Actually saw him in concert once at Jazz Alley." She rose and crossed to the stack of compact discs beside the CD player, rifling through them before holding one up. "This guy."

Ally took the CD and studied the black-and-white cover image of the handsome, dark-haired musician, a smile tugging at her mouth. "Yes," she said softly. "That guy."

"Paul adores this album. You really dated Josh Mitchell?"

"For a little while. In college."

"Have you kept up on his career?"

"Only enough to know he signed with a label. After we... broke up, it seemed better not to know too much." Flipping the case over, she scanned the playlist. She went still, her smile fading. Then, "You mind if I borrow this?"

"Not at all." She looked at Ally, curious, and started to ask something more, but then Ally picked up another framed photo from Darcie's nightstand.

"This must be you and Rees."

Darcie nodded, aware that Ally was deliberately changing the subject. "It was taken at the top of the Space Needle to celebrate Mom being halfway through chemo." Rees wore his dark-blond hair like a mop over his ears. Her own hair, neatly parted in the middle, fell in a shag cut below her shoulders. Both of them had dully glinting braces. He'd been about ten, she twelve on that day. Her mom had made it through the first tough months of cancer treatments, doctors cautiously optimistic as they decided to give her a three-week break from the drugs. It was the first time in eons Mom had felt like getting out of the house, so Dad took them all downtown for dinner at the top of the famous landmark. It had been a day infused with hope.

"How's your mom now?" Ally asked.

"She died two years after diagnosis. Didn't survive the treatments. My dad died soon after Paul and I were married. That's when we decided to move here, to Whidbey Island."

"So now it's just you and Rees?"

"Yep."

"You must be pretty close, then."

"We are." Or were, anyway. These days, she wasn't so sure.

"Has he ever been married?"

"Not married, but engaged once."

"What happened?" Ally returned the frame to Darcie's nightstand.

Darcie sighed. "She died."

"Oh. I'm sorry."

"Me too." Sometimes Darcie wondered if Rees would ever let himself love again. Losing their mom at a young age was hard enough. When she'd died, Rees had blamed himself, believing he'd not prayed hard enough to save her. It had taken him years to get over that. And then Julie, dying the way she did…

Irrational as it was, Rees blamed himself for that, too. Darcie feared these devastating losses had left her brother forever afraid of failing those he loved.

Her memory spun back to the day Rees had first introduced her to Julie. As Darcie was seeing Doug at the time, they'd planned a double-date. In those first minutes, she'd been taken by Julie's blond beauty and her easy-going warmth, but it was the discovery of their shared love for sushi that sealed the deal. *We bonded over raw fish*, they'd tell people later. "Julie was a wonderful person, a perfect match for Rees," she told Ally. "We all thought so."

Ally turned the rings around on her finger. "So how did she die?"

Darcie hesitated. "She was killed in the September 11 attacks." It still stunned her sometimes, saying those words aloud, so she anticipated the shock as it dawned on Ally's face. "She was on Flight 93, the one that crashed in Pennsylvania. She and Rees had flown out to Newark to attend a friend's wedding. While they were there, Rees got a call for a job interview in Seattle, so he returned early. She changed her flight to add a few days to see some family who lived out there."

At the time, Darcie was a newly minted hospice nurse. She'd heard the first reports of the attacks after an all-night vigil with an Alzheimer's patient, a woman who finally passed away at five in the morning. She was driving home, exhausted, through a gorgeous Northwest morning with summerlike temperatures and crystal blue skies, listening to the car radio to keep herself awake. Her sleep-deprived condition made her unsure, at first, of what she was hearing. Airplanes flying into buildings in New York City? Terrible. But that's all she'd thought. She hadn't known those planes were hijacked by terrorists, hadn't known Julie was scheduled to fly that morning, either. When she got to her apartment, she collapsed into bed and slept for two hours before Rees's phone call awakened her.

Are you watching the news? She would never forget his voice, stretched thin like a rubber band pulled from his throat. *We're under attack. Julie was flying home through San Francisco today. She's not answering her cell.*

"He never really forgave himself for her death," Darcie said.

"Why? It was hardly his fault that terrorists attacked."

"No, but his own change of plans led to Julie's being on that particular flight. He didn't have to come home early for that job interview. He chose to. Wanted to show them his commitment." She sighed. "But that was a while ago now." Thank God. She hoped she'd never have to relive such moments again, or watch Rees go through a similar ordeal. "It's been hard for him, but sometimes I think if he could just meet the right woman, it might help put this behind him for good." Though there would never be another Julie.

A door slammed. Voices came from the kitchen. "Sounds like the boys are back." Darcie stood, more than a little glad for the interruption. Even after all these years, Julie remained a painful subject. And if Darcie felt that way, she could only imagine how her brother felt. "Shall we go and say hello?"

CHAPTER 19

Ally took Jack's hand to hurry him along the lane to their house, listening with only half an ear to his chatter about Mr. Paul's promise to make homemade pizza for lunch next Saturday and the perfect ten-point starfish he found on their walk along the beach.

When Darcie had pulled that CD from her collection, with Josh Mitchell on the cover, Ally couldn't believe it. He looked exactly as she remembered him, down to the black button-down open at the neck, the dark hair long over the ears and forehead, the straight nose and disarming smile.

She'd not said a word about him to a single soul since the last time she saw him, though she'd thought of him often, tormenting herself with what-ifs, imagining all the while he'd forgotten about her. Until today, when she flipped Darcie's CD over and saw the title of the lead song on Josh's first solo album.

Cadence.

That's me, she thought as it all came back in a rush. Freshman year, fall semester. She'd been at Drake University a little over a month and was starting to believe she'd finally escaped the bondage of her bad choices, starting to believe she really could refashion herself into the kind of person she once dreamed of. Successful. Content. Free. But even then, as all the other pieces began fitting together to form a new whole, one piece remained missing. Not lost, just missing.

Lola. She hadn't played for nearly three years. Her longing to make music again, or to at least be around those who did, drew her to the Musical Arts Building that evening. She felt deprived of the passion that had driven her for so long. Even as a child, when home life was uncertain—when her father announced another move or her mother descended into another funk—music calmed her, gave her purpose, framed her identity.

She'd given it all up when her mother died, carrying her grief as a traveler would a suitcase. Awash with remorse and guilt, she'd buried that part of herself the day they'd buried her mom. But unlike her mother, who stayed irrevocably dead, this part of her rose out of the grave, refusing to remain dead any longer.

On that evening as her last class ended, a dull sociology class meant only to fulfill a requirement and not the yearnings of her soul, she felt starved for a taste of the feast she knew to be laid out right next door. A taste, she told herself, was all she wanted.

She mounted the steps to the Musical Arts Building, pushed open the heavy double doors, inhaled the smells of resin and wax. From down the polished hallway came the sturdy strains of Dvorak's *New World Symphony*. If they followed the same schedule as other classes, this one should have wrapped up fifteen minutes ago, but from the confident sounds emanating from the auditorium, it seemed this ensemble was having so much fun they didn't want to quit.

She remembered it well. The transcendent pleasure of joining her talent to others'. The awesome synergy of creating a whole greater than its parts. Sometimes joy expanded inside her chest so fast she feared her body couldn't contain it all.

She leaned against the cool, tiled wall, just listening. She couldn't have been there long when a voice spoke from behind her.

"I know who you are."

She spun, startled by the voice's nearness.

A boy—she still had a hard time thinking of her male peers as *men*. He must have come from one of the practice rooms. He grinned, showing white teeth. "You're Cadence Brennan."

"Yes."

"Josh Mitchell." He stuck out a hand, and she shook it. Even in that brief touch, she noticed his long, tapered hands. Musician's hands. "We're in European History together."

"Oh. Sure." Now it was coming back. "You sit in the back."

He gestured toward the auditorium with a tilt of his chin. "You like classical music?"

"Yes." Aware of his appraising gaze, she quashed the impulse to smooth her hair, which, as usual, flitted in unruly curls around her face.

"Figured you had to have more than a passing acquaintance with music." He grinned again. "With a name like Cadence."

She felt a flush begin. "You can thank my mother for that. She was a musician and hoped I would be one, too."

"And are you?"

"I used to be."

"Piano? Cello? Violin?"

"Viola, actually."

"Ah." His brown eyes crinkled at the corners in appreciation. "Not just any musician, but a smart one."

So he knew that old joke. *What do you call a violinist with brains? A violist.* A tweak on another old saw about sopranos and altos. She'd first heard it from her high school music teacher, Ms. Damiani, when she suggested Ally switch from violin to viola. "Violinists are like sopranos, Cadence, in that they don't have to think a whole lot about the music; they just need to learn how it goes. But altos and violists? They actually have to read the notes and figure out how their part fits with the rest. That makes them smarter. And better, in my opinion—though don't tell the violin section I said that."

She smiled now, sharing his laugh. "And you? You must play an instrument if you know so much about mine."

"Guitar. Acoustic," he added. "Not electric."

"I think I could have guessed that." He didn't strike her as a rocker. By now they'd moved toward the building's front doors, then outside into the cool autumn air, where they paused at the top of the stairs.

"Which way you heading?"

"Ballard," she said, naming one of the dorms. "You?"

"MacMillan."

"We're neighbors, then." Their feet crunched on the gravel pathway, lit by Victorian-era streetlamps. A gust of wind sent a whirl of leaves rattling across their path. She didn't have much experience making small talk while walking alongside a guy in the dark. The silence lengthened while she searched for something to say. Sending Josh a sidelong glance, she found him doing the same.

His teeth flashed. "This your first year at Drake?"

She nodded. "How 'bout you?"

"Second. You like our history class?"

"I find all that stuff fascinating." Although it was a bittersweet thing, learning about the European countries she'd given up opportunity to visit. Her high school ensemble had been planning a tour through England and Germany when Mom died. Still—maybe someday.

They reached the fork that branched in two directions, one to Ballard, the other to Mac Hall. "Guess I'll see you tomorrow," Josh said. "If you're nice, maybe I'll even save you a seat in the back."

"Only if *you're* nice."

"I'm always nice." Again, that flashing grin. "Especially to pretty girls. See you tomorrow…Cadence."

"What are you listening to, Mom?"

Jack's question yanked Ally back to reality. The first thing she'd done when they arrived home was insert the CD into Jack's player, sending its energetic strains pulsating into the room. She perched on the edge of his twin bed, listening. She looked at her son. "It's called jazz. Gypsy jazz. You like it?"

His brow furrowed. "Kinda. But I like what you play on Lola better."

"It's just a different style. Doesn't mean you can't like both." She handed him the CD case, pointed to the picture of Josh. "Believe it or not, your mom used to know this guy."

"Really?"

"Mmm-hmm."

He studied Josh's face a very long time, then looked up to search her eyes. "Is he my dad?"

"Your dad?" His question sent her stomach plunging right into her socks. "Why would you ask that?"

He dipped his head, not answering, just running a toy pickup truck back and forth along the edge of his bed. She reached for the CD player and pressed STOP. The room fell into quiet. "Jack?"

"Am I ever going to meet my dad?"

A long beat. Then, calmly, "I don't think so, Bubba." What she meant was, *Over my dead body*. But studying her son's downturned face, a glimmer of an idea began to form. An understanding maybe. Could this be at the root of the problems on the playground? She'd stopped asking Jack about it, adopting instead a wait-and-see approach. But now, with this new clue, Denny's advice came back to her.

Trust your gut. "Jack?" She drew him into her lap, the mattress sagging to accommodate the additional weight. "Remember that day a couple of weeks ago when I picked you up from school and you were crying?"

He ducked his head. "Yeah."

"I assumed it was because I was a few minutes late. But that wasn't the reason, was it?"

A head shake.

"It was for the same reason you tried to hit someone on the playground, wasn't it?"

A long pause, followed by a slow nod.

She felt relief bloom inside. Finally, progress. "Will you tell me about it now?"

Another silence stretched out, in which she heard only the steady in and out of Jack's breathing. "I'm afraid you'll be mad." His voice small and muffled against her shoulder.

"Why would I be mad?"

"I—I told someone to shut up. You always say 'shut up' is a bad word."

Ally fought a smile, grateful for his head buried in her shoulder so he couldn't see her face. "It's not something I like to hear you say. Why did you say it? Did someone say something you didn't like?"

"Yeah." Jack pulled himself upright, ran the truck wheels over his hand to make them spin.

"What did he say?"

Spin, spin. "He said, 'Jack, Jack, wants his Daddy back.' I told him to stop, but he wouldn't, so I said 'shut up.' And then when he wouldn't, I…I tried to punch him. To make him stop."

Ohhhh. She gathered him close. "Bubba, I'm sorry."

"He asked why I didn't have a dad. I said I just didn't. He said there had to be a reason. I said there wasn't. He said there was. Is there a reason, Mom?"

She cradled his head beneath her chin, his fine hair so soft against her neck. "Yes, Bubba, there's a reason."

"What is it?"

"Because…" How to unpack this so he would understand, but without revealing too much? "He wasn't the kind of man who would make a good daddy, Bubba."

He pulled himself away to look into her face. "How do you know?"

"He wasn't very nice."

"Did he tell you to shut up?"

"No, but he was not good to me in other ways. In grown up ways." *Please, don't ask me what that means.* Some things about his father Jack should never know.

"Did you love him?"

"I did, once. Or thought I did. I was pretty young. That's part of what was wrong."

His smooth brow furrowed. "It's just that sometimes… sometimes I wish I had a dad, too. Like other kids."

She kissed the top of his head, let her lips linger there. *Ah, the smell of my son is like the smell of a field, which the LORD has blessed.* The line from the book of Genesis came floating to her. How richly it described the scent of a boy: earthy, ripe, wholesome. "I wish you did, too."

Since he was little, Ally had tried to explain they weren't like most families, those with both a mom and a dad. She told him she'd always do the best she could, but it would never be the same for him as it was for kids with two parents.

He looked up at her. "I thought you'd be mad."

"I'm not mad. I'm sad I can't give you what you want. Especially since I know having a dad is really what's best for a boy. But I'm certainly not mad at you for wanting it."

"But you said we need to lay up our treasures in heaven and not be greedy for stuff on earth."

"It's not greedy to want a dad." She adjusted his weight on her lap, bringing him close enough to feel the steady *beat, beat* of his heart. "In fact, remember I said relationships are part of what Jesus meant by storing up treasures in heaven—investing in people who will live with us all the way into eternity. If you ever do have a daddy, it will be that kind of daddy. The forever kind. But those are pretty rare, Bubba, and very hard to find."

Jack fell silent. "What about that policeman from the playground?"

"Deputy Lewis?" The question surprised her, though she realized now it shouldn't. "He's just a friend."

"Not your boyfriend."

"I'm afraid not. He likes someone else."

"Do you think you'll ever have a boyfriend?"

"I hope so, Bubs. Someday."

CHAPTER 20

Jack's revelation continued to occupy Ally's mind a week later as she arrived at the elementary school to pick him up from class.

"The school day is over, the clock says we're done. See you on Wednesday, good-bye, everyone." In high, lilting unison, Jack's class sang their parting song, the sweetness of their voices blending with the desultory chatter of the parents congregated outside the classroom door. Ally exchanged a smile with another mom and took her place in the courtyard to await Jack's exit. Jack bounded over, trailing jacket in hand.

"Hey, Bubba, let's put on your jacket, okay? Season's changing, not so warm anymore." She felt grateful for the thick, kiwi-green scarf tucked beneath her coat, keeping the afternoon's chill off her neck.

After helping Jack into his jacket, she zipped it to his chin before waving goodbye to Mrs. Nichols in the doorway. She smiled and waved back. One of these days, Ally would probably have to explain to his teacher the reason for Jack's behavior on the playground. But not today. Today, she had something else in mind.

As they passed the blue and yellow Big Toy, she asked, "How'd you like to stop by the library on the way home?"

His brown eyes lit up. "Can I check out a movie?"

"Movie!" She feigned chagrin. "How 'bout a *book*?"

"Please?"

She squinted an eye. "*One* movie. As long as you check out at least two books, too."

They walked hand-in-hand from the school. Ally welcomed the chance to be outside again. Darcie had stopped by the night before to remove Ally's stitches, so that today, for the first time since slicing open her foot, Ally had left the car at home. The windstorm had ushered in the real start of autumn, with its nostalgic scents of ash and pine. Gone for good were the warmer days of Indian summer. Though the trees lining Langley's streets still retained most of their vibrant foliage, the crispness of the air and the angle of the sun's rays promised that soon even those leaves would fall.

"Mom?"

"Yes, Bubba?"

"Why do they make us sing so much in kindergarten?"

"Because setting words to music helps us remember them. That's why we learn to *sing* the ABCs before we say them."

"But why? Why is it easier?"

"We don't know exactly why. Something about the way our brains work, the way we make connections." It had always fascinated her, the impact of music on thought and emotion. To her, it suggested the handiwork of God Himself. How else did one explain the rise of joy as music surged to a crescendo? Why should a series of black dots on a page, when translated into sound, have such a visceral impact on her soul? Nothing else made sense other than to believe God had designed her to respond to music. The supernatural wonder of it provided a window to heaven, a glimpse of the beauty and majesty awaiting them there. "Some musicians are also scientists who spend a lot of time learning about how music affects us, but it's still a mystery." She looked down at him, loving the way his blond hair glinted in the sun's slanting light. "But I like mysteries, don't you? Life would be pretty boring if we understood everything. Nothing left to be curious about."

They reached the beige clapboard building with purple trim that housed Langley's tiny library. Jack ran ahead to punch the large square button that automatically opened the library's double doors. By the time Ally caught up, Jack had veered off the path to hang on the thick rope cordoning off the library's rustic rock garden. "Whatcha looking at, Bubs?"

"That." He pointed at the largest stone in the center. "Is that a grave marker?"

"You mean a gravestone? No."

"But it has words carved in it."

"It says, 'Given by the Friends of the Langley Library.'"

"Oh." He looked disappointed. "I thought maybe somebody read too many books and died of shock."

"Unlikely." Ally laughed and ruffled his hair. Inside the library, Jack shrugged out of his backpack and thrust it at her. "You know where to find me." As he scuttled off to the children's section, Ally headed for the bank of computers in the center of the room and claimed an unoccupied terminal at the end of the row. She logged in, navigated to the site of the *Spring Falls Sentinel*, and glanced around to make sure no one was near before whispering, "Hi Daddy."

It was the only link Ally allowed herself to her past. A paltry indulgence—and an empty one, since in all these years she'd never found a single mention of her father. But scanning the local headlines made her feel somehow closer to home, despite the regret and the doubt that twisted inside her.

She ran her fingers across the screen. After nearly six years, the sharp pain of loss was gone, but she doubted she'd ever outgrow the ache that throbbed deep in her spirit. *How're you doing, Dad? Do you miss me as much as I miss you?*

It hadn't been easy to leave him. Despite the tumultuous years of her childhood—the frequent moves, her mother's moods—she'd always known she was Daddy's girl. She may have gotten her talent and passion from her mother, but she'd gotten her resilience from her father. The ability to pick up and move on. And though she doubted she'd ever have the chance to explain, she hoped someday he might intuitively put the pieces together and understand why she had to disappear the way she did.

Have you forgiven me yet?

She wondered, sometimes, if her father had ever tried to find her, despite her asking him not to. Of course, he had. What father wouldn't? He'd probably enlisted the help of his law-enforcement stepson. And why not? She'd never told her father he shouldn't trust his stepson. She'd never told him the truth about Kyle Wylie.

Which was why she'd taken such drastic measures to escape attention when she moved to Langley. Why she'd fled her home state, changed her name, avoided any kind of national database that would enable Kyle to find her.

Even so, the first year after she arrived here, when the people and the place and the weather were still so strange, she fantasized about finding a missing persons ad in the *Sentinel.* What would she do? She never had, so the question remained unanswered, but it led to others. Had it been a mistake to leave the way she did, without telling anyone where she was going or why? Could there possibly have been another way? But every time she circled back to the same conclusion. There was no other way. For her sake. For Jack's.

Ally glanced once more toward the children's section and saw her son engrossed in a picture book. Settling back into her chair, she perused the most recent headlines, wondering if she'd find anything interesting. Very occasionally, she did. Two years ago, she'd found a wedding announcement for her teacher, Gina Damiani. "The bride is keeping her last name," the blurb had stated, making Ally smile. Naturally, her feisty music teacher was keeping her own name.

A year before that, she'd found Kyle's name mentioned in an article describing the capture of a serial burglar using dogs from his K-9 unit. She'd lingered long on this article. Though it had been like a knife twisting in her gut to read his name spelled out, she'd found it at the same time reassuring to see, in black and white, that he remained in Spring Falls. Had a life there. Had maybe forgotten her.

A wishful thought she had no intention of putting to the test.

She clicked on a new page of stories. The season's first major rainstorm was expected to move in by Friday. New DNA evidence had reopened a 1985 murder investigation. A Spring Falls resident had hired on with the Chicago Symphony. Here she paused, reading the article once, twice, wondering why the man's name rang a bell. A visiting conductor to her youth symphony? Modern composer of a piece she'd once memorized? Unable to place it, Ally shook her head and moved on.

She read a few more articles on the same page and was about to click to another when a different kind of headline caught her eye. **Witnesses sought in motorcycle crash**.

She wasn't sure why she read more than the headline. Perhaps it was the fact her father owned a motorcycle, never happier than when flying down the highway on his Suzuki at 75 miles an hour. Or perhaps it was some sixth sense drawing her attention to what she needed to see.

The Iowa State Patrol is looking for witnesses to a collision that badly injured a motorcyclist on Interstate 380 near 73rd Street NE in Spring Falls on Saturday. The accident occurred about 9 p.m., when a blue 2001 Honda Accord lost control and crossed two lanes of traffic before striking the motorcyclist.

Detectives are looking for anyone with information about the Honda Accord or its driver. The motorcyclist, identified as Patrick Brennan, has life-threatening injuries and was taken to Good Samaritan Hospital. The cause of the accident is under investigation.

Anyone with information is asked to call Detective Vince Slatterly at 319-502-8899.

The hum from the library faded as her heart stilled in her chest. *Daddy.*

"Mom?"

Ally looked up from the screen, dazed. "Jack. Yes?" It took a moment for her to focus on her son's face.

He frowned. "Why are you crying, Mom?"

She hadn't even known she was. "I—I was just reading something sad." She swiped at the wetness with her palms.

"I'm ready to go. Look what I picked out." He held up two Magic School Bus books and a VeggieTales video for her inspection.

Ally forced a smile. "Looks good, Bubba. Tell you what, why don't you go see if you can find another movie to check out?"

"But you said only one."

"We'll make an exception today, okay?"

"Okay." Leaving his books and video with her, he trotted off again.

Ally's face went numb as she stared once more at the cold words on the screen. "…striking the motorcyclist…. life-threatening injuries…. Good Samaritan Hospital…." The dateline told her the accident had occurred just yesterday. *Oh, Daddy. Why did this have to happen to you?*

Her fingers shook as she clicked out of the *Sentinel*'s website and navigated to Spring Falls Good Samaritan Hospital. Then she pulled her phone from her handbag and dialed the number listed. When the hospital operator answered, she identified herself as a family member seeking information on Patrick Brennan's medical status.

"One moment, please; let me connect you to that department."

Ally waited, barely breathing.

"Critical Care."

Ally swallowed and once more identified herself and her reason for calling.

"I'm sorry, ma'am, we're not allowed to give that information over the phone."

"But I'm his daughter."

"I'm very sorry, but it's the law. If you have a fax number, I can send you a copy of our HIPAA policy."

Ally bit her lip. "Could you at least tell me if he's still alive?"

Interminable pause. "I can confirm that Patrick Brennan is a patient at this hospital."

Ally let out a breath she didn't even realize she was holding. He was alive. After thanking the operator, she hung up and put her head in her hands. *Dear Jesus, what am I supposed to do now?*

Libby. When the name came to her, she turned it over in her mind. Libby, her father's wife. Her stepmom. She could call Libby. But that entailed risk. If Kyle was home and he answered, he would surely recognize her voice, even after all these years. And her cell phone number could be identified in the phone records. Then she thought of her father, critically wounded, perhaps fatally so.

It was a risk she would have to take.

Raising her head from her hands, she became aware of the librarian's concerned gaze. She forced a smile, scribbled the detective's number on a scrap of paper, and closed Internet

Explorer. Then she found Jack in the children's section. "Hey, Bubba, I have to make a phone call. I want you to stay here while I do it, okay? I'll be right out there in the lobby where you can see me, but you stay here. Understand?"

"But Mom, I can't find another video I like."

"Keep looking, okay?"

"But Mom—"

"*Jack*."

He scowled at her.

She held up a finger, forestalling further protest. "I'll be back in a minute."

In the lobby, she positioned herself so she could see her son, who hadn't yet lost his scowl, and then paused to figure out a plan. Finally, she drew a deep breath as she dialed the familiar number resurrected from memory.

One...two...three rings. Her heart sank. Of course Libby wouldn't be home. She'd be at the hospital with her husband. If she had a cell phone, Ally had no idea of the number. Deflated, she was about to end the call when someone answered.

"Hello?" A low voice, tight with tension, but one Ally recognized immediately as her stepmother's.

"Hello, Libby?" She attempted to make her voice throatier than usual.

"Yes"—warily.

"I—I'm sorry to bother you, but I worked with Patrick at Cameron Construction. I just heard about his accident. Can you tell me how he's doing?"

A silence settled, drawing out so long Ally feared Libby had hung up. Then, "Cadence? Is that you?"

Panicked, Ally disconnected. She should have known Libby would recognize her voice, too. If Ally wanted answers after all these years, Libby certainly wanted many more. Answers Ally was unprepared to give. Ally pressed herself against the cold bricks of the library foyer, clutching the phone, breathing hard and wondering how long it would take Libby to call her back.

But her cell phone remained silent. Ally's breathing stilled. For whatever reason, it seemed Libby was not going to call.

Leaning her head back, Ally considered what more could she do. Remembering the scrap of paper with the number of the police contact scribbled on it, she dialed once more.

"Slatterly."

"Hello." Her voice croaked. She cleared her throat before starting again. "Hello, are you the detective investigating the hit-and-run accident with the motorcycle? The one involving Patrick Brennan?"

"You calling with information?" She heard rustling and imagined the detective shifting papers, preparing to write down whatever she had to tell him.

"I'm sorry, no—I was hoping you could give me information."

"Such as?"

"Do you know how he's doing?"

"I'm sorry, ma'am, I don't. Last I heard, he'd slipped into a coma, but you'd have to speak to someone in the family for more than that."

A coma. *Oh, God.* Ally pushed a hand through her hair. Then she remembered something. In most states, crime reports were a matter of public record. If the accident that injured her father was a hit-and-run, it qualified as a crime, didn't it? "I assume an accident report has been filed?"

"Of course, ma'am."

"Can I access it online?"

"Not online, but I could fax it to you. Got a fax number?"

"No." Her spirits plummeting again, she stared down at the handbag at her feet.

"Would you like me to mail you a copy? If you give your address, I could—"

Ally's gaze sharpened as she focused on an object protruding from the clutter of her tote. "No, wait!" Ally grabbed her key ring and fumbled for the plastic tag, the one which read: Paul's Boats & Moor. And at the bottom, a fax number. "Yes, I do have a fax number." She read it off.

"I'll send it straight away."

Fifteen minutes later, she knocked on the Nielsens' front door. While she waited for someone to answer, she turned and bent to Jack's level. "Jack, look at me."

He glared at her from beneath spiky lashes, damp with tears. He'd pitched a fit when she hauled him without ceremony from the library, without his chosen books and videos. She probably should have taken the two minutes to check them out, but somewhere in the last half-hour she'd stopped thinking straight. It had taken all her strength to drag him here by the hand.

"I'm sorry we had to leave the library so fast, but something happened and Mommy had to go." She knew she was frightening him, but explanation would have to wait. Even then, she had no idea what she would say. *I'm very sorry, Bubba, but the grandfather I've never told you about is very sick, and I'm scared...*

As with Libby, the explanation would require much more than she could give.

The door opened. Paul gazed down on her. "Ally?"

"Paul!" She straightened. In her periphery, Jack dashed the tears from his eyes with his fist. "I'm so sorry to bother you, but I need your help."

Darcie joined Paul at the door. "Ally?" She drew her inside. "What's wrong?"

For the space of a heartbeat, Ally allowed herself to lean on her friend, welcoming her solid strength, absorbing her calm. "A fax," Ally said. "Paul, I asked for a fax to be sent to your shop. I'm so sorry to impose, but it's the only fax number I could think of." She held up her key chain with his shop's tag dangling from it. "But when I stopped by, your assistant said he hadn't received any, so I thought it might have come here."

"Let's go check." Paul was already moving toward the study. "When I'm not at the shop, I have my faxes forwarded here." Ally left Jack with Darcie and the dogs to trail Paul into the spare room he used as a home office. She'd never been inside this room; normally, the door was closed. When he turned on the light, she saw a small stack of papers in the in-tray of his fax machine. He glanced at the cover page before handing the rest to Ally.

She read them, trying to make sense of the words.

"Ally?" Darcie touched her shoulder.

Ally looked from her to Jack, who had followed her into the room. His angry tears had vanished, but in his wide brown eyes she read confusion and fear. Sick regret stabbed her heart. Wasn't it her job to protect her child from emotional trauma, not make him a part of it?

Paul seemed to understand the situation at a glance. "Know what?" Touching Jack's shoulder, he steered him toward the kitchen. "I think we have the fixings for some hot cocoa, *with* marshmallows. What do you say to that?"

Darcie didn't wait for Jack's reply. "Ally? What's going on?"

"It's my dad. I tried calling the hospital, but they won't tell me anything." Ally thrust the fax into Darcie's hands. "You're a nurse. If someone was in an accident like this, what do you think his condition would be?"

Darcie scanned the report, her frown deepening as she flipped to the second page, and then the third. Finally she looked at Ally. "I'd say anyone involved in an accident like this would have life-threatening injuries. Is that what you're asking?"

Biting her lips, Ally nodded.

"Did the hospital confirm he was admitted?"

She nodded again, hot tears sliding from her eyes.

When Darcie encircled her with her arms, Ally slumped against her. "You need to go to him."

Ally straightened and wiped her face, but her eyes wouldn't stop leaking. "I can't."

"Why on earth not?"

Ally shook her head. Even knowing her father was badly hurt, going to him wasn't worth the risk. Not to her, nor to Jack. What if Kyle was there? She couldn't take the chance, yet another consequence of the choice she'd made. "I just can't."

"Ally." Darcie took her by both arms, her gaze drilling into hers. "You *must.*" She gave her a gentle shake. "Listen to me, I'm not speaking as a friend but as a professional. For his sake and for yours, you must go to him. Immediately. Before it's too late. If you don't, you'll live with that regret the rest of your life. You don't want that."

Ally broke from Darcie's gaze, unable to bear its intensity. Darcie was right. Ally didn't want more regret. She had enough of it by now to see her to her grave. And given the anguish she'd put her father through, she owed him this much, to be with him once more before the end. Yet—

"I can't go to him, Darcie. I can't go. Not with Jack. I can't tell you why, but it wouldn't be safe for him."

"Fine." Darcie spoke without hesitation. "We'll take care of him while you go."

Ally searched her pockets for a Kleenex. When she came up empty, Darcie reached behind her to pluck a fresh one from the box on Paul's desk and handed it to her. From down the kitchen came Paul's easy baritone, followed by Jack's quick laugh. "You'd do that for me?"

"I've been around death long enough to know what's important. This is probably the most important thing you'll ever do for your father. For yourself, too, for that matter. So, yes, we'll do this for you."

Ally blew her nose, hard.

"You're not to worry about Jack. He'll be fine with us, and we'll enjoy having him. How soon can you leave?"

Ally wiped her nose and stuffed the tissue into her pocket. "I don't know. I have to call Sam. Tomorrow morning?"

Darcie nodded. "Done."

CHAPTER 21

Ally pulled her Saturn to the curb in front of the familiar, rambler-style house with an old Plymouth station wagon in the driveway, a pumpkin-sized tabby cat hunched on the car's hood. She cut the engine, listening to its pings and sighs as it stilled, summoning her courage to face Libby. After two full days on the road, her body craved release from its cramped position, but fear of the unknown kept her weighted to her seat.

She stalled the inevitable by looking around, as if understanding her surroundings would better prepare her for whatever was to come. At first glance, the single-story house, tan and unadorned, looked much as she remembered it. On closer examination, though, Ally noted the dark-brown trim peeling at the corners, and even from here she could see the gutters needed a good cleaning. One piece over the garage sagged with the weight of debris. At the intersection over the porch, a sapling sprouted skyward. This gave her a ripple of unease. The father she knew would never have allowed such a routine part of home maintenance to go untended.

The rambler's door opened. A woman, fiftyish with chin-length hair and bangs cut straight across her forehead, emerged from the house. Despite her lingering misgivings, Ally found herself smiling. Libby hadn't changed, except for the dark brown hair fading to gray.

This, finally, propelled Ally from behind the wheel. As she stepped out, the ground seemed to shift beneath her, and she realized her foolishness in skipping lunch. But her sense of urgency, her need to reach her father, had increased with every mile of I-90. So she had pushed through. Ally lifted a hand, words of greeting dying in her throat as her stepmother regarded her with thinly veiled hostility.

A silence of time and distance pulsed between them, broken only by the squeal of a neighborhood child. Libby crossed her arms over her thin chest. "Hello, Cadence."

"Libby." Ally watched her stepmother warily, seeking some clue for this animosity. After her long and unexplained absence, she could understand questions, even anger. But this? Something was off.

"So you've decided to come home at last," Libby said. "I guess he was right."

Ally licked her lips. "Who was right?" Her father? Kyle? Was Kyle here even now? She darted a look behind her, as if he might materialize on the street.

"Your father never believed you were dead, despite what Kyle told him."

Dead? Why would he think she was dead? The letter she'd sent all those years ago would have at least assured him of this. But her lips felt frozen. Before she could formulate the question, Libby went on.

"My son told him you were dead. You had to be, Kyle said, or else how would you have vanished without a trace? But your father wouldn't have it. Said he'd know if you were dead. Would know it in his heart."

"But... I don't understand. I mailed a letter..." She still remembered what she'd written because it had taken her half the night to decide what to say. Enough so her father wouldn't worry, not so much that he could find her. And most important, to remind him of her love.

Libby snorted. "A letter? There was no letter."

"But there was!" She'd posted it herself, dropped it in a mailbox the day she left Drake.

"There was no letter," she repeated flatly. "Kyle said you might send one, so he watched the mail like a hawk for months after you left. Are you saying an officer of the law would lie?" Her eyes narrowed. "When you disappeared from Drake, Kyle was as out of his mind with worry, as was your father. Neither of them sleeping or eating. Even though he couldn't afford it, Kyle took time off from work to ensure no stone was left unturned. He was the one who went up to Drake, talked to the police, your roommate, even the college president, trying to discover what had happened. Your father wanted to go, but Kyle persuaded him to stay put in case you came home. He insisted it made more sense for him to go since he had contacts and knew which questions to ask."

Ally felt sick. Kyle must have intercepted her letter, probably destroyed it. Though she'd said nothing about Kyle in her note, she'd hoped her father might have seen through the circumstances well enough to ask questions. Questions Kyle would not have wanted to answer. Yet for all these years, Kyle had led her father to think the worst. "Where is Kyle?"

"Not here." A hint of color in her face, her shoulders shifted off some discomfort. "Don't know where he is. Took off about a month ago. Left his job, didn't say where he was going. Calls sometimes, though. Checks in, lets me know he's all right."

Ally felt the tiniest flutter of relief. At least he wasn't here, if Libby was telling the truth. But if Libby had thought her dead, shouldn't she be happy to know Ally—Cadence—was in fact alive?

She knew better than to ask, at least not now. Instead, she posed the question that had haunted her every minute of the last forty-eight hours. "How's Dad?"

Libby's mouth twisted in a bitter grimace. "How do you think he is? Losing you just about destroyed him. Guess now it has. Might have pulled through the accident except he was in such terrible shape to begin with. Lost his will to live." Her whole face pulled tight. "You're too late, Cadence."

Ally felt her heart stop beating. "He's dead?"

"Not yet. Though he'll die soon enough. Any case, shouldn't matter to you. You got no business here, not after what you put him through. Breaking his heart." She put her hand on the doorknob. "There's no welcome for you here." The door slammed.

Ally closed the gap to the house, tripping over a soggy newspaper left on the walkway. "Libby. Libby, please." She pounded on the door, then flattened her palm against the wood. "Won't you at least talk to me? Let me explain?" But what could she explain? Libby would never believe her, even if she tried.

A sound behind her made her turn. A mom with a stroller and a toddler on a tricycle passed by on the sidewalk. The mom carefully avoided Ally's eye, but the boy watched her with open interest. Two houses down, a man watering his potted mums pretended not to listen.

Time to go before she made a spectacle of herself.

Ally returned to her car in stunned disbelief. Why had she not anticipated this? Why had she assumed they could pick up where they'd left off?

When she'd called Libby from Langley, their curt conversation should have tipped her off. Instead, she'd banked on the strength of their past relationship. Even in the wake of Ally's grief over her mother's death—when her teenage hormones ran wild—even then Ally had seen the way Libby loved her dad and was grateful for it. Ally knew little of Libby and Kyle Wylie's life before they came to live with them, but she did gather, from little things Kyle said, that Libby's first husband, Kyle's father, took off soon after he was born, never to be seen again. After a string of live-in boyfriends, when the last one broke three bones and knocked her unconscious, Libby had awakened in a hospital bed and something inside her snapped. She got help. She stopped drinking, joined AA, got her GED. Not long after that, she met Ally's dad. While she never pretended to be Ally's mother, she did provide a stable home environment.

Ally had admired her. Which was why she'd assumed Libby would receive her with the same acceptance she'd bestowed on her as a teenager.

Confused and discouraged, Ally leaned her forehead against the steering wheel as cold seeped into the car. *Dear Jesus…*

The prayer ground to a halt. She didn't even know what to ask for. Numb from fatigue and aching with disappointment, she lifted her head and caught movement from the house. Libby stood at the front window, holding back a section of drapery, watching her. She started the car, knowing she couldn't stay, not knowing where to go.

Well, I came to see Dad, didn't I? Her conversation with Libby had at least confirmed her father still lived. Her trip home was not in vain. She wasn't too late.

Good Samaritan Hospital sat in the heart of downtown Spring Falls. Ally drove the familiar roads, taking in both what had changed and what remained the same. For the most part, the town of her adolescence seemed unaltered by the years, though several windows of downtown shops posted For Sale and For Lease signs. Victims, she guessed, of the economic downturn that still crippled the country.

Arriving at the hospital, Ally parked and headed toward the covered walkway leading to the entrance. She found herself scanning every face she encountered, looking for Kyle. Libby would surely guess Ally would try to see her father. Would Libby tell Kyle she was in Spring Falls? Was Kyle at this very minute on his way to find her? Was he already here? Though Libby had said she hadn't seen Kyle in a month, that didn't necessarily mean he wasn't nearby.

In the hospital lobby, she greeted the volunteer behind the desk, an older man whose careful tan made him look as if he belonged on a golf course instead of behind a hospital reception desk. She requested the room number for Patrick Brennan.

"Critical Care Unit," he told her. "See the elevator on the other side of that fountain? Take it to the fifth floor. Critical Care's straight ahead."

She thanked him and followed his directions, passing a young mom sitting with her son. The boy, who looked to be about four, tossed pennies into the water, erupting in a small cheer every time a coin sank from the surface. Despite her desperation to see her father, she paused for a moment to watch him. Oh, she missed Jack. She'd never been apart from him for more than eight hours, had never even spoken to him on the phone before she'd called Darcie from the road this morning. Her son's piping soprano sounded strangely different on the phone. Younger. More vulnerable, somehow. Despite his good cheer and Darcie's reassurances, Ally questioned whether she'd done the right thing in leaving him.

On the fifth floor, Ally found the CCU and stopped at the semicircular nurse's station. "I'm here to see Patrick Brennan, please."

"I'm sorry." The woman looked up from her computer. Her badge identified her as Valerie Witten, Unit Clerk. "We're in the middle of shift change right now. You'll have to wait."

"But I'm his daughter." Ally leaned hard on the counter, exhaustion from the long drive finally catching up with her. "I've driven all night to be here. Please, may I just see him for a moment?"

"Not until shift change is over."

"How long will that take?"

"An hour? You're welcome to wait. The waiting room's just on the other side of that fish tank." She pointed a red lacquered nail down the hall and went back to clicking screens on her computer.

"Perhaps if I could just speak with his doctor? Or a nurse? Just for a moment."

Valerie looked up once more from her computer, the first hint of impatience flitting across her round face. "I'm sorry, we—"

"Can I help you?" A male nurse with a crew cut, wearing blue scrubs and a five-o'clock shadow, joined Ally at the counter.

She explained her mission.

"I already told her we're in the middle of a shift change and she'll have to wait," Valerie put in.

The nurse nodded. "It will only be an hour or so. Then you're welcome to visit him for as long as you like, so long as his status doesn't change."

"Please." Ally looked at his ID badge. Jamal Jones, Charge Nurse. "Please, Jamal, can you at least tell me how he is?" She heard her pleading tone, like Jack's when he wanted a cookie before dinner.

He shook his head. "Sorry, miss, no can-do. Come back in an hour and we'll get you in to see your father."

Trying not to feel defeated, Ally headed toward the CCU waiting room. On the long sofa, a woman in a sapphire-blue sari sat beside a man in a saffron turban. Both stared straight ahead at the CNN broadcast on the television that hung from the ceiling. Neither glanced at her as she claimed the room's unoccupied loveseat. Laying her head on the armrest, Ally settled in to wait.

CHAPTER 22

Bundled in jeans and a padded yellow jacket, Jack trailed behind Rees through the ankle-high grass behind the Nielsens' house. Though the afternoon sun shone and the day had warmed since morning, Darcie had insisted Jack take his mittens. He tugged them on as they reached the shed a hundred yards behind the house. Rees pulled on the door handle. The door opened with a creak, allowing a shaft of sunlight to fall on the hulking hunk of machinery inside. Rees surveyed it, hands on hips. "So, Jack. Ever been on one of these before?"

The boy shook his head, his gaze never leaving the green and yellow contraption twice his size.

Rees sighed. "Me neither."

Jack's eyes lifted, searched his.

Rees winked. "Kidding. I've been on one, but it was many years ago." He hoped the old adage about never forgetting how to ride a bike held true for lawn mowers as well. "Well, come on then. Let's see if we can figure this out."

Two nights ago at dinner, Darcie announced Ally Brennan's father had been critically, probably fatally, injured in a motorcycle accident. As Ally was leaving for Iowa the next morning and didn't want to take Jack with her, he would be staying with them while she was gone.

Rees had looked up from his plate of pasta Alfredo. "How will you manage that?"

"Jack will be in school most of the day. Beyond that, we'll figure it out." She glanced across at her husband. "Right, Paul?"

"Of course."

Rees couldn't help but notice how pleased his sister looked at the prospect. Maybe having Jack with them would scratch a long-neglected itch. Given how much his sister was wired for mothering, he wondered why she and Paul had put off starting their family.

Since his Skype conversation with Sheela, Rees had made an effort to be more conciliatory toward Darcie. He still hadn't had the heart-to-heart Sheela advised, but if he could keep their relationship on this even keel, perhaps he wouldn't need to. Which may have been why he found himself saying, "If you need a hand, let me know. I'll be glad to help out."

Darcie's surprised, gratified smile rewarded him. Later that evening, when he was stretched out on his bed reading, someone tapped on his door. Assuming it was Darcie, he laid aside the biography of Teddy Roosevelt and called, "Come in."

Paul entered and shut the door behind him. A smile bent his mouth upward, but the grooves etched across his forehead made him seem worried, or sad. Rees pulled himself upright, trying to recall if Paul had ever sought him out privately.

Rees liked Paul, appreciated his kindness and generosity. But he found his reserve tough to crack and had learned to be satisfied with a friendly but arm's-length relationship. He suspected Paul felt the same, for even now Paul was clearly uncomfortable, his color high as he cleared his throat. "I wanted to thank you for volunteering to help out with Jack," Paul said. "You know what a big heart Darcie has. She never hesitates to help a friend. That's great, but I was kind of wondering how she was going to manage."

"You're welcome."

Paul ducked his head. "I, uh…well, it meant a lot to her when you spoke up. And to me, too, because—well, because I know it's not been easy between you and Darcie lately. Not like it used to be."

Regret thumped dully inside his chest as he realized he'd allowed a private tension to become so noticeable. It couldn't have been pleasant for peace-loving Paul to live under the same roof as the two siblings. "That's probably my fault."

"No. No, I wouldn't say that." Paul looked around as if seeking a place to sit, but there was nowhere but the bed. He settled for leaning against the door and cleared his throat again. "I wanted to let you know about something Darcie probably hasn't mentioned. She hasn't told many folks, but you're her brother and I figured you should know. It might help explain some stuff. Thing is, we've been trying for a long time to have a baby, and, well, we're having some trouble." He glanced at Rees. His words came faster now, as if he wanted to get them over with. "You can't know unless you've been through it how awful it is not to be able to have a kid when you want one. Darcie stopped going to baby showers years ago, and I can't remember the last time we attended church on Mother's Day. Just hurts too much."

Rees stared at him, stunned. "I didn't know." Why hadn't he read the signs? He knew his sister better than almost anyone; certainly, he knew how much she loved kids. He just assumed she and Paul were waiting. Now he kicked himself for not guessing the truth.

Paul shrugged. "Most women are designed to want babies. When it's denied, it—well, it's like when my rhodies don't get enough water. Pretty soon their leaves start to droop. Then they turn yellow and drop off. They can go a long time without water before actually dying, but it's obvious when something important is being withheld."

"I—I'm glad you told me." He didn't know what else to say.

Paul sighed. "Darcie thinks I don't understand, but I do. If she comes across as overly controlling sometimes, try to remember it's just her way of coping with something she has no control over." He hesitated. "You know, she still says taking care of you when your mother was sick and after she died was the best thing that ever happened to her. Not your mother's death, but taking care of you. Says it helped carry her through her own grief." He offered a smile. "So be patient with her. She's hurting, but she loves you."

Rees remembered again Sheela's words. *If you find your sister different, I would ask, have her circumstances changed? That will tell you much about your sister's happiness.* Regret again sliced through him that he hadn't bothered to ask the right questions, leaving it instead to shy, reserved Paul to bridge the gap. "She's lucky to have you."

"I'm the lucky one." Paul shrugged. "She's struggling with some doubts right now, but she's strong, and I know we'll get through it. Just going to take some time."

Since then, as Rees replayed their conversation, it struck him that Paul's words echoed Sheela's when he'd raised his concerns over Jayashri. *These things take time.* At a certain level, Rees got it, saw the wisdom, could let it fuel his patience. But Darcie, on the other hand, must be feeling time was precisely what she did not have. As she neared her mid-thirties, the time for her to conceive was now. And what of Jayashri? Experience told Rees her damaged psyche was a ticking time bomb. That if they couldn't help her soon, she would explode.

There is a time for everything under the sun, a season for everything. A time to be born, and a time to die.

To die. Is that what happened when time ran out?

But standing in Paul's shed with Jack, Rees pushed weighty issues from his mind. He had a small boy to tend to. "Now." He circled the John Deere mower. "First rule to operating any machine is to make sure you're doing it right. Doing it right means doing it safe. So we're going to put on ear protection, because these puppies are loud." He snagged a couple of protective ear muffs from a hook on the shed wall. "Here, these are probably a little big, but they should fit all right. How's that feel?" He fitted them over Jack's head and tightened the band as far as it would go. "Okay?"

Jack's quick nod made the headband slip forward over his forehead. "Fine." He pushed it back into place with his mittened hands.

"Hmm." Rees frowned. "Well, it'll have to do." He raised his voice to ensure the boy could hear him through the muffs. "Okay now, let's check this out. See here, we've got what we call the choke. Then over here is the gas. Step on this, it moves forward. Unlike a car, this has no brake. To make it stop, you simply let up on the gas. Understand?"

"Yep."

"Easy-peasy, right? Okay, you sit here, right in front of me." Rees hoisted himself on the seat before positioning the boy between his legs. "Remember, it's going to be loud. Ready?"

Jack threw a grin over his shoulder.

Rees turned the key. The riding mower roared to life. Even with the muff, the noise rattled his eardrums, the vibration beneath him almost enough to jar him from his seat. Jack clutched the steering wheel, knuckles white. "I'm going to put this into reverse," Rees shouted. "Right, here we go!"

Rees backed from the shed, turned around and started on Paul's lawn. A bit herky-jerky at first, but his technique soon improved and their ride smoothed out. Every so often Jack looked back at him, his face plastered in perma-grin. After the third pass, Rees let Jack take the wheel. They neared the edge of the lawn again and were executing their turn when an object near the road caught his attention. A black pickup truck parked on the shoulder, a man in a red ball cap and shades leaning against it. Watching them. Rees's antennae quivered. He didn't recognize the man. How long had he been there? And what did a stranger find so interesting about them mowing the lawn?

By now, Jack had seen him too. Rees let up on the gas, letting the machine idle. "Hey Jack, who's that?" he asked, trying to sound casual.

Jack shrugged. "Dunno."

"Never seen him before?"

"Nope."

The man hadn't budged, though he had to know he'd been spotted. Rees killed the engine and pocketed the key. "Stay here. Don't go anywhere, promise? Be right back." He jogged up the hill toward the stranger.

But the man jumped behind the wheel of his truck and took off, skidding on the gravel shoulder. At the top of the rise, Rees stopped, panting a little. The sun was behind the stranger, so he'd not gotten a good look at his face. He'd not been close enough to catch the license plate, either, though he could tell it wasn't from Washington state.

Rees returned to the mower.

"Who was he?" Jack asked.

"Just someone admiring the view." Rees narrowed his eyes in the direction of the vanished truck. That guy had been watching them. *Why?*

Chapter 23

Ally roused to the smell of coffee, aware only in her awakening that she'd fallen asleep. A fresh pot rested on the credenza in the far corner of the CCU waiting room. The Indian couple was gone, the room empty, except for her.

Ally looked at her watch and blinked, sure she must have misread it. 8:15? Couldn't be. She squinted at the only window, where the faded sunlight of an overcast sky filtered into the room. Suddenly, she pushed herself off the couch, alarm tingling through her. She'd slept through the night. *Dad.* What if he'd taken a turn for the worse? Uncaring of her sleep-rumpled state, she scooped up her tote and stumbled to the nurse's station.

Valerie of the red-lacquered nails had been replaced by a heavyset nurse with tightly crimped, gray curls. A plump shoulder pressed a phone to her ear as she tapped into her computer. She glanced up briefly before resuming her work. Ally gripped the counter, knuckles whitening as she waited for an opening. When a full minute passed, she abandoned politeness and waved her hand to get the nurse's attention. "Patrick Brennan, room 507," she whispered, hoping that knowing the room number would convey her right to be here. "I'm his daughter." The nurse gave a vaguely irritated nod and Ally felt a pulse of relief. At least that answered one question: her dad was still alive. Ally scurried down the hall before anyone could challenge her.

She paused in front of room 507. Aware of the fluttering of her stomach, she felt she should be praying but couldn't find the words. Catching a big breath, she opened the door.

The harshly lit room smelled of stool and baby wipes. But who was stretched out on the bed? An old man with faded skin and hair, like newspaper print left too long in the sun, tubes protruding from his mouth, wires attached to his chest. And then there was his face…

The door behind her opened, and she swung around. Charge Nurse Jamal from the night before. "Oh, hey, didn't realize you were in here or I would have knocked. You get some decent sleep?"

"Sleep?" Her gaze darted to the man beneath the blanket. "Um, yeah."

"Last night I went to tell you that you could see your dad, but you'd fallen asleep. Kept thinking you'd wake up, but you must have needed your shuteye."

"I did." Even now Ally felt lightheaded. She swallowed the queasiness that crept up her gullet. "What's wrong with him?"

"His face, you mean?"

She nodded. It was bloated beyond recognition. If the name on the whiteboard at the foot of the bed hadn't identified this man as Patrick Brennan, she would never have believed it.

"Edema," Jamal said. "Swelling. The body's natural response to trauma, dumping fluids on the injury. It'll subside in a day or two."

Hope caught on these words. "He's going to make it?"

"I meant if—well, if he survives, the edema will eventually subside." He checked her father's IV site, the leads on his chest. Then, turning back to her, he frowned. "Hey, you okay?"

"Fine. I was just—I wasn't expecting…"

"No one ever does." Jamal's deep brown eyes softened. "When did you last eat?"

"I—I can't remember."

"Listen, you're not gonna do your dad any good if you end up on the floor. Go get some food. Lucky for you, I'm workin' a double-shift today, so I can make sure your daddy's all ready for you by the time you get back. You can have your visit then."

"He'll be all right?"

Jamal glanced again at the machines connected to her father. "He's stable. You go on now." When still she hesitated, Jamal said, "Would it help if I made it an order? You don't look so good. I've got all I can handle here without having you pass out on me."

Finally, she relented. "I'll be back in just a few minutes."

"We're not going anywhere."

In the cafeteria, she bought a bagel with cream cheese and a banana, the cheapest items on the breakfast menu. She ate them at a table near the window, thinking about the pitiful figure in the bed upstairs. Until the moment she'd seen him, she'd only known she had to see her father one last time. But now she knew she needed to do something more.

Though he might be incapable of understanding, her father needed to hear the truth. And she needed to speak it.

Feeling some slight relief in having reached this resolution, she stood to leave. A familiar figure coming up the outside walkway made her pause.

Libby. Ally's spirits sank. The quilted crocheting bag over her shoulder and thick hardcover in hand indicated her stepmom planned to stay awhile. The hem of her drab, brown raincoat fluttered as she passed through the entrance. She glanced neither right nor left as she approached the elevator. The doors whisked closed behind her.

Ally gnawed on her lower lip. What should she do? Not that she would let Libby keep her from seeing her father, but at the same time, did she really want a scene? Jamal had assured her that her father was stable, at least for now. Would it be better for her dad's sake to choose a different moment? Libby had made it clear she wasn't welcome. Ally had come here to put away old regrets, but that didn't mean she needed to create new ones. If Libby wanted to, she could make things very unpleasant. And Ally's father wouldn't want that.

Still, the desire to stay, to see him now while she still could, was strong.

Daddy, what should I do?

She knew what he'd say. *Don't make a fuss, Cadence.*

Swallowing her disappointment, she sank back into her seat. She would wait. But what now? She had no place to go, no place to stay. With a sigh, she returned to the counter and bought herself a second cup of coffee while she considered her next move.

An hour later, Ally pulled her car into a visitor's slot at Spring Falls High School. Like the rest of town, her alma mater appeared as she remembered it, with a few small changes around the edges: the shrubbery flanking the walkway had grown taller, and fresh royal blue paint coated the double doors. Inside, the familiar odors of dry-erase markers, radiator heat, and fried food yanked her backwards in time to her uncertain adolescence, when the hours she spent within these walls vacillated between torment and escape. At the front office, Ally paused, rethinking her impulse to come here. This place held few pleasant memories for her.

A blond office assistant looked up as Ally hesitated in the hallway. "Can I help you?" She sat in front of a glass partition, behind which the rest of the office administrators worked.

Ally squared her shoulders. Since she was here, she might as well satisfy her curiosity. "I'm looking for Gina Damiani. The music teacher?"

"I'm sorry, but she no longer—" She broke off, her eyes widening. "Wait. You're Cadence Brennan, aren't you?"

Taken aback, Ally studied the blonde. Did she know her? She reminded her a little of Brittany, with her flat-ironed hair in a clip, the low-cut pink blouse. But no, she didn't know this woman. "Yes, I'm Cadence." The name felt strange on her tongue. "I'm sorry, but do I know you?"

"No, but I recognize you from your picture. You look exactly the same."

"My pic—oh, sure, right." She must mean the wall of photos outside these offices, the Spring Falls Hall of Fame, where every student who won a significant award or broke a major athletic record was enshrined. Her image went up the year she took first place at the Iowa State String Soloists competition. "It's been so long, I forgot about that." She paused. "How many years ago did Ms. Damiani leave?"

"Oh, not years, just a few weeks, actually. She resigned when her husband took a position with the Chicago Symphony. Pretty big news around here. Not Gina's quitting, I mean, but Leif's getting on with the Chicago."

All at once, Ally remembered the headline about a Spring Falls resident joining the Chicago Symphony. So that was Ms. Damiani's husband. "Well, if you happen to hear from her, tell her I'm sorry I missed her."

"Not half as sorry as she'll be when she finds out she missed you." The young woman studied Ally's face for a moment, apparently debating something. Then she turned to her computer screen, tapped in a few keystrokes, and scribbled something on a sticky note. "Here." She handed the paper to Ally. "I maybe shouldn't do this, but I'll take a chance, mainly because I think Gina would want me to. She should still be at this address. She wasn't planning to join Leif in Chicago until their house sold."

Grateful something had finally gone her way, Ally easily found Ms. Damiani's address, a short two miles from the school. She stopped in front of the house with a SOLD sign in the front yard and eyed the tri-level with its sage-green door, potted marigolds and small, square lawn.

From the car, Ally couldn't tell if anyone was home. She got out and moved slowly up the front walk. The blinds were closed, the garage door shut, the driveway empty of cars. What if the receptionist was wrong and Ms. Damiani had already left? Suddenly, she realized how very much she wanted to see her old teacher again. She'd endured a mentor-void in her life these last few years that no one else could fill. She could only hope Ms. Damiani would be just as happy to see her.

Without warning, the door yanked open and a woman with a huge belly and streaming red hair burst onto the front porch. "Cadence?" The woman hastened down the walk. "Good gosh, it really is you!" Before Ally could react, Ms. Damiani's arms wrapped around her, pulling her as close as her distended stomach would allow. "The school phoned, said you'd stopped by and were probably on your way. Look at you!" She regarded Ally from arm's length. "You look exactly the same!"

Catching her breath, Ally laughed. "You don't." She looked down at the enormous belly. "How'd that happen?" Her teacher was the last person on earth Ally would have expected to be, well, expecting.

"The usual way." She pushed her manic auburn hair back from a high forehead. "Boy meets girl, girl chases boy, boy marries girl. Though I will say—" she touched her belly—"this took us a bit by surprise. But that's another story." She grabbed Ally's hand and dragged her toward the house where the front door gaped open. From a CD player buried somewhere beneath a jumble of packing paper came Bach's rolling rhythms, like waves over sand. "Come in! The place is a mess, but here, sit down." She swept an arm across a red suede sofa, clearing it of crumpled paper.

Every spare inch of floor space from the vaulted living room to the chandeliered dining room was stacked with brown boxes labeled in Ms. Damiani's bold, slanting scrawl. China & Crystal. CDs. Sheet Music.

"Are you hungry?" Ms. Damiani asked. "I was just about to order takeout when Sophie called. Had the phone in my hand, actually, and dropped it when it rang, had to chase it across the floor. Quite a feat for a person in my condition. Glad the blinds were closed so the neighbors couldn't see." Her teacher stood in the doorway to the kitchen, arms crossed over the shelf of her stomach. "I've missed you, Cadence."

"Missed you too, Ms. Damiani." She spoke around the throbbing ache in her throat. How like her impulsive teacher to behave as if nothing had happened between them. Ally smiled with sheer relief as a burden she'd carried for years shifted from her shoulders.

"Do you think you could possibly wrap yourself around calling me Gina? Ms. Damiani makes me feel so old."

"I'll try. And I go by Ally now."

Surprise chased across Gina's porcelain features. "What happened to Cadence?"

More than you'll ever know. "Cadence didn't fit me anymore. I use my middle name now, Alise. Ally for short."

"So." Gina disappeared briefly into the kitchen, reappearing with a printed menu. "Take-out. I was thinking Chinese; does that sound good to you?"

Ally blinked. "It's not even ten o'clock."

Gina shrugged. "Whatever baby wants, baby gets. That pretty much spells it out for the next eighteen years; might as well get used to it now. 'Course, I have no idea how I'm going to manage once we get to Chicago. Been turning over every rock to find a nanny we can afford, but so far, no luck, and there's no way on this green earth I can manage a baby on my own. Can you even imagine me a full-time mama? Poor child wouldn't survive a week. Neither would I." She planted both fists on her non-existent waist. "So. Chinese?"

It didn't sound half-bad, actually. The bagel and banana she'd scarfed at the hospital hadn't stretched very far.

After Gina called in the order, she returned to the living room and lifted an empty box onto a Queen Anne chair upholstered in tangerine. "You don't mind if I keep packing while we talk, do you? Movers will be here day after tomorrow, and as you can see, I've still got a ton to do. Shouldn't have left it until the last minute." Looking at Ally, she rolled a crystal vase in paper and placed it in the box. "I never thought I'd see you again."

"I know." Preempting the questions she knew would follow, Ally said, "I heard about your husband, but Sophie didn't say what you would be doing in Chicago."

"You mean besides changing poopy diapers?" She crossed to the baby grand in the corner and picked up a pair of Limoges candlesticks sitting on the bench. "Well, ever heard of ..." Trailing off, Gina's hand went to her belly, her expression glazing over. After a long minute, she exhaled. "Whooo. That's new."

"Contraction?"

Gina nodded. "Probably just a Braxton Hicks. All this excitement, right, baby?" She looked at Ally. "What were you saying?"

"You were telling me what you'll be doing in Chicago."

"Oh. Right." She gave her belly a hard rub before resuming her packing. "Ever heard of The System?"

"No."

"It's an idea Gustavo Dudamel brought when he came to L.A. Symphony from Venezuela. Disadvantaged kids are given instruments, which they learn how to play under some of the country's greatest musicians. In L.A., it's already getting inner-city kids off the streets, away from drugs and gangs. Giving them something worthwhile to do, something they can believe in. They're launching a similar program in Chicago and putting me in charge." When she leveled her gaze at her, Ally caught a glimpse of the old steel glinting behind the black-framed glasses. "It's the kind of thing I once envisioned you doing. Giving some of your talent back to the world, the way God intended it."

Ally dodged having to respond as the Chinese delivery arrived. Gina fell on it like a woman who hadn't seen food in weeks. "Gads, this baby makes me hungry." She doled fried rice onto paper plates. "You wouldn't believe how much I put down these days."

"I might." Remembering her own bottomless hunger during pregnancy.

"So tell me." Gina forked a heaping amount of orange chicken into her mouth. "What possessed you to show up on my doorstep after all these years?"

Ally swirled her chopsticks through her chow mein. She'd wondered when Gina would ask. "I came to see my dad."

"Oh?" Her tone cooled slightly. Ally guessed she was remembering the heated words she and Ally's dad had exchanged in the months following Ally's quitting the viola. Though deeply mired in his own grief, he had defended Ally's decision and had consequently suffered a good share of Gina's ire. "And how is your father?"

"Not good." She put her chopsticks down, feeling the sudden pull of tears beneath her cheeks. For the last hour or so, she'd managed to push thoughts about her father aside, but now they came rushing back. "He's in the CCU at Good Samaritan." She told her about the accident, her arrival at the hospital, her painfully brief glimpse of her father. But when she got to the part about Libby, she stumbled to a stop. She couldn't explain that part, not all of it anyway, without wading into murky waters. In the end, she settled for an abridged truth. "My stepmother and I had a falling out. If I show up again while she's there, I'm afraid it might get ugly."

Gina, whose expression had softened, set her empty plate aside and stood. "Well, come on then."

"Where are we going?" Ally asked, confused. Unlike Gina, she still had half a plate of food left.

"To the hospital. To get you in to your see your dear old dad."

CHAPTER 24

Ally refused Gina's offer to drive. With Gina's big belly, Ally didn't trust her behind the wheel. Plus, Gina's contractions were worrying. She'd had another one as they were leaving the house. So, her former teacher crammed her girth into the passenger seat of Ally's Saturn.

"What became of you after you graduated?" Gina asked as they drove. "Most of my students stay in touch for a while, but I never heard a thing more about you. It was like you disappeared."

I did. Her grip tightened on the wheel. Though she'd known questions would come sooner or later, she still had no idea how to answer them. She settled for another abridged truth. "I went to Drake University, but only for one semester."

"Why just one? You were college material if ever I saw it."

Ally shrugged. "Why do lots of girls quit college? I got pregnant."

She felt the warmth of Gina's astonished gaze. "You have a child?"

"Jack." She nodded, pride and affection rushing over her at the mention of his name.

"Is he here?"

"No." Again that pull of longing. "I left him at home, with a friend." She could imagine the questions piling up in Gina's head and felt grateful for their arrival at the hospital, which prevented her from asking them.

Ally remained in the lobby while Gina went up to see if the coast was clear. Ally paced the perimeter, wishing she'd thought to change her clothes before returning to the hospital. She'd been in the same jeans for three days now, and her scalp felt oily without a recent shampoo. Then Gina rang her cell. "Come on up."

On the fifth floor, Ally found Gina with an elbow propped on the counter of the nurse's station, talking with Jamal Jones. His brow furrowed as Ally approached. "You had me worried when you didn't come back. Was afraid maybe I'd lost ya."

Before Ally could answer, Gina said, "Jamal's a former student of mine, Ally. We can trust him to help us. Libby's gone to lunch now. Jamal says she's usually gone for at least an hour."

"What about other visitors?" Ally thought of Kyle.

"So far, his wife's the only one." Jamal tugged on his diamond stud earring, eyeing Ally. "Didn't know he had a daughter till you showed up."

Ally left Gina and Jamal chatting at the nurse's station and made her way down the hall. She drew a steadying breath before entering room 507. As the door closed behind her, she stood still a moment, absorbing the room. Earlier, she'd been so shocked by her father's appearance she hadn't really seen anything else. Behind the bed, above her father's head, were several screens, which she guessed, monitored his heart and blood. A ventilator the size of a large suitcase was positioned on the far side of the bed. In the corner, beside the only chair, rested Libby's crochet bag, from which protruded a half-finished afghan in blue and yellow. The cheery colors sounded a wrong note in this dismal setting.

Finally, Ally allowed her eyes to rest on her father, willpower keeping them there. Even though this time she knew what to expect, it still twisted her gut to see him this way. "Hi, Daddy. It's Cadence." She moved one step closer to the bed. "I'm back."

Her gaze traveled from his unmoving feet beneath the sheet to the harsh abrasion on his right cheek, which disappeared behind a thick bandage at his temple. She wondered, fleetingly, what had happened to his motorcycle after the crash. Did the police have it? Did Libby? Pushing the stray thought aside, Ally sat in the chair and took her father's hand, careful not to disturb any of the attached lines. "Daddy, I'm sorry this happened to you," she whispered, regret scratching behind her sternum. "I'm sorry you're hurt so badly. Sorry for a lot of things."

Her resolve to tell him the truth quivered. What if her desire to reveal everything was only a selfish impulse to unburden herself? She believed people in comas could hear and understand, but could he bear to hear everything she had to say? What if telling him now did him more harm than good?

Memories of childhood pushed forward. The baggy "dad jeans" he favored for working around the house. The aviator shades he might have stolen from Tom Cruise. The spicy scent of his Stetson cologne. The way he rode his Suzuki Bandit, leaning into the curves, as if he'd been born on a bike. Her throat constricted and she swallowed hard. She didn't want to waste precious moments with him as an uncontrolled, sobbing wreck.

The knowledge that her time with him was slipping away strengthened her resolve. In his last hours on earth, her father deserved to hear what had happened. She owed him that much. At the very least.

"I want you to know," Ally began slowly, "I never meant it to turn out like this. I'm sorry I put you through so much, but I'd like to tell you what happened." Saying the words aloud caused courage to well up from some unacknowledged source. She inched her chair closer to his bed. Maybe she could actually get through this without falling apart. "It started in the fall of my junior year."

Libby and her father had been married two years when Kyle moved home to save expenses while attending police academy. At first, her stepbrother had scarcely paid her any attention. He was six years older than she, already long out of high school. She had been a gangly adolescent, mired in grief and guilt over her mother's death, glued to her studies. But when Ally turned sixteen, everything changed.

"Suddenly, Kyle started noticing me. I went from being a brainy geek to someone a grown man thought was beautiful." It was heady stuff, being the object of desire for a man who seemed, to her young eyes, sophisticated and worldly wise.

It started with kisses in the basement after their parents were in bed. And then it was more. A lot more. Even now, Ally could conjure the feeling, that electric sense of oneness. To her lonely and needy heart, it was magical. "We told no one; it was this secret between us."

During the day, they'd pretend to be completely indifferent to each other, would even find things to fight about, the way siblings were supposed to, so her father and Libby wouldn't suspect what was going on beneath their roof. But at night they'd meet in the basement, in a lair they'd created for themselves in a half-hidden crawlspace.

Ally dropped her head to the thin green coverlet. "We carried on like that for a year. And then my senior year you were hounding me to start applying for college, remember?"

Too immersed in his own grief following his wife's death, her father hadn't protested her decision to quit her instrument. Music had always been the bond between Ally and her mother, who had named her Cadence.

Her father did, however, insist Ally keep up her grades, and—in part as a distraction from her grief—she excelled academically. When it came time to consider colleges, she could apply to the best of them. "It was about then I began to sense that…I don't know, that I was outgrowing Kyle. A whole new kind of life awaited me at college, one Kyle didn't fit into. But when I tried to break it off, he'd tell me how much he loved me, how I was the only one for him. And so we stayed together, until the day I graduated from Spring Falls. My dream school had accepted me, my whole future lay before me. I wanted to be completely unfettered, not attached to my old life. So the day I graduated, I finally got the courage to break up with Kyle.

I put a lock on my bedroom door so he couldn't come to me at night anymore, and that's—" She swallowed. "That's when the trouble began.

"He started following me, stalking me everywhere. After my shift at Pizza Hut, he'd be in the parking lot, waiting for me. If I spent the evening hanging out with friends, he'd follow in his truck and watch the house from across the street. One time, I went with some girls to a movie. When we got up to leave, I found him sitting behind me. He'd been there the entire time. I couldn't shake him. It was almost as if he knew my next move before I did. I was so scared, and I—"

Her breath caught in her throat. Had she felt the tiniest pressure on her hand? The barest twitch of her father's fingers. She studied her father's face for a sign she was getting through to him, but his features remained immobile. Had she imagined it? Impossible to say. But even if he couldn't understand her words, could he at least feel her love? Taste the same sour regret that they'd been forced apart all these years? Her hand tightened on his as the machines continued their steady beeping.

A memory surfaced, a game they used to play. Dad would lie on his back on the floor, placing his hands, palms up, just above his shoulders. Ally would step on top of his hands in her socked feet. Then her father would slowly, carefully, straighten his arms until he locked his elbows. Ally would balance over him, careful to make no sudden movements so she wouldn't tumble down on top of him. They practiced this move over and over again, until Ally could do it without assistance. The game continued until she grew too heavy for him to lift. She'd never realized at the time what a demonstration of strength and trust their game had been.

It sickened Ally to realize Jack would never be able to play with her father like that. She thought she'd resigned herself to that truth years ago, but now it hit her with awful finality.

She longed to be able to spend this moment in that place of trust. To know his physical presence as she had not known it these past five years. To take strength in his very nearness. But she also knew the reality that her time with him was very limited. And she felt an increasing urgency to finish her story.

"Kyle wouldn't take no for an answer," she continued, her voice low. "When we were together, I didn't see his obsession as something bad. I saw it as a sign of how much he loved me. But when it continued on even months after we broke up, that's when I knew that if I wanted a fresh life without him, I'd have to do something drastic. So I decided I wouldn't tell anyone except you I was going to Drake. I'd pretend I'd chosen Iowa State." She'd told her father she didn't want everyone to know she was going to such a prestigious college and had given that as the reason for her secrecy. No one else from Spring Falls High had applied there. If she didn't make the grade, she said, she didn't want to slink back home a failure. Her father hadn't questioned her request, although now, in hindsight, she wondered why. Did he suspect she was in trouble? Did he know what was going on between her and Kyle? "I left for school that fall hoping I was finally through with Kyle."

Now she reached the hardest part of the story. The part where she chose to deliberately exclude her father from her life. Ally ran a thumb over the thin skin of his hand, taut from swelling. For the first time, it occurred to her to question whose plan was more merciful: hers, or Kyle's? To know a child was safe and alive but choosing to live a life without you? Or to believe your child dead? Was a slow, infinite grief better than a quick, finite one? Which path the kindest?

Perhaps in a perverse sense, Kyle's way had been better. And yet, Libby said her father had never believed her to be dead, despite what Kyle had told him.

Ally shook her head. In either case, it had never been Kyle's choice to make. "I was about halfway through my first semester at Drake. I'd met another guy, a musician. He tried to persuade me to start playing again. I think I would have, but then—"

The door pushed opened. Ally swiveled to see who had come in.

Libby stood framed in the doorway, her face bleached with fury.

CHAPTER 25

Pumpkin guts covered the surface of Darcie's kitchen table plus the floor beneath it, while the nutty aroma of seeds toasting in the oven filled the room. Rain pattered on the roof as Jack bent over a pumpkin bigger than his own blond head. With his tongue sticking out in concentration, he put finishing touches on a jack-o-lantern's face.

Watching him work, Darcie thought it fitting that the presence of a child in her house had finally prompted her to visit a fertility specialist. She'd been putting it off for months. A form of denial, she supposed, hoping her body would finally produce the way it was meant to. But she'd gotten her period ahead of schedule this month. Having Jack around made her realize she no longer wanted to wait. So, heart in her throat, she'd called, using her friendship with the doctor's nurse to get her appointment moved to as soon as possible.

Yesterday she'd spent an hour with Dr. Chen. He gave her a thorough examination before announcing he could find nothing physically amiss. As she lay on the examination table, her body cold beneath the thin, blue gown, he explained, with appropriate gravitas, that this was bad news rather than good. "Had I found something wrong, a blocked fallopian tube, say, or endometriosis, we might at least have a chance at fixing it. Without a definite clue, we don't know which direction to head." He then talked about how the health of a woman's eggs decline as they hit their thirties, which significantly decreased their fertility. He suggested starting folic acid supplements and told her how to track her basal body temperature.

Darcie swallowed. "What about the blood work?"

"We'll have to wait a few days for those results, but I'm not expecting anything to turn up. We'll want to check out your husband too, rule him out as the source of the issue before we move on to the big guns."

"You mean IVF." Saying it aloud made dollar signs flash inside her head.

"Yes, although we might start first with artificial insemination."

"Is that less expensive?"

"No, but slightly less invasive, and statistically, you get better odds." Sitting on his wheeled stool, he pushed himself across the floor to the desk, where he scribbled something on her chart. "But first things first, right? Let's get your husband in here. Then if that turns up nothing, you'll want to think about starting fertility treatments. We do have your age to consider."

How well she knew it. Dr. Chen had sent her home with a packet of brochures on various treatments and their costs, advising her to call when she and Paul were ready to take the next step.

"I'm done," Jack announced, turning the pumpkin so she could see it.

Darcie pulled her attention back to the moment. "Let's see. Oh, my. Jack, that is truly amazing." Even using the flimsy tools of a kid-safe carving kit she'd bought at Star Grocery, his artistry was remarkable. Though the cuts were a little ragged, his imagination was sharp. He'd turned his pumpkin into a leering goblin with triangle ears and spiked eyebrows. "You are awesome, possum."

"Can I show Mr. Rees when he comes home?"

"Of course." It had taken no time at all for Jack to idolize Rees. "He'd love to see what you've created."

Paul had disappeared into the study after doing the dishes, but he must have heard them talking because he came back into the room. "Ready for jammies and teeth-brushing?" Seeing that he carried his favorite, food-stained cookbook, she felt a flicker of irritation. She'd assumed he was working on the shop's books. *If that man paid as much attention to his business as he did to his food, we wouldn't be in the financial fix we're in.*

But she quashed the thought and said nothing, allowing him to gush over Jack's work before leading him down the hall for his nighttime routine.

Darcie set to work scrubbing the pumpkin innards from the table and was nearly done when Rees came in, admitting a cold burst of air. As he wiped his feet on the mat and hung his damp jacket on a peg, a peal of Jack's laughter came like music from down the hall. Rees turned, smiling. "What's so funny?"

"Our sink burps."

Rees's eyebrows shot up. "Say what now?"

She couldn't help a chuckle. "When it drains, the water goes down with a gurgle. Jack says it burps."

"Huh. Never noticed."

"Some things take a five-year-old to appreciate." She looked at her brother, his spiky hair damp with rain. The man could use a haircut, though she refrained from saying so. Lately, she'd noticed a thawing in Rees's manner toward her. She didn't know if it was because she was trying to be less intrusive or what, but she didn't want to do anything to jeopardize the unspoken truce.

She moved toward the sink to re-wet her washcloth. "Where've you been?" Rees had taken off without a word right after dinner.

"In town." He pulled a Coke from the fridge. Leaning a hip against the counter, he unscrewed the cap. "Had to talk to Denny Lewis."

"Denny?" She paused, washcloth suspended above the table. "What for?"

"Thought I saw someone watching Jack and me today while we were mowing the lawn. Don't know how long he was standing at the road, but when I went to talk to him, he took off."

A stranger watching Jack? A dull sock of alarm hit her stomach. "What did Denny say?"

"That he'd seen the same thing recently." Rees swigged his Coke.

"When?"

"Few weeks ago when he was at the park with Ally."

Darcie pulled a chair from the table and sat. "And we don't know who he is?"

"Not yet."

"What'd he look like?"

"Five-seven, five-eight. Goatee. Couldn't see much hair beneath his baseball cap, but either light brown or blond. He drove a black pickup, recent model, probably a Chevy or Ford."

"Why would he be interested in you or Jack?"

"Not for any good reason I can think of," he said, his tone grim.

Something Ally said came floating back. She hadn't wanted to take Jack with her to Iowa because it wasn't safe. At the time, Darcie had been too focused on her friend's distress to think much of this, but now it struck her as an odd thing to say. Not convenient, Darcie could understand. But not safe? She repeated this to Rees and watched his features draw together in a frown. "Think there might be a connection?"

Before Rees could respond, Paul came to the doorway with Jack in his footed spaceship sleeper. "Hey, buddy," Rees said.

Darcie gave Jack a smile. "Ready to be tucked in?"

"You said I could show Mr. Rees my pumpkin." His mouth puckered.

"Go for it."

He trailed a scent of bubblegum toothpaste as he scampered across the room. He picked up his pumpkin and turned it for Rees's inspection. "See?"

"Dude!" Rees's eyes went wide. "Cool goblin. Look at those eyebrows!"

Jack beamed at the praise.

"Come on." Darcie rose. "Time for your bedtime story. Which one are we reading tonight?"

Since Rees had the spare room, they'd made a place for Jack with a sleeping bag on the floor in Paul's study. Darcie lowered herself to the carpet, feeling her knees pop with the effort. "So what did you like best about Fort Casey?" That afternoon she'd taken him to Whidbey's defunct, turn-of-the-twentieth-century military fort.

"The big ship."

"Big ship?" She had to think about what he meant. She'd expected an answer similar to what Rees would have given at this age. The magazines, maybe, that maze of dank rooms connected by concrete passages built into the hillside whose empty spaces were filled now not with ammunition but stalactites and lime. Or the big guns themselves, pointing out to sea.

Then she realized Jack was talking about the Chinese cargo freighter they'd seen bound for port in Tacoma or Seattle, weighted down with boxes of goods—and possibly refugees, though she'd kept this thought to herself. "Why was that your favorite?"

"Because it came from a million miles away."

"Well, maybe not a million, but certainly a very long way." Darcie brushed back a lock of hair from his forehead.

"Isn't China on the other side of the world?"

"Yes."

"Then it's a million miles. Someday I want to go there. I've never been anywhere, not even Canada. My friend Eric goes to Canada all the time with his family."

"Just you wait, mister." She kissed his forehead, making sure Fluff was tightly tucked against his chest. "I have a feeling someday you'll go a lot farther than Canada."

"Like China?"

"At least."

When Jack was asleep, she returned to the kitchen, where Paul was kneading dough for tomorrow's cinnamon rolls. From the severe grooves drawn across her husband's face, she guessed Rees had been telling him about the stranger. Paul's question confirmed it. "So what can we do to keep the boy away from this guy?"

"Make sure Jack's always with someone we trust," Rees said. Clearly, he was taking this thing seriously. "Has Ally called today?"

"This morning." Darcie glanced again at the stove's digital clock. 8:35. "Iowa's two hours ahead, so I doubt she'll call again today. Think we should tell her when she does?"

Rees shook his head. "It would only alarm her. There's nothing she can do for him right now. Any idea when she's coming back?"

"She doesn't know." It would depend on how things progressed with her father. Darcie had encouraged her to take as much time as she needed. But she also knew Ally was concerned about taking so much time off work and probably wouldn't linger longer than strictly necessary.

"I'll talk to her when she gets back," Rees said, "so she can be on guard."

When Darcie let the dogs out later that night, she stood at the door and thought about what she'd explained to Jack that afternoon, how Fort Casey was one of three military installments strategically placed around Puget Sound to form a triangle of fire. *That's what we'll do for Jack*, she thought. *We'll form a triangle of fire. Rees. Paul. Me.*

She looked out into the veil of rain, darkness obscuring everything beyond the circle of the porch light. Was someone out there, looking back at her? If so, who? And why? She shivered, feeling grateful for the dogs, who came galloping back to the house, eager to be out of the rain. Their untroubled behavior reassured her. No one was out there or Moses and Aaron would have let her know. Still, Darcie checked and double-checked the locks before retiring for the night.

CHAPTER 26

"I must not have made myself clear." Libby stood in the hospital room doorway, her faded blue eyes a furious indigo. "I want you to stay away from us."

Ally felt a rush of blood under her cheeks as she wobbled to her feet, clutching the bed's side rail for support. "He's my father."

Libby's gaze narrowed. "Should have remembered that before you put him through these last six years."

Jamal hurried into the room. "Ladies." Though he kept his voice low, his tone carried the weight of authority. "Not here, please. Whatever issues you have, work them out somewhere else. Not in front of my patient." He eyed them sternly.

Then Gina swept into the room, a swirl of hair and flowing clothing. "Cadence—" She gasped, doubling over as she clutched her belly. "Oh!"

Jamal moved swiftly to Gina's side, placing a supporting arm around her. "Contraction?" His close-cropped head bent to hers.

Gina, her black glasses stark against the white of her face, could only nod. After a long minute during which even Libby stared, Gina straightened with a relieved sigh. "Okay. Whooo, okay now."

Jamal's eyes narrowed. "How far along are you?"

Not far enough, Ally thought.

"Seven months," Gina said.

Jamal's mouth tightened into a grim hyphen. "All right, we're getting you down to obstetrics. Who's your doc?"

Gina told him.

"I'll have her paged right now."

"I am so sorry Libby came back before I could sound the alarm." Gina's face filled with regret as she lay on her left side in a hospital bed two floors down.

Ally waved a hand from the recliner at the foot of the bed. "Would you quit worrying about Libby? I'm a lot more worried about you." Gina's room in the hospital's baby wing looked nothing like Patrick Brennan's in the CCU. Here the rooms featured subdued lighting, earth-toned prints on terra cotta walls and easy chairs for visitors. Gina's OB had been waiting for them when Gina arrived in a wheelchair. She'd promptly ordered Gina to bed to monitor her contractions, and then left after performing an examination. Now garbed in a pink hospital gown and fuzzy cotton socks, Gina wore a strap across her girth to gauge contractions.

"I had to pee, and since it had been only half an hour since you went into your dad's room, I thought it would be fine." Gina continued as if Ally hadn't spoken. "Libby came back early."

"Probably suspecting I'd show up."

Gina eyed her from the bed, her auburn hair splayed like a fiery sunset across the pillow. "You mentioned an estrangement."

"Yes, but even I don't understand this." Libby had loved her once. If Kyle had told everyone she was dead, and if Libby had believed him...

Could it be she'd grieved for Ally, thinking her lost forever? Did discovering that Ally's so-called death was a lie make her angry for having been put through such anguish? Or perhaps the answer rested more with her father and the effect her presumed death had on him. Libby loved him, clearly. If her father hadn't been the same after she left, Libby must blame her for that.

The unfairness rose in Ally's throat. Kyle was the one to blame for that, not her. Kyle must have destroyed her letter. He had misled her father all these years.

Gina's nurse returned, an electronic chart tucked into the crook of her arm. "Ms. Damiani? I'm afraid your contractions aren't getting any better." A lanky platinum blonde with dark roots, she moved to the bed, adjusted some of the lines attached to Gina. "We need to get them slowed down. We're going to start terbutaline to try to control things. If that doesn't work, we'll need to keep you overnight."

Gina's eyes cut to the monitor tracking the fetal heartbeat. "How's my baby?"

"Baby's fine." The austere lines of the nurse's face softened. "His heartbeat is steady, see? But we do need him to stay put a while longer, so that's why we're going to try this. Have you been able to reach your husband?"

"No." Leif was on tour in San Francisco. "I left a message."

"All right." The nurse adjusted the band over Gina's middle before pulling the coverlet back up. "I'll return in a few minutes with the terbutaline. Hang tight."

"As if I'm going anywhere," Gina muttered, tugging at the strap. She caught a breath, hissed it out slowly.

Ally's eyebrows drew together. "Another one?"

Gina nodded.

"You doing okay?"

"Just peachy, thanks." Gina's hair rasped against the pillow as she turned her head toward Ally. "Same as I always am when things don't go my way." She leveled her a look through narrowed eyes. "Why is it life seldom goes the way we plan? We hadn't planned for Leif to get on with the symphony at the same time we got pregnant, but it happened. I didn't plan to have a complicated pregnancy, but it looks like I've got one." She paused. "I never planned for my star pupil to give up the most promising career I'd ever laid my hands on, but she did."

Ally's smile wobbled. "I was kinda hoping you'd forgotten that part."

"I may have forgiven it, but I won't ever forget it."

They held each other's gazes for a long minute. Then Ally stood. "I'll be right back." She grabbed her tote. "I've got an idea."

Ally took her time returning to Gina's room, to give Gina privacy with the nurse and also so she could pull a thick, lemon-colored turtleneck from her bag in the car. She stopped in the ladies' room to pull her hair into a fresh ponytail, splash water on her face and apply a coat of lip gloss. Staring at her face in the mirror, she realized fatigue was pulling her skin taut. Or was it sorrow over her father? With Libby now standing sentinel, would she ever see him again? Would he make it out of this hospital alive?

Pushing depressing questions aside, Ally returned to Gina's third floor room with Lola. Her teacher, still curled on her left side, faced the door with her eyes closed, one arm draped across her belly. She looked as if she'd fallen asleep. As Ally allowed the door to close behind her, Gina's eyes fluttered open.

"You're awake."

"Just resting." Gina yawned. "Everything's kind of catching up with me. Exhausting lugging this fella around."

"I remember. Everything okay?"

"Fine. That is, there's no change. Contractions aren't better, but they're not worse either. Nurse was just in to check on me again. I haven't started dilating, so that's a good sign." Her gaze fell on the case in Ally's hand. "Is that what I think it is?"

In answer, Ally placed the case beside Gina. Her former teacher hoisted herself up on an elbow and snapped the lid open. Inside, the viola nestled in its cranberry-red cocoon. "I never thought I'd see it again."

"It has a name now. We call her Lola."

"Lola?"

"When my son was little, he couldn't wrap his tongue around *viola*. It came out *Lola*, and it stuck."

"She's just as lovely as I remember." Gina ran her fingers over the wood's fine patina, lifted the instrument from the case and carefully turned it over, fingering the long crack. "From the first time I saw her in that pokey little shop in Budapest, I knew she had to belong to you." While on a summer European tour, Gina had ducked into an antiques shop to get out of the rain and discovered Lola. Three hundred years old, with no craftsman label, it still had perfect sound. Yet it was gathering dust. Because of the crack, it wasn't considered valuable. Gina talked the owner into selling it for a few hundred forints and brought it back to Ally.

"You remember the story about how Lola got cracked?" Ally asked.

"The Gypsies, you mean?"

Ally nodded. "You told me the shopkeeper said it once belonged to Gypsies, who threw it into the bushes while escaping the law."

"That's right." Gina pursed her lips. "I remember wondering what would have happened if those Gypsies hadn't run. Where it might have ended up."

"Ended up?"

"I mean, if the Gypsies had stood their ground and faced whatever it was that was chasing them—they'd still have Lola, wouldn't they?"

"I suppose." Ally shifted her weight. "Do you remember what else you told me? About why I should switch from violin to viola? You said good violinists were a dime-a-dozen, but if I made the switch, I could have the world at my feet."

"Still true. If you want it to be." She looked up at Ally. "I assume this means you're playing again."

"A little."

"That's something anyway. Will you play for me?"

Ally took the instrument and set it to her chin. "How about an Irish air." She twisted Lola's pegs, one by one. "*Naoise and Deirdre*?"

"You remember." Wonder filled Gina's voice.

It had been one of her mentor's favorites. "I remember everything." As Ally set the horsehair bow to the strings, Lola began to sing. Ally closed her eyes, swaying to the Celtic melody. She played as much for herself as for Gina, needing the music to wash away the lingering ache lodged beneath her breastbone.

With the final stroke of her bow across the strings, she opened her eyes to find Gina's thoughtful gaze on her face. "Something happened to you, didn't it?"

Ally lowered her instrument and bow. "What do you mean?"

"Something big. Something…bad."

Ally looked away. "Why would you say that?"

"It took something nearly cataclysmic to drive you away from music. Listening to you now, I realize it must have taken something just as big to draw you back."

Ally replaced Lola inside her case and tucked her bow back into its slot before closing the lid.

"Will you tell me about it?"

Ally shook her head.

"Okay." Gina nodded. "It's not important I know. What's important is you're playing again. And you're still playing like that." Her fingers fluttered at the closed case. "Like an angel on loan from heaven."

Her heart lifted. "Really?" All these years later, she still craved her teacher's praise.

"From the first time I heard you play, when you were hardly more than a twig, I knew your talent was superb. I'd never seen anything like it in someone so young. And you were mine! A child prodigy, my very own Mozart. I said then if you gave this instrument your all, the world would be yours. That's just as true now as it was when you were a kid. Maybe even more so."

"Good to know I haven't lost my chops." She'd been playing in a vacuum for so long, she'd wondered what she'd lost along the way.

She didn't have to wait long to find out. "Well," Gina drawled. "Don't get too cocky. There's room for improvement in the smoothness and accuracy of your shifting, your intonation could stand to be a lot more consistent, and I can only pray someday you'll finally manage to get your vibrato under control."

Ally's heart sank. "Is that all?"

"You want more?"

"Not really."

"I didn't think so." Gina looked away. "In any case, it hardly matters now, does it?"

"Why do you say that? It matters to me. I'd like to think I can still make beautiful music, even if no one hears it but me, my son, and God."

"That's such a waste."

"My playing brings me joy. What's wasteful about that?"

"It could do so much more." Straining against the strap across her belly, Gina pushed herself upright and leaned forward to thrust out a finger. "I don't care what you say, you're still squandering something great, a gift most of us can only dream of. You say your playing brings you joy. Hurray for you. But what about the rest of the world that could gain so much from your gift?"

Ally remained silent.

"Think about it." Gina gentled her tone. "How do you feel when you hear one of the greats perform? When Andreas Bocelli sings, or when Yo-Yo Ma draws sound from his cello like no one else in the world? It transports you to another time, or place, or mood. The gift of music. Is there anything else like it?"

The door swung open. The nurse needing a root touchup hastened inside. "Why did I lose my monitor reading?" Her gaze went to the wide strap that had slipped from Gina's abdomen. She *tsk*ed and ordered her patient to lie back down.

Gina ignored the nurse's fussing. "Music changes people from the inside out, Ally. How many things in this old world can you say that about? Not many. And you've got it in your bones. What's left now is for you to figure out what to do about it."

CHAPTER 27

By late afternoon, Gina's doctor was satisfied her contractions had slowed enough for her to return home, as long as she stayed on strict bed rest and took her uterus-relaxing meds. Gina invited Ally to stay at her place until the buyers took possession the following week.

Back at the house, Ally was just getting her teacher settled in bed when Gina's cell phone rang. Leif, at last returning her call. Ally scuttled across the hall into the guest room to give Gina privacy, listening to the murmur of Gina's side of the conversation as she readied herself for bed. When she emerged from the bathroom after brushing her teeth, Ally poked her head inside Gina's room to see if there was anything else she needed before turning in.

"Yes, actually. Come sit for a moment. I want to talk to you."

Ally took the room's only chair, a Queen Anne that matched the one in the living room. Keeping her eyes on Gina's face, which seemed strangely naked without her trademark black-framed glasses, she tried to ignore the weirdness of being in her former teacher's bedroom. Even with the personal touches packed away, the room's strong, inner-sanctum aura made Ally feel keenly out of place.

"I have a proposal for you." Gina cupped her cell phone between her palms. "Leif and I have been talking, and—well, how'd you like to come to Chicago?"

Ally's brow furrowed. "To visit, you mean?"

"No, to live."

"I could hardly afford to live in a place like Chicago as a part-time waitress." She could barely afford Langley.

"That's why I want you to come live with me. With us. With Leif and me, and the baby."

Ally smiled. "Just like that? Just…because?"

"Not just because. So you can finish your college education, and more importantly, to study music again. To play in a symphony or string quintet or chamber orchestra—or all three. To rub elbows with kindred spirits and unleash your hidden muse once more."

A zipper-like thrill ran up Ally's back as a shimmering vision glittered. Concerts, music to her heart's content, the intellectual and creative stimulation of others who shared her passion. But then the vision faded, making her reality seem drab by contrast.

Slowly, she shook her head. "That sounds amazing, but I can't. I have a son, whom I miss, and a job. When I leave here, I need to go home. I have another life now."

"What life?" Gina frowned. "You earn a living serving people scrambled eggs and ham sandwiches. That's not a life. It's a job, and not a very good one, at that."

Stung, Ally said, "Well then, what about my son?"

"We want him too, of course. Leif and I are proposing a trade. We will house you and Jack while making sure you get a world-class education. In return, you'll help me look after the baby."

"You mean, like a nanny?"

"Something like that, yes. Leif is completely on board."

"Don't you think that's an awful lot to ask of my son? He's only five. To uproot from the only home he's known so his mother can chase her dream of playing her fiddle?"

"I'd say the greater risk is staying where you are. How exactly are you helping your son when you don't let him see that passion matters? Pursuing our dreams gives life purpose." Gina leaned forward, elbow on the edge of the mattress. "You admitted something happened to you, something bad. I don't know what it was, I don't need to know, but I get the sense it still haunts you. Why not look at this as the chance to put it all behind you? To start over, once and for all?"

Ally opened her mouth to argue, then shut it again. Gina was right. Her past did haunt her. Despite everything, she'd never been able to leave it completely behind. Would a move like this finally liberate her from her mistakes, enable her to live freely once more? To immerse herself in music again. To pursue her college education, to finish what she'd barely begun. It sounded like nothing less than a dream come true.

But she had to consider what it would do to Jack. "I have more than just myself to think about now," she said, her words slow. "You say Jack's welcome. I appreciate that. But I can't assume he'll adapt to such a big change." Gina would find out soon enough that having a child changed everything about a woman's priorities.

"You're afraid he won't adjust? Make friends? Have fun? Kids are resilient." Gina shook her head. "Don't use him as an excuse for saying no, because that's all it would be. An excuse."

Unbidden, something Brittany said dropped into her mind. *You never take any kind of chance, afraid you'll get hurt. Or Jack will. How is he ever going to learn to be a man if all he sees is you avoiding risk at all cost?*

Still, Ally shook her head. "I don't know, Gina."

"Why are you hesitating for even a second?" Her voice rose high in frustration.

"I'm not sure." Gina was offering everything she'd once dreamed of. Why did she hold back? Because Langley was safe. She'd built a safe life for Jack there. And while Chicago held plenty of allure, it also held just as many unknowns. Unknowns she wasn't sure she was prepared to face. "It's complicated, Gina."

They talked for another hour, until Ally could no longer keep her eyes open. She planned an early morning, wanting to return to the hospital as soon as possible in hopes of getting past the lioness Libby to see her father. But even as she slept, the possibilities of what Gina offered tangled in her mind.

The bright opening bars of Vivaldi's *Four Seasons* penetrated her consciousness. She blinked her eyes open. A moment passed in disorientation before she realized the music was Gina's ringtone. Ally rolled to look at the digital clock radio on the nightstand. 6:07.

Cadence. From nowhere, the name dropped into her ear.

Daddy? Ally bolted upright, certain she'd heard her father say her name. Was she dreaming? Confused, she pushed back her tangled hair, taking in the unfamiliar surroundings. Bare cream-colored walls, double bed fitted with striped blue and white sheets, boxes stacked beside the door. From across the hall, the soft rise and fall of Gina's voice. Then silence.

A moment later, a light tap sounded on her door. Gina ducked inside, her hair wild around her head. Concern pushed a frown to Ally's face. "You're supposed to be lying down. Do you need something?" Still groggy, she swung her feet to the floor, the hardwood cold beneath her toes. "Get back in bed and I'll get it for you."

Gina's upraised hand stopped her. "Ally, wait. I'm afraid I have some news. The hospital just called."

"Dad?" Ally's gut tightened.

"I'd asked Jamal to call if anything changed." She paused, and in that pause, Ally's insides turned to liquid. "I'm so sorry, but he died this morning."

CHAPTER 28

"Thanks for everything." Showered and dressed, Ally leaned awkwardly over Gina's bed to give her teacher a parting hug.

"You're sure you won't stay until the funeral?" Gina looked up from her pillow. "I don't have to be out of the house for another week, even though the movers are coming tomorrow. You're welcome to stay."

"No point in that." She blinked hard, her eyes still stinging from the crying she'd done in the shower. "Libby wouldn't stand for my being at the service." Too risky, besides. She'd managed to avoid Kyle so far, but what if he returned to see his stepfather buried?

Gina hesitated. "Your dad waited for you, you know. It's not a coincidence he didn't die until after you arrived. He knew you were there."

Ally's throat closed as tears threatened again. "You really believe that?" Her time with him had been so brief. And yet, maybe it was enough. Darcie had told her about patients who lingered, waiting for an estranged loved one to arrive. As if their souls needed that closure before moving into the next realm. For her own part, she felt what she'd offered her father had been too little, too late.

"I do believe it." Gina frowned. "I wish you'd at least stay long enough for Leif to meet you. His flight gets in at ten."

"I really need to get back." She had a long drive ahead, her craving to see Jack a physical hunger.

Gina nodded, expecting this. "Guess Leif'll meet you soon enough anyway." She gave her a penetrating look. "I hope."

"Gina." Ally took a breath and let it go. "What you've offered—it's amazing, really."

"But?"

"I just can't. I can't uproot Jack like that." Gina had woven a spell last night, painting a masterpiece. But Ally had made her choice years ago. In the clear light of morning, she knew there was no turning back.

At midmorning the next day, Ally crossed the Washington state line. If she pressed on without stopping, she could be back in Langley in time to pick up Jack from school. Her arms tingled and her heart throbbed at the thought of holding her son again, making her push the speed limit. Finally arriving at the Mukilteo ferry landing, she called Darcie to let her know she was almost home. Precisely five minutes before Jack's class let out, Ally stepped from her Saturn, stretching tired, cramped limbs.

The kids were stuffing their backpacks with their belongings when Ally peeked through the half-open door to the classroom. One of Jack's classmates spotted her first. He nudged Jack with his elbow, whispering something. Jack looked up, a grin lighting his face as he hurled himself at her. "Mommy!"

Her heart thumped painfully. "Hello, my Bubba." She held her boy in her arms and inhaled the scent of him.

"What'd you bring me?" His eyes shined up at her. "Whenever Carter's mom comes back from a trip, she always brings him something. What did you bring me, Mom?"

Her sheen of pleasure faded. She'd been so consumed with longing for him that thought of a gift had never even occurred to her. She pasted on a smile. "How 'bout we do Pizzeria takeout for dinner? To celebrate my being home."

His face fell. Though he made no further mention of a gift, Ally's delight at being home dulled. She attributed her melancholy to grief and fatigue, but she still kicked herself. What kind of a mom didn't think to bring her son a treat after a long absence?

When at last she pulled in behind their cottage and parked, Jack leapt from the car and dashed to the back porch. "Mom?" Jack called. "What's this?"

Pulling the pizza from the passenger seat, Ally turned to look. Jack pointed to a slim package, wrapped in plain brown paper, propped against the back door. She frowned. She wasn't expecting anything. "I have no idea."

"Maybe it's for me," Jack suggested, cheering up at the idea of a present today, after all.

"Maybe." Wouldn't that be nice, something to make up for her failure. Balancing the cardboard pizza box in her arms, she managed to get the door open. "Let me put this down and we'll take a look."

Jack carried the brown bundle to the kitchen table. She set the pizza on the stove, grateful for its warm garlic and pepperoni smells to chase away the cottage's stale odor. Then she picked up the brown parcel and looked at it more carefully. About the size of a book, it had no markings on the wrapper. No name, nothing.

"Can I open it?" Jack asked.

"Of course."

Jack tore the brown paper from the package while Ally made one more trip to the car for her overnight bag. When she returned, Jack was staring in disappointment at the object he held. "What is it, Bubs?"

"Nothing," he said, disgusted.

"What do you mean, nothing? What is it?"

"Just an old picture. Broken, too."

"Let me see." As she took it from him, dread settled low in her belly.

The framed photograph of her and Jack was the one that had gone missing the day of the break-in. Only now the photograph was torn in two, with the halves paired roughly together and replaced inside the frame, the rip down the middle neatly separating her from Jack.

CHAPTER 29

"Who would do this?" Ally stared at the mangled photograph while Denny faced her across her kitchen table. She'd phoned him as soon as she'd seen the package's contents. "And why? It makes no sense." Her hand trembled as she tucked a stray strand of hair behind her ear. From the other room came cartoon-like explosions as Jack watched *The Incredibles* and munched on pizza.

Wearing latex gloves, Denny held the frame by its edges. "You say it's been missing since the break-in?"

"I think so, yes. That's when I noticed it gone, anyway."

"Why didn't you say so when I asked?"

She lifted her hands, palms up. "I never thought it was stolen. I mean, who would want to steal a personal snapshot in a cheap frame? I assumed I'd misplaced it, or Jack had put it somewhere. Honestly, it never crossed my mind."

Ally could tell by the focused look on Denny's face he disagreed. "Show me exactly where you found it."

"Jack found it, actually."

"Do you mind if I talk to him?"

Ally hesitated. "Just don't scare him, okay?" Although as far as she could tell, Jack was more disgusted by than worried about the strange package.

"I'll do my best."

"Jack!" she called over her shoulder. "Could you come here a minute?"

His quick appearance made her think he'd been poised for just such a summons. "Hey, Bubba, Deputy Lewis has a few questions for you."

"About the package?"

"That's right." Denny nodded. "I understand you were the one to find it on your doorstep. Can you show me where, exactly?"

Jack walked to the back door, opened it, pointed to the spot. "Leaning right there."

Denny looked at Ally. "Any idea how long it had been there?"

"I've been gone for most of the week. It could have been left anytime."

"You didn't have anyone stopping by to water your plants? Feed the cat?"

"We don't have a cat," Jack said.

"My landlady may have stopped by," Ally said, "just to check on things, but I doubt it. There was no reason for her to."

"I'll talk to her, just in case. Maybe she saw someone come to your house. Jack, you opened the package? What'd you do with the wrapper?"

"Threw it away."

"Where?"

"In the garbage."

"The can's under the sink," Ally added. "Should be empty except for the wrapper."

Denny brought the torn paper to the table. He then pulled two plastic bags from his kit and slipped the frame inside one, the wrapper inside the other. "I'll take these with me, have them analyzed. Has anyone touched them besides you two?"

"No one."

"Right, then I'll just have to get prints from the both of you."

Jack's eyes lit up. "You need my fingerprints?"

"Sure do. So our lab technicians can eliminate them from any others we find on the frame or wrapper."

"Why do you want to find fingerprints?"

"So we can figure out who wrecked your photo."

"Is that a crime?"

Denny smiled. "Destroying someone's property without their permission is always against the law. So is stealing something from someone's home. If it was the same man who stole your television and your mom's jewelry, this might help us catch him. We want that, don't we?" Denny looked at Ally. "Can you come right now? It won't take long."

Ally glanced at the pizza on the counter, grease congealed on its surface. "Sure." She had no appetite, anyway. Then her gaze fell once more on the destroyed photograph encased in

Denny's plastic bag. It was a recent snapshot, one of Ally and Jack on the beach below their house, her arms around him, their faces pressed together, cheek to cheek. Whoever had torn the photo had done it precisely, to make it look as if Jack had been ripped from Ally's embrace.

As Jack ran to put on his shoes, Ally looked at Denny. "It's like someone's trying to send me a message." It seemed like something Kyle would do. But it couldn't be Kyle. The break-in was weeks ago. If he had managed to track her to Langley, she would know by now. He would have made sure of it.

"More than likely, it's just someone messing with your head," Denny said. "All the same, we'll send a patrol car out here a little more often. Be sure to keep a close eye on Jack until we know who sent this, all right?" The smile he offered didn't quite reach his eyes. It struck her as more worried than reassuring.

CHAPTER 30

Though she tried to brush it off as the work of a prankster, the incident robbed Ally of a night's sleep, making her feel ragged and on edge when she arrived at the Front Street Bistro the next morning. She told Sam about her father's death, accepting his sympathy but declining his offer for any more time off. As everyone else assumed she'd taken a few days of vacation, she managed to cocoon herself in a gauze of unreality that kept her from feeling anything too keenly, which suited her just fine.

When the lunch crowd thinned, she took her break. She picked up a tub of scraps for Stormy, carried it outside and placed it on the bottom step, wondering if anyone had remembered to feed the cat in her absence. Brittany sat on the stairs, smoking, using a cracked ceramic saucer as an ashtray. Ally had hardly seen Brittany all morning. "Thought you were going to quit those cancer sticks." Ally sat beside her and cradled her Nalgene water bottle between her knees.

"Never said I would." Brittany stared out over the blackberry bushes toward the gray waters of Saratoga Passage. Silence stretched between them. As Ally lifted her water bottle to her lips, she heard a sniff. Glancing at her friend, she saw tears clearing tracks through Brittany's pink blush.

"Sheesh, sorry, Brit. If it bugs you that much, I'll lay off about the smoking."

"Don't be stupid." Brittany sniffed again. "It's not that, it's Rosie."

"Your parents' dog?" Brittany was dog sitting as well as house sitting for her parents while they were away.

Brittany puffed again on her cigarette before dropping it into the saucer. "Yesterday when I got home from work, Rose was unconscious in the front yard. I had no idea what was wrong, so I carried her into the house. Jamie was watching TV. I asked him when he'd last seen Rosie running around. He said he'd been inside watching TV all afternoon and had no idea. I was just thinking I should take her to the vet when she started to revive. Then she drank up all her water and curled up on her bed. This morning she was back to normal, except—"

"Except?"

"She won't go anywhere near Jamie. Like she's afraid of him." Her friend's shoulders rounded forward as she clutched her elbows with both hands.

Watching her, Ally knew her friend wasn't telling everything. "Brittany? Why would she be afraid of Jamie?"

Brittany stared down at her clasped arms. "I think he might have done something to her."

"Why would you think that?"

"Because he can't stand Rosie, the way she's always barking and jumping up on people. She's sweet, but she does kind of rule the roost. And—" She bit her lip. "Once I lost an earring and thought maybe it had gotten caught in his sweater. So I looked through his stuff and found a…a *Taser* underneath his jeans."

Ally stared. A Taser? Why on earth—

"I have no idea why, I don't want to know," Brittany hurried on. "But when I found Rosie like that, I remembered it. When Jamie wasn't around, I went online and—it all matches."

Ally sucked cold air into her lungs. "He tazed your dog?"

"I don't know. Maybe." Brittany dropped her forehead to her knees. "I don't know what to think."

"You didn't ask?"

"I couldn't."

"Why not?" In Ally's opinion, animal abusers were among the worst sort, their mistreatment of animals usually signifying only the tip of an iceberg of violence.

"Because I was afraid of what might happen to Rosie if I confronted him."

Against her will, Ally's mind winged back to the time during her senior year after she'd first tried to break off her affair with Kyle. She'd returned home from school to find her almost-finished, twenty-page English report on Beowulf erased from her hard drive. She'd known it was Kyle; it couldn't have been anyone else. It scared her. And yet, she'd dared not accuse him. Because if he was capable of that, what else was he capable of? Sabotaging her entire senior project to prevent her from graduating? So she'd redone the whole report from scratch, working from notes and memory. All of which earned her a barely passing grade.

"Brit—" Ally fumbled to say something, anything. But what? Words to commiserate? To sympathize? She couldn't. The suspicion that Brittany's boyfriend was an animal-abuser made anything she might say stick in her throat.

Brittany raised her head. She must have read judgment in Ally's eyes, for she stood suddenly, brushing the seat of her jeans. "Don't say it." She mounted the steps to the screen door. "I don't want to hear it."

Ally craned her neck, looking up at her friend. "I'm worried about you, Brit."

"Don't be. I can take care of myself. Besides, I don't know anything for a fact. I have to trust he's innocent. That's what love does, you know. It trusts." She disappeared inside the bistro, letting the door slap shut behind her.

CHAPTER 31

Her conversation with Brittany weighted Ally's mood for the rest of the day. When she picked up Jack from school, she made a deliberate effort to be upbeat, even promising his favorite macaroni-and-cheese-with-hot-dogs in an effort to make up for yesterday's fiasco of a homecoming. Hoping too that the effort might distract her from the first real stirrings of grief. Could she count herself past the denial stage even though she hadn't yet told her son his grandfather had died? She figured she could, given that Jack had never known his grandfather existed in the first place.

After tucking Jack into bed, Ally took a load of damp clothes from the dryer to the back porch, where she'd stretched a clothesline from one end of the porch to the other. It was dark and cold. She should have been wearing a jacket, but she planned to complete this chore quickly before getting back inside where it was warm. Pulling Jack's sweater from the basket, she clipped it to the line.

She was reaching for another clothespin when a sudden movement at the corner of the house made her turn her head. She gasped as a tall man stepped into view.

"It's me, Ally." He held up a hand. "Sorry, didn't mean to startle you."

Rees. "Good grief, what are you doing sneaking around in the dark?"

"Sorry," he repeated, mounting the steps. By the dim illumination of the yellow porch light, she saw he was again dressed for a run, this time in a lightweight jacket and long black spandex. In this light, his scar appeared as only a faint pink line, tracing upward from his jaw and right cheek. "I did try your cell, but no one answered." Then, taking in the scene, his forehead crinkled. "Are you actually hanging clothes?"

She pulled another clothespin from the bag. "Obviously."

"In the dark? It's cold outside." He came all the way up to the porch, his sneakers soundless on the wooden planks. After reaching into her wicker laundry basket, he pulled out a pair of Jack's jeans.

"My dryer broke today." She handed him a clothespin. "I didn't realize it until an hour ago. If I let things sit overnight, they'll start to stink." She'd not been thrilled to come home to discover the batch of clothes she'd put in that morning still damp. As Rees clipped a small pair of Superman underpants next to the jeans, Ally felt a fleeting pulse of gratitude it had been Jack's clothes caught in the dryer, not hers. She wasn't sure how she'd feel seeing Rees Davies hanging her delicates out to dry.

"I came by to say I'm sorry about your dad."

"Thank you." She looked down at the dwindling heap of clothes in the basket. "I'm not sure it's really hit yet."

"It might not, for a while."

"I think I'm afraid to let it be real." The last few days seemed cast in an aura of unreality, as if the events were something she'd seen in a movie instead of lived through.

"That's natural."

"But Dad deserves more than that, more than my pushing it aside, afraid to feel grief now he's gone. He was a good dad." She believed that, even though he hadn't always made the best choices. It was hard on them as a family, moving to follow his work or his whim, whichever came first. When her mother sank into her depression, he hadn't known how to handle it. And yet, despite it all, he remained a devoted dad.

She replayed her last moments with him in his hospital room, when he'd been all but unrecognizable, scraped and bloated and broken beyond repair. Only that one time had he given any indication he was aware of her presence, by the tiniest pressure of his fingers. So slight she might have imagined it. Yet she felt sure a connection had been made.

Ally glanced at Rees. "I was at my…friend's house when I found out he'd died. Right before we got the call, I thought I heard him speak my name." She surprised herself, telling him. But something about the cloaking darkness, Rees's warm gaze, and his protective presence made her want to say the words aloud. "I don't mean I heard his voice. I mean I think my spirit heard him, somehow. Do you think that's possible?"

"I think we know more about what goes on in the far reaches of the universe than we do about what goes on in the spiritual realm." He lifted the last sweatshirt from the basket. With no more room on the line, he draped it across the wooden railing. "Westerners tend to forget such a place really exists, if we even believe in it in the first place. In India, most people pay a great deal of attention to what goes on in the spiritual realm. I work with a woman, Sheela, who was Hindu before she became a Christian. She says the only thing she's brought with her from her former faith is her awareness of spirits."

"Spirits." The word itself had an odd ring to it, like something out of a Victorian novel. "You mean, like demons?"

"And angels and an entire world we cannot see. The same one the apostle Paul described when he wrote about our battles on earth not being against flesh and blood but against the spiritual forces of evil. Sheela maintains every struggle we face has a spiritual element to it, tempting us to lose faith in God's power over it all. She says too many Christians have lost sight of the prophecy made to Joel, in which God says He will pour out His Spirit into dreams and visions. That this will be the new norm for believers. But Westerners crave rational explanations and chalk up things like hearing your dying father's voice from miles away as emotion, or stress, or an overactive imagination. So yes, in very long answer to your question—" She heard the smile in his voice—"I'd say it's entirely possible God enabled you to hear your father speak your name."

"You don't think I'm crazy?"

"If Sheela were here, she'd tell you that since you heard your father's voice, God meant it for comfort. To give you hope."

Hope for what? That her father had found his place with Jesus? That God knew of her loss and understood it? "This Sheela sounds like a good person to know."

"She is. She's been through the fire herself. It's made her very wise."

"What happened to her?" Darkness obscured his expression, making it impossible to tell whether Sheela was more to him than just a coworker and friend.

"Her Hindu husband divorced her when she became a Christian, and then her family disowned her. She came to Sanctuary because of a vision she had in a dream."

"A dream?" So far, this didn't sound like too much of a trial.

"Shortly after Sheela's husband kicked her out and her family shunned her, she lost her job because of her husband's family's influence. Back then she was too proud to ask for help, so she lived on the streets until she finally understood how women could resort to selling their bodies. Her last meal had been three days before. She was unable to do anything but pray. Eventually she fell asleep and dreamed of a peacock-blue door, one she'd seen many times as she passed by on her way to market. In her dream, Jesus told her to knock on that door and tell whoever opened it, 'I am the woman you've been seeking.'

"When she woke up, Sheela knew she'd received instructions. But you can also imagine she was more than a little afraid to follow through on them. To say to a stranger, *I am the woman you've been seeking?* As a housekeeper? A wife? She didn't know, but it didn't matter. Her job was to obey. So she set out the next day. The door she'd seen in her dream was clear across the city. She had no money for the train, so she walked. Miles and miles. It was dinnertime when she finally arrived, nearly passing out from hunger and fatigue.

"She knocked. The door was opened by a man with thinning gray hair and black-framed glasses. By his clothes, Sheela guessed he was British, so she addressed him in English. 'I am the woman you've been seeking.' You can guess what *he* must have thought. Here's this strange woman with unwashed hair, filthy feet, clothes torn and dirty. She looked like a beggar. But he took her hand and drew her inside. With the door shut, he turned to her. 'My name is Nigel. I was about to have some tea. Will you join me?'

"Sheela hadn't eaten in days but she had to know first. 'Have you been seeking a woman?'

"'Let's start with tea,' Nigel said, 'and then I'll answer your question.' That's how Sheela learned Nigel Helmsley, an atheist-turned-Christian, had turned his back on his upward rise on the corporate-attorney ladder in order to pursue his dream of starting a foundation in India, with the purpose of freeing women and children from sexual slavery. He'd sold his assets, assembled a team of attorneys and investigators, and moved to Mumbai. But then he realized rescuing women from slavery was only half the battle. Without rehabilitation, these women were destined to return to their former way of life within months. He had his legal team, but he also needed a therapeutic team, a group of caring counselors who would teach these freed women how to take care of themselves. To feed and shelter them, but more importantly to help them heal from their psychological trauma. But finding people both qualified and committed to his Christian vision was harder than he'd imagined. The previous month, he'd been praying for God to bring him such a person. And since, despite his best efforts, he'd been unable to find one, he asked God to bring the right one to him. To his own doorstep.

"But even Nigel hadn't expected God to take his request quite so literally, so one of the first questions he asked Sheela was whether she had any formal education. Judging from the way she looked and smelled, he expected none at all. He was shocked when she told him she'd received her masters in clinical psychology from Cambridge University.

"That's when Nigel told her that the week before, acting on God's leading, he took the last of his own personal money to purchase a small walled compound on the outskirts of Mumbai to use as an aftercare home, trusting God would fill the position of aftercare supervisor in His way, in His time."

As Rees reached the end of his story, Ally became aware of something hard clutched in her hand. Looking down, she saw a clothespin. She turned it over in her palm, then closed her fingers over it again. "So Sheela works for him now?"

"She's our aftercare supervisor."

Ally nodded, unsure of what else to say. What would it be like to feel that God's grip on you was as real as her grip on this clothespin? She realized she tended to think of His care as a distant thing, remote as her own father's had been. Certainly not the up-close-and-personal variety Rees had just described. Even though she worshipped Him in her heart and with her music, even though she brought her concerns to Him, she realized that while she hoped for His help, she scarcely expected Him to take her requests so…personally.

Fingers numb from cold, she became aware of how long she'd kept Rees standing there, prying him with questions. Slightly embarrassed, she dropped the clothespin into the empty laundry basket. "Well, thanks for telling me about your friend. And thanks for helping me with my laundry."

"You're welcome." To her surprise, he didn't leave. Instead, he cleared his throat. "Actually, I had another reason for stopping by. A question I need to ask." His huff of breath appeared as a cloud of steam in the chilled air.

"Oh." She shifted the basket to her hip. "Would you like to come inside then? It's chilly out here."

He hesitated. "Is Jack inside?"

"He's sleeping."

"Let's talk here then. I'll only keep you another minute."

"Is something wrong?"

He paused again, and in the gap of his silence, her antennae began to vibrate. "The other day, when you were away, Jack and I were outside the Nielsens' house. I thought I saw someone watching us."

"Watching you?" Alarm tightened her voice. Watching Jack, he meant.

He nodded. "Loitering at the top of the road, looking down on us. You haven't noticed anything like that recently, have you?"

"No, but—" Something tickled her memory. That day at the park. She'd forgotten it until now. "Denny Lewis did a few weeks ago, when Jack was playing at The Castle."

Rees nodded. "Yeah, he mentioned that."

Surprise pinged inside her chest. "You've talked with Denny?"

"I was concerned." He drew in a breath. "There's no easy way to ask this, so I'm just going to ask straight out. Ally, what's the situation with Jack's dad?"

Her mouth went dry. "Why would you ask that?"

"Because if this creep is stalking Jack, chances are it's someone Jack knows."

A tiny measure of relief slivered through her. "Then it's not him. Jack's father doesn't even know he exists."

"You're sure?"

"Absolutely." She'd taken every possible precaution to make sure of it. And yet—

A thought needled her, the same one that came to her yesterday when she realized the torn photograph was something Kyle would do. But once again, she circled back to the same questions. If Kyle had been here for several weeks, where was he? Why had he not come to her before now? "What did he look like, the man you saw?"

"Medium height, maybe a goatee or a beard. I couldn't get a good look, the sun was wrong. He was wearing a cap and a bulky jacket. Denny Lewis said it sounded like the guy he saw."

She was aware of his scrutiny, his watching for her reaction. She quickly shook her head. Though the height was right, Kyle wouldn't have facial hair, it was against police regulations. "It's not him."

"Denny mentioned something else. A photograph?"

"He told you about that?"

"If the guy we saw isn't Jack's dad, it's possible he could be the same guy who broke into your home. Perhaps he took the photo, seeing an opportunity to frighten you."

"Well, it's working."Ally hugged her arms to herself, the cold heightening her fear.

Rees's expression softened. "I know. I'm sorry. But it's better you have your guard up. Try not to worry. Keep in mind guys like these are cowards at heart. We can take precautions.

Talk to Jack's principal. His teacher can keep an eye out while Jack's in school. When he's not, the rest of us will make sure nothing happens."

Rees said goodnight and Ally returned to the house, grateful for its enveloping warmth. Locking the back door behind her, she moved quickly to the front door to check that lock, too. When she was sure she and Jack were secure inside their home, she sank onto the couch, suddenly and overwhelmingly drained. Even the idea of picking up Lola, as she'd planned, offered no joy.

Admit it. Pushing a throw pillow beneath her head, she curled onto her side and brought her knees to her chest. *What Rees said freaks you out.* Nothing mattered more than knowing her son was safe. Wasn't that why she'd made the countless sacrifices over the years? Only now to learn a strange man had his eye on Jack. But who, and why? She didn't care for any of the possibilities.

A fragment of their conversation came to her. *Every struggle we face has a spiritual element, tempting us to lose our faith.*

In that moment, she wished she had faith like the Sheela person Rees so admired. Faith that would keep her strong and unafraid.

But then, she told herself, Sheela had only herself to think of. She had no son. Would even Sheela's faith be strong enough to carry her past the temptation to doubt God if it meant endangering the child she'd give her life for?

CHAPTER 32

When Ally arrived for work Monday morning, she'd no sooner tied on her apron than she knew something was wrong. Susan, the other morning waitress, passed by as she delivered an order to a family at the back booth at the same time that Sam dinged his bell. "Order up!"

"Be right back for that," Susan tossed over her shoulder at Sam, while giving Ally a harried look. "Ally, can you take care of the espresso bar? Customer's been waiting five minutes."

"Of course." She was already moving toward the alcove. "Where's Brittany?"

"Never showed."

Never showed? Unease rippled through Ally as she took her place behind the counter and asked the customer for his order. She had no chance to question Susan further until the breakfast rush slowed. Then she caught her co-worker as she wiped down the table at station eight. "Susan, what do you mean, Brittany never showed? Is she sick?"

Susan shrugged, pushing fingers through her short, black hair. "No idea. When Sam and I came in this morning, she wasn't here. And she's not answering her phone."

That didn't sound good. Unbidden, fear for Brittany swam to the surface. What if Jamie was worse than an animal-abuser? What if he'd hurt her? "I should go check on her." Susan didn't disagree. Ally glanced around the restaurant. Only one table awaiting their check, and the espresso line had slowed to a trickle. "Can you manage for half an hour if I run out to her place?"

"I've been managing, haven't I?"

"Thanks. Can I borrow your car?" Ally had walked to work that morning. Brittany's house was two miles outside of town.

Before Susan could answer, a cry arose from the family at the corner table. The toddler had tipped over the syrup carafe. The mom signaled frantically to Susan as she grabbed paper napkins to sop up the sticky mess. "Yes, go." Susan headed toward the table with a damp cloth. "Keys are in my purse, inside pocket."

The Westcotts lived on an acre of land hidden from the road by a stand of fir trees. As Ally pulled Susan's car into the paved circular drive, she noted Brittany's Jetta parked on the gravel spit beside the garage.

The two-storied house, painted a creamy yellow, had a wide front porch with a bench swing facing the road. At the door, Ally knocked—once, twice—and when that roused no answer, she rang the bell. Still no response. Where was Jamie? According to Brittany, he spent most of his time watching TV.

Glancing around, Ally stepped from the porch and into the flowerbed, trying to peer past the lace draping the living room window. No sign of anyone in either the living room or foyer, the only rooms she could see, but Brittany might be in her bedroom upstairs.

Ally stepped gingerly from the flowerbed to the porch and tried the front door. Locked. She circled the house. Maybe from the back she could see more. Brittany's mom was a master gardener. Flowering bushes interspersed with perennials dotted the immaculate backyard.

In the back corner, partially hidden by shrubbery, Ally caught a flash of movement. Drawing her coat more tightly around her, she moved toward it. As she rounded the shrubbery, she found Brittany hunched over a small, brown mound on the ground. At the sound of Ally's approach, her friend sat back on her haunches and looked up with a tear-stained face.

"It's Rosie." Brittany's voice emerged flat and strange. "She's dead."

Ally's stomach went queasy as she dropped to her knees, unmindful of the mud as she ran her hand over the cocker spaniel's smooth side. Vomit, flecked with white, pooled around the dog's open mouth.

"I think she was poisoned." Brittany stared at Rosie, whose brown eyes showed through slitted lids. Then she roused, as if suddenly aware of the reason behind Ally's presence. "Sorry about work. I should have called. But when I let Rosie out this morning and she didn't return, I had to find her. I went driving around, looking. I didn't see her until just a few minutes before you showed up."

Ally watched the strange, wooden way Brittany's face moved while she spoke. Did she suspect Jamie of this, too? When tasing Rosie hadn't killed her, had he poisoned her instead? Ally's insides trembled. "Where's Jamie, Brit?"

"I don't know," she said dully. "He never came home last night."

The sound of a vehicle pulling into the drive made them both look toward the road. Out of sight beyond the shrubbery, a car door slammed. Without a word, Ally took Brittany's unresisting hand. Together, they started toward the front of the house. As they rounded the corner, a black Chevy pickup came into view. On the porch, inserting his key into the lock, a man wearing jeans and a plaid flannel shirt. A goatee framed his chin, and though his hair was longer than Ally remembered, it was thick and blond. Just like Jack's.

Kyle. Fear lanced through her, heart racing against her ribs. *Fight or flight.* The phrase, learned long ago in high school psychology, ran absurdly through her head. It was all she could do to keep both feet planted on the ground. She squeezed Brittany's hand so hard, Brittany cried out. The man turned his head.

His surprise transformed into pleasure as he stepped off the porch, closing the distance between them. "Cadence," he said warmly, as if this were a happy tryst and not the nightmare that had haunted her for six years. "I've been wondering when you'd finally show up."

"Cadence?" Confusion pleated Brittany's forehead as she pulled her hand from Ally's. "No, this is Ally."

Ally found her voice. "Why are you here, Kyle?"

"Kyle?" Brittany's glance bounced between them. "Jamie, what's going on?"

"A reunion, baby." His eyes fastened on Ally. "Come on, Cadence, don't you have a kiss for your long lost brother?"

Brittany shook her head. "I don't understand."

"She never told you about her stepbrother?" His gaze never left Ally's face. "I suppose there are lots of things she never told you. Like who stole her virginity."

Ally felt the blood drain from her face, pooling somewhere above her heart.

Brittany flushed a dull red. "You're lying."

He shrugged. "Ask her if you don't believe me."

Ally couldn't bear to look in her friend's eyes. Her own fear and shock were too great, she couldn't handle Brittany's as well.

With a small cry, Brittany fled to the backyard. A moment later she reappeared, hugging a still and silent Rosie to her to her chest. She moved past them without a word. After carefully placing Rosie in the backseat of the Jetta, she slid behind the wheel. Her door slammed, the engine revved. Brittany roared out of the driveway, onto the road.

Ally's knees felt liquid as she looked at Kyle. "Please tell me you didn't kill that dog."

He shrugged. "That dog was a pain in the butt. But that's not why you're here, is it? To talk about unpleasant things." He took her hand. "It's so good to see you again."

His touch burned. She snatched her hand away. "How'd you find me, Kyle?"

"Took some doing," he admitted. "First time was easy, cell phone with GPS tucked away in your car. This time, well, a bit more of a challenge. Forced me to be methodical. But I was patient. And you see? My patience paid off."

She felt a chill as what he said sank in. When he'd found her at Drake University all those years ago, she'd blamed her father for betraying her secret. But there had been no betrayal. Her father had protected her trust. She closed her eyes as nausea clenched her stomach, sick with regret.

Opening her eyes, she found Kyle gazing at her with laser-like intensity. Her skin prickled as she realized she was alone with him on this vast property, no one else in sight. If she screamed, would anyone hear?

From her jeans pocket, her phone rang. She fumbled for it as she would a lifeline.

"Ally?" It was Susan.

"I'm so sorry, Susan!"

A pause. "Are you all right?"

"Yes!" Never taking her eyes off Kyle, she backed toward the car. He followed. She tightened her grip on the phone. He wouldn't dare do anything while she was still talking. Would he? "I'm coming right now."

"Did you find Brittany?"

"Yes, she's all right. Her dog died, and she's upset." She reached the car, opened the door, slipped inside. "She'll be taking the rest of the day off."

"We need you back here. Things got busy."

"I'm on my way—"

Kyle grabbed her wrist. The motion made her phone skitter across the passenger seat, out of reach. She sucked in a breath, ready to scream, when Kyle clamped a hand over her mouth. "Don't yell."

If she did, would Susan hear it and wonder what was wrong? Or had she already hung up? What if she bit Kyle's hand? Apparently reading her mind, Kyle shifted both hands to pin her shoulders against the seat. "Don't leave."

"Let go of me." She tried in vain to wriggle from his grip.

He leaned over. She smelled spearmint and stale cigarette smoke on his breath. "Do you have any idea how much I've missed you?" He moved one hand to cup her face. "So beautiful, even more than I remember. That's saying something." She coiled, preparing to lunge free when his next words made her freeze. "I see motherhood suits you." Her heart stopped. He pulled back to gaze, smiling, into her eyes. "So when do I get to meet him?"

She swallowed. "Meet…him?"

"Our son."

"My son, you mean."

His eyes hardened. "Don't play games with me." His thumb stroked her neck, just above her windpipe. "I know he's mine. He looks just like me. I can't wait to meet him."

Panic jolted her with strength she didn't know she had. Muscle and sinew bunched beneath her skin. She flexed, thrust him hard away. He stumbled back, she slammed the door, fumbled for the lock. His face reared up, twisted in a snarl, filling her window. Hands shaking, she shoved the car into drive and hurtled down the driveway.

Oh, God, he found me. Oh, God, he knows about Jack.

She burst onto the road. A horn blared. A red SUV bore down upon her. Ally stomped on the accelerator and twisted the wheel hard to the right. The car careened onto the narrow shoulder. Her head bounced off the steering wheel, and she rolled to a stop.

CHAPTER 33

Rees emerged from the barber shop, running a hand down the back of his bare neck. He'd told Stanley to cut his hair short as he was leaving for Mumbai in six days. It might be months before he saw a barber again.

Mumbai. He let that idea spool out, feeling a familiar kick in his gut at the thought of returning to the trenches with Nigel and Sheela. Normally that gut-kick was a sure sign of his eagerness to jump back into the saddle. This time, though, he was pretty sure it meant something else.

Jack. A stranger watching him. Rees felt no great assurance Denny Lewis could prevent the boy from getting hurt, if harm was what the man intended. If, on the other hand, Rees was to stay in Langley, *he* might be able to do something about it.

But he wasn't staying.

He couldn't. In a week's time, a jet would carry him halfway around the world. From there, he could do nothing to protect Jack. Nothing except pray. He wished the idea gave him more comfort.

Pushing these thoughts away, he set about finishing his errands. He always stocked up before returning to Mumbai from stateside. Today, Star Grocery was his final stop, where he picked up items impossible to find in Mumbai: Jif extra-crunchy peanut butter. Reynolds aluminum foil. Wrigley's chewing gum. Old Spice deodorant and multi-packs of Hanes underwear.

As he left Star Grocery, he silently admitted to the reason he'd kept this stop until last. His route back to his truck took him right past Jack's school. Some part of his brain recognized that a sunny day like this meant Jack might be outside at recess, where Rees could catch a reassuring glimpse of the boy.

Rees stopped at the fence and peered through the wire, looking for Jack. The sun shone boldly, leaves shimmied in the breeze lifting off the sound. The whole schoolyard writhed with movement, the very air vibrating with childish joy. A blond boy wearing Spiderman sneakers scampered past. For a second Rees thought it was Jack. But no, this boy was older, at least seven. Where was Jack? Inside with the teacher? On a beautiful day like this? Unlikely. Home sick, with Ally? Possible. Still, he frowned, uneasiness rippling through his abdomen.

I don't want to leave. The thought hit him like a blow to the head, the truth so strong he took a step back from the fence. He bumped against a metal garbage can anchored to the sidewalk. One of his plastic grocery bags snagged on a protruding piece of metal. It tore a hole, sending twelve sticks of Old Spice clattering to the pavement. He scooped them up and tucked them into another already bulging bag. As he straightened, a person hurtling down the sidewalk jostled his arm, loosened his grip on the bags. He had the impression of swirling, long dark hair as everything went flying, scattering his purchases once more across the pavement.

He held back a mild expletive while the woman gave a cry of apology. Not until he heard her voice did he lock eyes on her familiar form. Shock rippled through him. "Ally!" She whirled around, wide eyes on his. Her face was pale as paper. Her hair, pulled free from its usual barrette, tumbled across her shoulders. A red welt marked the center of her forehead. "What happened to you?" His mind leapt to his worst fear. "Where's Jack?"

Tears trembled on her lower eyelids, ready to spill. "Here, at school."

"You're sure?"

"I just called. They got him out of class. I'm taking him home." His question seemed to register. "Why wouldn't I be sure?"

"I looked for him on the playground just now and couldn't find him. What happened to you? How'd you get this bump?"

She touched two fingers to her forehead. "I'm fine." But when she raised her eyes to his, he saw they were dilated. From fear or concussion, he couldn't be sure.

"Tell me what happened."

"I can't. I have to get Jack."

"If you've already called the school, he's fine where he is. You can at least tell me what's wrong." Leaving his stuff on the sidewalk, he led her to a nearby bench and made her sit. She didn't resist, probably from shock. "Ally, I can't let you go until you tell me what happened." He took her ice-cold hands in his. "Talk to me."

She tucked her chin into the wooly scarf askew around her neck and drew a shuddering breath. "He's here."

Something cold chased down his spine. "Who's here?"

She swallowed. "Jack's father." She caught his eye and nodded. "You were right."

He didn't care about being right, he wanted to know why the presence of Jack's father had Ally terrified.

"He's been here all along. All this time, he's been playing his games. I had no clue. What am I going to do?" She bit her lips together.

Rees realized she was too rattled to give him any useful information. And a public bench was no place to carry out this conversation. Ally clutched a set of car keys. These he gently pried from her clenched fingers. "I'm going to drive you home—"

"No! I have to get back to work." She held out her hand. "Give me my keys, please."

Fat chance. "Ally," he said, speaking slowly, "here's what you're going to do. You're going to go inside the school and sign Jack out of class. Then you're going to call your boss and tell him you're taking a personal day. Let him think you're having a hard time with your dad's passing. Then you and I are going to go someplace where we can talk. We'll take Jack with us; he'll never be out of our sight. Okay?"

"But I've got Susan's car."

He didn't know who Susan was. It didn't matter. "We'll return her car as soon as we're done here, but I'm driving. Got it?"

She stared at him, her chest rising and falling with each rapid breath. When her shoulders slumped, he knew he'd won. "All right."

"Good girl." He squeezed her hand. "Now you go get Jack. I'll wait for you right here."

He watched her disappear inside the school. As soon as the door closed behind her, he pulled his phone from his pocket and was glad when Darcie picked up. "Hey, it's me. I'm going to be late for dinner."

"Something wrong?"

"I just ran into Ally." He paused. "I need to talk to her about Jack's father."

"Jack's father?"

"I'm afraid so." Rees scanned the perimeter of the playground, wondering if even now the man might be watching. "We know who's been stalking Jack."

CHAPTER 34

Ally signed Jack out of school, exchanging pleasantries with the secretary, a plastic smile on her lips, trying to act as if it was perfectly normal to remove a healthy child from his classroom in the middle of the day. All the while thinking, *Rees is a legal investigator. He knows the law. He'll know what to do. About Kyle. About Jack. About us. Please, God, let him know what to do.*

"What's going on, Mom?" Jack looked up at her as she led him from the school. "How come you're taking me home early?"

Ally gave him a tense smile and squeezed his hand, too rattled to find a plausible answer. She was still trying to come up with something Jack might swallow when he spotted Rees on the sidewalk, groceries gathered back into bags and piled neatly beside him. With a happy cry, Jack dropped her hand

and took off running. He threw himself at Rees, who caught him up off the ground and hoisted him into a bear hug.

Her son's joy turned her heart inside out.

"Hey, big guy," Rees said. "You up for a field trip to the beach?"

"The beach?"

"Too nice a day to be cooped up inside. Even your mom's taking the day off work. So whatd'ya say?"

Jack looked from Rees to Ally, clearly trying to process this unprecedented event. "Is it really okay?"

"It is if we say so," Rees said heartily. "Right, Mom?"

She hoped her smile didn't wobble too badly. "Right." She lifted her eyes to Rees's but then quickly looked away because what she saw there made her want to dissolve into a puddle on the sidewalk. He wore his worry plainly, but beneath that she glimpsed something more. Something deeper, stronger… something she didn't dare to think about in this moment.

They returned to the side street where she'd left Susan's car. With Rees behind the wheel, they found his car, left his purchases inside, then went to the bistro, where Ally returned her coworker's keys and requested the rest of the day off from Sam. Her boss took one look at her face, muttered something about taking time to grieve, and shooed her out the door.

Rees waited for her on the sidewalk, Jack balanced on his wide shoulders. Her son wore a gleeful grin at finding himself at this new height. Ally said nothing, too consumed by fear as she fell into step beside Rees. They walked the few blocks to Langley's rocky beach, the silence punctuated only by Jack's occasional happy exclamation. Glancing up at his face, Ally felt a pulse of gratitude her boy was, at least for now, oblivious to the danger at their door.

They left the pavement, their pace slowing on the coarse sand. The shore curved in a half-moon. On their left, one of Langley's posh hotel resorts overlooked the water, but this wasn't tourist season so it stood eerily quiet. Ahead, a lone fisherman stood knee-deep in the water, spooling out his line. Otherwise, they were alone.

Rees swung Jack from his shoulders to the ground, then crouched to look into his eyes. "Want to play a game?"

Jack nodded, all ears.

"Here's what you do. Find as many sand dollars as you can on this beach. For every one you collect, I'll give you a *real* dollar. How does that sound?"

"A dollar!" Jack shouted.

"You heard me."

"What if I find a hundred?"

"I dare you to find *two* hundred. Here." He pulled a wadded plastic bag from his back pocket. "Put them in this bag. But here's the thing. None of them will count until you've found all you can. That's why it's a game. You can come back to get a new bag to fill. But once you quit, that's it. So you're going to want to find as many as you can, even if it takes you all afternoon. Just don't go anywhere your mom and I can't see you. You have to stay on this beach and not run too far ahead. Got it?"

"Got it!" Jack took off at a sprint, plastic bag flapping in his hand.

Ally watched his small feet kicking up tufts of sand in his wake. It would be at least an hour before he wandered back to them, bag overflowing with sand dollars. Even with worry pressing on her shoulders, she found a smile for Rees, who'd thought of a way to keep Jack within sight and yet out of earshot. "Impressive."

He shrugged. "Job requirement, thinking outside the box."

She shook her head. "You do realize this beach contains thousands of sand dollars. You'll go broke before we're finished."

"So long as it keeps him happy and occupied. Put the money in his college fund if you think it's too much." Already Jack was bending and dropping sand dollars into the bag. "Come on, let's walk. We'll follow at a distance. You talk, I'll listen."

"I don't know where to begin." She felt glad for the bracing wind whistling past them, the occasional screech of a gull. She didn't know if she could say anything at all into pure silence.

"Why not start with why you're so scared." They walked several more paces, but she couldn't push the words past her lips. He glanced at her. "I know it's hard, but you need to talk about it. For Jack's sake. Whatever you have to say, you know I've heard worse. Seen worse. You don't have to be afraid anymore. Talk to me."

Something like relief bloomed inside. Of course. Of all people, Rees would understand. She drew a deep breath. "I'd gone away to college, Drake University. No one knew I was there except my father. I'd gone there to get away from Kyle."

"That's his name?"

"Yes. Kyle Wylie."

"Why'd you need to get away?"

"He was stalking me. Following me."

"He was your boyfriend?"

"Stepbrother, boyfriend. For about a year, he was my everything." The admission scraped raw inside her mouth. She looked at Rees and saw he understood. "When I tried to end our relationship, he wouldn't let go. I was scared. I thought I could get away from him if I just disappeared." The problem with running away, she thought, is you have to keep running. You're never free, not completely. Even after she'd come here, to Langley, when years had passed and she began to feel safe, safety and freedom were mere illusions. Kyle had been behind her, hunting her down. "I was wrong."

With sand crunching beneath her feet, she cast her mind back to the time before today when she'd last seen Kyle. She was at Drake, on her way back to the dorm after spending the evening at Josh's. The mild fall had begun its descent toward winter, with forecasters predicting snowfall by the weekend. Josh promised her a snowball fight in the Loop if the weathermen were right.

As she started down the path linking the two residence halls, a flash of movement turned her head. It was dusk, and the parking lot between Mac and Ballard was crowded with cars and poorly lit. Her gaze landed on her own faded red Honda parked beneath one of the few streetlamps. And beside it, a black Chevy pickup truck.

She stopped walking. It couldn't be. Could it? Her heart scudded inside her chest. Her breath came faster, appearing as quick puffs in the wintry air. After a moment, she resumed walking, starting toward the truck, thinking she would check the plates, just to be sure. But at the edge of the lot, she stopped, chiding herself. *Don't be ridiculous. He doesn't know you're here. Hundreds of people drive black Chevy pickup trucks.* Squaring her shoulders, she continued on. Wasn't that why she'd come to Drake in the first place? To leave all that paranoid nonsense behind. Not that there hadn't been good reason for the paranoia, but still.

Even so, she kept a wary eye on the parking lot as she closed the gap to the dorm, until a dry rustle behind her, much closer now, made her wheel. Heart pounding, she scanned the pathway, wishing she'd accepted Josh's offer to walk her to her door. The crackle came again, from the direction of the wrought-iron trash can positioned beside a laurel bush large enough for a man to hide behind. Without warning, a squirrel exploded from the mouth of the can. She screamed. The squirrel gave a startled shiver before racing away.

She ran the rest of the way to her dorm and yanked the door open. Stepping inside, she welcomed its familiar comfort: the shabby upholstered furniture positioned in groups of twos and threes throughout the common area, a chess game left out on the coffee table. The fire in the gas fireplace, lending its glow to the room.

As she paused to unwind her scarf from her neck, a man peered from the side of an easy chair facing the fire. Comfort vanished like smoke up the chimney when he spoke. "Hello, Cadence."

Dread claimed her. She clutched her scarf to her chest, like a shield. "Kyle." She barely managed the word, so parched was her mouth.

Kyle rose in graceful motion from the chair and moved toward her. "Why did you leave without saying goodbye?" The pucker above his eyes made him look honestly wounded, bewildered she would do such a thing.

She licked impossibly dry lips. "What are you doing here?" How did he find her?

"I missed you." He stood before her now, cupped her face in his hands. "You have no idea how much. I came to see you. Had to see you." The side of his mouth tipped up in the way that once made her insides melt. "Aren't you going to ask how I am?"

She swallowed. "How are you?"

"Not so good, actually, but I've done my best to carry on, even passed my exams at the academy. Shows how determined I can be, when I put my mind to it. That's why I haven't been able to come until now. But I made it into the K-9 Unit. Even missing you the way I have, I made it." He smiled. "Aren't you happy for me?"

"Of course."

He lowered his head. She submitted to the light brush of his mouth on hers. "Ahhh." He shuddered with pleasure. "I've missed that. Haven't you?"

She stepped from his embrace. "Please, Kyle, not here." She cast an anxious look around. If someone should see her with him, how would she explain to Josh?

"Where then? Your room?" When his eyes brightened, she realized her mistake.

"We can't." Trying to undo the damage, she lied. "My roommate's studying, she doesn't like me bringing people up." In truth, Maggie welcomed any excuse to keep from studying and was probably at this very moment out somewhere trying to start a party. But the lie formed easily on her tongue. Kyle had taught her well.

But it was too late. Kyle took her hand, leading her toward the stairs, the cool twinkle in his eyes telling her he knew better. She should have known she couldn't fool a master of deceit. "Let's just check, shall we?" He continued in a soothing tone, as if coaxing a reluctant dog from its cage. "If she's home, you can introduce me. Then we'll find another place for some quality time together."

She allowed herself to be led. They passed two girls on the stairs, another in the hall, none of whom she knew beyond a passing acquaintance. None whom she could stop with a glance, silently communicating something was wrong. One girl carried a bag of freshly popped microwave popcorn. Its trailing buttery scent made her stomach lurch into her throat.

As she and Kyle reached the fourth floor and approached her room, her brain remained in deep freeze. *Please, Maggie, please be home.* The half-prayer formed as she slipped her key into the lock. "Maggie?" she called, pushing the door open. But the darkness revealed what she already knew. Maggie wasn't home.

"Too bad." Kyle pulled her into the room and shut the door. "I'd have liked to meet one of your new friends. Would still like to meet that other one, actually."

"Other one?"

"That guy you were with tonight. Noticed you've been spending a lot of time with him. Made me a wee bit jealous, actually."

A chill descended, shivering down her spine. He knew about Josh? She tried to bluff. "Oh, you mean Imraj?" She named her biology T.A., with whom she actually had spent an hour at the library that afternoon. "He's just helping me with an assignment. You know how I always sucked at science."

He blinked slowly at her. *What, you think I'm stupid?* "I was referring to Josh."

He even knows his name? She gulped air, tamping down panic as Kyle cupped her cheek with one hand, stroking it with his thumb. She felt the ragged edge of a hangnail as he rubbed back and forth against her skin and fought the urge to whimper. His mouth descended. He kissed her thoroughly. After a long moment, her unresponsiveness made him withdraw.

"What's the matter?" The deep brown eyes searched hers. "You used to like this. Used to be we couldn't get enough of it. Used to be you couldn't keep your hands off me. What's changed?"

I've changed. "It's over, Kyle." How many times did she have to say it?

"For you, maybe. Never for me." He lowered his voice. For the first time she recognized a hint of menace in his tone. "You hear me? Never."

Now real fear lanced through her. "I was just a kid. You took advantage of me. Can't you see that? I didn't know what I was doing." *But you did.* To her horror, tears leaked from her lids.

Seeing her tears, his gaze turned tender. With his tongue he licked the wetness from her cheeks. "Advantage?" His mouth moved to her lips. "I'd say you came quite willingly," he murmured between kisses. "Don't try to deny it. You enjoyed it. I was there. I remember it well."

She shut her eyes as shame curled low in the bottom of her belly. "Please."

"You said you loved me, Cadence. God knows I love you." He tugged her toward her narrow twin bed covered by one of her mother's quilts. "We can have that again, you know. You just have to be willing to try." He came down on top of her. She struggled against him, but he was strong, passion making him stronger. He tugged at her clothes. She cried out. He smothered her mouth with his own. Realizing her struggles only excited him, she finally went limp.

When it was over, he pressed his face into her neck, slick with tears. To her horror, he began to cry. "Oh, God, Cadence, don't you know how much I love you? No matter where you go, no matter what you do, I'll still love you. I've tried to forget you, but I can't." He'd raised himself above her to gaze into her eyes. Tears ran from his face, falling to mingle with hers. "And I never will."

CHAPTER 35

Her secret bared, Ally glanced at Rees, expecting disgust twisting his features. But his eyes reflected only care and concern. Inside, she felt a lift of relief. Rees was right, she had needed to tell someone.

"And then you discovered you were pregnant?" he prompted.

"Yes." She'd stopped taking the pill when she broke up with Kyle, figuring she didn't need it anymore.

"But you didn't tell him?"

"No. He left messages on my phone every day, but he was too busy with his work to come see me again, so I was able to hide my pregnancy. For a while anyway." She was afraid of what would happen if he knew he'd fathered a child. Become as obsessive about it as he was about her? "But I knew it was only a matter of time. Pretty soon he'd come back, and he'd know. I was so sick I couldn't even get out of bed in the morning, much less go to class." She closed her eyes, remembering Maggie's smug remarks. She'd assumed the father was Josh, naturally. As for Josh—well, it was better not to think about him, how hurt and angry he'd been when she refused to see him anymore without a word of explanation. But better for him to assume the worst about her than for him to know the truth.

It struck her, then, the irony of choosing Drake University, with its motto of *Veritas*. Truth. Not for one minute of her short tenure there had she lived a life of truth.

"A month after Kyle left Drake, I came up with a plan." A second plan, much like the first. As the end of the semester approached, while everyone else studied for finals and anticipated Christmas break, she plotted her escape route. Because as impossible as it was to think of herself as a mother, it was ludicrous to consider Kyle as a father. She entertained no illusions. Fatherhood would not change Kyle. "I researched online until I found a place where I could have my baby. I mailed a letter to my father saying I had to leave but not explaining why. Asking him not to look for me but telling him I would call him when I could. And I left." With only Lola and a small bag of clothes, she'd boarded a Greyhound bound for Angel's Alcove in Mt. Vernon, Illinois.

"Until the moment I held Jack in my arms, I thought about returning to Spring Falls. But once I had Jack, I realized there was no way I could subject my child to Kyle. I'd realized by then what a big place America was, how easy it would be to disappear. Even knowing how determined Kyle would be to find me, I figured if I put up enough roadblocks, it might take a while. Maybe I'd even get lucky and he never would."

She'd chosen Langley because of its remoteness. Even with Kyle's access to law enforcement databases, she figured he wouldn't think to look for her there, so long as she flew beneath the radar. She used a derivative of her middle name. She never left the country, renewed her driver's license, or got insurance. When she stumbled on Penny's advertisement for a tenant willing to do yard work in exchange for reduced rent, she knew she'd found their new home.

"So what happened today?" he asked.

She told him about Rosie, the shock of Brittany's boyfriend turning out to be Kyle. "He must have been biding his time." She could imagine his private amusement these past few weeks as he waited for the right moment to let her know he'd found her. Mocking her, mocking her friend. Poor Brit. To know Kyle had used her in such a heartless way brought a sour taste to the back of Ally's tongue. "Now that I know he knows where I am, I don't know what to do." Everything in her cried, *Run!* But where?

Chicago. The answer came like a flash of light. Gina's invitation now appeared as a godsend. The chance to escape this place, to start over again. But she'd told Gina no. Was it too late to change her mind?

Jack chose that moment to return to them, lugging a bag bursting with sand dollars. "I need another bag!" he gasped, dropping the first bag at Rees's feet.

Rees fished a second bag from his pocket, handed it to Jack without a word. Jack ran back to the place he'd left. Rees waited until he was well out of earshot to speak. "I promise I won't let Kyle hurt you again." A muscle beneath his scar moved as his jaw hardened. When he met her gaze, she took a measure of courage in the resolve she found there.

CHAPTER 36

He'd heard a hundred worse stories, seen many of them with his own eyes. Every day, in the course of his work, he personally encountered women who dealt with the aftermath of trauma inflicted on them by men. Until now, Rees would have said he'd seen it all. But Ally's story ignited in him an angry flame he hadn't felt since his first brothel raid, when he smelled for himself the squalid stench of evil. Ally didn't need to fill in every detail. He knew what men were capable of.

He thought he did a pretty good job of hiding his reaction. His gut told him it would distress Ally if she knew how her story disturbed him. How it made him want to inflict physical pain on this whack-job, Kyle Wylie. So he adopted a practical approach that seemed to calm her. Or maybe it was simply the relief of sharing her secret after all these years. He knew from experience, people weren't meant to shoulder burdens alone.

By the time he and Ally were ready to leave Langley's beach, Jack had managed to collect one hundred and sixty-seven sand dollars. As promised, Rees paid him for each one. Ally had shaken her head with a tiny smile when Rees stopped at the nearest ATM and counted the appropriate number of bills into Jack's open palm. She'd tucked most of it into her tote to deposit in an account for Jack, promising her son he could use a portion of it on a shopping spree sometime soon.

They didn't talk much on their return to the cottage. Rees got her and Jack settled with Moses as their temporary guardian. Then he went home and called the law offices of Culpepper, Wright & Spelling, making an appointment with his old college roommate for the next morning. Sleep eluded Rees that night. He kept replaying portions of what Ally told him and awakened several times, once even going to his window to look out toward Ally's cottage. There, a single light burned through the night.

At dawn he was up, half an hour later on his way to the Clinton ferry terminal. On the mainland, he hit morning rush hour, but his early start afforded him plenty of time. If everything went as he hoped, he'd make it back to Langley before Ally got off her shift that afternoon. She'd promised she'd not send Jack back to school until they figured out a plan to keep Jack safe. Both Paul and Darcie had promised anything to help.

Clouds scuttled across the sky and a smattering of rain sprinkled the pavement as Rees pulled into the lot beneath the Seattle high-rise. He took an elevator to the twenty-second floor. He gave his name to the receptionist and had just plucked a *Newsweek* from the coffee table when Andrew Spelling's office door opened.

"Holy smokes! It *is* you!" In two long strides Andy crossed the room and wrapped him in a bear hug. "When I saw your name on my schedule, I thought Kim must have spiked my morning coffee." He stepped back, gripping Rees's arms. "I thought you were in India, man."

"Home on leave. But heading back next week, actually."

"Well, I'm glad to see you. It's been too long." He ushered him into his office and shut the door. "How about some coffee?"

"Sounds great."

While Andy depressed the intercom button to request the coffee, Rees took stock. His old roommate's office was decorated with heavy furniture and fine prints on mocha walls. The view demanded attention, overlooking Elliott Bay with both the Cascade and Olympic Mountain ranges in view. A black walnut desk the size of Rees's first car took up most of the space in front of the window. Closer to the door, four red leather club chairs clustered around an oval coffee table. Fat legal tomes lined two entire walls. Everything spoke of prosperity. But he was relieved to note Andy himself, wearing a simple white oxford shirt, dark slacks, and a gold wristwatch, exuded the same relaxed, ah-shucks self-assurance Rees remembered from their college days.

"So." Andy leaned back in his chair, crossing one leg over the other knee. "I doubt you've come all this way merely for a social call. What can I do for you?"

Andy always had been one to cut straight to the chase. "I'm looking for a favor."

"Tell me how I can help."

"I have a friend who's in trouble."

Andy tilted forward. "What kind of trouble?"

While Andy took notes on an iPad, Rees sketched Ally's history through to yesterday's discovery that Kyle Wylie was in Langley. Twice he had to stop when his words grew heated. "He's obsessed with her," Rees concluded grimly, "and he's not going to stop stalking her unless we can find a way to make him stop."

Andy pursed his mouth and took Rees's measure. "And what exactly would you like from me?"

"A background check. Your resources here are better than mine. I figure the more info we have on this creep, the better our ammo."

Andy jotted notes. "Full name?"

Rees gave it and the birth date Ally had supplied him with. "One other thing. My friend has a son. Wylie's been stalking him, too."

Andy gave the slightest lift to his eyebrows. "Know why he'd be interested in the boy, other than as a way to get to the mom?"

"Jack is his son. He must have figured it out. Not too hard, once he laid eyes on him. Jack looks just like him."

"All right." Andy tapped out a few more keystrokes. "There. I just sent it to my investigator. He should have something to us by the end of today. I'll email you the file as soon as I get it." He placed the iPad on the table before leaning back in his chair, hands clasped behind his head. He shot Rees a knowing half-grin. "I don't suppose this friend of yours is something more than just a friend?"

The question caught Rees off-guard. An unaccustomed flush ignited inside his chest. "No. Why?"

Andy's grin broadened. "Just asking. Been an awful long time since Julie."

The arrival of coffee forestalled Rees's reply. He was still searching for a change of subject when Andy found one for him. "So how's life in Mumbai treating you?" He poured the steaming brew into heavy white mugs.

Rees was only too glad to follow his lead. "Keeps me busy."

Andy squinted at him, smiling faintly. "Mumbai can't be the kind of place you'd want to raise a family. Ever think about coming back? Taking the bar, hanging out a shingle? You wanted to do that once."

"Still crosses my mind sometimes," Rees admitted. "But only on the tough days. Most times, I know I'm where I'm supposed to be."

Andy eyed him for a long moment before reaching for an additional packet of sweetener. "Goes without saying, but if you ever change your mind, there's a place for you here."

Rees only nodded, preferring not to pursue this line of discussion. His glance snagged on a framed family photo on the desk. From this angle, he could catch only a portion of it. "Is that Kim? How is she?"

"Pretty good. Got two little ones now, another due in February." He handed over the photo. Rees looked at the family foursome. Handsome dad, smiling mom, two blue-eyed blond children, one girl, one boy. The perfect American family. "They're beautiful." Unanticipated longing tugged at him as he passed back the picture.

"Thanks." Andy gazed down at the photo, something unreadable clouding his features. He started to say something, but his buzzing intercom cut him off.

"Sorry to interrupt," said his assistant, "but Kim's on line one."

"Thanks, Pam." To Rees, he said with a wink, "Speak of the devil, I'd better take this."

"Sure." He stood and crossed to the window, where he had a clear view of the Space Needle and Vashon and Bainbridge Islands. He tracked the green-and-white ferries inching like slugs in purposeful migration.

"Hey, babe, what's up?" Andy listened a few minutes. When he spoke again, his voice changed tenor. "How is he now? Was he hurt?" Rees turned to look at his friend, whose forehead creased with concern. "What did Dr. Benson say?" A longer pause, Andy's expression smoothing somewhat. "Well, okay. Hang in there. We'll talk about it tonight, figure out a plan. I'll be home early." Then, meeting Rees's gaze, he added, "By the way, you'll never guess who's standing in my office taking in the view. Rees Davies." Kim exclaimed something unintelligible. "Hold on," Andy said, "I'll ask." To Rees he said, "She wants to know if you can join us for dinner."

He hesitated. On the one hand, he would love to spend an evening with these old friends. On the other, he wanted to return to Ally as soon as possible in case Wylie started causing trouble. He deliberated a moment longer before striking what he hoped was a compromise. "As long as I can still catch the seven o'clock ferry."

After another brief consultation with Kim, Andy hung up. "We'll make it an early dinner. I'll knock off around three-thirty. We can still have you on your way to the ferry at a decent hour."

"You sure that's okay? Sounds like you might need some time with Kim."

Andy blew out his cheeks. "It's Jameson, our three-year-old. He has autism."

The word hit Rees like a cold wave. He deliberated how to respond. *I'm sorry,* didn't seem right. Neither did, *It must be hard.* He finally settled for, "How long have you known?"

"They diagnosed him last summer. We feel fortunate we caught it so young. As you've probably heard, early intervention is critical. But it's been a rough go. We have him in a specialized preschool, but Jameson's a runner. Any chance he gets, he escapes. This time he was halfway down the block before his teacher caught up."

"Maybe we should skip dinner."

"No. Something a little more normal is exactly what Kim needs today. She wants you to come. Please. It'll be good for all of us."

Chapter 37

"Morning, Sam." Ally hung her handbag and coat on the peg inside the door.

Her boss merely grunted, not looking up from eggs frying on the griddle. She paused in tying on her apron. "Everything all right?"

He flipped a couple of pieces of French toast. "Guess you haven't heard the news. Brittany quit."

Remorse squeezed her heart. She'd hardly given her co-worker another thought since fleeing her house the day before. But Brittany had nearly as much reason to be traumatized by what had happened as she did. "Did she say why?"

"Only that she couldn't work here anymore. Said she'd stay through her shift today, but then—*pfttt*. She's gone." He paused as the espresso machine roared from the alcove. "Now I gotta find me another barista, and fast."

"I'll go talk to her."

"Please. She won't tell me nothing, not even when I said I'd bump her pay fifty cents an hour." He shook his head.

Entering the alcove, Ally blew out a breath, like an athlete preparing for an event. Susan leaned an elbow on the counter as she waited for Brittany to complete an order. Brittany was dressed in black, her face drawn into a tight mask. Ignoring Ally, Brittany handed over a steaming espresso drink. Susan brushed past Ally with the drink in hand, her glance holding something Ally had never seen before—interest, or maybe curiosity. Unease settled on Ally's shoulders. Brittany would almost certainly have figured out Kyle was Jack's father. Had she told Susan?

"Hey, Brittany," she ventured. Brittany's eyes were red, her face puffy and gray, as if she hadn't slept at all. "How are you?"

"How do you think I am?" Her voice sounded rough, like it had been brushed over with sand. "My dog died, and I found out my boyfriend has been lying to me. He's gone now, by the way."

"Gone?"

"Took off. Left the island. Didn't even give me the pleasure of throwing him out."

Ally said nothing.

Brittany lifted her eyebrows, hostility barely concealed. "You don't believe me?"

"That he's left the island? I—well, no. I don't." She knew Kyle and his ways too well for that.

Brittany turned her back and scrubbed at the steaming spout. "He specifically wanted me to tell you he was leaving."

I'll bet he did. He wanted her to let her guard down so he could catch her unawares again. Well, she wasn't going to let that happen. Not this time.

She gazed at her friend, who looked as if she was barely holding it together. "I'm awfully sorry, Brit. Honestly, I had no idea who Jamie really was."

"Of course you didn't." Brittany put on fake cheeriness. "How could you?"

Ally eyed her warily. She had the sense of treading through a minefield, aware any misstep could blow up in her face. "Have you—have you called your parents?"

She barked a laugh. "To tell them what, exactly? That the guy I was living with in their house without their permission used me to get to my co-worker? And he also, by the way, killed their beloved pet?"

"You should tell them."

Brittany's complexion grew mottled. "Now you're telling me what to do?"

Ally tried another tack. "Sam says you're quitting."

Brittany didn't respond.

Ally came around the counter and laid a hand on Brittany's arm. "Don't make things worse by quitting, Brit. Don't let Kyle win like this."

Brittany moved away from Ally's touch. "This isn't about Jamie, or *Kyle*, or whatever his name is." Her voice took on that same flat, strange tone she'd used yesterday as they crouched together over Rosie's lifeless form. "Look, Ally, I like you. You've been a good friend to me. But this thing with you and Jamie… your own stepbrother. I'm sorry, but that's just weird."

A beat as this sank in. Brittany was quitting because of *her*. "But you need your job." She thought fleetingly of telling her about Chicago but changed her mind. "What will you do?"

Brittany moved from behind the counter, began wiping down the tables out front. "I'll find something."

Ally followed. "What about Sam?"

"That's his problem. I've got my own to deal with." Her voice raised a pitch toward meanness. "And my guess is, so do you."

Chapter 38

Standing at her kitchen counter, Ally diced vegetables into fine, uniform pieces, the way Sam had taught her. Tomatoes first. Then bell pepper and onions. The rhythmic motion soothed her somehow. On the stove, ground beef simmered in taco sauce, sending out tendrils of zesty aroma. In the other room, Jack sprawled on the floor watching *Finding Nemo*, his head propped on Moses' broad side. She offered a quick prayer of thanks Jack was unaware of the drama playing out around him. She intended to keep it that way.

He had spent most of the day "helping" Paul at the shop. She'd called the school first thing and explained because of her father's recent death, they needed some extended family time together. Not exactly the truth, but not far from it either. In any case, the school hadn't questioned it. Neither had Jack, who was only too delighted to spend a "field trip" day with Mr. Paul.

She looked at the stove clock. 6:15. After Rees dropped them at home yesterday, she'd left a frantic message, telling Gina she wanted to join them in Chicago after all. But Gina hadn't returned her call. Ally struggled to tamp down her rising panic. Had something happened to either Gina or the baby? Had Leif thought better about allowing strangers to join his new-formed family? If Chicago didn't work out, what other option would she have?

Her thoughts flipped back to Brittany. Her friend's hostility had rattled her badly. She felt guilty, responsible not only for Brittany quitting but for Sam losing his barista. On top of that, worry swirled through her brain like leaves in a dust devil. Kyle hadn't left Langley for good. No way. Which left her feeling wound tight. She'd lost sight of the enemy. Who knew when or where he might appear next? Or what he might try to do.

Making a meal had helped to keep her anxiety in check. Then it occurred to her she hadn't heard from Rees, either. He'd said he wanted to check out a few things, but she had no idea what that meant. He'd promised to call. What had he been doing all day?

One thing she did know: She trusted him, and that trust felt good. Not just good but *right* in a way nothing else did just now. As if Rees's being here in this time and place was meant to be.

A clatter from outside caught her ear. She tensed and looked out the window, but only saw a gull flapping away, likely having dropped a clamshell onto the shed. Moses remained sprawled serenely on the carpet. She was thankful Rees had insisted they borrow him for a few days. His presence comforted her. He'd not allow anyone near the house without alerting her first. Still, she kept her phone within easy reach, prepared to dial 911 at the first sign of Kyle.

"What are you looking at, Mom?" Jack asked from the floor.

"Nothing." She forced a smile. For Jack's sake, she had to keep pretending everything was fine. She eyed him as he wrapped an arm around Moses' neck. "You like having Moses here, don't you?"

He grinned and nodded. "How long can we keep him?"

"Only for another week or so."

His face puckered in a frown. "When we give him back, can we get a dog of our own?"

"We'll see, Bubba." She returned to her chopping and dicing. "Dogs are nice, but they're also a lot of work."

"I can help."

"We'll talk about it later, okay?" A debate with her five-year-old over the pros and cons of dog-ownership was the last thing she needed tonight.

She and Jack ate picnic-style in front of the fire while Moses presided Sphinx-like beside them. Afterwards, she read to Jack from a *Jigsaw Jones* book before tucking him in. Then the house grew quiet. She considered going to bed but felt too unsettled for sleep, her mind filled with too many questions, her fate shadowed with too many unknowns.

Moses snored before the fire as she turned on some Elgar, hoping the music might relax her. The rich strains of a cello concerto had just begun to curl into the room, when Moses lifted his head and uttered a low rumble. Her breath caught. A light tap sounded on the front door. Moses sprang to his feet, growling. Then came a welcome sound, Rees's voice. "Ally? It's me."

Her muscles relaxed as she hastened to let him in. It had started to drizzle, speckling Rees's light windbreaker. His broad shoulders were hunched against the chill.

He stepped inside. "Sorry to stop by so late. Yes, Moses, I see you." He stroked the Lab's head as the dog pushed his snout into Rees's palm. To Ally he said, "I apologize for not calling first."

"That's okay. I thought maybe you'd forgotten about us."

"I would never do that."

She stood just a few feet from him, so close she could smell his skin. For a long moment, they regarded each other in silence. When the pause stretched into awkwardness, Ally moved to the fireplace. She tossed another log onto the fire, the room flaring into brightness as the wood flamed. "Can I get you something? Cup of coffee, glass of wine? I was just thinking of having one myself."

"Which, coffee or wine?"

She smiled. "Wine."

"I could go for that."

She fetched a bottle of syrah and two glasses and set them on the coffee table. She felt his eyes on her as she poured a measure of the burgundy liquid into both glasses. Her nervousness mounted. "Kyle left town." The words fell between them, too abrupt. She gave him his wine, hoping he didn't notice how her hand trembled. "Brittany told me today. I don't believe it, of course."

"Smart girl." Rees nodded. She felt a strange, small uplift at his approval. "This guy won't stop harassing you until we force him to."

She bit her lip, not liking the sound of that. "What did you find out today?"

Rees sat on the couch, giving Moses an absent pat as the big dog settled at his feet. "A friend of mine ran a background check. Wylie got kicked off his K-9 squad three months ago. Authority issues. Guess his captain finally had enough." Rees adopted a businesslike tone, speaking in terse spurts as if reading from a bulleted list. "Like any good sociopath, he knows how to manipulate the system. Same qualities that make him a menace to society also made him a good cop. Determination, quick wits. Knowing how to lie his way through a psych exam. He looked good on paper. Unfortunately, the real deal's a lot more scary. As you know." His blue eyes delved into hers. "He spent six years tracking you down."

Ally set down her glass and rubbed the goose bumps that exploded on her arms. The thought of Chicago as a refuge slammed into her, an almost physical force. Why hadn't Gina called back? Ally wanted to tell Rees she had a plan but knew she couldn't until she talked to Gina. "What do you think he'll do next?"

"I don't know." His frown told her he didn't like any of the possibilities that came to mind. "But he'll make himself known, I'm certain of it. And you need to be ready for him when he does." He continued to eye her steadily. In the depths of his gaze, she found a melding of steely resolve and compassion. "The man raped you, Ally. Don't forget that. That's the bad news. But there's good news in that, too, because it means you've got some leverage, some serious legal recourse. That's how we're going to get him to leave you alone for good."

A chill raced down her body. "Legal recourse?"

"You can take him to court."

She looked down at the hearth, where flames leapt and danced. "I can't do that."

A short, thick silence. "Why not?"

"Because of Jack." Her voice scraped low along the bottom of her throat. "I can't let him know the reason he was born is because his father raped me."

"Ally." Rees stared at her. "What Kyle Wylie did to you is not about you or Jack. This man committed sexual assault. That's a *crime*. You're the one holding the cards here, not him."

No. Her spirit recoiled at the very idea. Her son existed because she was the victim of violence. What kind of damage might that knowledge do to a child? She thought of Jack getting into trouble on the playground. How much worse would it be if he knew what kind of blood ran in his veins? No matter what Rees said, she wouldn't set Jack up for that. Besides, it was her word against Kyle's. She had slept with him for months before he raped her. How would she make anyone believe the final time had been against her will? "What about a restraining order?"

"Restraining orders are a joke." Standing, he set his glass beside hers and began pacing the space between the kitchen and front door. "If the man's determined enough to follow you halfway across the country to exert his domination over you, what good will a piece of paper do?"

The first Elgar concerto came to an end. She stared down at the hearthrug, where a corner had begun to unravel. Silence gaped between her and Rees. Not until the next concerto started did she speak. "But to have him convicted for raping me, won't I have to prove it?"

"The burden of proof does rest with the prosecution, but given Wylie's history, that shouldn't be too difficult." Rees came to her, standing so close she could see the faint flecks of indigo in his eyes. "Do you really want to live like this the rest of your life? Always worried he might show up? Afraid he might do something to Jack? Why not confront him and be done with it?"

Ally's flesh tingled as he took her hands in his. His skin was warm and surprisingly soft.

His grip tightened slightly. "I told you before. Men like Wylie are cowards. Bullies who pick on people they think are weaker than them. That's why he took advantage of you when you were a teenager. Because he could. But you're not a teenager anymore, Ally." His gaze held hers. "You understand that, don't you?"

She stepped away from his touch, hugging her arms across her chest.

He sighed. "Has it occurred to you stealing a photograph and returning it to you torn in half is just the kind of manipulative stunt Wylie would pull?"

"Of course it has." Now it seemed so obvious. Even the timing fit. Brittany had first mentioned her new boyfriend about the same time as the break-in. And Kyle, an ex-cop, would know all about how to break and enter into someone's home, as well as which pieces to take and how to exchange them for quick cash. "I wish that—"

Moses raised his head and growled. Hackles up, he moved to the door and uttered a sharp bark. Ally and Rees exchanged glances. Rees swiftly crossed the room. The big dog growled again. "Moses, quiet," Rees commanded softly. He subsided, hackles still raised. Rees glanced through the window. "Does your landlady usually pay you visits at nine o'clock at night?"

A sigh pushed its way up. "When it suits her."

He lifted an eyebrow, inquiring. "Should I answer?"

"Yes." She moved to join him at the door. She greeted Penny and introduced Rees. Ever since the debacle with Jack on Penny's front porch, Ally had been stepping carefully around her landlady.

Penny's sharp brown eyes glittered as she peered inside, taking in the fire, the wine, the music…the man. "Saw your lights on and wanted to remind you the leaves didn't get raked last weekend. You plan on getting to them soon?"

She forced a smile. "Next weekend, I promise."

Penny squinted at her. "What happened to your head?"

She touched the spot where the goose egg had subsided, leaving only a bruise. She'd all but forgotten it. "I wasn't watching where I was going."

"First your foot, now your head. You should be more careful." Penny shifted her gaze to Rees and eyed him appraisingly, as if suspecting him of administering the bruise. Smiling faintly, Rees moved closer to Ally, rested his hand on her shoulder. The protective gesture sent comfort quivering through her. She met Rees's glance, catching the tiniest hint of a wink before she turned back to Penny.

Her landlady narrowed her eyes at Rees. "That your dog?"

"My sister's. He's staying with the Brennans for a while."

Penny crossed her arms. "No dogs allowed."

"It's just a temporary—" Ally began.

"No dogs," Penny repeated. "Read your contract."

"Mrs. Watrous." Rees angled himself between Ally and her landlady. "I encourage you to rethink that policy."

"Oh?" Penny's mouth pulled down, etching deep grooves along her cheeks. "Why?"

"For your own sake. Ally is borrowing my sister's dog because of the recent break-in. It's made both Ally and Jack a little nervous, living as they do down here off the beaten path. Especially since, as I'm sure you've heard, there's been a rash of thefts in Langley. The dog is for their protection. Now if you, as their landlady, prevent Ally from protecting herself and they're burglarized again, you could be held liable. You don't want that."

Penny frowned. "You're making that up."

"You're welcome to check for yourself."

The landlady gnawed her lower lip. "Well, I guess it's all right. But only if it's temporary."

"Of course." Rees smiled. "You might even consider getting a dog yourself."

"No, thank you." She sniffed. "I like cats, and I'll stick with cats." She pointed at Ally. "Just be sure to pick up after him. He better not dig up my azaleas, neither." The door shut behind her.

In the silence that stretched out, Rees raised his eyebrows to Ally. "She always like that?"

"On her good days." Ally pushed a hand through her hair and moved to the fireplace, drained by the encounter. Suddenly, all she wanted was to crawl into bed and slip into slumber, pretend for a time she'd never known Kyle Wylie.

When Rees tilted his head appraisingly, she wondered if he'd read her mind. Somehow she didn't think he would approve of her head-in-the-sand thinking. "Right before your landlady arrived," he said, "you said, 'I wish that—' What do you wish, Ally?"

"Oh." She looked away, fighting her fatigue. "I was thinking about the break-in. About how much trouble I might have saved people if I'd just reported it when it happened."

"It wouldn't have prevented Wylie from coming after you."

"I know, but—I don't know. I just wish things were different."

He moved a step closer. "That's what I'm trying to tell you, Ally. Everything can be different. If you choose to make it that way."

She frowned. "You make it sound so easy."

"Not easy. But do you really want to spend the rest of your life looking behind you?"

She lifted her chin. "If that's what keeps us safe."

He regarded her for a long minute, allowing silence to fill the space between them. "But there's a big problem with that, Ally." Then he surprised her by lifting a hand and running the backs of gentle fingers over her upturned face. "When you spend all your time looking back," he said softly, his eyes never leaving hers, "it means you can't see what's right in front of you."

Her breath caught. For one long moment, she looked deeply into those blue eyes that seemed to reflect her own soul. Heat flooding her cheeks, she looked away, unable to bear his searing gaze. "For my son's sake, I can't do that."

"Oh, Ally." Sadness and regret edged his voice as his hand dropped to his side. "How can you not?"

CHAPTER 39

Darcie eased her car into an empty space in front of the Good Cheer. The thrift shop was located next to the Honey Bun Bakery, or what used to be the Honey Bun Bakery. The space now had empty display shelves and a For Lease sign in the window. *Another business bites the dust.* She shook her head. They were all dropping like flies, Margit Olsson's bookstore the latest casualty. In an economic climate like this, how much longer could Paul's Boats & Moor hold out?

But everyone else's waning business meant the thrift shop was thriving. As Darcie pushed open the door, she found at least a dozen customers browsing the racks of second-hand clothing. Brittany from the bistro leaned a hip on the front counter as she talked to Ally's landlord, Penny, who manned the till. Brittany broke off mid-sentence, pinching her pink lips together as the mechanical ding-dong announced Darcie's entrance. She muttered something more to Penny before swiveling on her heel and disappearing into the back room, a cheerless, airless cave of a place where donations were received and sorted.

Brittany's distasteful expression and abrupt departure struck her as ominous, though she couldn't imagine why Brittany would have anything against her. Had she and Penny been talking about her? As unlikely as it seemed, she sensed they had been. Darcie rarely crossed paths with her neighbor, but since Jack had started spending Saturdays with Darcie, she'd picked up hostile vibes when she did run into Penny at Star Grocery or the post office. She would have thought twice about coming here today if she'd remembered Penny occasionally worked the cash register.

A teenage boy in a black t-shirt and a nose ring rifled through LP records in a bin near the front. Penny eyed him narrowly before turning to Darcie. "Can I help you?" Penny wore a white cardigan sweater over a yellow button-down blouse. The steel-gray curls clinging tightly to her scalp smelled faintly of ammonia, evidence of a recent trip to the beauty salon.

"I'm sure you can." Darcie ignored Penny's look of thinly veiled resentment. "I'm looking for a dog costume, maybe one of those furry one-piece outfits that zips up the front, has a hood with ears on it? You have anything like that?"

The corners of Penny's mouth pulled down as she ran her gaze from the tips of Darcie's white hospital clogs to her hair pulled into a loose ponytail. "You're looking for something in your size?"

"In my—? Oh, no. Sorry, it's for a boy, a five-year-old boy. Jack Brennan, actually."

Penny lips puckered into a prune. "So he's decided to be a dog, huh? Last year, it was Bob the Builder."

"His mother's been so busy lately, I don't think she's had two minutes together to think about his Halloween costume, but Jack mentioned wanting to go as a dog, so I thought I'd try to help out." Seeing her nervous babbling wasn't lightening the tension, she stumbled to a halt.

"Too busy to put a costume together for her own son, huh?" Though her expression of disapproval deepened, Penny started around the counter. "We do got some costumes." She spoke over her shoulder, apparently expecting Darcie to follow. "All together on the rack in the corner, but not sure we got anything exactly like what you're looking for."

As Darcie trailed behind, she eyed Penny's swaying hips and thought that a woman with a bottom like Penny's should not be wearing stretch pants. The older woman halted at a rack where children's costumes were arranged by size. "You need a size five, I suppose." Penny flipped through the hangers. "Don't see anything. We got a firefighter and a frog, but no dogs. Sorry."

Sure you are. She should have read that as her cue to take her impulsive idea and get out. Instead, she let her neighbor's sour shrug goad her. Darcie spun and headed for the cave Brittany had disappeared into. "Well, let's check in the back, shall we? I'm feeling lucky today. Maybe we'll find just the thing."

"You can't go in there. Employees only."

"Oh, shush. I've done my share of volunteering here. No reason I can't go back and take a look myself."

Brittany looked up, startled, as Darcie strode into the room. She stood behind a long, folding table on which sat newly arrived donations. She'd evidently been sorting clothing into plastic bins, separating adult sizes from children's.

"Mind if I take a look?" Darcie slid behind the table before the girl could protest.

"Be my guest." Brittany stepped back, tucking her fingers into the back pockets of her snug jeans.

With Penny watching from the doorway, Darcie pulled the bin with a small Superman sweatshirt on top toward her, hoping her dismay didn't register on her face. Everything was a random mess, girls' and boys' clothing all dumped in together in every size. How would she spot what she was looking for, if it was even here?

A flush crept up her neck as silence filled the room. Darcie dug nearly to the bottom of the bin and was about to cut bait when she spied a possibility. A pair of black sweatpants. With a ping of relief, she tugged them from the pile. The tag read size seven, a bit big for Jack, but they would do. Her fingertips scraped the bottom of the kids' bin, but then she spotted a faded black sweatshirt in the pile Brittany had been sorting. A size small adult. That would do too.

She snatched up both. "Not exactly what I had in mind, but we can make this work. With some mittens and felt, and a little help from the Internet, we got ourselves a costume."

Brittany eyed the items askance. "He's going to swim in those."

She was right, but somehow having this option to offer Ally and Jack felt better than none. Maybe, too, she wanted to best Penny in this matter, though to be honest, she wasn't sure she was coming out on top. "At least these give us something to work with."

Brittany shrugged. "I'll ring you up."

She led the way to the cash register, followed by a still-silent Penny. "So." Darcie fished out her wallet as Brittany began the transaction. "How long have you been working here, Brit?"

"A few days."

"What happened to your job at the bistro?"

"I quit."

"Why?" Not for better pay, surely.

When Brittany didn't answer, Penny did. "Company got too crowded at the bistro. Wasn't comfortable anymore."

Not comfortable? What on earth did that mean? Too late, she realized she'd opened a door for Penny to walk through.

"'Course you probably know something about that, seeing as you've gotten so chummy with Ally Brennan lately." Penny crossed her arms, pale eyes glittering. "With her ex-boyfriend playing Brittany for the fool, who could blame her for wanting to find other employment? You can imagine the awkwardness, them still working together. Of course, the clincher was when Brittany discovered the man was Ally's stepbrother."

Her stepbrother—what? How could Brittany not know—

Like a puzzle piece locking into place, Darcie understood. The man wasn't Brittany's stepbrother. He was Ally's. Well. That explained a few things. Little things that had always perplexed Darcie. Ally's reluctance to share the details of her past. Her refusal to take Jack to Iowa with her. Her lack of family connections.

Darcie stiffened, angry this gossip had landed so quickly in Penny's lap. It wouldn't be long before everyone knew, churned up by the small-town rumor mill. It was the main reason she hadn't told anyone about her infertility. She could imagine the label it would automatically earn her: sterile.

Poor Ally. She'd be labeled with worse. Incestuous. It wasn't, of course, but close enough for a lot of folks to make that leap. What would it mean for Ally? Even worse, what would it mean for Jack?

Darcie narrowed her eyes at Penny. "Anyone with a shred of decency would understand why Ally wouldn't want news like that to get around." How dare this woman gossip about Ally, who worked herself to death to live in Penny's scrap of a house?

Penny lips grew tight, as if drawn across a ruler. "She should have thought of that before she got tangled up in a relationship she didn't belong in."

"That was a very long time ago. Few of us would want our pasts too closely examined."

"You're just defending her because of what's going on between her and your brother."

Between Ally and Rees? "Nothing going on there except friendship."

"Is that what they're calling it these days?" Penny eyed her with a brittle smile, clearly delighted to be the deliverer of such news. "I seen them together. I know."

Darcie pinched back a retort. She didn't know what Penny thought she knew, but Darcie knew her brother, and she knew Ally. There was nothing there. But saying that to Penny would only fan the flame. "I *defend* her," she said, using Penny's word, "because Ally's my friend, too. And whatever she did or didn't do when she was young, it's certainly not Jack's fault."

Penny's chin lifted. "'Because of their parents' sins, children will waste away.'"

Something inside her snapped. Ignoring the Goth-looking young man who approached the register to purchase his record, Darcie snatched up the plastic bag containing Jack's costume. "You're the one who's wasting away, Penny. You and your small-town soul. Have you no heart? Can't you see what that girl has gone through?" Darcie glared at her, so angry she was shaking. "Shame on you, Penny. Shame."

She let the door punctuate her exit with a satisfying slam.

CHAPTER 40

Rees feared he'd pushed Ally too far. After leaving her cottage that night, he'd returned to his solitary room, almost queasy with regret. Not that he'd do it any differently, given the chance. He'd told her straight out what she needed to hear. Still, he was afraid he'd crossed a line, surrendering further opportunity to help her. As for when he'd reached out and stroked her soft skin—well, he hadn't planned it but he wasn't sorry about it, either. Truth was, he'd been wanting to touch her like that for a long time. The reality was just as sweet as he'd imagined.

The next day, the silence that stood between them made him increasingly uneasy. As the hours ticked by, Ally didn't call or stop by. Not wanting her to feel pressured, he was reluctant to make the first move. Yet urgency underscored his apprehension: in two days, he would be on his way back to Mumbai. He hated the idea of leaving her and Jack on a bad note.

That night, as he went for his ritual run along the beach, the sight of Ally's laundry hanging again from her back porch gave him the excuse he was looking for. When he knocked on her back door, she didn't seem surprised to see him, allowing him to hope she, too, wanted to end the silence between them.

She barely let him finish his apology. "I'm the one who's sorry, Rees." Beside him on the porch, the door shut behind her; she shivered in the dim light. "I shouldn't have unburdened on you like that, especially when I'm not prepared to take your advice. But you have to understand, this isn't about me." When he opened his mouth to speak, she hurried on. "I'm grateful for what you're trying to do for us, but there's only so much I'm willing to bring on Jack. Please don't ask me to do more than that."

Wariness again guarded her eyes. Helplessness surged over him in a hot wave. He'd come here to apologize, to let the matter rest. If he'd believed that was his sole intent, he knew now he'd only been fooling himself. "You asked for my help. I gave you the best I know."

"And I appreciate that. But there's…I have another idea that might work. A plan I want to try."

"There is?" He couldn't help his surprise.

"I—it's not certain yet, but I think it's going to work out." She chewed her lip and her eyebrows puckered, making him question if she really had the confidence she pretended. "Jack and I will be okay. The other day, I was just—scared, that's all. Seeing Kyle freaked me out because I wasn't expecting it. I've had time to think about it. Now I know he's found us, so the worst is over."

Was she honestly standing there trying to *minimize* this? He knew Kyle Wylie or men just like him. He wasn't about to quit, not now when he had his prize within in his sights. Rees started to argue, but then he caught the hard glint in Ally's green eyes, a hint of challenge that told him despite her apparent vulnerability, he'd better step carefully or lose any chance of helping her. Besides—*You came here to apologize, remember?* The air left his lungs.

"If you're sure." He overcame his misgivings by reminding himself she'd managed to take care of herself and Jack so far.

"I'm sure."

"Good." He tried on a smile. It felt strained but was the best he could do. "Then how about you let me do one last thing for you before I go?"

She crossed her arms over her chest. "What's that?"

He flicked one of Jack's socks hanging above his shoulder. "Let me fix your dryer."

Somewhat to his surprise, she agreed. And since the next day was Sunday, her day off, she even offered to feed him lunch in return.

Now he wielded a wrench in Ally's cramped utility room, where a guy had barely enough room to stand, wads of lint littering the floor. In the next room, water splashed in the kitchen sink as Ally washed up after lunch. A cell phone rang. The sound of running water stopped as she answered. As she greeted her caller, her tone lifted in unmistakable relief. Then her voice faded as she took her conversation into another room. Five minutes later, with a final twist of his wrist, he drove home the last bolt. He secured the cover and turned the switch. The machine droned to life. Satisfaction washed over him as he gathered up his tools and went in search of Ally.

He found her sitting on the couch, her phone silent beside her, a distant look in her eyes. "Everything's working."

She moved her head slightly, as if shaking herself back to reality. "Is it really?"

"One-hundred-percent operational."

She tipped her head and listened, a smile spreading across her face as she heard the murmur of a working appliance. "Thank you." She took his hand. "*Thank* you, Rees. Really. For everything."

"You're welcome." Caught off guard, his pulse quickened as he stared down at her upturned face. "Glad to be of service."

Her hold tightened. "You've gone to so much trouble, now I feel kind of bad."

"For what?"

"Sit down for a minute?" Finally letting go of his hand, she gestured to a place beside her on the couch.

"Sure." He claimed the far end. Except for the dryer humming in the next room, the little house was quiet. Sunshine streamed through the window overlooking the lawn, where Jack was playing Frisbee with Moses. "What's up?"

She picked up her phone and cradled it between her hands. "I just got the news I've been praying for."

"News?" He didn't much like the way she said this, nor the unexpected way it made his stomach turn over. "What news?"

She drew a breath. "Jack and I are moving to Chicago."

"Chicago?"

She nodded.

"But why? How?" It would have made more sense to him if she'd said she was flying to the moon.

"Everything's set. I haven't told anyone, but when I was back home, I kind of reunited with my old music teacher. Gina. She invited me to go to Chicago with her to help look after her new baby. In return, she'll give me the chance to study music again and complete my degree."

Rees sat back, at a complete loss. "Why didn't you say something before?"

"I wasn't sure if the offer still stood. She was in the hospital, that's why I hadn't heard from her. But she and the baby are okay now. She wants us to come."

At last the picture was beginning to sharpen into focus. "Is this what you meant when you said there was another plan you wanted to try?" She nodded. "Tell me more about this Gina person." He asked not because he cared but because he needed time to marshal his scattered thoughts.

"Her husband is Leif Svalgard. He just got on with the Chicago Symphony, which is why they're moving. If I go with them, it'll open doors for me that wouldn't be open elsewhere." With every word, her face grew brighter with hope and relief. She really believed this was a good idea. "Gina pointed out if I can get solid work doing what I'm gifted at, I can quit waitressing. I'll be able to provide better for Jack, not to mention give him untold opportunities."

"How will you afford all this?"

"We'll live in their house. Room and board. Jack and I will be safe there, with them."

"Safe?" There it was, the wrong note he'd been listening for. Everything Ally said about the opportunities that awaited her and Jack might be true, but they weren't the real reason she was willing to uproot herself and Jack. The real reason was she saw Chicago as a new place to hide.

Ally was getting ready to run. Again.

Don't you see how fear drives you, Ally? You let it do your thinking for you. He longed to say it, better yet to take her by her pretty shoulders and rattle her teeth until she saw the truth. Did she think because Chicago was a huge place, Wylie wouldn't find her, a needle in a haystack? "If Wylie tracked you here, he can track you there, you know."

She gave him a look. "It's not like I plan to leave a forwarding address."

It hit him then that despite his best intentions, he was not ready to let this matter die. He put on what he hoped was a neutral expression. "How long will you stay?"

Her reply was cut off as Jack burst through the front door. Ally shot Rees a cautionary glance. "What's up, Bubba?"

Jack slouched onto the couch between them. "I'm bored."

"Well, you can't just leave Moses outside." Ally touched her son's head with a hint of a smile.

"I'm tired of playing Frisbee. Can I watch a movie?"

"No, you may not watch a movie. It's a beautiful day. We won't have many more of these. Go back outside, but stay in the front yard where we can see you." Rees heard the steel in her voice. Faint, but definitely there. A woman who had to be both mom and dad to this child.

"I don't wanna." Jack looked at her with a hint of defiance in his eyes

"I don't care, Jack. Go." He didn't move. "*Now.*"

Scowling, Jack dragged his sneakered feet every step toward the door. Rees half-expected the boy to slam the door on his way out, but he didn't. Instead, he waited until he was outside, well out of his mother's reach, before turning toward the window and scrunching his face into the most horrific grimace.

Ally sighed and turned away. "Sorry."

"No problem." Despite himself, Rees had to fight a smile. "Anyway, you were saying?"

"Was I?" She rubbed her forehead. "What were we talking about?"

"How long you'll be in Chicago." Over Ally's shoulder, he watched Jack lean down and pick up something from the ground. A sharp stick. Jack studied it for a moment before applying it to the porch rail, picking off peeling paint.

"As long as it takes to complete my degree, I suppose."

"And then what?" Outside, Jack grinned as a quarter-sized patch of paint chipped off into his hand. Rees cringed.

Ally shrugged. "That's a bridge I'll cross when I get there."

A bridge. An idea sprang at him. With another glance outside, he stood abruptly and headed for the door. "Hey, I have a thought. How about a drive?"

A startled silence. "What?"

"Come on. I think it'd do you both some good to blow the cobwebs out. I'll get Jack." And maybe spare the kid a spanking if he could stop him before Ally clued into his mischief. "Grab your coat. We'll take Moses too."

She stared at him as if he'd lost his marbles. Maybe he had. All he knew was he had to knock some sense into this woman. Her and Jack's safety was more important than Rees's desire to preserve goodwill between them.

Minutes later they were all in Paul's borrowed truck, heading north out of Langley, following Saratoga Road along the island's perimeter until they reached Highway 20, where autumn foliage created a richly hued canyon that enveloped them from both sides.

Jack, wriggling with happiness at this unexpected turn of adventure, shared the backseat with Moses. When Rees refused to tell where they were going, Ally fell silent. Hands clenched, she kept darting him uneasy glances. He'd unsettled her. Good. Maybe that would make her more open to reason.

Any other time, he would have enjoyed the drive. The island was at its autumn peak, a riot of color so vivid it seemed almost overdone. But the splendor of the day barely penetrated his senses, so intent was he on the problem at hand. Before he knew it, he was signaling his exit from Highway 20. Seconds later, he pulled into a small, paved parking lot and slid the truck between two other vehicles.

Ally couldn't get her mind to calm down. She kept jumping from her relief that Gina had finally called to Rees's reaction to her news. He didn't like it, that much was clear. Although *why* he didn't like it wasn't nearly so obvious. When Rees parked the truck in the gravel lot, she spoke for the first time since leaving the cottage. "Where are we?"

"You don't know?" Unlike her, he seemed calmer now, almost cheerful as he stepped from the cab and held the door for Jack and Moses.

She got out and looked around. A bracing, salt-laden wind struck her full in the face. Behind them, old growth firs towered above, their tips spiky against the gray-clouded sky. Ahead and below, far below, the waters of Puget Sound ran like a green river beneath the long, arched bridge just visible to their right.

"Awesome!" Jack shouted. The brisk breeze seemed to exhilarate him as it pushed his blond bangs away from his forehead. He kept one hand on Moses' collar as if he feared the wind might sweep him away. "Look at the bridge!"

"Deception Pass," Rees said.

Deception Pass. She cut him a glance. She'd heard of this place at the northern end of the island. She looked around. Despite her uneasiness, the beauty of her surroundings filled her chest. "It's…amazing." Breathtaking.

He smiled. "Come on." He called to Jack and Moses, pointing to the trail entrance visible at the far side of the parking lot. Boy and dog scrambled ahead of them and disappeared on the wooded path.

Rees gestured for her to follow. She started down after him on the graveled trail, which descended steeply to the water below. Majestic Madrone trees and mammoth Douglas firs tangled their branches above, while a low, stone wall ran along one side. When Ally's booted foot slipped on loose pebbles, she skidded several inches. "Here," Rees said. "Take my hand."

She hesitated but he reached back, warm fingers folding over hers. His grasp remained strong and steady until they reached the bottom of the trail, where a small-pebbled beach opened before them. Jack and Moses were already fifty yards down the shore. Jack picked up a stick and tossed it into the waves. With a happy bark, Moses splashed in after it.

Ally unclasped her hand from Rees's and took a few steps over the rocky terrain. Aside from another couple taking pictures farther down the beach, they were alone. She turned in a slow circle, taking in the trees, the water, the green bridge arcing high above, the red draining from the horizon. A hawk—or was it an eagle?—wheeled overhead. The only sounds came from the rustle of water moving past, the low hum of traffic from the bridge above.

She felt rather than saw Rees's presence behind her, anticipated his voice before he spoke. "Do you know why it's called Deception Pass?" She turned to look at him. Against the gray sky, his eyes were startling blue. "Over two hundred years ago, when George Vancouver was exploring Puget Sound, naming every island and body of water in sight, he gave this place the name 'Deception' because what he assumed at first was a river turned out to be a narrow strait. I brought you here because I wanted you to see things aren't always what they seem. Even as they appear right in front of us, what we see can deceive." His hand brushed her shoulder, his touch transmitting a reassuring warmth even through the layer of her sweater. "What's in front of you now seems impossible, but there is a way out." He pointed above. "This bridge is the only way you can drive directly from the mainland onto Whidbey Island. The bridge we see is actually two bridges, with a short bit of land, a tiny island, in between. And that's how we're going to find our way out of this. From bridge to solid ground to bridge to solid ground. And you'll not have to do it alone, Ally." He stood before her, so close she caught his scent, clean and manly and true. "I promise you that."

She searched his eyes. "You mean that."

"Yep." Holding her gaze, he spoke so softly she could barely hear his words above the whistle of the wind. "The Lord will fight for you. You need only to be still."

"Still?" She stared. "I'm not sure I know what that means."

"It means you're not alone. You never have been."

Something hard uncoiled deep inside her chest, releasing warmth along her limbs. Rees's words made her feel un-tethered, as if gravity no longer had the power to hold her to earth. The feeling scared her. She took a step back.

His gaze bore into hers. "Do you believe that?"

"I want to," she whispered. Unable to look away, in his eyes she caught a glimpse of what the future might hold. A future without fear or regret. So close she could almost reach out and grasp it. Almost.

CHAPTER 41

The previous week had seen the deterioration of one of Darcie's patients. Three months earlier, when treatment had failed to stop Patty Nelson's lung cancer from spreading to her liver and right kidney, she'd moved in with her middle-aged son, Leslie. A shy, square bachelor, Leslie ran a computer repair business out of his double-wide trailer, but he made room for his mother's hospital bed in his dining room.

On Friday, Darcie had recommended Leslie advise his sister of their mother's decline so Shirley could fly out from Kansas to say goodbye. "I don't do timeframes," Darcie cautioned, "but I doubt your mother will be coherent for much longer." Patty's periods of wakefulness were ebbing, her breathing becoming more labored. Darcie increased the morphine to control her discomfort and administered lorazepam to ease her shortness of breath. She'd left instructions with Leslie to call her anytime, day or night, if his mother's condition took a nosedive. She fully expected the turn to come that weekend.

So, when Monday arrived and Leslie had not called, Darcie was surprised. As she drove to Leslie's trailer park twenty minutes from Langley, she tried to guess what she would find. A coma Leslie had mistaken for sleep? If so, she hoped Shirley had arrived in time to find her mother conscious. Or would Patty, despite Darcie's predictions, have rallied? Stranger things have happened, Darcie thought as she knocked on Leslie's flimsy aluminum front door.

She stood there grateful for the warmth of her parka as she waited for Leslie to answer. When he opened the door, she took one look at his face, as pale and as round as the moon, and knew something was wrong. The first words out of his mouth confirmed it. "We should have called, I'm sorry."

"I'm too late?" Her heart plummeted. In all her years of nursing, she had missed only two patients' deaths. Both times she'd been summoned and was en route, but the end had come faster than anticipated. When this happened, it grieved her. Though her weeks or months of care were important, she considered it her particular calling to usher a soul from this world into the next. To have missed Patty's passing saddened her. More than most, Patty reminded her of her own mother in her refusal to accept the inevitable without a fight. Not two weeks before, Darcie had helped Patty hobble to the Langley marina, her final farewell to the place where she and her family had spent so many happy hours.

This memory lingered at the forefront of Darcie's mind. "Why didn't you call me?" She craned to see past Leslie into the double-wide, but he stepped onto the tiny front porch and closed the door behind him.

His eyes dropped to his battered moccasins, held together by duct tape. "Shirley didn't think that was such a good idea."

"She got here in time, then?" This, at least, was good news.

He nodded, still not meeting her eyes. "She flew in early Saturday morning."

The weight of her medical bag grew heavy as her mind moved ahead to what came next: the final paperwork, the transport of the body to the funeral parlor. She was about to ask what time his mother had died when it occurred to her Leslie wasn't showing the grief she'd have expected. Was he in denial? "Leslie? Are you all right?"

"I'm fine." The watery blue eyes met hers for a nanosecond before skittering away. "But Mom's not."

Darcie frowned, her confusion deepening. "May I see her?"

"Sure." Leslie shifted his weight. "I mean, I guess so." But he made no move to open the door.

"Well? Aren't you going to let me in?"

"Oh. No, she's, ah…at the hospital. With Shirley."

At the hospital? Was there a mix-up? Had Patty's body been taken to the morgue? If so, who had transported it? She opened her mouth to ask just as an inkling of the truth presented itself. "Leslie, your mother didn't die, did she?"

"Die?" he repeated, as if surprised by the word. "No, she didn't die. She was having trouble breathing, so Shirley took her to the ER."

Darcie sucked in a breath through pursed lips, like a pole-vaulter before a big jump. She thought about reminding Leslie what he knew already, that for a patient on hospice care, a trip to the emergency room was the number-one no-no. The whole point of hospice was to do nothing to speed death or to slow it down, but to let the end come naturally. If his mother was struggling to breathe, it was because her end was drawing near.

But she also knew how pointless it would be to say any of this to Leslie. She could imagine the scenario. His sister, unfamiliar with her mother's wishes, had panicked to see her mother struggling for breath. So she'd done what she'd believed was the best, quickest way to ease Patty's discomfort, with Patty helpless to stop it. "When did this happen?" Darcie resigned herself to the irrevocable.

"Um—" Leslie looked up at the blanket of clouds, as if hoping to read the time there. "About an hour ago?"

"All right. Fine. Thank you." Without another word, Darcie returned to her car. She waited until Leslie slipped back inside his trailer before calling her supervisor. Briefly, she explained the situation.

A short silence spooled out before Wendy sighed. "I hate it when they do that."

"I know." With her free hand Darcie rubbed her left temple, where a dime-sized area of headache had begun.

"Try not to take it personally, okay?"

"Hard not to."

"I know, but it's not your fault. You can explain until you're blue in the face, but some people just don't get it."

Obviously. "Well, I'm off to visit her in the ER now, see if I can get things back on track."

"Which hospital?"

"Whidbey General."

"I'll send Juanita to meet you there." Juanita Gomez, their hospice chaplain.

"I'd appreciate that."

When Darcie returned home three hours later, her spirits were at low ebb, having exhausted her powers of diplomacy to get Patty's hospice care back on track. Shirley, who turned out to be as strong-willed as her brother was weak, "didn't believe in hospice care." The battle that followed left Darcie feeling as wrung out as a dirty dishrag. She couldn't help feeling she had failed Patty. On Friday, when she'd known the end was near, why hadn't she insisted on remaining at Patty's bedside? She could have done that, but hadn't. Now Patty was suffering unnecessarily.

Paul's truck was already beneath the carport when Darcie pulled in. As she parked and set the brake, a sigh slid past her lips. She didn't want to go inside. When had home stopped being a haven? Funny how the absence of something could make a place feel so crowded. Too many unfulfilled dreams, too many words unspoken.

Leaving her kit in the car, she exited its cocoon. Entering the kitchen, she was met by warm, edible odors as Paul pulled a batch of scones from the oven. Pumpkin scones, she guessed, by their orangey color and the tang of nutmeg in the air. Aaron came immediately to greet her.

"You're home." Paul greeted her, his shoulders lifting in guilty surprise.

"So are you." She wasn't even going to ask why he was here at this hour. By the looks of the kitchen, he had been for quite some time. Paul always baked neatly, concisely, cleaning up after himself as he went, but a tower of dishes remained stacked in the drain. Sugary goodies arrayed in military precision rested on cooling racks across the counter. Chocolate drop cookies, peanut butter morsels, and were those pecan tarts? Enough to feed half the town. She couldn't even guess what had brought him home from the shop to cook up this much food at this hour. Then again, she'd given up trying to understand what was going on inside her husband's head. Ever since he'd gotten the extra business from Jerry over in Freeland, which would allow them to climb out of their financial pickle, she'd hoped Paul's passion for his shop would reignite. For a while, it seemed it had. He'd remarked he and Diego had enough work to keep them busy until Christmas. So what was he doing here?

As she dropped her handbag beside the phone, Paul slid a golden scone from a baking sheet and held it out to her. "Just in time to taste test."

Barely glancing at the confection balanced on the flat of the spatula, she crossed to the fridge. "Not right now, thanks." Aaron loped back to his bed.

"Not even a bite?"

"I said no thanks. I'm not hungry."

"Just a taste, to tell me what you think."

Knowing the quickest route to time alone in the tub was to accept Paul's offering, she sighed and took the scone, tore a teeny bit from its tip, popped it into her mouth.

Paul watched for her reaction. "Well?"

"Good." She took another bite, bigger this time. "Very good." Dense, buttery texture filled her mouth. She set the rest aside on a napkin.

"I fiddled with the recipe a bit, added honey instead of sugar and a pinch more nutmeg. You think it might be good enough to sell? For people to want to buy?"

It finally occurred to her that her husband, in his roundabout way, was trying to make her understand something. She struggled to set aside the day's events long enough to guess his message. Then—*Of course. The Harvest Festival this weekend. He heard me on the phone with Lauren yesterday planning the treats table.* She felt touched, despite herself, that he would go to so much trouble for her event. "They'll be a hit at the bake sale."

His face fell. "Bake sale?"

"For the Festival. Isn't that what you mean?"

"I—no, not exactly."

"Just tell me, then." She was tired of guessing games, wanted only to sink into a frothy tub of hot water.

Paul put down his spatula and faced her. "I want to sell the shop."

Her heart thudded. "I thought you said business was okay now. That you had enough work to keep us afloat."

"It is. I do. That's why I want to sell now."

"I don't understand." The first shock of his announcement passed, leaving in its wake something else. Absurd as it seemed, she felt relieved that at last someone under this roof was daring to say straight up what was on his mind. "If not the shop, what will you do?"

"Sam and I are talking about going into business together."

It took several ticks of the cuckoo clock before she understood what he was talking about. "Sam? Bistro Sam?"

He nodded. "The bakery that's been supplying the bistro's pastries went out of business." A trace of pride entered his voice. "Sam's the one who came to me with the idea."

He means the Honey Bun Bakery, she thought, remembering the For Lease sign in its window. The news hit her at the back of the knees, causing her to sink into the nearest kitchen chair. "How long have you been thinking about this?"

"Working with Sam or getting out of the boat business?"

"Both."

He hung his head. "A long time."

Since the day after the storm when he'd invited her out to lunch? He'd been the one, come to think of it, who'd suggested they meet at the bistro. Was that what that had been about? "It's a crazy idea. No way you can make it work, not enough to support us anyway. Not in this economy."

His head came up. The bruised, helpless look on his face made her heart clench. "I can't go on doing what I'm doing, Darce. My soul's not in it anymore. I hate it. Hate going to work every morning."

"Who would buy your shop?"

"Diego, if he can get the money."

"Diego's just a kid."

"A kid who knows what he's doing. Besides that, he enjoys it in a way I never did."

She stared at him. In the silence, a chilling new thought came to her. "Do you realize what this would mean for us?" Her pitch rose as the full weight of his disclosure collapsed on her. "It means forgetting our plans for fertility treatments."

His face twisted. "Not necessarily—"

"Yes, necessarily!" She'd read everything she could about what they'd need to do to try to conceive. It would be thousands of dollars every month. Just as it would take thousands every month to get this new venture off the ground. Paul knew this as well as she did, having bootstrapped a new business when they first moved to the island. They'd need more than the bistro's business, more than whatever pittance of a profit they might manage from selling the shop to Diego. She understood, even if Paul didn't, just how much this lark would cost them. "All our money will go to investing in your new venture. Even with me working full-time, we can't do both, Paul. We can't have a baby and a new career."

Paul's face tightened. "I don't know what else to do. I'm miserable at the shop. I should never have continued in the boating business. I only did it because it was familiar. Safe. It was a mistake, but don't you see? I can get out of it now, before we have children, so we can be settled financially again once we have the responsibility of a child."

"And how much time will that take? Three, four years?" By then she'd be in her late thirties. Their chances of having a healthy baby would dwindle, if they could manage to conceive at all. "I'm running out of time. If we're going to try for a baby of our own, we need to do it now."

Paul opened his mouth but closed it again.

Darcie rose from her chair. "I'm taking a bath."

"Hon—"

"Please." She held up a hand. "If you're going to take away what matters most to me, the least you can do is to give me time." She left the kitchen. In her bedroom, she shut the door behind her, hoping Paul wouldn't be fool enough to try to follow her.

In the bathroom, Darcie stared at her face, taut with tension, and then sank to the edge of the tub.

The house fell into silence. What was Paul doing right this minute? Crying? Praying? Probably better for their marriage if they could do both together right now. But at this moment, she couldn't even bring herself to face her husband. The dream crusher.

And what of Paul's dreams? The thought came unbidden and unwelcome. She squashed it as soon as it broke free inside her brain.

She couldn't let herself think of Paul's dreams right now. After all, which was more important? A career or a child?

She leaned her forehead against the tiled wall, welcomed its coolness against her hot skin. She'd ignored the headache that had begun hours ago at Leslie's place, but now it swelled like a balloon behind her temples. *Oh, God…* She hardly knew where to begin, her thoughts and emotions an untidy swirl. One of them untangled itself from the rest. *Dear God, if we're not meant to have a baby, won't you at least remove this longing from my heart?* A sigh hefted itself from the bottom of her empty womb.

I know the plans I have for you. Plans to give you hope and a future and not to harm you.

As the familiar Scripture came to her, it brought not peace but a quiver of fear. *I know I'm supposed to find that comforting,*

Lord, but somehow it only scares me. I'm so afraid your plans are far from my own.

She waited in the quiet of the darkening room until she heard Paul call to Aaron and leave by the backdoor. When she was sure he was really gone, she crept into the kitchen in search of Advil. Paul's unwashed dishes remained beside the sink, a sure sign of his own distress. Under other circumstances, this might have elicited at least a tremor of compassion. But today? Nothing.

After finding the bottle of ibuprofen in the pantry, she swallowed two pills while eyeing her unfinished scone on a paper napkin. She sat down, polished it off, and then dropped her head onto her arms on top of the table. Outside, she heard a vehicle pull into the drive, a car door slam. Whistling.

Rees.

The kitchen door opened. Cool air swirled around her ankles. "Darcie? You okay?"

Raising her head, she managed a weak smile. She was still getting used to his shorn look. "Have I mentioned I like your haircut?"

"Thanks." He took a scone, ate half in a single bite. "This is good."

"It should be, seeing as it's Paul's own special recipe." She heard the edge in her tone but could do nothing to stop it.

He peered at her. "Something wrong, Sis?"

Sis. He hadn't called her that in ages. "You could say that."

"Want to tell me?" He pulled out a chair, sat down.

Tears pricking like needles behind her eyes, she blew out a slow breath, not wanting him to see her cry. "I ever tell you why I chose hospice nursing?"

"Because you're good at it?"

She shook her head. "Toward the end of nursing school, we all had to choose our specialties. I'd narrowed the field to three options: ER, OB, or hospice. I decided against ER because I didn't want to deal with the crazies who come to the emergency room for a cold. So that left obstetrics or hospice. For a week, I shadowed a nurse on the maternity ward, thought for sure I'd found my calling. The first time I delivered a baby, I knew I'd never experience anything so thrilling as bringing a new life into this world. I'd made up my mind. But to be thorough, I followed through on my week with a hospice nurse. I shadowed an older nurse who'd been doing hospice nursing for over twenty years. She called herself a midwife to the soul. I was so struck by this. It seemed such a beautiful thing, even more beautiful than being a midwife to a new life. Life in this world eventually ends. But to usher a soul into eternity, and to do it with dignity, without pain or fear? I couldn't aspire to a higher calling."

"I never heard that story." Rees paused. "I'm glad you made the choice you did."

"So am I." Bitterness tightened her throat. "Because it looks as if that's as good as it gets for me." She looked at him, the features she loved blurred by tears. "I'm never going to be a mom, Rees."

His hand closed over hers. "Why do you say that?"

His touch felt so familiar, so good, she almost laughed for the pure pleasure of feeling it again. "Because it's true."

"Did something happen?"

"Paul wants to start a new business. He hates his boat shop and wants to get out of it. But in order to get him started in a new business, we'll have to throw all our money into that. Which means we can't start fertility treatments as we'd planned. We can't afford to do both."

His thumb swiped across her skin. "I'm sorry."

She swallowed. "Do you have any idea how hard it is to accept that I will never know what it means to nourish a life? To give birth? Do you know how my body craves that?"

"No." He squeezed her fingers. "I can't even imagine."

She turned her hand in his and squeezed, grateful he didn't pretend to understand something he could not. His presence with her in this moment was enough, and he knew it. Darcie looked down at their clasped hands. When they were young, they'd been like this, so close they were practically intertwined. As a child, she used to pretend they were twins. Even amidst her current heartache, gratitude pulsed that their intimacy had somehow been restored.

Another Scripture fragment came to her. *I, the LORD, will repay you for the years the locusts have eaten.* Her father had first shown her this verse and taught her what it meant. It was God's promise to His children that He would restore what had been lost at the hands of their enemies. This had helped carry her through those years when she'd lost her mother to cancer. But now she wondered if even the LORD God could restore that which had never been. Was it wrong to consider He could not? Or would not?

Her thoughts took an unexpected turn as she recalled what Penny Watrous had implied about Ally and Rees. Darcie straightened, slipping her hand from his. "Ever find yourself saying something you never in a million years believed you would?"

"What'd you say this time?" Her brother's chiseled mouth quirked knowingly.

"I told Penny Watrous she had a shriveled soul, that she should be ashamed of herself for—" She stopped and stared at him. "Why are you smiling?"

"Because this reminds me of the time I was having a hard time in school after mom died. Remember? I'd cry in class. I couldn't help it; the tears would just come. One of the boys called me a crybaby, teasing me every day at recess. Until you found out about it. You told him if he didn't knock it off, you'd tell everyone he still wet the bed. You were friends with his sister, that's how you knew. Never had any trouble with him after that."

She smiled in spite of herself, remembering.

"Sorry," Rees said, "getting distracted here. What made you say that to Penny?"

She told him, watching his scar whiten like lightning across his cheek as her story spilled out. Rees rose from the table, raking his fingers through his hair. "Have you told her this?"

"Ally? Of course not. Only you."

He paced the room like a courtroom lawyer. "This is just the sort of thing she was afraid of."

"You already knew?"

"She told me everything, but she doesn't want Jack to know about his father."

"Why?"

He hesitated. "All I can say is she doesn't want her son to know his father was her stepbrother."

"I'm afraid it's too late to stop the gossip." Darcie winced. "What did you tell her to do?"

"To file rape charges against Kyle Wylie. But she's refusing."

"Why?"

"She's scared."

"Of him?"

"Of what it might do to Jack. I've tried telling her it's okay to be afraid, but it's not okay to run from what she's afraid of."

Darcie flattened her hands against the tabletop, feeling renewed shame for letting her anger get the better of her. "I shouldn't have said that to Penny. I probably made things worse for Ally."

Rees shook his head. "Don't worry about that."

"People have big memories in small towns." She could think of half-a-dozen ways Penny could make life unpleasant for the Brennans without even trying.

"I meant, Ally won't be around much longer for it to matter. She's moving to Chicago."

For the second time in an hour, Darcie felt the wind knocked from her. "*Chicago*?"

"When Ally was back in Iowa, she reconnected with an old teacher." He told her the details.

"When is she leaving?" It seemed so unlike Ally.

"As soon as possible. A week. Sam asked her to give him that long to find a replacement. Jack won't go back to school until after the new year, though. She thinks it'll help make the transition easier."

"It's going to make for a lonely Christmas, for us and for them. Thanksgiving too." She said it lightly, ignoring the pang of loss as she realized how soon she'd have to say goodbye. "I'd been looking forward to sharing the holidays."

"I can't help but think she sees this as one more opportunity to escape." Rees sank into his chair. "I don't think she realizes it. She's already fled from him twice. Twice, he's found her again. Only this time, he's the one who's disappeared from the scene. But he'll be back, and she knows it. She somehow hopes she'll be able to hide herself in a big city, even though a place like Chicago won't make any difference to someone like Wylie. And when he finds her again, then what?" His voice caught as he dropped his head into his hands. "She can't keep running forever."

His distress yanked hard on her sympathy, while the truth slammed her in the chest. The truth Penny had snidely hinted at, which even Paul had guessed. *Rees loves Ally.* Darcie would have known it for herself if she'd not been so attached to her own ideas of what was right for her brother.

She laid a hand on his broad shoulder. "So that's it? You're just going to let her leave?"

CHAPTER 42

Rees lifted his head. "What choice do I have? Her mind is made up, and I'm leaving for Mumbai in the morning."

"So why not take her with you?"

Rees's heart pounded. Until his sister said it aloud, he hadn't realized how much it had become his heart's desire, crazy as it was. "That's impossible."

"Not if you care for her the way I think you do."

I don't want to leave. When it hit him outside Jack's school, he'd assumed his wanting to stay in Langley was all about the boy. He was wrong. Jack may have walked through the front door of his heart, but Ally had sneaked in through the back. Yet to stay here was not an option. He had responsibilities in Mumbai. More than that, he had a calling. It was his chosen life.

He didn't bother denying the truth of Darcie's words. "She deserves a chance at a normal life with Jack." She'd certainly not get that in Mumbai.

"Is that what she wants?"

"It's everything she's fought for these last five years."

"Yes, but what if she wants a life with you more than she wants a normal one? Don't you think she deserves the chance to make that choice herself?"

He thought of her carefully shuttered face when they'd said their goodbyes after their visit to Deception Pass. The softening he'd seen just a few hours earlier had vanished, the wariness locked back in place. She'd barely allowed him to touch her, had held herself as stiff as a statue when he'd hugged her goodbye. He shook his head. "It's too late for that now. Her course is set. I have to make peace with that." Somehow.

Darcie frowned. "That doesn't seem right. You've got to at least leave the door open. Who knows what lies ahead? No one's saying you have to get married tomorrow. Even though"—she smiled faintly—"I've always wanted a sister."

He looked at her, surprised. Darcie would never admit it but saying that had cost her something. She liked Ally. He knew that. But Ally would never be the kind of woman she'd once envisioned for him. Darcie had loved Julie, considered them a perfect match. So Darcie's acceptance of Ally now underscored her devotion to him. He smiled at the pleasure of having his big sister on his team again.

Then his smile faded as a new truth hit him like a rock between the eyes. Whatever heartache he might face when he left Ally and Jack behind, it was nothing to what Darcie was going through. And he'd contributed to her unhappiness. Knowing she'd craved their old intimacy, he'd done nothing to change it, even when it was in his power to do so. *I've been selfish, telling myself I've been harming no one by keeping my business to myself. What kind of a donkey's butt does that?*

His sister had raised him better.

"Darcie." He waited until those blue eyes, a mirror image of his own, settled on him. "I know I haven't been the easiest company to have around these past two months. Thanks for letting me stay here and putting up with all my—well, me."

Her eyes softened. "Anytime."

"I know you've wondered how this happened." Running his thumb along his scar, he remembered how he'd persuaded Ally to open up to him. Telling her to be honest for Jack's sake, knowing if she didn't, what she kept to herself would fester like a cancer. Yet he'd done exactly that himself, out of stubborn pride, even after Sheela, one of his most trusted friends, told him he should talk to Darcie. It had poisoned his relationship with the sister who loved him more than anybody on the planet. "I'll tell you the story now, if you want to hear it."

"You know I do."

A short silence drew out, with only the sigh of the cooling oven to fill the room. "It happened during the last brothel raid before my home-leave." Rees let the memory come flooding back. "It was so blazing hot, at the tail end of a stifling summer. I remember wondering if I'd ever breathe clean air again." He'd planned to be onboard an Air India flight to Seattle within forty-eight hours. For weeks his daydreams had been filled with visions of long runs along Langley's rocky shores, lung-cleansing breaths of Puget Sound's pure, salty breezes. But on days like that one, he questioned whether the reek of Mumbai would ever leave his nostrils, a smell so thick he swore he could rub it between his fingers. More than just the stench wafting like unholy specters from the sewers, the smothering humidity anchored him like a lead cape to earth.

"I was waiting in a parked SUV across the street from the brothel we'd targeted." Sweat had traced tiny rivers between his shoulder blades as he slouched in the passenger seat. Beside him, his partner, Arundhati, chain smoked behind the wheel while he waited for the signal from the plainclothes cop stationed outside the building. Obscured by tinted windows in the back of the SUV, their Swedish intern, Rickard, hunched over his video camera, taping the proceedings. Both Rees and Rickard were confined to the car for the duration of this waiting period. As white men in this part of town, they would draw unwanted attention to their presence and risk sabotaging the mission.

To the casual passerby, the targeted building appeared like a thousand others in the island city—squat, cement, ordinary, on a busy corner where two dusty streets intersected. The front door was intricately carved but there was nothing else to draw the eye, nothing to identify its purpose.

"It was getting toward late afternoon. We'd been waiting for hours." Years of living in Mumbai had acclimatized him to the sluggish pace of Indian society, from the chai-wallah brewing a cup of tea, to the local police chief responding to their summons. Unable to do anything else, he passed the time by praying. *God, you train our hands for battle. You make it so our arms can bend a bow of bronze. Give us Your shield of victory.*

"We usually do our raids at night, but we'd chosen to conduct this one in the afternoon. We suspected the pimp knew he'd been under surveillance, so we were hoping to throw him off by moving in during broad daylight." He and his investigative team had had their eye on this place for months, had specifically targeted it because about half its sex workers were Nepali. No Nepali woman worked the Mumbai sex trade voluntarily. Most of these women had been abducted by traffickers or sold into slavery by people they trusted.

In most of Kamathipura, the red light district, business was conducted behind the doors of the brothels and dance bars, but here on Grant Road, sex was sold openly on the street. At barely four in the afternoon, women lounged outside, waiting for their next customer. Each could expect to service twenty or more men that night, each time for a handful of rupees that went straight into her pimp's pocket.

Sanctuary always partnered with the local police. It took months of groundwork to prepare the way: learning which of the officers could be trusted, which could be bribed, which were so corrupt (sometimes as the brothel's most regular customers) they needed to be avoided altogether. Rees's job was to figure this out beforehand and to ensure no law was broken during the raid, while Arundhati's was to receive the signal from his man inside. This man was wired with a hidden microphone and button camera for obtaining evidence of the pimp committing a crime. Once they had that on tape, the police could move in.

The blast of a train's whistle pulling into the nearby station shook the SUV. In his periphery, movement caught Rees's attention. A woman and girl stepped outside the building next door as the whistle's echo faded. Squinting in the sun, their heart-shaped faces eerily identical, they sank into squat positions beneath the sagging wooden balcony. The taller of the two was perhaps twenty-five, the smaller one scarcely more than a girl. Both wore tight white tee-shirts stretched across their chests. A man strolled by, glanced their way. Beneath her voluminous hot-pink skirt, the older one spread her knees in unspoken invitation. The passerby looked away.

The girl's gaze followed the man's progress as he continued down the street. As she lifted her eyes, a cold stone dropped onto Rees's chest. Those topaz eyes, he'd seen them before. He knew these two women. A mother and daughter who had first appeared on Sanctuary's radar years earlier, in one of Rees's first investigations, when he'd targeted a former U.S. Army captain named Phelps. At that time, Phelps, then a civilian, taught at one of the universities. But his respectable day job hid a dark side.

He had cultivated a taste for young girls and hired a former prostitute to procure them. After getting the girls addicted to morphine to keep them compliant, he repeatedly raped them. When tired of them, he sold them to brothel owners for a profit. All except for one. Phelps had a favorite: Salila. He kept her even after she got pregnant, both her and the daughter she birthed. The girl, Jayashri, was eight when Sanctuary finally nailed Phelps. While the police took Phelps into custody to face prosecution, Sanctuary ushered Salila and Jayashri into the aftercare home. But by then, Salila was so indoctrinated that she ran away a few months later, Jayashri with her, back into their old lifestyle. They'd not been seen since.

Until now.

Without thinking, Rees opened his door. Immediately, Arundhati jerked him back inside. "What are you doing?"

Reaching past Rees, he slammed the door shut as a bicycle carrying two men careened by on the sidewalk.

"Look." Rees pointed. "Recognize those two?"

Arundhati squinted before he hissed a sharp intake of breath. "Salila!" He and Rees had partnered on the Phelps case. When Salila and Jayashri had disappeared into the streets, Arundhati'd spent weeks searching for them. Now, though, his black eyes meeting Rees's, he shook his head. "We can do nothing for them, today. We cannot blow our cover."

"But—"

The walkie-talkie crackled. Arundhati snatched it from the dusty console. He listened to the rapid issue of Hindi and responded in the same language before nodding at Rees. "It's time." Almost before the words left his lips, he'd stepped from the vehicle. Rees and Rickard stayed behind as Arundhati joined the flood of police and rescue workers pouring from every nearby doorway and alley. When he disappeared inside the building, Rees heard the click of Rickard's camera as he began recording.

At the burst of street activity, pedestrians and pedicab drivers had stopped to gawk. Rees held his breath, waiting to see whether a mob would form. It happened sometimes. Finally, after what seemed like hours, Arundhati and the police emerged from the brothel, the pimp handcuffed between them. One of Sheela's social workers followed, her arm around a young woman in a soiled yellow sari who covered her face with her hands.

Rees, who had briefly abandoned his interest in the pair beneath the balcony next door, leaned forward to see how Salila and Jayashri were reacting to the raid. The man Rees assumed to be their pimp had emerged to investigate the commotion. As the police led arrested men to their vehicles, this pimp rushed into the fray, waving his arms, yelling in unintelligible Hindi. Salila and Jayashri rose to their feet, Jayashri's heart-shaped face frozen in fear as she clutched her mother's arm.

Go. Sensing the Lord's prompt, he found himself emerging from the SUV. Then he was on the street, walking away from the vehicle, toward the pair crouched beneath the balcony. Salila's wide brown eyes locked on his. Did she remember him? Though he could never be sure, he would swear he read recognition in her startled glance. As to what happened next, he'd never know the why of it. Did Salila misunderstand his intent and think he was coming to arrest her? Did he remind her too much of the white man who'd abused her? Or did she simply see a chance for escape and take it? Whatever the reason, she grabbed Jayashri's thin wrist and ran.

Rees took off after them, dimly aware of Arundhati's shout behind him. As the women had only a brief head start, he thought he'd close the gap quickly. But he had to fight for every foot of ground he gained, squeezing past pedestrians and sidewalk vendors, hurdling squawking chickens and even a goat. The crowds pressed in on the pale Westerner, while Salila and Jayashri slipped through like water through a sieve. Every several meters, Salila glanced behind, sometimes locking eyes with him. After two blocks, when at every obstacle he feared he'd lost them, he realized she was not wandering aimlessly. A Hindu temple loomed across from the train station. Did she seek sanctuary within its walls, believing he wouldn't dare to follow her inside a holy place?

But a block from the temple, she veered sharply right, on direct course for the train station. Did she plan to hop the tracks, thinking she'd lose him on the other side? The tracks here were at ground level. People crushed in close as the roar of an approaching engine drowned out the city's drone.

Salila tossed another look over her shoulder, as if to see if Rees still followed. He remained about a half-a-block away but was gaining ground now. Her glance lingered. She slowed, sure now she'd caught his attention. Then she changed her trajectory, aiming not for the boarding platform directly in front of her, but for the tracks themselves.

Jayashri had remained in her grip, following compliantly if without comprehension. But now, as if sensing something different in her mother's intent, she began to resist. She tugged on Salila's arm, with increasing strength. Rees closed the gap. Jayashri shrieked as her mother continued to pull her toward the oncoming train.

The train.

Rees froze. Salila was going to throw them both in front of the train. It bore down on them like a fire-breathing dragon. *Dear God, help us.*

The horn blared. Rees's eyes cut to the engine. Too late. The engineer could not halt this beast in time. Salila straddled the tracks, her daughter's wrist tight in her grasp. Jayashri struggled like a trapped animal. The girl's mouth opened in a scream, the sound lost as the train thundered past.

In Darcie's kitchen, Rees pressed his fingertips into the sockets of his eyes. "I don't know exactly what happened next. So many people, all of them getting in the way. It happened so fast. The crowd surged. Next thing I knew, I was covering Jayashri with my body. She was screaming, writhing like a landed fish, terrified but unharmed. That's how I got this." He traced the wound on his cheek. "Something on the tracks the train kicked up when it flew by."

Silence sat back down on top of them as he finished his story. Suddenly Rees understood why he'd not been able to bring himself to tell Darcie what had happened until now. He hadn't wanted to disappoint her again. She'd been so shattered when Julie had died. He'd never been able to shake the feeling it was his fault. If he hadn't been so eager to impress, changing his flight to start his new job ASAP, Julie wouldn't have changed hers. She'd still be alive.

And now, because of his choice, yet another woman had died.

Darcie's voice broke the quiet. "So Salila took her own life so her daughter might live."

"What? No." Hadn't he made it clear? "She tried to kill them both." A murder-suicide. Not so uncommon in Kamathipura.

Darcie shook her head. "I don't think so. I think when Salila saw you, she recognized you and saw a chance to give her daughter a better fate than the one she'd chosen for herself. She must have believed herself to be beyond redemption. After all, she'd been rescued once but had returned to the brothel by choice. Worse, she'd dragged her daughter back with her. But she knew what kind of life outside the brothel you and your people offered. Don't you see? You didn't cause a loss of life. You saved one."

He sat back, stunned. Could Darcie be right? He recalled the way Salila kept checking back over her shoulder. The way her dark eyes locked with his. As if she had been trying to communicate with him. A message. What if it was no accident

Jayashri had escaped the train? What if at the very last moment, her mother had shoved her free, knowing Rees would take her and return her to Sanctuary?

Was it possible?

Yes. Relief flooded him in a drenching wave.

CHAPTER 43

Mumbai, one week later

The Madonna with Child reminded him of Ally, but that wasn't the reason Rees bought the exquisitely painted icon. Not the only reason, anyway. He was drawn to the fine-featured, brunette beauty of this depiction of Mary, the dark hair rare for a Renaissance rendering. Even more, he liked the gentle way this Madonna cupped the Christ Child's head and how the baby was swaddled, obscuring His gender.

On the long flight from Seattle, images of Ally's face kept colliding with Jayashri's, what he had left clashing with what lay ahead. When he'd boarded his plane, he'd known only time would ease the pain of leaving Ally and Jack in Langley, allowing them to find their way without him. Knowing this, he didn't even try to banish her from his mind. Somewhere over the polar cap, an idea sprang up, which led to a prompting that persisted after he'd landed in Mumbai. It fueled his days. He spent hours scouring the bazaars, searching for exactly the right image to serve his purpose. A purpose he wasn't sure would be sanctioned by Nigel, who insisted on running an ecumenical Christian organization. This artwork was flagrantly Roman Catholic. Even so, he thought it worth the gamble.

As a hired pedicab carried Rees to Sanctuary's safe house on the city's outskirts, he cradled the icon, wrapped in a strip of cream muslin and tied with a white ribbon. He stopped the driver a block away from the safe house, handed him a fistful of rupees, and walked the remaining distance. He couldn't remember the last time he'd been here. Under normal circumstances, once he'd done his job in freeing the victims from their traffickers, there was no need. But these weren't normal circumstances.

The wrought iron gate squealed on its hinges as Rees pushed past it into the private compound, set apart from its neighbors by an eight-foot brick wall topped with broken glass and barbed wire. An ancient banyan spread its shade over the enclosure. From the depths of its branches, cicadas thrummed in raucous harmony. Beneath the thick canopy, a woman in a saffron-colored sari sat erect on a bamboo mat, while in the dirt nearby, a naked toddler, a girl, pushed a toy car through the rugged topography of the banyan's roots. The woman glanced at him before calling to the child, drawing her into the encircled protection of her arms.

Rees moved past her wary gaze and mounted the steps to the two-story, stucco dwelling. At the intricately carved door, he knocked. Almost immediately, a young woman answered. Dressed in a modest blue *salwar kameez*, her black hair was pulled into a neat braid and a *bindi* punctuated her forehead. She took him in at a glance and asked in careful English, "May I help you?"

Despite the polite greeting, he wasn't sure how much English she understood. "My name is Rees Davies. I work for Sanctuary." At her nod of understanding, he continued. "Is Sheela here? May I see her?"

"Yes, of course." She opened the door wider, revealing four other women bent over tables making jewelry. "Please, come in. I will get her for you. May I also bring you some tea?"

Scents of cinnamon and ginger tantalized him from some unseen source. He guessed somewhere inside, a pot of chai tea was brewing. "If it's not too much trouble."

"It is my pleasure." Her bare feet made no sound against the teak floor as she glided through a doorway out of sight. No sooner had she disappeared than one of the women stringing polished stones onto delicate wiring murmured something in Hindi. A titter of giggling rose from her three companions. All four darted curious glances at the package Rees held, so he moved it behind his back while attempting a smile. This set off another round of subdued laughter. Increasingly ill at ease, he shifted his gaze to the sheer drapes billowing inward from the open window, through which came the melancholy caw of a peacock.

Sheela swept into the room, the gauzy scarf of her crimson salwar kameez trailing behind. Rees set his package on a nearby table. Hands outstretched, she took both of his into hers. "Rees. It is so good to see you again."

He felt a lift of real pleasure. "And you."

Sheela turned aside as the young woman who had first greeted him offered Rees a battered, handle-less cup containing chai tea, thick with cream and—he knew even before tasting it—a crazy amount of sugar. When he thanked her, she smiled. Sheela addressed him as the woman withdrew. "I knew you returned this week, but I did not expect to see you here. What brings you to our part of the city, my friend?"

"I came to see Jayashri."

Sheela's fine eyebrows fluttered over her gold-framed glasses. "That is kind of you."

"Is she better?"

"She is here." Sheela clasped her slim brown hands at waist-level in characteristic pose. "For now, that is enough."

Rees retrieved his package. "I brought her something." Swiftly, he described what the gift contained and watched as surprise fluttered across Sheela's face. Surprise and something else, too quick for him to catch. "I know it's unorthodox to bring the girls gifts, but I was thinking this might help her somehow." He had some vague idea of the icon making her feel connected to a mother figure, but he couldn't bring himself to voice it.

Sheela had listened with her head cocked to one side, as if expecting God's voice to tip into her upraised ear. "Come," she said when he finished. "Let me take you to her."

"So it's all right?" Rees fell into step behind her.

She glanced back over her shoulder, a smile blooming on her bare lips. "We will find out in a moment."

Puzzled by this response, Rees followed her along an airy hallway to an open door that gave way to a white-painted room with two narrow twin beds. A quick rap and Sheela stepped inside. As she spoke briefly in Hindi, the room's only occupant turned from the window, where she'd been gazing at the sprawling banyan outside. When she faced them, Rees experienced a jolt. Those rich topaz eyes set in the heart-shaped face were as arresting as always, but they weren't what stunned him. Although thin strands of black hair traced across her shoulders and back, bald patches sprawled from her forehead to her crown.

Hoping his smile concealed his shock, Rees greeted her. "Hello, Jayashri. I stopped by to see how you were feeling."

Sheela translated, eliciting no reaction from the girl.

"Does she remember who I am?" he asked.

"Possibly, but I doubt it. Her memory of the day her mother was killed is mercifully unclear. It's probably best not to remind her of your role. Let her to assume you are someone who is interested in her well-being." Sheela smiled. "Which is true enough." Then, taking the wrapped package from Rees, she held it out to Jayashri, offering a brief explanation in her language.

As Jayashri took the package, her long sleeve slid to her elbow, revealing an untidy criss-cross of scabs like scattered toothpicks running up the inside of her forearm. Rees's stomach clenched at this visible reminder of her self-abuse, but she seemed oblivious as she unwrapped his gift, letting the cloth and ribbon flutter to the floor. She stared a long moment at the icon before cutting a glance to an object sitting atop the plain table beside her bed. Following her glance, Rees received another jolt.

An icon identical to the one he'd just given her.

Though she didn't speak, questions flashed in the wide, topaz eyes. Sheela spoke at length in the language they shared. When she finished, a silence fell. Then, for the first time, Rees heard the girl speak. Her voice low, she uttered what seemed to be a single sentence. Sheela answered. Jayashri said something more before returning her gaze to the window. She cradled Rees's gift close to her heart.

Sheela touched Rees's arm to guide him from the room. "What happened?" Rees asked as they retraced their steps down the hall. "What were you saying?"

"Let us go outside to talk, where we can have some privacy. But first I will ask, did you notice?"

"That she already had an icon exactly like the one I gave her? Yes."

"Good. That was important for you to see. For both of you," she added enigmatically.

"But Sheela—her baldness." He followed her to a door at the rear of the building, and they passed outside. "Is she ill?"

"When we took the piece of pottery from her so she was unable to cut herself, she took to pulling out her hair, instead. One strand at a time."

"It's terrible." Keeping to a broad stone path, he fell into step beside her as they walked the length of the compound.

"Another thing for which she must find healing." Dappled sunlight fell across the smooth planes of Sheela's face as she looked up at him. "You do not blame yourself so much now for what happened to Salila, I think."

"I still feel responsible, but I don't feel guilt."

"I'm glad. Those are two very different things. One leads to wholeness and healing. The other to—well, destruction."

He looked over the great expanse of yard. "You do good work here, Sheela. This is a good place." A tree-shaded plot of land, still in Mumbai, but away from the crowds and the smells.

She nodded. "Nigel did well to find it. It was once a convent, I believe."

Rees turned to her. "Is that why she has that icon in her room?"

"No. She has that icon in her room because about a month after she came here—about the same time you and I began our long-distance communiqués, come to think of it—I felt prompted to give it to her."

Rees's pulse quickened. "Prompted, how?"

"I awakened one morning with Jayashri on my heart and a vision in my head. I went to the bazaars and searched for what I'd seen until I found it."

The wonder of this settled over Rees like a gossamer veil. "Don't you find that…strange? That I should bring her the same icon you did? The exact same one?" Of all the hundreds, thousands on the streets of Mumbai.

"Why should I find that strange? Is it not the same Spirit speaking to you that speaks to me? There is One much greater than you or I at work here. This is something Jayashri is just beginning to understand, I think. I explained you had no idea I had already given her that icon. I told her God had led you to find the same one to give her. I also told her you were praying for her. And that is the first time I've seen her accept such words without exploding into a rage. The first time I told her I was praying for her, she picked up a paperweight from my desk and hurled it at me. The Lord is working in her life, with or without her permission."

"The Lord will fight for you. You need only to be still."

"Exactly so."

"I said that recently to a…friend who needed to hear it."

"And did it help?"

"I think so. I hope so."

Sheela watched him for a moment, a smile tugging at one corner of her mouth. "This friend. Where is she now?"

Rees crossed his arms. "Why do you assume it's a she?"

Sheela's smile grew. "That, my friend, is not an impossible guess. The truth is written all over your face."

Warmth spread through his chest. He hadn't meant to be so transparent. "She's in Langley. My sister's neighbor, actually. She was a musician once. Still is, I guess. Gave up it all up when—well, she ran from something. Someone. She's still running. Afraid to stop, afraid to be still. Afraid what she's fleeing from will catch up to her. That she won't be strong enough to face it down."

"Not so very different from what we find here, is it? Well, it is a process. We do not give up. On your friend, or anyone."

They rounded the corner. The mother Rees had seen when he'd first entered the gate was still in her position beneath the tree, stitching a hem on a piece of fine linen, singing to her child as she worked. Rees and Sheela stopped to watch.

"God sets the lonely in families," Sheela observed. He glanced at her, knowing she was thinking of her own estranged family. "He leads forth the prisoners in singing." Her glance swept the enclosed compound. "This is my family now. He gave these women to me. We are family to each other."

Rees nodded at the pair beneath the banyan. "What is she singing?"

Sheela paused, listening. "It's about women and freedom."

Our people, our people, how we long to be free.
But until the least of us find freedom
How will it ever come to be?
The women, and our girls,
Who grow to be women,
When we have not education, respect, or honor,
We remain enslaved.
Until we are set free,
Like birds to fly on the wind,
Our people will never know, truly know,
What it means to be free.

As she finished, the idea Rees had toyed with in the States catapulted back to him. When it first came to him, the concept of using music as a therapeutic tool for these women had seemed innovative. But once he'd returned to Mumbai, he wasn't so sure. If it were such a great idea, wouldn't Sheela have already thought of it?

But now he was doing another re-think. Maybe this woman singing this song at this particular moment was a sign. "This song she's singing," he asked, "where did she learn it?"

"I'm guessing she made it up."

"To express herself?"

Sheela looked at him curiously. "Yes, of course."

"Do many of the women do this? Make up music like that, I mean."

"I suppose." She watched him with patient eyes.

"At home, I was thinking how to help these women unlock their emotional baggage, and I wondered if we could use something as basic as music to get at their pain. I don't know how to articulate it. Maybe if I gave you an example." He told Sheela what he'd seen the night he had dinner with Andy Spelling and his family. "Their son's just a little guy, three years old, with autism. They use music to communicate with him. His mother plays simple tunes on the piano to get him to behave in certain ways. To call him to come to dinner, for instance, she plays a song he knows means it's time to wash his hands and go to the table. From what I saw, it really works. His mother says they're experimenting with music as a way to come in through the back door of his mind, since the front door is locked to them. And it occurred to me there are similarities between autistic children who are trapped inside their minds, unable to connect, and our women who are also trapped by the trauma they've endured."

Sheela nodded. "Psychologically, of course, there are many differences, but there are also similarities. Our problem remains a much more practical one. I think it is a good idea, but how would we implement it? You know we are short-handed. No one on our staff knows anything about music, certainly not to the degree you are suggesting. So who could we get to put it into practice?" She paused. "What about this friend you just mentioned, the musician. Was it she who put the idea into your head?"

"I picked her brain a bit."

"Might she be willing to come to Mumbai, to use her gifts here?"

He shook his head. "She's going to Chicago to finish her musical studies."

"You're sure?" The lenses of Sheela's glasses winked in the sunlight, obscuring her dark eyes. "Because if not, it would be something to consider, wouldn't it?"

He looked away from her gaze, unwilling for his friend to see how much he longed for this very thing.

CHAPTER 44

"It's totally dorky, Mom." Jack folded his thin arms across his chest and stuck out his lower lip.

"No, it's not."

"Yes, it is."

Standing in the doorway to Jack's bedroom, Ally pressed her palms to her thighs, fighting the impulse to throttle her child. The object of their debate, the dog costume Darcie made for him, lay spread out across Jack's bed. Jack sat on the floor, surrounded by LEGOs.

"Why is it dorky?" A sense of her inadequacy coiled around her, rendering her helpless in the face of Jack's defiance. He'd been like this for days, worrying her. What had happened to her sweet, compliant son? If he acted like this now, what would he do when she uprooted him from the familiar and moved him to Chicago?

"Look at it." He poked a finger, the disdain in his voice thick as tar. "Doesn't even look like a dog."

Ally huffed an exasperated sigh. Couldn't he at least pretend to show a little gratitude for Darcie's thoughtfulness? With everything else going on, Ally herself had not given a thought to Halloween. For her, Darcie's gift had been an answer to unspoken prayer. Until Jack refused to wear it.

"Bubba, please. At least try it on." She heard the wheedling tone in her voice and cringed. Who was in charge here anyway? "Halloween's tomorrow. We should at least see if it fits."

Jack added another piece to his LEGO creation, not bothering to look up.

"Miss Darcie went to a lot of trouble for you." Darcie had thought of everything, even included several printouts from the web with ideas for doggie face paint. Ally's glance shifted to Moses, spread out beside her son on the carpet. "And it's black, just like Moses."

Jack latched onto the shift in subject. "Why can't we get a dog?" His high whine set Ally's teeth on edge.

She looked at the ceiling, as if she might find patience there. "Because dogs are a lot of work." She'd already explained this half a dozen times. "And right now you're all I can handle." Then, in an attempt to regain control of the conversation—"Are you going to put this on or not?"

"No."

"You're disobeying me now, young man. You want a consequence?"

"But Mom." Tears filled his eyes. "I'll feel like a baby wearing that thing. And the top is way too big. I'll be embarrassed."

She sighed. "It's the only costume we've got, Bubs. If you won't wear this, you won't have a costume for the Harvest Festival and trick-or-treating."

"I don't care. I'll go as myself."

Fine. She turned away, realizing she'd lost the battle but not having the strength to care. "I'm going outside to rake leaves. You can either come with me or stay in here and play by yourself."

She left without his answer. Stepping outside, she sucked in a breath of sea-laden air. For once, she was glad for some time away from her son. Truth was, she felt unsettled, like an unresolved minor chord. She sensed at least part of her son's foul mood was because Rees was gone. Probably the reason for her foul mood, too.

A strong breeze shook leaves from the trees with a noise like a snake's rattle. Sometime over the last few hours, the sky had darkened from soft flannel to an ominous slate gray. The temperature had also dropped. She shivered in her fleece sweatshirt. Better get to work if she hoped to finish before those clouds unleashed their burden.

She trudged toward Penny's house, relieved to see her landlady's car gone from the carport. Penny's strange behavior lately made Ally uneasy. She'd failed to return Ally's calls, and when Ally had swung by to ask about pro-rating her November rent, Penny had refused to answer her knock, though Ally knew she was home by the car parked outside. Was Penny still miffed by Jack's refusal to spend his Saturdays at her place? Well, it hardly mattered now. She wouldn't have to deal with Penny Watrous's whims for many more days. That knowledge ought to please her more than it did.

Nearing the tool shed, Ally's glance fell on one of the towering Douglas firs at the perimeter of the yard. Instead of the deep, rich hue of a healthy tree, this one had faded to a pallid green, tipped by shriveled brown at the uppermost branches. Ally frowned. It looked half-dead. If they didn't take it down soon, the next good storm would do it for them, just as had happened to the tree in Brittany's front yard.

Brittany. Her insides curdled as she recalled the distain frosting Brittany's blue eyes the last time they'd spoken. It still caught her off-guard how their friendship had crashed to an end. She'd tried phoning several times since that day, though she wasn't sure what she could say to make things better. In any case, it was moot. Brittany had never answered or called back. Ally hoped someday they might have a chance to bridge the gulf that gaped between them. She also knew quite possibly they never would.

With a sigh, she pulled the rake and wheelbarrow from the shed and set to work, hoping the rhythmic motions would smooth her frazzled edges. She was so tired. The thought of Chicago should have energized her. Instead, she felt as if she were running a marathon, with the finish line nowhere in sight. She was like Lola's fleeing Gypsies, who in their desperation had tossed into the bushes anything that might slow them down. And she—well, she was tossing away the chance of a different kind of life.

The LORD will fight for you. You need only to be still.

Ally closed her eyes. When Rees had taken them to Deception Pass, she'd caught a glimpse of the peace that might be hers. That night, after Jack was in bed, as she and Rees were saying their final goodbyes, she'd known if she gave the word, she could choose a different path for her and Jack. A different path for her and Rees. She sensed that despite the distance that would soon separate them, their futures might be linked. When she'd stood beside him at Deception Pass, that choice had seemed tantalizingly close. But away from that time and place, fear came crowding back. She believed her chosen course was the right one, so she'd turned her back on what Rees offered.

But now, with Rees gone, she saw with stinging regret an unanticipated cost of her decision. The loss for Jack, who cared for Rees. No, who loved him.

Pushing these thoughts from her mind, Ally filled the wheelbarrow with its first load and took it to the compost heap behind the cottage. As she emptied it, a sound drew her attention: a car turning in at the lane, shells popping beneath its tires. Tensing, she pushed the wheelbarrow around the corner of the cottage, then relaxed when she caught sight of Denny Lewis emerging from his squad car.

Her polite smile of greeting faded as she saw Denny's face, drawn and grim. Tucked beneath his arm was a large manila envelope. She eyed the package warily.

Denny closed the space between them. "Ally." He doffed his hat. His solemn show of courtesy further tightened the qualm in her gut.

"What's wrong?" Her eyes flicked again to the envelope.

He answered her question with another. "Is your full name Cadence Alise Brennan?"

"Yes." Alarm zipped through her. How did he know her real name?

He held out the thick brown envelope. "I've been instructed by the law firm of Mulhoney, Johnson & Johnson to serve you these papers."

His words struck like a rock to her chest. Her lips went numb. "Why?"

"Better read it for yourself." A tortured expression twisted his features. "It's all there."

She swallowed. "And if I refuse to accept this?"

"You'll be in contempt of court." His official demeanor cracked. "Don't do that, Ally. It'll only get you in a whole lot more trouble than you're already in. Get yourself a lawyer just as quick as you can." He took her hand and wrapped her unbending fingers around the envelope. "What you do at that point is between you and your attorney." He looked at her long and hard. "I'm really sorry, Ally."

She waited until his car left the property before, with a trembling hand, she pulled the papers from the envelope. The first few lines made all the blood rush from her head.

YOU ARE HEREBY COMMANDED TO APPEAR at the offices of Mark D. Mulhoney, Johnson & Johnson, PLLC, 1502 Fourth Avenue, Suite 3300, Seattle, Washington, 98101, on the 22 day of November, 2010, at the hour of 10 a.m., then and there to testify as a witness at the request of the Kyle James Wylie in the above-entitled action, and to remain in attendance until discharged. You are further directed and required to have ready for review and/or reproduction the following papers, information, and documents regarding the birth and custody of Jack Christian Brennan....

Kyle was suing her for custody of Jack.

Ally's world tilted and she slipped, plummeting toward cold, unfamiliar waters. *Oh, God. Oh, no.*

She ran for the house. In the kitchen, she grabbed her cell from the counter and dialed Rees's number. He'd scribbled it on a scrap of paper the night he'd said goodbye. Her hands were shaking so badly she could scarcely press the right numbers—so many of them!—but finally she hit the last one and the call went through.

One ring…two… A scraping sound made her whirl around, expecting to see Kyle's leering face at the window. Only a tree branch bent by a rise of wind, but she lost her grip on the phone. It tumbled to the floor. The plastic cracked open and the battery flew out. As she swooped to pick up the pieces, her gaze caught on a plastic bag on the floor. Her son had wadded up his costume, put it inside the bag and dumped it where she'd be sure to notice.

Then another sound, the scuff of socked feet. Jack came to the doorway. His brown eyes wide and wary, he clutched Fluff to his chest like a shield. A wave of déjà vu spun her back, back to the day their home had been invaded by Kyle. The day she'd met Darcie, and Rees. Jack had stood in that same doorway, clutching Fluff, just like now.

He shuffled across the linoleum and took the phone from her. "I think it's broken, Mom." His face puckered with worry.

When she pulled him into her lap, he wrapped his arms around her neck, warm and tight. "It's okay, Bubba. I didn't really need it." What had she been thinking, anyway? Rees was half a world away, much too far to do them any good now. She thought fleetingly of Rees's lawyer friend, but what could he do? Only file a restraining order, which would make Kyle angrier.

Jack burrowed his face into her side, closing every distance between them. "I'll wear the costume, Mommy," came his muffled voice. "Really, I don't mind."

She tucked his head beneath her chin. "You don't have to wear the costume, Bubba." She'd told Sam she'd give him a week to find her replacement, but she couldn't afford even that much time now. Her red-hot instinct was to leave this very second, but she had to do it carefully. She couldn't overlook a single detail or leave anything behind that might enable Kyle to find them again.

She'd pack tonight. They'd leave tomorrow morning, just as soon as she could get everything in the car. By the time the kids of Langley had donned their Halloween costumes, she and Jack would be long gone. She would make sure of it.

CHAPTER 45

In his third floor flat, lying on the futon that doubled as his bed, Rees stared up at a dark ceiling. He'd been back in Mumbai over a week, plenty long enough to get over his jet lag. Yet this was the third morning in a row he'd awakened before four and been unable to return to sleep. With an impatient grunt, he flipped to his stomach and searched in vain for a cool spot on his pillow.

Whatever was keeping him awake wasn't jet lag.

For the first few days after his return, a combination of traveler's haze and brute willpower had allowed him to maintain a laser-like focus on work. His visit to the compound had also helped to distract him. But now, as he settled into his old routine, he found control slipping, his thoughts turning more and more to what he'd left behind. Or rather, whom.

Why not take her with you? Darcie's question circled relentlessly inside his head, chased by his response: *That's impossible.*

He'd believed it at the time. Problem was, he'd not been considering the big picture, nor taking into account One for whom nothing was impossible.

Seeing Sheela again had reminded him of that.

Though daylight wouldn't paint the city's whitewashed buildings for hours yet, traffic outside began to rumble. Knowing it was useless to hope for more sleep, he rose from the futon and went into the miniscule kitchen of his studio apartment, where he put the kettle on and scooped four generous spoonfuls of Sumatra coffee grinds into his French press. While he waited for the water to boil, he logged onto his laptop. He would use these hours to catch up on paperwork.

But he couldn't concentrate, even the strong coffee sweetened with condensed milk unable to dispel the fog from his brain. His thoughts kept wandering to Ally. Had he been wrong not to tell her his feelings before he left? Would it have made a difference if she'd known what he was willing to put on the line for her?

He had no idea if she would return his feelings. She'd never given him any sign she felt the same. Except once.

When you spend all your time looking back, it means you can't see what's right in front of you. The look in those green eyes when he'd said that to her—she'd known what he was saying. A light had sparked and flared, sizzling for one long moment before she looked away. And she'd blushed. Did that mean something, or nothing at all? And why didn't he have the guts to find out?

He crossed to the window. In dawn's first light, he could just make out the outline of the scaffolded building across the street. An abandoned apartment complex encircled by a low wall, half-destroyed, with jagged bits of masonry sticking up like rotted teeth. Yesterday, he'd watched a brown-skinned man in a white loincloth move like a monkey around the scaffolding as he applied spackle to the myriad cracks and crevices.

I'm like that building. The thought ripped through him. Ever since losing Julie, he'd built scaffolding around his heart. Then he'd spackled over the cracks in his soul by embracing a high-octane career that risked his safety, even his life, every day. But it was mere camouflage, carefully controlled risks calculated to keep his heart untouched.

In the quietness, Rees's cell phone rang. He gave a startled glance to the clock. 4:10. Who would be calling at this ungodly hour? Darcie never called him this early. Across the display, an unknown Washington ID flickered. His heart leapt. Ally?

He snatched the phone to his ear and spoke her name.

Silence.

"Ally?" He pulled the phone from his ear and saw the call had ended. He waited a moment for her to call back. When she didn't, he fumbled to find her number stored on his phone. But when he dialed, his call went straight to voicemail. He asked her to call him back as soon as she got his message.

Unsettled, he put the phone down and tried to return to the report he was drafting for Nigel. Every minute he expected the phone to ring again. Thirty minutes passed. Still no call. He gave up trying to concentrate on Nigel's report and called Ally again. Same result.

Something was wrong. Ally always carried her phone with her because of Jack. She'd have seen by now he was trying to reach her. Why wasn't she responding?

He rose to take his shower, hoping the tepid water would clear his head and dissipate the worry wrapping itself like a strangler fig around his brain. Instead, his unease increased. As soon as he was shaved and dressed, he dialed his sister's number. She answered on the third ring. "Rees?"

"Something's wrong with Ally." Not even bothering with a greeting.

Darcie's startled silence stretched across oceans. "Is it Jack?"

"I don't know. She called my phone an hour ago. I've tried calling her back, but all I get is voicemail. Have you seen her lately?"

"I stopped by her place before work this morning to drop off some of Paul's cookies. She was fine then. She knows she can rely on Moses to alert her to the first sign of trouble. Seemed a little down, maybe, but otherwise good."

"Jack, too?"

"Yes."

He wanted to feel reassured, but worry still encroached like fog. "You're sure?"

"We talked a little. She had a day of yard work planned. She didn't mention anything else. You want me to call?"

"Please, and text me when you reach her. Or no, tell her to call me, would you?"

As Rees ended the call, Julie's face rose before him. A flashback that felt more like a premonition. He remembered the hours on the morning of Julie's fateful flight, when he'd been unable to reach her by phone. Despite every rational assurance otherwise, he'd known something was wrong. And he'd been right. In fact, by the time he began to worry, Julie was already dead.

The memory made him choke. Had Wylie come back? Was that why Ally called? Was she scared…or worse? What if Wylie wasn't content merely to frighten Ally this time, but to harm her? He'd done it before. And now there was Jack. What if Wylie intended the worst?

His phone rang. He fumbled to answer, nearly dropped it. "Ally?"

But it wasn't the strange emptiness of an international connection that met his ear. "Rees?"

"Sheela." His heart plummeted.

"I am sorry to call you so early."

Rees stood, raking his fingers through his hair. Why was Sheela even awake at this hour? Then he thought, *Jayashri*. "What's wrong? Is it Jayashri?"

"She is fine, that is not the reason I'm calling. You will forgive me, I hope, for awakening you."

"I was already awake."

"Well, I was not. Until five minutes ago, I was sleeping, but my dream awakened me. I have spent these last minutes questioning whether I should call. I had the strongest impression I should. I decided to risk waking you, and perhaps angering you for my foolishness, rather than wait for a more human hour to call."

More humane. Though Sheela's English was nearly flawless, sometimes she stumbled. "Why did you think you should call me?"

"Because of my dream. May I tell you of it?"

"Yes." The weight of his increasing foreboding dropped him to the edge of his futon.

"There was a woman. I saw her at a distance, standing at the edge of a great body of water. It looked...alive. I don't know how else to explain it. The water was a rich green, deep and jewel-like. Like an emerald. I've never seen water that color except in photographs."

Puget Sound. Rees's insides tensed.

"This woman stood at the edge of a structure of some sort, something man-made, like a platform, or a dock. I somehow knew she needed to get to the other side, but this structure, whatever it was, I couldn't see if it stretched to the other side. She kept looking behind her. I knew by her expression she was pursued. I have seen that same look many times on the faces of our rescued women. What, or who, pursued this woman, I could not tell, but she was very frightened. She wore no clothing, but this was not provocative. It showed only how very vulnerable she was." She paused.

Rees closed his eyes, apprehension swelling inside his chest.

"In my dream, I viewed all of this from behind the woman, seeing only her back. Her form was beautiful, her long, dark hair streaming down her back halfway to her waist. But then a wind rose up, sweeping her hair aside, and that's when I saw it. A crack. Running lengthwise up her back."

A prickle began low on Rees's own spine. "A wound?"

"No, not a wound, not like what you'd imagine. There was no blood, nor even a scar. I don't know how to describe it except to say it was like a piece of fine wood had splintered right up its middle. And just as her nakedness spoke to her vulnerability, this crack revealed her brokenness. She was not whole. Fear hovered over her like an aura. I've never thought of fear as a color, but it's black. There was a darkness surrounding her." Rees's throat felt stuffed with cotton as she continued. "She turned her head once to look behind, and her eyes were a beautiful emerald green, like the water."

CHAPTER 46

The day of the Harvest Festival arrived, along with steady rain and a forecast for a whole lot worse by nightfall. Darcie skipped church that morning in order to meet with the other committee members to begin set-up in Langley's Community Hall for the afternoon's festivity. She welcomed the diversion. It got her mind off her anxiety over Ally and Jack.

When Rees had called yesterday so worried about Ally, Darcie had been at the Holcombs'. She'd called Ally as soon as she was off the phone with Rees, but she too had gotten only voicemail. Darcie finished with the Holcombs quickly, anxious to swing by the Brennans' to see for herself what was going on.

Ally had met her at the door, Moses beside her.

"Rees is worried about you." Darcie peered past Ally into the cottage, the front room stacked with boxes. "Neither of us could reach you on your phone."

"I dropped it today and it broke. Sorry."

"But otherwise everything's okay? You look pale."

"I'm tired." Ally anchored herself at the threshold, making no move to invite Darcie inside. "You know how it is, a million things to do before we leave."

"Rees mentioned he missed a call from you. Why did you call him?"

"Oh, that." Ally's eyes darted behind her, as if checking to see who might be listening. "Jack had wanted to talk to him, so we called, but no one answered. And then my phone stopped working. I'm sorry we worried Rees."

"Where's Jack?" She stooped to scratch the top of Moses' head as he stood patiently beside Ally.

"In his room playing LEGOs. Why?"

"Wanted to see if the costume worked out okay."

"Oh, yes. Thank you again. That was so thoughtful of you." She pulled Moses out of the doorway and made a move to shut the door. "Sorry, but I really do need to get back to packing."

Darcie had to let it drop after that, afraid further questions would only alienate. Moses' presence attested to their relative safety. Reluctantly, she'd left Ally and phoned Rees as soon as she reached the house. When she got his voicemail, she described the situation and urged him to call her back. He never had.

But this morning, what little reassurance she'd had evaporated when she emerged from the shower to discover Ally had delivered Moses back to them. "What about Kyle Wylie?" she'd demanded when Paul told her. Rees would not be happy. She debated whether to let him know. But how would that help?

"That's what I said, and she said not to worry, she had everything taken care of."

"What does that mean?" Frustration coiled around her, making her wish she'd been available to question Ally. *She* would have gotten better answers.

Paul had leveled her with a look. "She's a grown woman, Darce, and a responsible mom. We can't go around second-guessing her every decision without damaging her trust."

He was right. It was that same reason she'd quit grilling Ally yesterday. Still, she'd determined then to ask Ally about all of this when she saw her at the festival this afternoon. She would insist at the very least she take Moses back until she left for Chicago.

Outside the community center, thick, steel-gray clouds clustered overhead and gusts of wind tipped the waves of the sound white. Darcie tried to focus on the task of hanging orange and yellow streamers. She and Lauren pushed bales of hay around the perimeter of the room and debated whether the predicted storm would be good for the festival. "It might end up keeping families at home." Lauren positioned decorative gourds on top of a stack of bales. "They say it's going to get pretty stormy."

"On the other hand, we might get more people to show up," Darcie countered. "Not many kids will want to be out trick-or-treating in this rain. They'll wind up here instead."

Lauren paused, loops of pumpkin-shaped twinkle lights draped over her arms. "I think you're right, in which case we're going to need more candy for prizes."

"I have several more bags of donated candy at home." She'd not brought them because she thought they'd have enough. "I can go get them now if you'd like."

"If you don't mind."

Outside, the wind blew across the sound, hard as a slap, and rain came down in a steady, drenching pour. As she dashed to the car, Darcie felt confirmed in their consensus. No mother in her right mind would take a child out in this weather.

On the five-minute drive home, she tuned her car radio to the weather station. "Puget Sound residences are being asked to stay home to wait out the storm," the DJ said, "which promises to be a big one. The weather has grounded flights at SeaTac, and gusts of wind of up to 60 miles per hour are expected to close the Washington State ferries by late afternoon."

At home, Darcie felt a flicker of surprise Paul's truck wasn't beneath the carport. Church would have ended half an hour ago. He hadn't mentioned other plans. But she didn't dwell on it, more relieved than otherwise to let herself into an empty house. Ever since Paul had dropped his bombshell, a coldness had taken up residence in their home. If she hadn't been so frustrated by what he was doing, the atmosphere would have frightened her.

Who knows what lies ahead? Her own words dropped into her mind, a fragment of her conversation with Rees before he'd returned for Mumbai. She'd encouraged Rees to consider Ally's hopes and dreams as well as his own, insisting they needn't be mutually exclusive. Yet in her own marriage, she was doing exactly the opposite, refusing to believe her husband's dreams might be compatible with hers. Why should she assume they weren't? Could there be a way forward by means neither could yet see?

The idea momentarily interrupted her swirling thoughts, but she brushed it aside as Moses and Aaron greeted her at the door. Moses whistled low in his throat as his tail swept side to side in wide, anxious waves. "Storm making you nervous, boy? Don't worry, it's just wind." As Darcie took a minute to soothe him, she remembered why Paul had said Ally returned the dog. That she had everything "taken care of."

What on earth is that supposed to mean? Darcie pulled the bags of extra candy from the pantry. She could think of no answer that satisfied. Despite having determined to question Ally further at the festival this afternoon, she knew now she couldn't wait even that long. Before rejoining Lauren at the Community Center, she would drop in at Ally's again. She no longer cared about respecting boundaries. To silence her worries, she had to know.

Feeling a tiny peace at reaching this decision, she shut the dogs in the kitchen once more and was returning to the car when she noticed the door to the back shed standing open. Paul must have left it ajar. Now the wind had blown it wide.

Oh, brother. She dumped the bags in the trunk and grabbed the umbrella from the front seat. Before she'd walked ten feet, her loafers were soaked through. Her annoyance toward Paul returned. Where was he, anyway? Maybe with Diego, working out the details of the sale. Paul said it was moving along swiftly.

She supposed she should wish for this. A quick and easy sale so they could move on with their lives. Which might, if she could just accept it, contain enough possibility to see both of their dreams fulfilled. In ways as yet unforeseen.

A strong push of wind nearly ripped the umbrella from her hand as she reached the shed door. That's when she thought she heard a sound coming from inside the shed, a soft snuffle. An animal? Not a raccoon, she hoped. They got vicious when cornered. Why hadn't she thought to bring a shovel or broom? Wielding her umbrella as a weapon, she peered carefully around the door.

A small child huddled on a seat of the John Deere mower. *Jack*? Here she was, all anxious about Ally and her son, and one of them had found his way to her backyard. She found this somehow reassuring. Then, taking a closer look, her insides squeezed tight, like a sponge wringing dry. The boy was dressed in the black sweats she'd given him for Halloween. Though he had his back to her, she could see the costume looked pathetic. Nothing at all like a dog, even with the felt ears and tail. What had she been thinking?

All at once, she knew in her body what it meant to love someone more than she loved herself. *I would do anything for this child. I love him.* The thought spiraled from its niche, jolting her on impact.

A beat of silence, as if the Divine wanted this astonishing fact to sink in. And then—*As if he were your own?*

Yes!

She could almost feel the warmth of His smile blooming inside her chest. *Well, then.*

This new knowledge filled her with colliding surges of fear and wonder as she stepped into the shed's relative darkness. "Jack?"

He jumped, whirled to face her.

"Hey, it's okay, it's just me. What are you doing here?" No answer. She moved inside. "Does your mom know you're here?"

A quick headshake, the floppy, felt ears tipping forward over his bangs. "She told me to go away."

Darcie frowned, her uneasiness returning. No way Ally would have told Jack to go anywhere alone. "I doubt she said that."

"She told me to go to my room, but it's what she meant."

"You shouldn't have left the house, Jack. Your mom will be very worried. But I see you're ready for the Harvest Festival, so that's good. All your friends will be there. It'll be lots of fun."

He tugged at the felt tail lying across his lap. "We're not going."

"Why not?"

"We're going somewhere." Then he looked up at her, his eyes large and anxious. "I wasn't supposed to tell anyone that."

"You mean, to Chicago?" Ally wasn't due to leave for another week.

"Someplace else, but I don't know where. Mom wouldn't say."

Uneasiness flared into full-blown anxiety. Rees was right. Something was very wrong.

Moses burst into the shed, his thick coat glistening. He went straight to Jack, his plumey tail fanning droplets of rainwater over him. "Moses!" With joy in his voice, Jack slid from the lawnmower and encircled the dog with his arms, oblivious to the wet.

Darcie groaned. "Moses! How'd you get out?" She must have failed to latch the door securely when she left the house. Telling herself to stay calm, to focus on one problem at a time, she hooked the dog by his collar. "Come on, ol' boy, let's put you back in the house. And then, Jack, I'm taking you home."

He thrust out his lower lip. "I don't want to go home. I want to stay here."

"Sorry, kiddo, you can't. I need to talk to your mom."

CHAPTER 47

Wind hurled rain like an endless blast of shotgun pellets against the house as Ally tossed clothes into suitcases. Sweaters went in on top of shoes, socks beside jeans, the entire contents of her underwear drawer on top of everything else. She no longer cared about being methodical, the important thing was to keep moving. Constant motion was the only thing keeping her from thinking about all the *what-ifs* and *what-might-have-beens.*

She wheeled the suitcase from the bedroom to the kitchen and propped it beside the backdoor. They couldn't take all their belongings, or even half. Only what they needed most to start over.

But food. She should take food, whatever she could squeeze into the Saturn. She ducked into the utility room, grabbed the largest cardboard box she could find from the shelf, and dumped its contents of cleaning supplies on the floor. On her way out, her glance fell on the dryer Rees had fixed. She touched its cold, smooth surface. Rees. Her eyes squeezed shut as memory bumped the ache in her chest that refused to go away.

She spun on her heel and returned to the kitchen. From the pantry she pulled an unopened bottle of apple juice, granola bars, turkey jerky and peanut butter. Spaghetti O's, tuna, kidney beans and macaroni-and-cheese. Once she'd emptied the shelves, she shoved the box beside her suitcase and turned to start on the refrigerator. That's when her glance fell on the papers scattered across the kitchen table.

The legal summons. The very sight of it turned her stomach queasy, but at least it had bought her some time. She'd played his game, signed on the dotted line, even gone into town to hire a courier to get it back to the attorney who had sent it. She'd let Kyle think he'd won. Demanding custody of Jack? A hideous idea, but she should have seen it coming. The photograph he stole and tore in half was his way of telling her what he'd planned all along.

She wished she'd seen the warning for what it was so she could have acted first. Because if she filed charges now, it would be seen as defensive. Retaliatory. She should have trusted Rees. Then she could have minimized the damage to Jack. He was all that mattered. She no longer cared what Kyle might do to her. But Jack…

She had to get him out of here.

They would leave this place. Not for Chicago, where Kyle's lawyers would find her. No, they'd go where no one knew them. She would start over from scratch. She'd done it once;

she could do it again. And she would tell no one. Not Gina. Not Darcie. She dared not think about the steep price because it was the only way her plan could work.

With the cooler filled with the contents of the fridge, she had only one suitcase left, the one for Jack. Heading toward his closed door, she called his name. No answer. She frowned. Was he still pouting? She'd banished him to his room an hour earlier when she'd grown impatient with his fussy demands. He didn't understand that she was doing this for his own good. "Jack." She opened his door. "It's time to—"

He was gone, his room empty except for the coloring book splayed open on the floor.

"Jack?" She turned from the room, hot panic flooding her chest. The cottage was too tiny for her to have missed him in any of the other rooms. He must have gone outside. A glance through the window made her stomach drop. In this storm? Already the wind had ripped almost every remaining leaf from trees bowing beneath the strength of its gale force. She tripped over her suitcase in her hurry to reach the back door.

She wrenched it open. "Jack!" The only answer was the roaring rush of white-capped waves beating against the rocks just yards from the cottage's foundation.

Think, Ally. Think! What was Jack wearing today? She drew a blank, she'd hardly seen him all morning. Clutching the door-frame, she scanned the beach, searching for a splash of color, any color that didn't belong to the landscape. Jack had grown up with the sound as his backyard and had a healthy respect for the water, but these waves were vicious. Ravenous. If he'd gotten too close, he could have lost his footing on the shifting rocks, gotten pulled under. Easy prey for the roiling black beast waiting to devour.

Darcie's blue jeans were soaked, and water oozed from her leather loafers by the time she and Jack reached the cottage. Before she could knock, the front door flung open and there was Ally, looking a bit wild, her green eyes dilated to almost black, her dark curls escaping their hair band. When a gush of wind snatched the doorknob from Ally's grasp, she let it go and dropped to her knees in front of her son. "Thank God," she breathed, pulling him to her. He wrapped his small arms around her neck.

The mother-son reunion made Darcie's heart thud painfully. She prodded them gently inside so she could shut the door. The sudden quiet seemed, by comparison, as if someone had twisted a volume knob, silencing the raving elements outside.

"Where did you go?" Ally pressed kisses into Jack's damp hair. "I was worried."

"I didn't think you'd notice I was gone."

Ally drew back and seemed to really see him for the first time. "You're wearing your costume." Her voice choked and she hugged him again. "Bubba, I need you to do something for me. Would you please go into your room and choose three things you'd like to take with us? Just three, okay?"

"Does Fluff count?"

"No, Fluff's a given. Three things other than Fluff, okay? You can bring your whole box of LEGOs if you want, that counts as only one thing."

"Okay."

As he shuffled off, Ally rose slowly from her knees, rubbing her eyes. "Where did you find him?"

"In our tool shed."

"Tool shed! How long had he been there?"

"Not very long, I think. Moses let me know."

Ally turned her face toward the cold stone fireplace. "Sometimes I think I'm the worst kind of mother. I didn't even notice he was gone until five minutes ago. Thank you for bringing him back."

From somewhere at the back of the house, a window screen came loose and banged against the cottage like a drum. Darcie raised her voice to be heard above the racket. "Jack says you're going somewhere."

"We are." Ally bit her lip, an expression Darcie could not read shuttering Ally's eyes. Ally's gaze shifted to her viola's hard case resting by the fireplace. She picked up the case and carried it into the kitchen.

"To Chicago?" Darcie followed her.

"No."

"But you're still going to Chicago, right?"

"Not anymore."

"What changed?"

"Everything." She set the case by the back door. With growing alarm, Darcie took in the boxes of food supplies, the packed cooler. This did not look like any kind of overnighter. This looked like Ally taking off for good.

"Is this why you brought Moses back this morning?" Ally's shrug sent a chill through Darcie. If Ally disappeared...she didn't even want to think about the effect it would have on

Rees. Not to mention what it would do to her if she never saw Jack again. "Are you going to tell me what's going on?"

"If I do, it'll ruin everything."

"Will you at least tell me where you're going?"

"I can't."

Darcie crossed her arms. "Well, you can't leave anyway."

"What's going to stop me?"

As if in answer, the lights flickered—once, twice. "That is." Darcie jerked an arm toward the roof, where pelting rain roared like an airplane taking off. "Haven't you been listening to the news? There's a major storm moving in. Airport's closed. Ferries are shutting down. You can't get off the island tonight. Ferries will start up again in the morning. By then, we'll have figured something else out. We'll call Rees; he'll know what to do."

For a moment, Ally's expression clouded, allowing Darcie the fleeting hope she'd succeeded in dissuading Ally from her crazy course. But then she squared her shoulders. "Then I'll drive off the island."

"There's only one way out by car."

"I know. Deception Pass. Rees showed me."

"Are you nuts? Crossing that bridge in this kind of wind? They've probably closed that, too."

"It's a risk I'll have to—" She paused, listening. "What's that?"

Darcie cocked her ear. Above the wind's steady howl rose another noise, the sharp staccato of a dog barking. The sound grew steadily louder. Nearer. She let out an exasperated breath. "It's Moses. He keeps escaping. I'll go let him in or he'll never shut up." She hurried from the kitchen to intercept him at the front door.

"Did you say Moses?" Jack appeared, Fluff dangling from one hand.

"He must have followed you, Jack." Darcie opened the door, gasped, and stepped back.

On Ally's porch, hand raised as if to knock, stood a man of medium height with dark blond stubble shadowing a narrow chin. His brown boots were soaked, the shoulders of his red jacket dark with moisture. Though she'd never seen this man, she had seen those large brown eyes before, set in someone else's face. And she knew.

She was looking at Jack's father.

Somewhere over the Canadian Northern Territories, the posh inflections of the British Airways pilot came over the intercom. "Ladies and gentlemen, we regret to inform you of a change in plans. A weather system has arrived over Puget Sound making landing at SeaTac impossible. We will be diverting to Portland. Our agents will be standing by to assist you in finding additional transportation to get you to your intended destination."

Rees suffered his first real qualm since leaving Mumbai as his seatmate—a portly Londoner with gin-tinged breath—swore robustly. Had he launched himself on a very expensive wild goose chase?

But Sheela had been so sure. When he'd identified the woman in her dream as Ally, Sheela's response had been immediate and decisive. "You must go to her. She is in trouble. She needs you."

"But how?" Though he shared her sense of urgency, his rational side told him to slow down. Objections lined up: Nigel needed him, he was scheduled to testify in court in two days, he couldn't afford another plane ticket. And what if they were wrong?

But Sheela, harboring no such doubts, had refused to let him debate. "You hop on a plane and go, my friend. You take care of the possible and leave the impossible to God."

Take a risk, man, the one you were too chicken to take before. In the end, his heart had decided for him. But then everything had happened so fast. It had been a dash to get him to the airport in time to catch the only flight that would put him back in Washington within twenty-four hours. He'd not even had time to let Darcie know he was flying back.

Now he had to wonder if it was all just wishful thinking. He even doubted Sheela's advice. The years they'd worked together at Sanctuary had taught him to trust her instincts, but if this journey was really God-ordained, would He allow him to get stuck in Portland? Rees might as well have stayed in Mumbai.

His British companion in the window seat jabbed at the call button with a stubby finger, summoning an attendant to their row. "Yes, sir?" A trim flight attendant, her blond hair pulled into a chignon, materialized at Rees's elbow.

"Another drink, if I may," the man said.

"Of course." She switched off the call light and looked down at Rees. "How about you, sir? May I bring you something?"

"I'm fine." *Ha, hardly.* The blasted flight was landing in Portland, a good four hours from Langley under the best of circumstances. What could he do from Portland? Call Andy? Or Denny Lewis? And say he suspected what, exactly? In her last message, Darcie had told him she had personally seen Ally at the cottage with Moses and Jack. She reported them all to be fine. Which did nothing to assuage his fear. He wanted to hear from Ally herself. He thrashed under the weight of all the unknowns.

Be still.

As the voice dropped wordlessly into his ear, Rees gripped the arms of his seat. Be still? He'd made a career out of rescuing women from harm, and now it looked as if he would be destined to fail the woman he loved when she needed him most.

Be still and see the deliverance I will bring today.

Hoping it really was God's voice and not more wishful thinking, Rees blew out a slow breath and focused on untying the knots that clenched his stomach.

Inside the Portland Airport, Rees joined the endless queue of irritable, jet-lagged passengers at the rental-car counter, each hoping to complete their passage to Seattle. But when his turn came, the red-headed agent told him, with careful regret, that the last car had just been rented. "There is, however, a chartered bus leaving for Seattle in two hours."

Two hours? "Nothing before then?"

"No, sir. I'm sorry. We've had to call a bus up from Eugene as it is. It's not scheduled to arrive before then."

Rees closed his eyes in defeat and was about to step away when someone jostled his elbow. He opened his eyes and found himself looking into the florid face of his British seatmate. The man had already been helped but he'd returned, having shoved his way to the front of the line.

Inserting himself in front of Rees, he glared at the rental agent. "What kind of customer service is this?" he demanded loudly enough to turn the head of every agent behind the counter as well as those waiting in line. "You gave me a manual transmission when I specifically told you I needed an automatic."

The young woman's face paled beneath her freckles. "I'm sorry, sir. I must have missed that." Her keyboard rattled as she did a quick search of her database before lifting her reluctant gaze again. "I'm so sorry, but that was the last available car. If you'll– "

He didn't allow her to finish. "That car is no good to me!" He shook the key in front of her flustered face. "I don't know how to drive a manual!"

Rees took the key dangling from the man's beefy fist. "I do."

Chapter 48

Ally froze as the big dog launched himself at the man on her porch. *Kyle*. Her brain barely registered this before Kyle whirled toward Moses' snarling lunge, pulling a Taser from his puffed jacket. With a resounding *crack!* the Taser made contact. Ally screamed as Moses yelped and fell to the floor, unmoving.

Darcie sank to her knees beside him. With an anguished cry, Jack dropped Fluff and ran forward. Ally grabbed him as he darted past. She clutched him to her chest, heart beating like an angry fist.

Ignoring Darcie, Kyle locked eyes with Ally. Rain matted his blond hair to his head, moisture glistening on the thick stubble of his chin. But his eyes. There was something wrong with them. They were changing, the pupils widening so his eyes seemed more black than brown. "That was quite a greeting, Cadence." He stepped over the threshold. Rain driven sideways by the wind poured through the open door, showering Darcie as she crouched over her dog.

Kyle smiled at Ally, exploding a bubble of fear inside her. She stiffened as he crossed the room to crouch in front of Jack. The smell of stale cigarette smoke clung to him. "Hey, fella." Jack pressed himself into the soft flesh of her abdomen. "You have no idea who I am, do you?"

Jack shook his head. Kyle shot Ally a reproachful look. When he straightened, she glanced at the Taser in his hand. Her mind felt shredded, every thought scattered. She couldn't outrun Kyle now, not with Jack. Did she dare try to swat the Taser away?

He quirked an amused eyebrow, as if sensing her intent, and tightened his grip on the weapon. "You signed the papers my attorney sent." He angled himself so as not to turn his back on Darcie, who hadn't moved from the doorway. His voice was strange. Blurred. Had he been drinking? "When he told me that, I got a hinky feeling, knowing how you have a way of disappearing on me." He glanced at the pile of luggage in the kitchen. "Looks like I was right to be worried."

"What do you want, Kyle?" How calm she sounded. Amazing, because beneath her sweater, she could feel sweat drenching her skin. The little cottage seemed to close in on her. She felt trapped. No escape. No chance for help. No one on earth besides the people in this room knew the trouble they were in. *Dear God, please help us.*

"Same thing I've always wanted." He touched her cheek with a bent knuckle. "You."

And then it struck her. The summons. It was all a ploy. He didn't want Jack. He wanted her. And in order to get her, he would use Jack to distract her mentally, exhaust her financially, wear her down physically and emotionally. He'd pull her through the fire until he got what he desired.

She held back an icy shudder. "You can't have me, Kyle."

"No?" He rubbed his thumb thoughtfully across her lips. She willed herself not to flinch, afraid of angering him. "He's a beautiful boy, Cadence. I can see why you're so attached to him. I look forward to getting to know him better myself."

"That's not going to happen."

"I've got a lawyer who says it will."

A sudden swoop of wind came in, so strong the cottage trembled in its grip. And then, a terrible ripping sound, like the rending of thick cloth. A deep, rustling rumble, a jarring crash. The tree! Lights flashed to darkness. Jack screamed as the world dimmed. Ally felt him torn from her arms.

"Jack!" By the gray light from the living room window, Ally saw him in Kyle's grasp, Taser at his neck. When Darcie lunged to her feet, Kyle glared at her, pressing the gun deeper into Jack's soft skin. Jack whimpered. Darcie withdrew, her face framed with all the fear Ally felt.

Jack's terrified gaze met Ally's. Ice slid across her skin. "Please." It came out as a whisper. She tried again. "Please, Kyle, let him go. Please don't hurt him. He's just a child."

"I don't want to hurt him. I really don't. That's never what I want, to hurt people."

Ally glanced toward the door. In the dim light, she could see the outline of Moses' inert form sprawled on the porch. He still hadn't moved. Had the jolt stopped his heart? Moses easily weighed twice as much as Jack. If the Taser had done that to Moses, Jack wouldn't stand a chance.

She had to get Kyle away from him.

She sucked in a breath. "You win, Kyle."

His eyes narrowed. "Win?"

"I'll go with you."

Darcie gasped, but Ally refused to look at her. Like the doe, she would run to draw the hunter's fire from her fawn.

Stepping toward Kyle, Ally tried to ignore the pounding of her heart. She dropped to her knees before her son, all-too-aware of the Taser pressed like fangs into his neck. She looked into the brown eyes she adored. Touching his face, she caught the tears collecting beneath his chin. "No matter what happens, remember Mommy loves you." Straightening, she looked at Darcie. "Take him. Keep him safe."

And to Kyle, "Let's go."

Rees had been driving for hours, wipers going full speed as wind buffeted the little Honda Civic. He flew by Olympia. Tacoma. Kent. Spent one precious half-hour detouring into Seattle to drop his British passenger at the Westin before hitting I-5 again. Outside, trees flashing by were bent over like balsa wood. The only good thing about the driving conditions was few other people fool enough to brave them. He pretty much had the road to himself. He kept the radio tuned to KOMO 1000 as he raced north, volume cranked high so he could hear the broadcaster's reports above the roar.

Leaving Seattle behind, he felt a lift of hope. Less than an hour to go.

But then the Washington State Department of Transportation announced all ferry runs shut down. No ferries? Rees pounded the wheel with the heel of his hand. *God, are you kidding me?* He nearly screamed his frustration.

And then he remembered. Deception Pass. He could still cross over to the island by the bridge. It would double the time to reach Langley, but it was the only way.

Chapter 49

Kyle's truck shot down Ally's driveway, his breath coming quickly. Ally turned her head away from the sour smell. Outside, the sky was like night, black clouds rolling toward them from the mainland. He headed north. For miles he said nothing, only occasionally squeezing her knee, stroking it as he vigilantly watched his rearview. Was he worried someone would give chase? But who? Darcie? Denny Lewis, if she managed to alert him? But first Denny would have to correctly guess Kyle's route.

They passed few other drivers insane enough to be on the road in this weather. Only wind-tossed trees and houses, no yellow-lit windows shining into the unnatural darkness. Apparently satisfied no one was following them, Kyle pulled the truck to the shoulder. Her heart thumped as gravel crackled beneath the truck's wheels. Leaving the engine running, he took her face in his hands. "You're what I want, Cadence." He searched her eyes. "All I've ever wanted. You know that, don't you?"

She said nothing.

His expression hardening, he tightened his grip on her chin. "Don't you?" Her teeth pressed into the soft flesh inside her cheeks. "Tell me you know it."

"I do." Though everything inside her recoiled from his touch, a voice told her to say what he wanted to hear. "I know it, Kyle."

He kissed her, his tongue invading her mouth. She fought back a wave of nausea.

He leaned in, fingers fumbling at the hem of her sweater. Heart in her throat, she pressed her hand flat against his chest, searching frantically for a distraction. "What did you tell Libby, Kyle? She used to love me. Why did you turn her against me?"

He hesitated. Withdrew his hand from her sweater. "I didn't have to tell her a thing. You did the damage all by yourself, just by staying away. When you disappeared, it was hell on your dad. Ate away at him like a cancer. Nothing Mom said or did could fix it. That's what she couldn't stand. Couldn't stand he needed you more than he needed her." He shrugged. "Gave me peace of mind, actually, knowing my mother wouldn't welcome you with open arms if you ever did show up again. I couldn't afford for her to become your ally. Who knows how you would have bent the truth. I might have lost you then."

Ally closed her eyes as another wave of nausea clenched her stomach. At least now she knew.

A blast of wind swept rain hard against the truck. Enough, apparently, to remind Kyle of the urgency of their escape. They took to the road again, Ally sending her mind far away from this place, this man. She felt intensely aware of her movements, the way her skin pushed against her seatbelt with every breath, the cold curl of her toes inside her boots. She thought of Jack. Leaving him was a calculated risk. She hadn't thought much past the moment of her decision. What if she never saw him again? The possibility felt very real as Kyle sped across the rain-slick asphalt, swerving recklessly over the double yellow line.

She crossed her arms over her chest, trying to stop her shivering. She felt her heart beating. One, two, three, four…too fast, too fast…

The tires on the wet road hummed. *Key of B minor*, she thought wildly. Through the trees flashing by, she caught glimpses of the blackened water of the sound. The wipers danced frenetically, scarcely keeping the windshield cleared. Right, left, right, left. *What-if. What-if.* The refrain caught inside her head, an endless coda. *What-if. What-if.*

Rees's face rose up in her mind. She tried to push away the image but couldn't. She longed for him so viscerally that her heart ached deep inside her chest. *I could love him.* The thought came without surprise, dropping neatly into place. *Maybe I already do.* Hadn't she at some level known it all along? She just hadn't dared to admit it. Because she'd been afraid.

Fear. Was there even one minute of the last six years when it had not ruled her heart? How much longer would it trump her emotions, dictate her course? Not only hers, but Jack's.

Her breath expanded inside her chest as the truck began a long ascent, the road twisting upward in front of them. Ally stared out her window as a sign blurred past, signaling their approach to Deception Pass. *Leaving Whidbey Island: We wish you fair winds and calm seas.*

Kyle downshifted. The hum of the tires against the road changed keys to E major. She heard the sustained note inside her head as clearly as if she held Lola in her hands, her memory of music. Ally closed her eyes and heard that note again. The bow drawn across the strings, the pure tone as only Lola could sing it. And a then new voice entered her mind: *Be still.*

A thread of peace uncoiled inside her, wrapping around her terror. Whatever else happened, she was not alone.

They rounded a curve. Deception Pass Bridge sprawled before them. At its entrance, four orange-and-white barricades stood sentinel, shoulder to shoulder, blocking their passage.

Kyle swore and slammed on the brakes, then fought for control as they spiraled across the road. Trees flashed by in a watery green blur. The truck grazed the guardrail. Ally caught sight of the darkly textured waves far below. Kyle jerked the wheel, turning into the skid. Finally they came to a shuddering halt, mere feet from the wall of barricades.

Ally's world slowed to stillness.

Go. The command came, sure and steady at the center of her spirit.

I will fight for you. Her heart throbbed as truth thrummed to life deep within her soul.

Go—now!

Kyle remained hunched over the wheel, his breathing labored, as if he'd sprinted a mile. She unclasped her seatbelt, and her fingers curled around the door handle. She tugged. The door swung open, letting in a blast of frigid air. She launched from the vehicle, beyond Kyle's reach. In a flash, she was drenched to the skin, the wind pressing rain like cold needles into her scalp and face.

"Get back inside!" Kyle yelled above the force of the gale.

"I won't!" Ally faced him. Her focus narrowed, sharpened, aware only of the flame that flared inside, hot and steady. "And if you try to take my son from me, I'll fight you all the way. You won't win. I can promise you that. I won't let you hurt me any longer, Kyle."

He wrenched open his door and stood glaring at her across the hood of the truck. His chest rose and fell as he caught each breath, the downpour blurring features twisted in anger and pain. "My life is nothing without you!" From inside his jacket, he withdrew his Taser. With his thumb, he flicked it on. The weapon crackled as rain fell on its prongs. Kyle rounded the front of the truck, his eyes never leaving hers.

"What are you going to do, Kyle, kill me?" She took a step back, seeking a way out. Not the way they'd come, back down the road. She had no hope of outrunning him. On her left, just over the guardrail, the land fell away. A hundred feet below, black waters churned white as they crashed against the bridge's pilings.

She moved toward the bridge and edged around the barrier.

Kyle's glance cut to the roiling waters below. Fear flashed across his face. He hesitated, shook it off. Took one step closer. "I love you, Cadence." The wind whipped his plea away.

The barrier stood between her and Kyle, but here, with nothing to stop it, the wind pounded her body with such force she felt the bones of her face rattle. The pedestrian railing reached barely above her waist. Looking down, she fought a swirl of dizziness and clutched at the top rail. Her fingers slipped on its rain-slick surface.

Kyle edged onto the mouth of the bridge, Taser in one hand, his other gripping the barrier.

A flash of light made him turn his head. Ally saw it, too, reflected in the sheen of Kyle's truck. She wheeled in the light's direction. Headlights. A car approaching fast from the opposite side.

The car fishtailed, skidding to a stop mere feet from the barrier on the mainland side of the bridge. The driver emerged. Ally's throat closed. *Rees?* Not pausing to question whether he was real or imagined, Ally ran toward to him.

"*No*!" Behind her, Kyle roared. A scuffle, a clatter, then her feet pulled out from under. Her chin crashed to the pavement, teeth clacking hard as breath whooshed from her lungs. She could not breathe. *God, help!* Terrifying seconds. A heaving surge as she inhaled. Kicking, she fought to free her ankle from Kyle's grasp. He held her fast, even when she landed a blow to his head.

"Ally!" Rees sprinted toward her.

"Rees!" The wind thrust her cry down her throat. Rees closed the distance and hurled himself on top of Kyle. Kyle raised both hands to shield himself from impact. Ally broke free.

Kyle grunted as Rees landed hard. Ally scrambled out of reach. The men rolled toward the mouth of the bridge, edging the sheer drop to the churning waters below. Kyle lurched upright, hauled back and landed a kick to Rees's ribs. Rees doubled over. Kyle fell on him with his fists.

"No!" Lunging forward, Ally tripped over a something hard. The Taser. She snatched it and advanced on the grappling men. "Stop it, Kyle!" Her hands shook as she aimed the weapon. Kyle swung another kick at Rees but missed. Rees rolled beyond his reach. "I said, stop!"

Kyle whirled. His face twisted into a sneer when he saw the Taser. "What are you going to do, Ally, use that on me?"

"I swear I will." Her hands trembled. "I won't let you hurt anyone else again."

Kyle spat. "You don't have the guts."

Rees groaned, struggling to regain his footing. Kyle spun, aimed a hard-soled boot at Rees's face.

Ally swung hard with both arms. The weight of the Taser connected with the back of Kyle's skull. He staggered toward the rail, grabbed on. Hanging half-over the black waters below, a shudder shook his frame. He sank, moaning, to his knees.

Rees reached Kyle in seconds, captured him in a headlock. Then a new noise. Another vehicle, this one coming from the island. A sheriff's car skidded within inches of Kyle's truck. Denny leapt out.

"Kyle Wylie," Denny yelled, jerking him out of Rees's grasp. "You're under arrest for trespassing and kidnapping."

"Ally?" Rees's voice was near her ear.

She turned. His shirt was soaked through, his chest rising and falling with every hard-fought breath. She brushed away the rain blurring her vision, questions piling up but finding no release.

Rees took her by the shoulders, his searing touch warm against her skin. "Are you okay?"

She could only nod, vaguely aware of Denny shoving Kyle into the backseat of his car, while every word vanished.

Rees's eyes searched hers before he raised his hands to cup her face, as if unwilling to believe his eyes. "I was so afraid…I thought I would be too late."

"You weren't." Finding her voice at last. "Your timing was perfect."

A smile started in the depths of his eyes, changing swiftly to something deeper. And then a question, which she must have answered somehow. Without wasting another second, he claimed her mouth with his. Heat suffused her limbs as his arms came around her, tightening their embrace. She clung to him, and everything else disappeared.

CHAPTER 50

"You're sure he's all right?" Jack asked for the third time in as many minutes.

It was the next day. Darcie shared a smile with Paul before glancing at the boy strapped into the car seat in the backseat of their Camry. "Yes, kiddo, Moses is just fine." *God, I still say that boy has the most beautiful eyes You've ever set in a child's head.* The sight brightened the new hope blooming inside her chest, one she now dared to believe included a child of her own. Not this child, but one like him. One whom she would grow to love. Because that's who she was, that's what she did. She and Paul both. She reached across the console and took Paul's hand, a gesture he promptly answered with a reassuring squeeze. They loved children. It was that simple.

She smiled into Jack's anxious face. "I spoke to the vet this morning on the phone. Ol' Moses had a close call, but he's going to live to see the Promised Land, after all."

Jack didn't answer, only shifted his gaze out the window, the worried look still on his face. Darcie knew he wouldn't stop fretting until he could actually touch Moses and know for himself the dog had survived his ordeal.

Today, Whidbey Island was a world washed clean by yesterday's crashing windstorm, the worst the island had seen in nearly twenty years. The tree that toppled in Ally's yard had not been the only one to fall. Power lines were down all over the entire county, where fully a third of Puget Sound Electric's customers were without power. Which was why they were headed to the vet in Coupeville. That was where she had taken Moses yesterday, as soon as Rees and Ally had returned to the cottage for a tearful reunion with Jack. Darcie had never been more thankful for Denny Lewis's quick reflexes and clear thinking. When she'd called 911, frantic after Kyle Wylie sped away with Ally, Denny had known exactly where Kyle would go. The fact Rees had been there too—well, that was a miracle of a whole different category.

Darcie had offered to take Jack with them on this errand, to give her brother and Ally some privacy. She knew they had much to talk about, and she doubted it involved Ally's going to Chicago or Rees's returning to Mumbai alone. At least not for long.

As for her, she realized she could not go on blaming Paul for shutting her out when she was doing the very same thing to him. Now they were talking again, talking *and* listening: a good start. While neither knew how they would find the light at the end of their tunnel, they at least believed it was there. She harbored a secret confidence that if Rees and Ally, with all their differences and complications, could find their way forward, so could they.

A block from the vet's office, Paul pulled into a parking lot still gleaming slick with rain. Taking Jack's soft hand in hers, Darcie guided him around the fallen branches littering the sidewalks. Road crews worked to clear the streets of debris, while shopkeepers repaired broken windows with particleboard and duct tape. "There's the vet's." Paul pointed it out to Jack. "In just a few minutes, you'll get to see—"

Jack's tug on Darcie's hand halted them in front of the antique store next to the vet's. *Dominique's Antiques. Consignments welcome*, read a sign tacked to the door. Jack pressed his nose to the window display. "What do you see?" Darcie wondered what object inside had caught his interest. The model airplane, perhaps, or the red Radio Flyer wagon beside the cash register?

Instead, Jack's gaze was drawn down to a shelf just inside the window, where pieces of Victorian-era jewelry were artistically arranged on black velvet. He lifted his nose from the glass to glance up at Darcie. "Look." He pointed to an antique diamond engagement ring sparkling alongside a simple gold wedding band.

"Pretty, aren't they?" Darcie exchanged a bemused glance with her husband. Alongside all the toys, she was surprised the boy would even notice some old jewelry. "Well, are you ready?" She put a hand on his back to move him forward. "Let's go see Moses."

But he refused to budge. "Don't you see?" A note of impatience crept into his tone, prompting Darcie to take a second look at the object capturing Jack's attention. "Those are my mom's." He pointed again. "Her grandma's rings."

CHAPTER 51

Mumbai, six months later

It was a day edged in gold, ideal for an afternoon on the beach.

They came here often as a family, to Mumbai's Juhu Beach, so Jack could run and play as he did back home in Langley. In a city of beaches, this one was closest to their flat, but despite its convenience, it wasn't Ally's favorite. Inexplicably, the sand brushing across her sandaled feet felt more like dirt than sand, and this stretch of waterfront teamed with humanity. Really, the crowds were impossible. Most people came here to enjoy the sand, the water, the view. But also, everywhere, there were those for whom the beach meant business—the chai wallah who wanted to sell Ally tea, the snack vendor who wanted to sell her a *vada pav*, the balloon guy, the *mendi* woman…and on and on. Rees told her she'd get used to the crowds in time. Perhaps he was right. He usually was.

He had been right about Kyle. When she'd at last found the courage to face him, he'd backed down from his legal action against her. Confronted with the evidence, he admitted burglarizing not only her house but many others in and around Langley. He also confessed it was Jack's starting kindergarten that had finally tipped him off as to her whereabouts in Washington. Among all the other papers Ally had signed to register her son for school, she'd signed one that allowed a criminal background check, which state law required before she could volunteer in Jack's classroom. Her name showed up in a national database. For Kyle, the rest was easy.

Already facing charges for breaking and entering, trespassing and kidnapping, Kyle agreed to drop all claim to Jack in exchange for Ally's agreement to not press rape charges.

Rees was also right about the futility of looking back, so she made it a point now to look only to the future. A year ago, her life here in Mumbai was one she could never have envisioned for herself. But she was playing Lola for an audience again. She and Sheela talked almost daily as they fine-tuned their fledgling music therapy program for rescued women. Neither knew yet how it would all work out, but Ally felt a sustained satisfaction in knowing one of her great joys had found a way to meet one of the world's great needs.

Ally and Rees had invited Sheela to join them at the beach. She and Ally shared a blanket as they kept a watchful eye on Jack. He'd already made a friend today, another little boy about his age. The boy didn't speak English, and Jack spoke little Hindi—though fascinated by the foreign sounds, he was eager to learn. Instead, he and his playmate drew pictures in the sand, managing to relate in the universal language of children.

Ally leaned back on her hands as she spotted Rees at a distance, tanned and shirtless, weaving his way through the maze of people as he ran along the water's edge. Nearing their blanket, he paused to pluck an object from the sand. When he reached Ally, he dropped it into her lap before collapsing beside her on the blanket, sweating.

"How was your run?" She offered him a kiss.

"Hot."

Sheela turned her head, humor glinting in her black eyes. "You Americans." She shook her head. "So concerned about your bodies. Do you think running five miles along this hot beach will help you live a few years longer?"

Rees smiled at her teasing and tipped his face toward the sky. Ally placed a hand on her husband's thigh, the diamond on her finger glinting in the sunlight. Her grandmother's rings once more graced her left hand, placed there by Rees in a quiet ceremony shortly before their departure for Mumbai.

Their courtship had been swift but sure. After Rees's surprise return to the States, he had been granted an extension of his home leave, while Ally postponed her move to Chicago. In the weeks that followed, Rees and Ally scarcely left each other's company. Jack grew so attached to Rees that Ally could hardly imagine their lives without him. So when Rees proposed on Christmas Eve, Ally's answer was a quick, fearless yes.

"We should go soon," Ally reminded Rees now, "or we'll be late for the party." Today marked nine months since Jayashri had come to Sanctuary. Though she still struggled to open her heart to those who cared for her, she was content to remain with

Sanctuary. And that, for now, was enough. Together, Sheela and Ally had decided to throw her a party, not just to celebrate Jayashri's life, but those of all the other rescued victims as well. They had planned it for weeks: the decorations, the food, the dancing…and music, of course. In honor of the occasion, Ally had even purchased her first salwar kameez, a purple and black ensemble with silver sequins.

"Pretty soon," Rees answered, his gaze on Jack and his new friend. "We still have time."

The boys, one with ebony hair, the other with yellow gold, bent their heads together over some piece of treasure in the sand, probably a bit of sea glass or an odd piece of metal. The boys shared a chortle, their laughter carrying to her like grace notes on the breeze.

Ally picked up the object Rees had dropped into her lap: a whole seashell, perfect and curled, like a child nestled in its mother's womb. A rare find on this populated beach. Her soul rose with joy as she remembered her secret, which she'd been waiting for the right moment to share. In a few weeks' time. Perhaps on the eight-month anniversary of her father's death. It might seem morbid to some, but Rees would understand. Life to death, and death to life, intertwined.

Darcie would understand, too.

Ally's thoughts turned to her sister-in-law. She and Paul were playing the waiting game, hoping to receive their first foster child soon. It occurred to Ally if everything went well, she and Darcie would be raising children together. Close cousins, a world apart.

Rees's hand brushed hers. She turned her head, smiled. Then she twined her fingers with his as together they looked out to open sea, where calm water met the sky.

Dear Reader ~

Jayashri wasn't in my original story outline. *That* plan detailed the story of a young mom hiding from a frightening past who encounters a troubled sex-trafficking investigator home from India on furlough. So far, so good. But as I wrote, I realized that in order to give the investigator's side of the story greater substance, I had to do some research. And that's when Jayashri materialized onto the page.

Even then I meant for her to be a mere mention, a tiny slice of Ally and Rees's bigger story. But the more I researched what it meant to be Jayashri—and the more investigators and psychologists I questioned—the more I realized Jayashri could not remain a footnote.

Beyond that, I realized I could not remain still, knowing as I did now that Jayashri represents millions of girls who are very, very real. Understanding what these girls endure on their way to rescue and healing made me want to do something tangible to keep real girls out of a real sex-trafficking trade.

Thousands of children are forced into trafficking every year, mostly because their families cannot afford to keep them alive. They lack the resources for food, clean water, shelter, education—all the things we take for granted.

But it's hard to know how to help because unlike Ally and Rees, you and I are unlikely to move to India. It's also easy to question whether one person really can make a difference in the lives of so many. But I believe we can. Because while no one can do everything, everyone can do one thing.

For me, that one thing includes sponsoring through World Vision a little girl in India who is exactly my own daughter's age. I also trained to become a World Vision Child Ambassador because I want to be a voice for children in the hopes that they, unlike Jayashri, will not be forced to into trafficking in order for a family to survive.

If you'd like more information on how you can make a difference by sponsoring a child, I encourage you to drop me a line at www.katherinescottjones.com. I love hearing from like-minded readers who seek opportunities to make a world of difference.

Together, we can change how a child's story ends.

**"He will take pity on the weak and the needy
and save the needy from death.
He will rescue them from oppression and violence,
for precious is their blood in his sight."
~ Psalm 72:13-14**

The author with a photo of her sponsored child.

ACKNOWLEDGEMENTS

Writing *Her Memory of Music* has provided me one of the greatest joys and challenges of my life. Thank God He didn't leave me to do it alone but provided support every step along the way. With a full heart, I offer deep gratitude to these who have been a part of the journey:

Athena Dean Holtz for reaching out and giving me the opportunity to get my story out there. Thanks too to the godly professionals at Redemption Press who have made the publishing process a joy, especially Hannah McKenzie, who helped keep my head on straight.

Jenny at Seedlings Design for the beautiful cover that exceeded expectations.

Anne Mateer for making my work shine. I am beyond grateful.

Isaac and Andrea Conver for sharing their experiences in India and providing behind-the-scenes insights into the fight against sex trafficking in Mumbai.

Sybil Dyrness, Gwyn Kopp, and Janet Phelps for sharing their experiences as musicians; and most especially to Bryn Cannon for introducing me to the world of violists, and whose own cracked, centuries-old viola provided the inspiration for Lola.

Kathy Anderberg and Rachael Lyons for their nursing expertise, and for my beloved brother, David J. Kopp, M.A., for insights into psychology.

Early critique partners, Connie Brzowski, Ocieanna Fleiss, and Paula Bicknell for knocking off the rough edges; and to Kim Galgano for countless hours of kindred-spirit encouragement.

Sherri Sand, my valued critique partner and cherished friend. Iron sharpens iron. We both know God brought us together for a reason, and this is one of them.

Mom and Dad for believing it would happen.

Jack and Madeline for allowing me peace and quiet (most days) so I could get words onto paper.

Scott for your faithful love and support. Always.

Father God for giving me a heart for story and the desire to speak for those who cannot speak for themselves. Thank You for fighting for me.

Order Information

To order additional copies of this book, please visit
www.redemption-press.com.
Also available on Amazon.com and BarnesandNoble.com
Or by calling toll free 1-844-2REDEEM.

CPSIA information can be obtained
at www.ICGtesting.com
Printed in the USA
LVOW11s0738170517
534761LV00005B/6/P